DARK HORSE

MAGGIE RAWDON

Editing by Kat Wyeth – Editor (Kat's Literary Services)
Proofreading by Vanessa Esquibel – Proofreader (Kat's Literary Services)
Chess Piece Illustration - Emma Rottersman
Cover Design – Maggie Rawdon

This is a work of fiction. Any names, characters, places or events are purely a work of imagination. Any resemblance to actual people, living or dead, actual events, or places is purely coincidental.

CONTENT NOTE

A list of content information you may want before reading can be found on maggierawdon.com/content-information

PROLOGUE

G RANT

TEN YEARS EARLIER

"OH FUCK..." Jesse mutters as we get to the car and load the bags in the trunk.

"That bad?" I ask.

The deal hadn't gone well. Frankly, everything had gone to fucking shit the way I thought it would, but if he wanted to break out on his own, I didn't want to be the one to stop him.

"Hurts like a motherfucker. I think when I fell, I broke a rib or something. My chest, my stomach... Doesn't fucking feel right. I might have to go to the hospital." He pulls up his tattered shirt, and both of us go silent. There's a bullet wound just below his ribs on his right side.

I close the distance between us, circling him and lifting his shirt at the back. Nothing. No exit wound.

Fuck.

Fuck.

FUCK.

"Sit down. I'm going to call 911."

"You can't fucking call 911. Are you insane? Bring them and the cops here while we're sitting on dirty cash. No. No fucking way," he yells, shoving me away from him and making his way to the passenger side of the car.

"You caught one. There's no exit wound. You need a doctor now," I insist, following him as I pull out my phone. He bats it down, his brow furrowing.

"I just need to get in the car. You can drive me and—" He collapses backward into the car seat, and the overhead light illuminates just how pale he is.

"Okay. I'll get you to the hospital," I mumble, my heart racing with the need to get him there as fast as possible. We don't have time to wait on emergency services to come to us. He doesn't have much time left, and we're miles away from a hospital that could deal with this kind of injury.

"I don't think I'm gonna make it, brother. I think this might be the last one."

"Don't talk like that."

"Listen to me."

"No. Not if you're gonna say shit like that. We're gonna get you to the ER down here. They'll stabilize you and get you on a medical flight. They'll treat you in the Springs. Just let me drive while you save your energy." I have a plan. I always have a fucking plan. Tonight might not have been my plan, but me getting him to a hospital in time? That's a plan I can make happen.

"Grant..." His head lulls to the side, and he looks at me. "I need you to be my friend right now. You have to listen."

"I'm listening. But I'm driving while I listen." I gun the engine and peel out of the spot. The roads are slick, and the car fishtails for a moment before I can straighten her out.

"You've got to take care of her. If I don't make it. It has to be you. Dakota, she..." He tries to take a deep breath, one that sounds almost as weak as he looks. "She's on the verge of going down a bad path. I put her in that private school to help keep her out of trouble. You gotta keep her there. She needs someone who cares about her. I don't want her going into the system. It'll destroy her." I can hear the panic in his voice as he realizes that he might not be around to take care of his younger sister.

"What am I gonna do with a seventeen-year-old? I'd be a terrible replacement. So you're not done. You gotta hang on. Fight to stay with her. She needs you, not me. Not anyone else. Just hang on, okay? I'll get you there." I make a promise I don't know if I can keep, but I need him to focus his energy on himself right now.

"She's gonna need you..." He struggles to take another breath. "She won't trust anyone else. You know how hard she's had it..." His next breath is even shallower than the last. "Promise me you'll take care of her. Keep her safe. Keep her out of our kind of trouble."

"*You* have to do it. *You're* her brother. She needs *you*. Not me. Save your energy, and just let me get you to a hospital." I plead with him. "You'll keep her safe. You'll keep her out of trouble."

"Grant... please. I need to know you'll..." His breath rattles in his chest, and my eyes dodge off the road and over to his side of the car to make sure he's still with me. His lids start to fall shut, but he fights to keep them open. His chest still rises and falls, but it's barely perceptible, and his hand slides off his side where he'd been holding the wound.

The life is slowly draining out of him while I watch, helpless to do anything but try to drive faster in this snow. His eyes plead with me, silently asking what he no longer has the breath to say.

"I'll take care of her. If the worst happens... I'll protect her with my life. I'll keep her out of trouble. Whatever I have to do. I promise. Just fight for her. Please fucking fight. I'll have you there in a couple of minutes." I swear to him.

"Keep her safe." The words are barely audible as his eyelids get heavy and his head droops to the side.

"Jesse!" I yell, shaking him harder and harder as I yell his name over and over. But he doesn't answer me—not in the car, not as I drag him into the emergency room, and not as they wheel him away.

An hour later, Jesse's sister, Dakota, comes crashing through the doors of the waiting room, her eyes red and her cheeks stained with tears, confirming what I already knew but didn't want to believe. She rushes at me, and I'm half worried she's going to slap me, blame me for everything that's gone wrong in his life, but instead, she just holds out her arms and wraps them around my waist. She presses her face to my chest, sobs racking through her while she can barely catch her breath. We don't talk. She just clings to me, holding on to me like I'm the last life raft she has left.

Her dad died when she was a baby, then her mother before she turned ten, and now her only brother. All with six months left before she even graduates. She hasn't even tasted how cruel and bitter the real world is outside those walls.

And it's all my fault.

I'm the one who put her here tonight.

The one who didn't keep him from joining the Horsemen.

The one who didn't stop him from taking this job even though he wasn't ready. The one who didn't talk him out of going tonight. The one who didn't call 911 when it might have been his only chance. The one who didn't drive fast enough to save his life.

I'm the asshole who left her without a single fucking soul in the world to watch out for her.

ONE

D AKOTA

THE DEVIL:

I'm here

I GLANCE SURREPTITIOUSLY down the bar when my phone dings with a message on the counter in front of me. He's in his usual spot, my brother's place, on the far side of Seven Sins Saloon. It keeps him near the door, away from the rabble, with his back to the wall as he surveys the room and tucks his phone away into his pocket. He makes quick, one-handed work of the buttons on his suit jacket before he eases onto the bar stool.

Heads swivel around the room, despite the loud atmosphere and the blaring country music; most of them don't need a text to know he's arrived. There's a cold snap and a rise in whispers and low voices chattering, like a slow wave that travels through the bar.

It's always the tourists who try to grab his attention. A good number of them just want to fuck him because he's tall, dark, and handsome. But the locals know who he is—what he is—the head of The Quiet Horsemen. Our very own living, breathing devil in the flesh, and for them, he owns too many souls in this town to ever see him as anything other than a pretty face to be observed from a distance.

For me, he's an extortionist. A tyrannical landlord who owns this building and my home upstairs and uses both as an excuse to keep tabs on me like I'm a child he's put in charge of. Which I was for six brief months between my brother's death and my eighteenth birthday. Before that, he'd been my brother's best friend, the one my friends and I giggled about whenever he showed up, and the man we'd fantasized about marrying when we played marry, fuck, kill. Something that's hard for adult me to reconcile with, since these days I mostly imagine wrapping my hands around his throat until the lights go out in his eyes.

"What's wrong, gorgeous?" The young guy's voice snaps me back into the present, and I finish shaking the drink he's asked for, grabbing a glass to pour it into. I force myself to fix my face and flash a bright smile at him.

"Death, taxes, and the devil himself," I answer as I slide the glass across the bar top.

His brow furrows immediately, and he looks between me and the drink. "What?"

He's far too drunk to process words and too young to understand that life comes with certain guarantees. I envy him for that. I feel at least a decade older than my twenty-eight years, and some days, I'd give anything to be a bright-eyed college kid again. One without the burden of the future always weighing me down.

"Nothing, handsome. That'll be ten dollars. You want it on your tab?" I flash a fake smile that he accepts as real before his eyes drift down to my breasts.

"Yeah." He nods too emphatically for my liking. I'm going to have to watch him to make sure he doesn't get overserved because I'd bet money that he's a raging asshole when he's drunk. I just hope his friends decide to move on to the next bar before we get there, and he remembers how heavy my pour is when he scrawls his name on the receipt before stumbling out.

The next guy bellies up to the bar in his wake. This one's got bright-green eyes and curly red hair, a smattering of freckles across his nose and cheeks, and a smile that's so sweet I can't imagine he's ever seen a bad day. His buddies creep up behind him, mischievous grins on their faces as he holds up a fifty.

"What can I get you, handsome?" I slide a napkin in front of him, and he stares at it for a moment before he blinks.

"Hey! I want to order a... uh..." He looks back at his friends, and one of them shouts something in his ear before he turns back to me with a little more confidence. "I want a Sinner's Shower."

"It's his birthday!" One friend leans forward to tell me.

"Twenty-one!" the other adds.

"I'll give you the birthday bonus then. What do you want as a chaser?"

"Uh." He stares back at me, clearly clueless.

"Anything that's on tap." I nod back to the blackboard behind me.

"Umm..." he answers, his brows knitting together for a moment as he studies the list. "A Yeti?"

"Good choice. Have a seat while I get it all ready." I point to the bar stool tucked between two gold bars.

The Sinner's Shower is a new drink I came back with when I saw the girls at the MC bar I visited doing them. They were charging thirty bucks a piece to have guys take shots and then slap them before they splashed water in their faces. I'd upped the ante and the price—for fifty, I'd spit the whiskey in their mouths, slap them, and drench them in ice water. Catharsis for me for dealing with all the assholes every night, and a fun story for them to take back to the frat house.

I pull a waiver and a pen out from under the counter and slide them in front of him.

"Sign this." I had the waiver drawn up to cover my ass in the event that some asshole thought he liked to be slapped but then decided he didn't like that particular kink as much as he anticipated. He starts to bring it closer to his eyes, reading carefully before his friend slaps him on the back.

"You want her to spit in your mouth or not? Just sign it." His friend taps the pen, and he quickly flourishes his name across the paper. I grab the Jack, pouring a shot before I get a glass of ice water and pour his draft.

"Another taker?" Hayley smiles as she dodges behind me. She pulls the expensive whisky from the shelf above the Jack. There's only one person who ever drinks it, but if he wants to come in and be charged triple the going rate for what he could get for free at the bar in his casino, I'm not about to be the one to stop him. He takes it right back out the door with him at the end of the month with rent anyway.

"Another taker." I nod.

"You're an evil genius, you know?" She elbows me gently.

"I wouldn't go quite that far. But if it keeps the lights on." I shrug as I line up all the drinks on the right side of the counter before I climb up on the bar after them.

Hayley disappears with the devil's drink, and I turn my attention back to the wide-eyed boy in front of me. He doesn't know where to put his eyes as I slide to the edge of the bar.

"Scoot in." I draw my fingers back toward me, and he drags the bar stool in between my knees. His eyes crawl up my legs, studying my tattoos for a moment, before they find where my cut-off jeans end at the apex of my thighs.

"Up here," I remind him, and his attention snaps to my face. I raise a brow at him, only giving him shit because he seems so sweet. His cheeks blush bright fucking red, and I have to suppress a smile.

"All right. Whiskey first. Then a slap. Then a shower. Got it?" I glance down to make sure he's signed the waiver, and I tuck it behind the bar before we start. I don't need water bleeding the ink.

"Got it." His eyes drift down and then snap back up again.

"Good." I knock the whiskey back into my mouth.

Then I lean forward, grabbing his cheeks and forcing his mouth open wider as I press on the place where his jaw hinges. I spit the whiskey into his mouth, and he gags on it a little, sputtering and wheezing as I slam the shot glass down. I let go of his cheeks and haul back like I'll hit him hard but slow the movement until it's more like a love tap. This kid can barely hold his liquor, and I don't need him choking on it.

His friends are hollering and cheering by the time I pick up the glass of ice water and toss it into his face. I don't hate that it catches all of them in the process. They take a step back, wiping their faces right along with him.

"Holy shit!" Birthday Boy cries out as he wipes at his eyes.

"Fuck me," another yells.

"That was hot as fuck!" His friend looks up at me in awe.

"Me next!" another guy their age yells from one of the tables, waving money in the air and jumping up to head my way.

"Thanks." Birthday Boy shoves a twenty-dollar tip into the empty shot glass before he backs away slowly, wide-eyed as he still processes what just happened. I can see the wheels churning in his head, deciding just how much he liked that and what it means for his future that he likes women slapping him around.

"Happy Birthday, handsome." I grin at him before I gather the glasses.

"Me next!" His friend shoves past him and holds out another fifty.

"Give me a minute to reset." I roll my eyes and shake my head as I climb back over the bar. When my feet hit the rubber mat, I hear Hayley's laugh tinkle its way across the room, and I look up to see what's so funny. She's still standing with the devil, her hand on his as she throws her head back in laughter, but he's not meeting her with his own. In fact, he looks pissed, and I feel my phone vibrate again as I see him set his down onto the bar with his free hand before he takes the last swallow of his drink. I risk a peek.

THE DEVIL:

Scotch neat. Now.

And that last word is exactly why I give out five more Sinner's Showers before I even think about making my way to his end of the bar.

TWO

G RANT

SHE CONTINUES DOLING out shots and ignoring me like I didn't see her pick up her phone and read my message. I'm gripping the glass so tight I'm about to shatter it by the time she finally starts to saunter my way, a glass of whisky in hand. She was the one who summoned me here in the first place, complaining that there's a maintenance issue in the apartment she lives in upstairs. I'd planned to have a drink while I waited for her to have a free moment, not watch a live show of her spitting down the throats of a half dozen college guys before she slapped and drenched them. I have work I need to return to at the Avarice.

"Your whisky." She sets the drink down in front of me without any fanfare.

"Funny, I thought it was Speyside, not spit side," I mutter, and she raises her eyebrow in return.

"Jealous? Because if you want it served that way, it can be arranged." She's always sassy, but it's turned up a notch tonight.

"I think I might be too old to be impressed by that sort of thing." I glance back at the college kids who are still shouting and cheering as one of their own chugs beer from a boot-shaped glass. Seven Sins and Dakota lean into all the kitsch of the country dive bar and then some.

"Oh, Cowboy, it's okay. I know that big birthday's just around the corner for you, but we don't judge around here." She speaks with a saccharine tone and points back at the glowing red neon sign behind the bar that says Sinners Welcome.

I narrow my eyes at her. I don't need to be reminded that I'm closing in on forty; the gray hairs that keep popping up handle that daily reminder just fine.

"Not worried about my age as much as I'm worried about you not being able to handle the extra whiskey you're swallowing and falling off this bar," I taunt her. She nearly slipped the last time getting down, and I pictured her falling backward, a mess of limbs and shattered glass. I'd lose my fucking mind if I lost another Hartfield right in front of me.

"Hayley! Get me a water, please!" she calls over her shoulder before the false smile returns. "I think you'd be surprised what I can handle." She looks me over in one slow rake before her blue-green eyes come back up to meet mine. "Unless you're scared?"

"Scared of what?" I bluster because I'm fucking terrified when I watch her climb up on the bar in front of me. Not about her falling, at least not in this moment because she's nimbly navigating the counter and already perched in front of me, but that this is only going to give the crowd and her more encouragement. I can't back down though. I'll look like I cower from a twenty-something woman simply teasing me a little, and it'll be hard to get anyone to take me seriously after that.

"That you might like it." Her lips pull up at the corners as she spreads her legs in front of me. She studies my face for a moment, the sly smile growing as she reaches forward and grabs my tie. She wraps it around her fist once and tugs. "Come closer. I won't bite."

"You always fucking bite," I mutter.

"At least not hard," she says softer, and I'm starting to see why this works so well with the men in this bar. The proximity would knock me off guard if she wasn't Jesse's sister.

The college boys have their full attention on her, and they're practically rabid. Screaming, hollering, and cheering her on. A low rumble erupts as I scoot forward on the seat, and her knees bump my shoulders. I look down at her long legs in front of me, studying the curve of her calves in her boots, and for one blackout second, I'm tempted to run my hands up the backs of them.

At least until I see her grab the expensive glass like it's another shot of bottom-shelf liquor.

"That's fifty dollars' worth of alcohol," I protest as she presses it to her lips.

"Then let's try not to spill it." She smirks as she knocks back the whisky. Despite her self-assured taunting, some of it dribbles down the corner of her chin, and she presses her fingers to her lips as she smiles.

"Fuck that's hot! I want to be that fucking whisky!" one guy chimes in loudly.

The way I'm tempted to drag her upstairs to lecture her on how fucking stupid and risky this little routine is—how stupid it is to rile these guys up like this—but I don't have time to think more. Her hand is under my jaw, pressing me to open my mouth wider, and I follow her lead. We're in this now, whether I like it or not.

The rest is a lightning-fast blur. She spits in my mouth, and I barely have time to swallow it before her hand comes flying toward my face. She pulls the punch more than she would've with anyone else, but I can feel each and every ring on her finger as her open palm strikes against my skin, leaving a crisp burn of contact in its wake before it's doused with ice-cold water.

I gasp, nearly choking on the last bit of whisky. I haven't swallowed it all before I run my fingers through my wet hair and sweep it out of my face. When I look up, she looks surprised at her own work, just before it morphs into a smile so sweet, you'd almost think it was real instead of what it is—an act for everyone in this room.

It's working too. The howls and hoots get even louder, and her college boys are chanting her name from the other side of the bar. In the midst of it all, we just stare at each other, like the first one to blink loses.

"You all right there, Cowboy? Don't choke to death on me," she teases, her eyes lighting with amusement as they fall over the water stains on my suit and the drips of whisky still caught in my beard.

"As I've ever been." I glare back at her, swiping at the mess, but it's hard to keep the malice in it when I see how delighted she is.

Hayley leans forward past her and hands me a napkin. I smile and thank her, losing Dakota's eyes in the process. She takes it as a victory and swings her legs back over the counter, gathering the glasses and tucking them under the bar in the dirty bin before she grabs a rag to wipe down the last of the water. She tosses it back into the sterilizing solution and tucks a strand of hair behind her ear—drawing out every little motion, like she's doing her best to avoid looking at me again.

But for a split second, as if time is frozen, I can't stop looking at her; the way her blue-green eyes catch the neon, the way it halos around her highlighted dark brunette hair, how she rolls her lower lip between her teeth when she works, the way the sun has already colored her cheeks with freckles this season —it's hard not to notice. If she were anyone else, I might tell her how gorgeous she is, but with her, I can't. With her, I've only got the well-worn track the two of us travel side by side. She's the reckless, wild-hearted one who won't listen to reason or me —now or years ago when I was responsible for her. And I'm the sad fucking excuse for a replacement older brother—the one she lost thanks to me.

But I won't stop trying to get her to rein in some of her worst impulses. Like this one.

"This isn't smart, you know?" I toss my napkin up onto the bar next to a hundred-dollar bill and wait for her attention to return to me.

"Which part?" Her eyes meet mine in challenge.

"Any of it. The spitting. The climbing on the bar. The part where you slap your patrons. You're asking for a lawsuit." I keep my voice low. We're alone at this end of the bar. All the college boys are crowded together at the other end for the moment, playing pool and hovering around a couple of pitchers of beer. But I don't need to give anyone ideas.

"That's why they sign a waiver." She rolls her eyes.

"A waiver won't protect you if they argue they were too drunk to understand what they were signing. Or you forget to have them sign one at all because you're too eager to humiliate them in front of a crowd of your fanboys." I give her a pointed look.

"Oops." She shrugs half-heartedly and goes back to grinning while she finishes cleaning up. "I guess I'll let my lawyer know to expect a call from yours."

"I'm serious, Hartfield."

"So am I. I can tell mine to ask when your slumlord ass is going to fix the damn sink." Her temper slips.

"That's what I'm here for."

"You're here for the rent check. I've got it upstairs. But I'm deducting money since you haven't fixed the sink."

"You're deducting it, or you don't have it?"

"When is the handyman coming?" Her eyes narrow.

"You're looking at him." I shove back off the stool. I'm headed for the stairs in the back, the ones that lead up to her apartment, before she can say another word. But I hear her shouting my name, and in my peripheral vision, she's chasing down the backside of the bar, headed for the exit so she can cut me off.

She darts out in front of me just as I reach the back door, putting herself between me and the stairs like a roadblock.

"You're not fixing my sink." She looks over my suit with disdain.

"Why not?"

"There's no way you know how. And getting your hands dirty? Since when?"

"You'd be surprised." I repeat her earlier claim. "Now, let me upstairs."

She blinks, her eyes wandering over me for a moment as she runs her teeth over her lower lip. While she tries to make sense of the fact that I can actually do minor repairs, I slide past her and charge up the steps. I want this done and fixed so I can get back to business at the Avarice. Then I want to go home and crash out for the next ten hours.

"You don't even know which sink!" She chases after me up

the stairs. "Grant!" she screeches as the lock tumbler clicks, and I turn the door handle.

"What the fuck are you so worried about? Something illegal going on up here?" I turn and study her face.

"No, it's just my private space. You don't respect anything."

"Your private space." I huff as I look at her with frustration mounting in my chest. "The same private space you're fine with having some random fucking handyman in?"

"It would be better than you!" she argues.

"I can fucking fix it in five minutes without paying two hundred plus dollars." And without a guy who would probably be trying to root around in her panty drawer while he was at it —or straight up angling to get her clothes off, depending on how much of an ego the fucker had on him. I'm already punching the imaginary handyman in the face, and now I know I've lost my fucking mind along with my temper. I take a breath even as she shouts the next sentence at me.

"Because you're so fucking broke you can't afford it, right?" Sarcasm leeches through her tone.

I close my eyes, counting to five before I open them again.

"Because I'm here, right now. Do you want it fixed, or do you want to wait for someone to come out? It's the weekend, and they might not even get someone here until Monday or Tuesday."

She's still looking at me like she wishes she could backhand me under the guise of playfulness at the bar, but her shoulders relax the slightest bit. I can tell her gears are turning. The two of us always manage to rile each other up over something mundane, and it takes a minute for us to come down from it.

"Fine," she agrees, a hint of bitterness still in her tone before she waves me in, and I open the door.

She breezes past me, her cat, Vendetta, zooming out to greet her and only sparing me a threatening glance before she jumps up to a perch on the TV stand to keep an eye on her mom. Dakota's hurrying around, gathering things up off the table and the counter. I suspect she's trying to hide anything she thinks I might ask questions about. So maybe nothing illegal, but definitely things worth questioning. Unless she's just worried about it being messy.

"I don't care what it looks like." I'm used to messy. I just happen to have maid service every day.

"Right," she answers sarcastically. "I bet your place is just as messy."

"It is usually, but I have easy access to housekeeping."

"Yeah, well, I live in a bar and have easy access to needing more sleep in the mornings," she grumbles.

"Can't argue with that. Which sink is it?"

"The kitchen." She nods to it as she clutches the items she picked up to her chest, her body half turned away from me as she answers. "I'll be right back."

THREE

D AKOTA

I HURRY TO MY ROOM, tossing things on my bed and tucking a few things away in drawers. The last thing I want is for him to see the mail that has FINAL NOTICE scrawled in bright red letters across the top or the lingerie I put on earlier and took photos in for a new side hustle. Bristol, one of my best friends, jokingly mentioned selling pictures of her feet online last month for some extra cash, and it sent me down a rabbit hole. A girl had to know her options, especially when circumstances were dire. And mine are about as dire as they get, especially considering I have to go back out there in a minute and tell Mr. Casino Cowboy that I don't have all the money I need for rent this month. Right after he fixes my sink for free or hires a handyman to do it.

I glance in the mirror as I make my way back out the door

to the kitchen and stop short. I'm covered in whiskey stains, and my body glitter has started to clump along my cleavage. My lipstick is smeared, and the clasp on my necklace has dropped to the bottom, ruining the cute aesthetic I'd started the night with. In the bright light of my bedroom, I look as disheveled as my apartment is right now. I don't need another thing for him to judge and find wanting.

I stop and grab another crop top out of my drawer, wipe the glitter with a tissue, and adjust my necklace before I swipe another round of gloss on my lips. I run a brush through the curls that have started to tangle at the long ends of my hair too. I'm in desperate need of a trim and a dye, but it's one more thing I can't afford at the moment. At least not until I get paid for this last month.

I need to be able to afford my bridesmaid dress and the makeover that I need to look the part. Our best friend Hazel is getting remarried to a pro football player (and regrettably, Grant's younger brother) in a few short weeks. Between the family money and the rich pro-sports friends, I'm going to have to whip up a miracle to make it look like I even remotely fit in with the bridal party. But I'm not about to let Hazel down.

When I get back out to the kitchen, Grant's under the sink, messing around with the pipes. His jacket's off, the tie's gone, his shirt's unbuttoned, and his sleeves are rolled up neatly to his elbows. The muscles I thought his jacket perfectly accented? They're even better in the shirt. And the way his body is stretched out, one leg bent to help give him leverage on what-ever tinkering he's doing, is doing things for me. Especially since I don't have his disapproving glare or his impatient tone aimed at me right now.

"Hartfield?" He calls out my name louder than he needs to, probably still thinking I'm in the other room.

"Yes?"

"Do you have a tool kit of any kind? I need a wrench." He softens his voice this round.

"You need a wrench?" I repeat it like a question because I'm baffled at this series of events—that Grant Stockton is on his back under the sink in my kitchen at midnight, that he needs a wrench, and that he appears to know what to do with it.

"I have Jesse's above the cabinet," I answer. Or at least I think I still have my brother's old tool kit. I haven't touched it in years.

"Can you get it, please?" The please is a little more impatient than the rest of the question.

"Yes," I say as I walk into the room. "But it's on the cabinet above the sink, and I'll need the ladder."

"Fuck!" he curses. "I don't want to let this go. It's loose, and if I do—"

"Okay. Okay," I reassure him. "It's fine. I'll just climb on the edge of the sink. Hold on... Let me just—" I place my feet carefully around his body until I'm standing over him, place my palms on the counter, and boost one knee up onto the edge of the sink. One more boost, and I'm up to the level I can reach the top of the cabinet.

Thankfully, the tool kit is still there dusty and a little worse for the lack of use, but still where Jesse always kept it when we lived here together. I pull it down and set it carefully on the counter next to the sink.

"Got it?" Grant asks when he hears the thunk of it hitting the surface above his head.

"Yep. Just getting down, and I'll get the wrench." I dangle one foot back down, trying hard not to step on the man beneath me. That's the last thing I need because I'll never hear the end of it if I crush his precious hand or—

"Fuck!" I scream as my knee slips on the pool of water at the edge of the sink Grant created when he tested the faucet. I fly off the counter and fall to the floor—a fall that's only broken by the body of the man beneath me.

"Holy fuck!" His curse echoes mine as he catches me. I land in the most awkward position imaginable—practically sitting on the man's face.

I'm spread across his chest, one knee on either side, his hand wrapped around my thigh from where he tried to stop my fall. It's currently resting just under my left butt cheek. He's gripping the back of his head with his other hand, where he hit it on the back of the cabinet door as my body slammed into his chest. He's forgotten to hold whatever he had been keeping shut under the sink, and water starts to leak out from under it.

"Are you okay?" He rubs the back of his head, apparently not registering anything other than the immediate potential for injury to our bodies.

"I'm fine. Are you okay?" I ask as I try to move carefully and only manage to entangle us further.

"I'm fine. Just be careful sitting up. Fuck. I let go, and now there's more water. Don't trip—" He finally looks up to see me practically riding his face. Well, not quite—there's still clothing and two inches of air—but too close for comfort by the way his face contorts.

"Hartfield." The pained way he says my name makes me want to die. My face heats, and I scramble up, twisting my ankle in the process but managing to get away from him. I fall back onto the carpeted dining room floor and stare up at the ceiling. I'm trying to think of something funny to say. Or maybe something bitchy. Anything that's going to stop the awkward silence.

"Fuck!" He ends it for us. "It's wet again." Wait... what? Oh. Right. The sink. The pipes. Shit. "The water's starting to come faster. The wrench?"

I leap up and hobble over to the counter to get the wrench

as he dives back under the sink to try to re-secure it manually. I unlatch and root through the tool kit until I get the wrench and hand it to him. It's a few more curses and twists plus a handful of grunts, and he resurfaces again.

"That should hold it for now," he explains as he sits back up again. I hobble my way to the dining chair and sit down. He frowns at the way I'm favoring my ankle. "Are you okay?"

"Just twisted something. It'll be fine in a minute." I waive it off, but as he stands to put the wrench back, I don't miss the blood on his hands.

"You're bleeding!" I jump up out of instinct and nearly fall again.

"I'm fine. Just sit down." He gives me a glowering look, and I take a step back as he grabs a paper towel off the roll and wipes the blood from his hand. He reaches back to touch his head, and his fingers are stained crimson again. "Well, fuck," he mutters.

"Let me see," I insist, his grumpy threat forgotten as I hobble my way around to look at the back of his head. I raise onto my tiptoes and see a small abrasion from where the cabinet must have dug in when I fell on him. My cheeks heat again as I remember our position, and I shake my head. "The cabinet got you. Give me a second, and I'll get my first aid kit out of the bathroom."

"I'm fine," he insists.

"You're not fine. Just let me get it cleaned up."

"It's just a scratch. I'm fine. I can clean it up when I get home."

"I've got it."

"You need to get off your ankle," he insists.

"I can be the judge of my own ankle. I can walk ten feet to get the kit." I make my way into the bathroom, open the cabinet, and pull it out—holding it up for full effect. "See?"

"I just don't want you to fall again." The man worries even when he's grumpy.

"I fell because there was water. There's no water on the carpet."

He presses his lips together in irritation but doesn't say anything as I open the first aid kit and pull out some alcohol wipes. I rip one open, tossing the wrapper onto the counter.

"Sit." I pat a chair in front of me. He glares at it, but he follows the order. I gently press my fingers to the crown of his head, my fingers slipping through his hair as I tip his head forward. "I'm just gonna clean it up."

I swipe the pad across the small wound, and he grunts loudly, jolting in his chair. You'd think I shot the man.

"It's just a little alcohol," I say softly.

"It fucking stings," he grouches. Wounded animals never like to be touched.

"You can handle it." I take another swipe, and he complains under his breath, but he holds still. I eye the lollipops that are still sitting out on my counter next to the toolbox from a promo event we did last weekend. "If you quit complaining, I'll give you a sucker for being a good boy."

"You'd be better off giving them to the children you're entertaining downstairs," he deflects.

"This again?" I ask, dousing the wound with one last fresh wipe before I throw them all away and close the kit. There's too much hair for a Band-Aid to do anything other than get tangled, and the bleeding is slowing anyway.

"What again?"

"You hypocritically giving me shit for flirting with younger men when you date younger women."

"I don't date younger women."

"I've seen you with younger women."

"I might spend time with them, but I'm not dating them."

"Potatoes, po-tah-tohs," I counter. "You know what I mean."

"You're literally luring them with candy and treats. Spitting in their mouths. Spreading your legs."

"Slapping them. Dumping ice water on them," I fire back.

"Yeah, well after all that, they need the fucking ice water." His eyes follow me as I drop the used wipes and wrappers in the trash on the far side of the kitchen.

"I'm doing just fine. Those guys are paying fifty dollars for a half shot of Jack and a glass of ice water."

"Christ," he curses, shaking his head.

"See. You're just jealous you didn't think of it first."

"I didn't say it wasn't clever." He shakes his head. "I just said it's asking for trouble. Lawsuits. Guys thinking it's an invitation for more when you—" He stops short.

"When I do what?" I dare him to finish his sentence.

"You know what you're doing." His eyes lift to meet mine.

"I don't think what I do with my body is any of your business. And if they think it's an invitation, that's their problem." This is exactly why I hid everything when he got here.

"I would fucking make it their problem. But if Jesse was here..." His gaze drifts to the toolbox that has Jesse's initials engraved into the side.

Grant has a point there. No way in hell would Jesse ever let me sell that shot if he was still alive. He'd be giving me the same lecture Grant is, but I'd be talking back less. Because I looked up to Jesse. Grant is... complicated.

"Well, he's not, and someone has to pay the bills."

"I thought things were doing better?" His head snaps up, and he looks at me with surprise. "You said New Year's and Valentine's were good."

"They are. People still come here. But the competition around here is stiff." I narrow my eyes at him, and he has the decency to look a touch sheepish. The Avarice's new bar is slowly drawing some of my regulars away with its fancy specials and glittery new interior. Not that I want to admit that to him outright.

"We don't have the same clientele," he notes defensively.

"We don't? You're telling me that those college guys wouldn't be at your bar if you had hotter bartenders?"

"My bartenders are plenty fucking hot. I hand selected most of them, and we don't charge fifty dollars for an under-poured shot." His jaw ticks with irritation, and I stand straighter as I imagine him handpicking his staff.

"You also don't deliver that shot with a side of public humiliation that gets his friends cheering and him wondering what kink he's been missing his whole life." I press my lips together, shaking my head as I cross my arms in challenge.

"What kink he's been..." he scoffs. "Do you hear yourself? Do you run a bar or a sex club?" he asks derisively. I inhale sharply and bite my tongue to keep from snapping at him. I wish I had a whole bottle of alcohol to douse his wound with.

"Whatever I have to run to keep the doors open and the lights on." Every time he tells me not to do something—it just makes me want to do it that much more.

"Again, Jesse would—"

"I don't give a shit what Jesse would or wouldn't do. He's not here. He's gone because of decisions he made—the two of you made, really. So let's not pretend either of you was particularly good at them. I make my own decisions, and I don't give a shit what you think of them. You're not my brother, Grant. You have zero say. I'm tired of you treating me like I'm some lost sibling of yours who needs your constant oversight." I lash out, and I hate how bitter I sound and how invested I am in his approval—the way his lack of support for anything I do grates on my nerves until they're raw enough to make me say things like this.

Grant stiffens and then stands. He grabs his jacket off the chair without another word and heads for the door.

"I'll call a handyman in the morning. He should be able to fix that for you." He's terse now, all business, and it pricks that he's refusing to even fight back. He always fights back. It's just the way we work through things. We're both too strong-willed to cede ground easily.

"Don't you want your rent? If you give me a second, I can get it for you." I'm just trying to buy time; find some way I can apologize for the bitchy thing I said without letting him think he's run the board. But if I apologize now, he'll seize it. He'll see me as weak, someone he can manipulate. Just like everyone else in this town.

"Fine." He pauses at the doorway.

Unfortunately for me, I forgot the part where I need to ask him for a pass on a few hundred dollars-ish of the rent. A thing I'm fairly certain is gonna go over like a lead balloon now. I cringe as I go to my safe.

"I'm a little short this month," I say softly as I press the code into the door.

"How short?" he asks in a scolding tone.

"A thousand."

There's a long pause, like he's holding back other words he might say.

"Fine." The man has a new favorite word.

"I'll pay you back next month." I hedge.

"You won't. Not if things are bad like you say. And with the wedding, you'll be working less, which means fewer tips," he states sharply.

"So what do you want me to do then?" I pull the money I do have for him out and then lock the safe. He watches me as I walk toward him, holding out the stack of cash and raising a brow expectantly when he stays silent.

His eyes catch mine, and he studies me for a minute.

"If I was your brother, I'd just let it slide. But I guess since I have zero fucking reason to care, you'll have to find another way to make it up to me." He's got the door open and is halfway down the hall before I've processed what he's just said.

"What does that even mean?" I call after him.

"I'll send a handyman over here Monday. I'll text you the time later today. Try not to have lingerie scattered over half the fucking place when he comes!" He calls back down the hall. The door to the outside slams behind him, and I'm left pondering what the hell I've just walked myself into now.

FOUR

G RANT

BY THE TIME I get to Dakota's apartment, I'm pissed. She didn't show up to meet the handyman, so he called me to see if I could let him in. I'd had to excuse myself mid-meeting with my floor and resort managers to figure out what the fuck was going on. I expected that she was just in the basement of the bar counting inventory or had stepped in the shower and forgotten to take her phone off silent. But now that I'm here, she's nowhere to be found, and she's still not answering her phone.

The handyman is standing against the wall, bag at his feet in the back hallway where Hayley had sent him when he arrived. She didn't have any idea where Dakota was, either, and hadn't seen her this morning, assuming she was still in bed after a late night.

I unlock the door and ease it open, calling her name out as I take one step inside. I don't want her to come flying across the room, baseball bat in hand, trying to smash my face in because she couldn't remember she was having maintenance this morning. But there's no response, and the apartment seems quiet and empty.

"Just give me one minute to make sure she's not asleep or something." I turn back to the handyman.

"Sure." He nods, and I step the rest of the way inside, closing the door behind me so that her cat, Vendetta, doesn't get out. The damn thing dodges in and out of the shadows like she's part of them, and I don't want to be responsible for her being loose in the bar.

There's plenty of light streaming in through the living room and bedroom windows, but otherwise, the place is dark—no lights, no TVs. However, the place is in disarray. The lingerie from the other night is gone, but a new set of lingerie and clothing is strewn over the couch and one of the chairs. Papers are scattered on the table and a couple of boxes sit out on the counter. Dakota wasn't the neatest person I'd ever met, but the last couple of times I've been in here, it's been messier than usual. Like she's too busy to even stop and put things away.

"Hartfield?" I call out for her as I approach the half-open bedroom door. She doesn't answer, and I gently press the handle to push it open.

The bed is empty and unmade. There's more clothing lying about on the footstool at the end of the bed and hanging out of the drawers in the dresser. The place almost looks tossed from this angle. My heart skips a beat.

Dakota has a temper and a habit of not giving a shit about who she's talking to when she runs her mouth. She says things to me no one but my family would dare even think in my presence. I mostly let it slide, though, given that her brother was like a brother to me and left her in my care when he died. She's as much family as anyone in my eyes even if she isn't keen on the association. But I'm not the only asshole she's threatened and derided, and if she finally said the wrong thing to the wrong person...

I hate to go into her room and invade her privacy. I've done my best to give her a wide berth for the last decade. The six months she'd been my ward hadn't gone well, and she's hated me pretty much every day of her adult life. If it were up to her, I'd never step foot in this place again. But I promised her brother I'd make sure she was looked after. The second she got financially stable, bought a house, or got married, I'd be happy to shut the door and let her live her life. Unfortunately for both of us, stable has never been a word close to her heart.

I grumble quietly to myself about being stuck in this position as I ease the door open the rest of the way and step inside. I needed to be sure there weren't more signs of a struggle or that she wasn't passed out in the bathroom.

I edge inside, careful not to touch anything, and step over the clothing items scattered over the floor. I call her last name one more time before I open the bathroom door. It's quiet. No running water or humming or any sort of noise to indicate she's there, and I'm half relieved not to find her lying on the floor. At least until I look up on the bathroom counter and see a handful of toys charging.

"Fuck." I scrub a hand over my face and make a quick glance around the rest of the bathroom to make sure I'm not missing any vital details before I hurry back out.

I definitely didn't need to know what kind of toys she enjoys. I pinch the bridge of my nose, hoping there's some way I can forget the size of the double-pronged vibrator and the delicate rose toy sitting next to it. The question of whether she's using them alone or with one of her college boys crosses my mind. A thought I curse myself for even having.

"Everything all right?" the handyman calls from the hallway, and I chase out the images that begin flashing in my head and pull my shit together.

"Yep," I answer, hurrying around the corner and shutting the doors behind me. He doesn't need the same eyeful I got.

Dakota's always sort of stayed a kid in my head, even though it's been a decade since she was anything close to one. Fuck, even when she was my ward for those brief few months, she was unwilling to be treated like she was anything less than grown—insisting on being involved in all the tedious details of her brother's small estate, wanting to be responsible for all the bills, and begging me to let her take over the bar as soon as she was legally able to do so.

I wave the handyman through the door and point out the sink and the problems to him so he can get started. Meanwhile, I'm still surveying the room, and the more I look, the more nervous I get. Her laptop's still open on the coffee table, a cup of coffee sits half-finished next to it alongside a half-eaten piece of toast on the plate. The spot in front of it looks mussed, like she had been sitting there and then jumped up unexpectedly.

Whatever she left for came up quickly. It must have been important that she would take off without finishing her breakfast or closing her laptop. Her place was messy the other day, so it didn't shock me that some things were lying around, but this seems borderline chaotic. Like someone else was rushing her out.

The blood chills in my veins, and I can't shake it. I call her one more time.

It rings once, twice, three times, and then it goes to voicemail.

A bleak feeling creeps up my spine.

I glance back, and the handyman's working away under the sink, completely unaware that I'm worried the tenant might have been kidnapped. I pull out my phone and shoot off a text to my brother Levi.

> Can you check the cameras at Seven Sins?

Dakota and I have never discussed the security system at the bar in much detail, so I never bothered to tell her that I'm still plugged into it and can view it remotely from the casino. I promised myself that someday when she got proper bouncers at the door, I'd stop checking in at night. But then she was adamant that she and her bartenders could handle it all just fine and that the baseball bat under the counter was security enough. I'm hoping like hell it was if something happened last night.

My phone dings, and my heart skips at the prospect of it being her telling me to go fuck myself for bothering her in the morning. But it's Lev's name on the screen.

LEV:

> Sure, anything in particular I'm looking for?

> Find what time Dakota goes into her apartment last night, and when she left. If she's alone or not.

> We have a problem?

> She's not here, and I had to let the handyman in. The place looks… messy. More so than usual.

> On it.

> Thanks.

"ALL RIGHT. It's just a few quick parts that need to be swapped out. I think that'll have her up and running again. I just need to run to my truck for one I don't have up here," the handyman announces.

"Sounds good."

"Is it all right if I leave the back door ajar so I don't have to ring again?"

"Sure thing." I nod. I could keep an eye on it from the apartment's front door anyway, and hopefully, this guy would be quick.

"Thanks." He disappears out the door, and I hear the clod of his boots on the steps.

I take the time alone to survey the room again, and my eyes land on her computer once more. I'm torn. The last thing she was doing could give me a clue about where she is. But I could be reading too much into everything I'm seeing, and then she'll be furious I invaded her privacy.

I pick up my phone again and dial her number. This time, it doesn't even ring. It goes straight to her voicemail. My chest feels tight. I barely register the handyman's return as my mind reels with possibilities.

I fucked up when I couldn't protect her brother. I can't do it again. If something's happened to her, I'll never fucking forgive myself. He'd never forgive me.

I return to the couch without considering the consequences any further. I move the mouse, and I'm immediately stymied when the computer screen is locked with a six-digit passcode. I rack my brain for ideas. Unless...

I type one, two, three, four, five, six into the screen... and it unlocks.

Fucking hell. We'll be having a conversation about that the second I find her.

The screen lights up, and my jaw drops.

My heart stops.

I'm not sure I'm even breathing anymore.

That conversation would have to wait because this one... what I'm seeing right now is going to be a much harder one to have. One I could have lived the rest of my life without having.

"Fuck me."

"What?" The handyman is back to work on the sink, and his brow furrows as he looks at me from across the room. I can see the skepticism written all over his face.

"My sister. She's just buying a ton of makeup and clothes again. We're gonna have to discuss her credit limits." I lie through my teeth like it's second nature.

"Oh shit. I got one of those. Not a sister but a daughter. She always wants something new. First, it was them big steel cups, and now it's shoes. Always somethin'." He shakes his head, a grin on his face as he gets down on the floor to fix the sink.

"Yeah. Always something," I agree absently.

My mind's too busy processing what I've just seen. I have to look again. I need to be sure I didn't just imagine it. I angle the computer screen away from the kitchen, opening it and checking to be sure that he can't catch a glimpse before I enter the password again.

The screen lights up, and I'm greeted with an image of Dakota. She's spread out on her bed, mostly naked with a strategically placed cowboy hat just below her navel. Her face is cut off. Her tattoos have been edited out. But otherwise, it's her.

There's a ding, and a conversation window pops up, a small icon of a sword in a stone next to the screen name.

SWORDMASTER782:

You're on early.

Couldn't stay away?

I scroll upward and realize the photo's on a website. It's a subscription site—Dakota's subscription site.

Or rather, RideHimCowgirl's subscription site.

I'm through the fucking looking glass and in alternate reality where Dakota has a subscription site where she posts naked photos of herself and pretends to be a cowgirl living on a ranch when she's not entertaining her subscribers. Our family ranch, judging by some of the photos I see in her feed.

I ignore the message from Swordmaster and go to the inbox. Dozens of messages are there. Some opened, others not. A few of them look to be much longer chains, and I open one with another subscriber. This one is GirthyGuy1020. There are messages of them saying goodnight to each other, but when I scroll up, there's a much more heated conversation. One where he's asking her to tell him how she'd ride him. I see a dozen voicemail attachments from her. I skip them for later; it's not like I can listen to them with the handyman here.

I scroll further down, and there's another image. She's in a set of pale-peach panties with her fingers slid under the waistband.

GIRTHYGUY1020:

I bet you like to ride 'em big.

What's the biggest dick you've ever had?

I bet I'm bigger. I bet I could bust that pussy wide open.

I bet I could break his fucking neck without even trying.

I slam the screen shut.

"That bad?" The handyman chuckles from under the sink when he hears the loud clink of plastic on plastic.

"That bad." I grunt.

My thoughts are racing. She'd been smart in lying about who she was. In getting rid of the identifying marks on her body before sharing the photos. But there's enough there. Enough that she could be identified by someone who was really trying. Lev could find her in minutes if I asked him to.

So what if they were tired of teasing photos and texts? Maybe they wanted her for real. My gut twists.

I have a high tolerance for a lot of things—cruel, gruesome, horrible things. But imagining what the wrong person might do to her has my stomach on the verge of retching and my blood pressure through the fucking roof while I think about tearing the imaginary man limb from limb.

I grab my phone back out.

> You have anything yet?

LEV:

> Takes a bit to get through all this footage.
> Forwarding as fast as I can.

> Can you still track her phone?

I put tracking software on her phone last year when she disappeared for a long weekend and didn't let anyone know where she was going. She has a right to do whatever the fuck she pleases, but if something happens, I need to know how to get to her. If I need to get to her.

LEV:

> Theoretically.

> Do it. Do we have anyone we could pull to
> put on the streets?

> Do you want to read me in on what's going on?

> She's gone. The place looks like it could have been tossed. And I just found out she has a dangerous side hustle.

> What kind of danger?

I fire off the website and her screen name to him.

LEV:
> Fuck.

> Can you hack into it? I want the names and addresses of every single one of these fucks. And I want the site offline.

> Yeah. But you want the footage first, right?

> The phone first. Then the footage. Then the site.

> Got it. Give me two.

The two minutes pass at an impossibly slow pace. I'm listening to the sounds of the handyman's wrench turning and the shuffle of plastic and the tear of cardboard while I wait to find out if she'll ever be back to use the sink again.

LEV:
> Last location on the phone is the ranch.

> Our ranch?

> Yeah. It's not tracking. Looks like it lost her headed into the woods.

My mind turns on that one. No way would some guy be

able to drag her onto our ranch to harm her unannounced, not after the additional security measures we put into place last year. And there's absolutely no chance that anyone on our ranch would touch a hair on her head. So she must be safe.

LEV:

Coverage is spotty out there. Possible she's on a hike.

Or a horseback ride?

Yeah. Would make sense.

She does go horseback riding with Hazel at least once a week when the weather holds up. I've seen her on the ranch enough times to know that much. But it doesn't explain the state of the apartment.

I'll call Ramsey.

"I'm just gonna make a work call really quick. Back in five?" I say to the handyman as I head for the door.

"Sounds good. Should be wrapping up by then."

"Perfect."

I slip into the hall and walk down toward the far door, the one that gives access to the outer stairwell that leads to the back parking lot, before I hit the call button on Ramsey's number. It rings twice before he picks up.

"Hey."

"Hey. Have you seen Dakota today?"

"Yeah. Got here an hour or so ago. She and Hazel went out on the trail. Need something?"

Oxygen seeps back into my lungs, and my heart starts to beat again at an unsteady pace. A frustrated sigh leaves my lips before I can stop it. I highly doubt Hazel or Ramsey know about Dakota's side hustle. If I had to guess, no one knows.

"She just forgot an appointment with the handyman," I explain. But as the dread recedes, anger fills the crevices it left behind. "Will you let me know when she leaves?"

"Sure."

"Don't tell her or Hazel I was looking for her."

"Okay..." Ramsey trails off, sounding skeptical of my intentions.

"I don't want her coming up with a list of excuses before she talks to me."

"Fair enough," he concedes.

"You doing all right?" I ask. The man is in the last few weeks of the run-up to his second wedding. "No cold feet? We could always run off to Monte Carlo for a few weeks. Take a yacht up to Portofino." I know he'll say no to all of that but as his brother I feel like I need to make the offer.

"Nah. Too excited about being able to call her the little wife again." Ramsey laughs.

"All right."

"See you tomorrow?" We're meeting for drinks along with Levi. Ironing out some business details and talking about what he wants for his bachelor party.

"See you then."

We hang up, and I close my eyes, pressing my phone to my forehead while I breathe a sigh of relief. She's fine. She's safe. On the family ranch out on some trail riding horses with her best friend. Not locked in some psycho's basement as his personal plaything.

Except now she has another problem. *Me.*

FIVE

D AKOTA

I'M EXHAUSTED by the time I get back to the apartment and trudge up the steps. There was an issue with our liquor license that I had to drive down to the county seat to deal with. Then Hazel called, crying and worried about the centerpieces and seating arrangements that she wanted to hash out together in person. Since I was already there, we ironed out details for the pre-wedding party that was fast approaching. One that was turning into a massive event, but one she was so excited for; it makes me smile every time I think about the animated description of her plans. After all of that, she talked me into going for a ride, one that was a much-needed escape, except for the fact that I managed to slip when we let the horses stop for water, ending up a muddy mess. So I showered and had a quick dinner with them before I made my way back home.

I need to get changed out of this Queen City Chaos shirt and into something sexier before I have to start my eight o'clock chat with my best subscriber. An appointment I'll have to cut tactfully short so I can make it to cover a shift at the bar tonight and hopefully grab a scoop of sorbet to keep my spirits up.

I shut the door behind me, locking it, and sliding down the back of it in exhaustion. I wonder for the briefest of moments why Vendetta isn't in my lap already before I nearly have a heart attack when I open my eyes and see the silhouette at the table. I open my mouth to scream, but he cuts me off.

"Long day?" It's the fucking devil himself, lurking in the late-day shadows.

"What the fuck are you doing in my apartment?" I'm furious. He's rarely even been in my apartment, and now in a week, he's been in here twice. "Just because you have a key doesn't mean you can let yourself in."

Anger and panic swirl around one another, tightening into a knot in my stomach. There are lots of reasons I don't want him in here. Too many secrets he could uncover and things he could never unsee that would kill me for him to find out.

"No, but it does mean I have to let the handyman in when you forget to meet him."

"Oh shit." I press my hand to my mouth. It had completely slipped my mind with everything else going on. "I had to put out fires today, and I guess I forgot."

"I guess." His eyes drift over my shirt. "You have fun with Hazel?"

"Mostly." I'm not about to admit I fell in the mud. It would just be another failure he could add to the column of things he finds annoying about me.

"Good. I'm glad one of us was enjoying ourselves."

"Listen. I'm sorry about the handyman. I fucked up. Was he able to fix it?" I ask as I make my way into the kitchen. I set my purse down in one of the chairs at the dining room table, and my eyes fall on my computer. It's sitting square in front of Grant in a place I definitely did not leave it.

"He was." He doesn't flinch as he watches me.

"What are you doing with that?"

"With this?" He holds up the laptop and then looks between me and the device.

"Yes." I eye it nervously, grateful when I remember I left it password protected.

"Well... funny fucking thing is, when you weren't here and the apartment was so messy it looked like it could have been tossed over by someone, I got real fucking worried. Especially when I called your phone a dozen times, and you didn't bother to pick up."

"Yeah. Sorry about that. I was on the trail."

"And after the trail when you were showering? When you got in the car to come back home? At any other fucking point today?" I hear his temper rising in his voice.

"I saw you called and figured this was more bullshit about the shots or the money I owe you. I didn't care to hear about either when I was dealing with every other problem under the sun, so I decided to wait to call you back." I give it back to him two-fold. I don't need his lectures tonight. I need him gone so I can get on to chat with my subscribers and then get down to the bar. Gemma had called off, and that meant I was up. This day refused to end. "Can we please just do this some other time? I have shit to do."

"Nah. You can have a seat though."

"I have work to do," I insist, refusing to sit down.

"It can wait."

"It can't. I'm busy, and I don't need whatever asinine lecture you're about to give me about answering my phone and putting things on my calendar."

"Oh, this lecture's going to be a lot more than that."

"Yeah. I don't need your bullshit. I thought we covered this the other day."

He slams his open palm on the table.

"Sit. The. Fuck. Down. Hartfield." He booms, and his lashes barely lift to reveal blue eyes that are positively glacial. My heart clicks up a notch in my chest. I normally don't fear him, but sometimes, like right now, even I worry I've pushed him too far.

I drop my ass in the chair reluctantly and give him an expectant look. He doesn't say another word; he just opens the lid of my computer, and I nearly choke on my words trying to stop him.

"What are you doing? Don't touch that!" I reach for it, trying to tear it out of his grasp, but he artfully dodges me, punching numbers into the keyboard and then turning the screen around.

"Why? Because of this?" he asks as I'm faced with my mostly naked body on full display.

The heat races up my neck and colors my cheeks. I thought no one would ever find these. At least, not anyone I knew. I'd gone to great lengths to keep it a secret. And now the last person on earth I'd ever want to know is staring at it. Has possibly seen all of it. I want to *die*.

He hits another button, and a voice memo I'd sent to one of my subscribers starts playing. It's my voice, husky and over-heated. The sound of my vibrator in the background.

"I wish it was you with me right now. Wish it was your hands on me." Voice-memo me gasps and then lets out a soft whimper. "Would you fuck me with your tongue or would you —" Grant cuts me short when he presses another button.

The silence between us stretches on, moving from deeply uncomfortable to tortuously long in nature.

"Should I keep going?" He breaks it finally, nodding to the computer.

"You've made your point."

"Have I? Because when I was worried something happened to you and I went looking for information..." His tone is lethal as he speaks. "Finding this? I thought one of these sick fucks could have taken you. I thought you could be lost to the fucking wind. Stuck in his basement being used for some madman's amusement."

"Well. I'm not." I state the obvious.

"You're *not*. Instead, you just disappear. Blowing off your responsibilities—"

"I was not blowing off responsibilities." It's my turn to cut him off, and he doesn't like it. "I had an issue with the liquor license, and then Hazel had a wedding emergency."

"What liquor-license issue?" His lips flatten.

"I forgot to check something. Betty always made sure to remind me, but I guess she's gone now. They've turned over a lot of the staff at the county office, and I missed a date. But I fixed it. I can take care of things myself." I don't want to hear him say that he'll take care of it. He always "takes care" of everything and then lords it over me like I'm a child who can't be responsible.

There's a low scathing laugh on his part as he considers my defense.

"So you're spending so much time talking to dirty old men on the internet, you can't keep up with your actual responsibilities?"

"I'm not talking to them for fun. I need the money."

"Yeah. I saw the thousands sitting in your account, and yet you haven't been able to make rent for months. Why is that?" Accusation scorches through his tone.

"Because the bar isn't doing well. You know this." It hurts my heart to admit it, but it's true.

"And you couldn't use some of your porn money to pay the rent?"

"It's not porn!"

Another derisive chuckle bubbles up from his chest. "No? What is it then?"

"It's just some pictures. No different than the kind I'd share with a boyfriend. You're making it sound lewd."

He runs his hand over his lips like he's half in disbelief and half incapable of speech. It's distractingly attractive, and I hate it. He blinks and refocuses his attention on me.

"*I'm* making it sound lewd? Do you need me to replay that voice memo? Or the half dozen other ones I found? These men aren't your boyfriends. They don't care about you."

"You listened to all of them?" I'm having trouble breathing, and I hear a faint ringing sound in my ears.

I can't hear the rest of what he's saying because I'm too busy coming to terms with the fact that Grant fucking Stockton has just witnessed enough private content to make me want to dig my own grave and jump in it.

"I told you. When you were missing..." There's the slightest catch in his voice before he speaks, though, like he was thinking of the lie he was going to tell before he spoke.

"There's no way you looked through all of that before you started calling your brothers if you really thought something happened to me."

"I don't call Ramsey for this kind of thing."

"So you called Levi."

"To see if he could find out where you were. It took time for him to get that information." The middle Stockton brother is half genius and half enforcer. He's always the one they call when they need the important jobs done. If we weren't in the middle of a humiliating argument, it might be a little bit touching he was that worried about me.

"So then you—" He cuts me off before I can finish.

"I'm done acting like this is a fucking democracy. You owed me rent. You didn't pay, and now I find out you had the money all along."

"It's in arrears. I don't have the money yet."

"You didn't have the money for the rent, but you had money for all these clothes and lingerie?" He points to the mess on the couch. I was trying to find something cute to wear for my client earlier. He's particular about what he likes, but he tips well.

"It's part of doing business. You have to spend money to make money." I state the obvious.

"You spent *my* money," he snaps, his tone growing more impatient each time he speaks.

"Like you fucking needed it!" It's my turn to slap my palm on the table.

His eyes follow the motion, staring at my hand before the bright blues slowly lift to meet mine.

"I think you're forgetting who you're talking to."

"I know who I'm talking to—the one who thinks he's better than everyone in this town with his fancy fucking suits and his expensive liquor, when in reality, he's the person in this town everyone tries to avoid like the plague because they all hate him."

He's quiet again. A long minute passes before his lips form their way into a wry smirk.

"They don't hate me, Hartfield. They *fear* me." His eyes lock with mine, and I can't seem to tear them away no matter how much I want to. "But you're right. It's high time I stopped treating you differently just because I loved your brother like one of my own. You want to learn the hard way? We can make that happen."

"Sounds good to me." I know I sound petulant, but I can't bring myself to care.

"Perfect. You owe me all the back rent in full—tomorrow."

I let out a stuttered laugh. "You're insane. I don't have it."

"You seem to have plenty from giving keyboard warriors blue balls in your spare time."

"I told you—that money gets paid in arrears. I won't even have the first installment until a week from now."

"Not my problem."

"Well, there's no way you're getting the money tomorrow."

"Then expect an eviction notice."

I scoff. "Be serious."

"I'm the most serious I've ever been in my life. And your little side hustle? It's mine now. Every ounce of income you have coming from it goes toward the back rent plus interest and late fees."

I laugh. "I'd like to see you try."

"I don't have to try." He shoves the computer toward me. "Hit refresh."

I do, and in a blink, the page is gone. The pictures, the messages, the subscribers. All of it is poof—gone. My heart bottoms out into my stomach.

"What did you do?"

"Deleted it. But not before I had the money forwarded to my account."

"You can't be serious, Grant. I need that money. I need at least another month of that work. I have things I have to pay for!" I protest.

"Then you'll have to pay it from the money you make at the bar."

"It's not enough!" Tears start to well in my eyes, and my

stomach churns. It was barely going to be enough with what I was earning with the subscribers. It would take forever to build back a subscriber base, if I even could. I'd never do it in time to pay all the bills I have coming due.

His jaw ticks, and he studies my face. I try to bite back the burn of the tears down my throat, holding his gaze, but it's a useless fight. They crest over the edge and stream down my cheeks. Humiliation burning a trail down my skin in their wake. I can add this to the list of things I didn't need him to witness today.

"Not enough for what? What could you possibly need all this money for? Do you have an addiction or something you haven't told me about?" His brow furrows, and his tone changes. A hint of the brotherly concern I've known before seeps through the coarse impatience of the gangster who's sitting in front of me now.

"Hazel's wedding. The pre-wedding party. The bachelorette. The dress and shoes. The hair. Do you have any fucking idea how much it costs to be a maid of honor when the bride's marrying a pro football player and everyone but you has money?" I glare at him bitterly.

"That's what this was for?"

I nod, looking away and swiping at the tears running down my cheeks.

"I just started it recently when the bar started to go downhill thanks to the extra competition in town." I pause to give him a pointed look. "Bristol was worried about paying for everything too, and she joked about selling pictures of her feet. I don't have cute feet, but I do have other things men can't stop staring at. So I thought, what the hell... if it gets the bills paid, and I can do it without showing my face, who does it really hurt?" I shrug and shake my head, barely able to make eye contact with him.

"You. It hurts *you* if one of these men turns out to be a fucking creep." He sounds genuinely concerned in this moment but still unable to grasp that I'm an adult fully in charge of my own life. One who gets to decide whether something is worth the gamble or not.

"Then it's a risk I'm willing to take. I need the money, Grant. I can't let her down. I can't. It's humiliating enough as it is telling you."

He closes his eyes and scrubs a hand over his face. A rough sigh escapes from his chest while he lets the silence stretch on.

"Fine," he says at last.

Hope blooms again. I glance at the clock. There's still time. We could fix this.

"Is there some way to get it back? Some way to undo the deletion of the account? I have someone I'm supposed to be online with in an hour."

"No." His thumb swipes over his lips as his eyes fall over me while he considers my situation. "You're done with that."

"I thought we just established that—" The look he gives me stops me mid-sentence. He shakes his head and sits back in the seat, surveying me in a way that makes me shift in mine.

"I'm done being your fucking guardian angel all the time. Fuck, I don't think I can handle another day like today." He looks up at the ceiling like he's saying a prayer to a higher power. "I'll give you the money in advance so you can pay for the things you need for Hazel's wedding. But you're going to pay it all back. Anything over and above what you already earned, the back rent, all of it—with interest and fucking penalties for lying to me. You don't want me to be family? Fine. I'm not gonna treat you like family. You're gonna learn what it means to be in debt up to your fucking eyeballs with the Horsemen."

"The bar is barely in the black most months after I pay the

staff. Without more subscriber money..." I shake my head. "There's no way I can pay you the money back. You might as well tell your minions to slit my throat or take a finger or whatever it is you all do now. Save us both the trouble of waiting around for it."

"I don't outsource my dirty work, and I didn't say you were going to pay me back in cash."

"What?" I frown in confusion.

He glances at the clock and stands abruptly like he has somewhere important to be.

"I have to get back to the Avarice. We've got VIPs in tonight. Cover the bar shift. But when I go back to my room after last call tonight, I expect to hear from you. Don't make me wait for the text."

"What do you mean hear from me? What am I texting you?"

"What were you doing for him in an hour?"

"I was..." The words fade on my lips, trying to make sense of what he's asking of me. It can't be what I think it is. I have to be misunderstanding him somehow.

"You were?" He looks at me impatiently and smirks when he sees the blush returning to my cheeks. His eyes drift down over my body. "You're gonna have to get over that embarrassment. It's gonna make it real hard for you to show me how wet you're getting while you beg for my cock later, Cowgirl."

SIX

D AKOTA

I SWIRL my straw through the ice and oat milk, churning up the chai at the bottom of the cup while I sit in the corner of Hotcakes. Marlowe, the owner, is one of my best friends, and another of Hazel's bridesmaids. She's working with a couple of her employees, finishing up their closing routine before she can come sit with me. The place opens at the crack of dawn, so they close just after the lunch shift, which leaves me plenty of time to chat with her before I have to go back to Seven Sins across the street for my shift.

I hadn't been able to sleep in like I wanted this morning. Grant let me off the hook late last night, but the events of the evening just kept playing in a loop in my head. The way he talked to me. What he asked for in exchange for the help he was giving me—if you can call destroying my side hustle help.

Don't get me wrong. I wasn't thinking of leaving behind my bar and changing careers, but I didn't hate the subscription site work. The men were easy enough to talk to, and several of them had even been nice. I expected to be wading waist-deep in creeps when I leaped into this whole thing. Still, I was pleasantly surprised to find it was mostly guys who were lonely and wanted someone to talk to about their days or escape their daily routine through fantasy for a half hour or two. It isn't nearly as scandalous as I'd made it out to be in my head. It felt a lot like running the bar—look cute, flirt, show a little cleavage, keep the discussion light and the patrons smiling. Simple stuff really.

I still know that it's the sort of thing I'd be scorned for in this small town. I already took enough shit for being the wild child who'd been running a bar since she turned twenty-one. Grandmas clutched their pearls, and mamas didn't see me as the type you took home for family dinner on Sunday nights. I'd learned to live with that over the years, but this would bring out the gossips in full force if they found out.

Which is why I don't know whether or not to tell Marlowe. Not that she'd tell anyone. In our friend group, she's the vault— the one you can tell anything to without fear of judgment or overbearing advice, and the same one who would take all your secrets to her grave. But we don't usually keep secrets from each other in our tight-knit group, and I'd be forcing her to do just that.

I can't imagine telling Hazel with the wedding looming and her former and future brother-in-law at the center of it. Bristol, our other best friend, is drowning in her own money and time problems. I can't add mine to the pile just to ease my mind. So it's Marlowe or no one. I look up to see her putting a few baked goods on a plate and grinning at me from across the room. I smile back.

She'd never get herself into this situation. In addition to

being the secret keeper, she's also the good girl. The one who dutifully took over her mother's bakery and charms every single person who walks in the door with her sunshiny disposition. Some days, I wish some of it could wear off on me, but it never seems to take, no matter how many years we've been friends.

She sits down across from me and immediately clocks my mood. She pushes a plate of chocolate croissants, cookies, and mini cupcakes in front of me.

"Dealer's choice for your troubles, but you gotta spill." She raises a brow.

"What makes you think I have something to spill? Maybe I just wanted some afternoon tea and company," I counter.

"You look like you haven't slept, and if you're here instead of in bed grabbing the last few hours before you have to be ready for work, then it's dire—whatever it is."

"It is dire." I sigh and tear off a piece of the chocolate croissant. "But I don't know if I should pull you into it or not. It's messy."

"How so?"

"I can't tell the girls. I can't tell anyone. It's..." I look out the big picture window to see a pair of couples walking by. "It's embarrassing and awkward."

"But?"

"But I need perspective."

"All right. Then I'm here. Spill." She insists.

"Okay. I'm sparing details about the whos and the hows in order to simplify this and keep you out of the mud."

She nods and sips her drink while she lets me continue.

"Say someone needed extra money, and instead of joking about that whole selling pictures of their feet thing, they actually did it." I look up at her to check her reaction, but she's unmoved, simply waiting for me to continue. "And then one of the people who saw those pictures of her cute feet decided that he wanted to be the only one seeing them."

"A subscriber who wants to date you?" She tilts her head and drops the pretense of this being about my friend. She knows me too well. Well enough to know I'd be exactly the friend who would try something like this for shits and giggles.

"Not date me but be an exclusive subscriber. I'd still be selling pictures of my feet, but he'd be the only one buying them."

"But he'd make up for the lost revenue?" She's all business while she considers this.

"Yes, and then some."

"Is he a creep?" Her brow arches up in concern.

"No. He's... Well, he's not boyfriend material or anything like that, but he's not a creep."

"Not going to cause you any sort of trouble or harm?"

"Not in the way you're thinking."

"But there's a problem." She looks at me thoughtfully, tearing off a piece of croissant and taking a nibble.

"I know him outside the subscription website." I run my finger over the edge of my nail as I explain.

"A regular at the bar?" Her brow creases.

"Yes." It was technically true, and I was running with it.

"Okay... so you're worried he'll say something to other people you know?"

"No. I don't think he would. It wouldn't do him any good to do that."

"Is he married?" She looks up from her glass, and her eyebrow climbs a little higher.

"No. Nothing like that just... if you were selling pictures of your feet and a guy who came into the bakery every day was suddenly the only one buying them. But then he was still coming into the bakery, getting his bread and muffins. Wouldn't that be weird for you?"

"I suppose it would be an odd arrangement, but if he's not creepy and not married or anything. I don't see the problem." She shrugs but then blinks and gives me a curious look. "Unless I liked him as something more than a customer."

"I..." Don't know about the word like. I'd had a crush on Grant when I was younger. The same way every other girl in this town grew up having a crush on at least one of the Stockton brothers. But the older I got and the more we clashed, the less it was a crush and more of a complication. A weird echo of a feeling that I couldn't put words to.

"Let me guess. It's complicated." She knows me well.

"Something like that."

"Wait... is he hot?" She pauses mid-sip to ask the question.

"Yes. Very." That's one I can be honest in answering because it's ridiculous to lie about, even if I do hate him most of the time. She grins brightly, and I feel like she's about to do a little dance on my behalf.

"Dakota!! Oh my god. Okay then. I don't get it—what's the problem, or I mean... what's your question that has you worried?"

"Am I stupid for getting into this situation? I mean, it's going to backfire somehow, right?"

"As long as you think he can be discreet, it honestly sounds perfect. You get your money. He gets his feet. He's hot, has disposable income, and he keeps your secrets? What's not to like there?" When she puts it like that, it's hard to argue with.

"I don't know. It just seems risky." I sigh.

"Less risky than taking feet pics for hundreds of guys who could be creeps," she counters, playing devil's advocate.

"I suppose that's true." I nod.

I could trust Grant. His loyalty to my brother had been

unwavering, and even if we don't see eye to eye on much, he would never try to hurt me. Not on purpose. Even with the rival bar situation, it'd been a natural thing for him to do. He ran a casino and a resort. The place having a bar just made sense. We'd both thought, and I'd hoped, it wouldn't have any effect on my sales.

"So if it were me then... I'd do it. Too many upsides to worry about the slim chance of a downside." She shrugs. "Simple economics."

"This is why I need you for advice." I smile at her practical assessment.

"I've got you. I'm guessing this is vault?"

"Yeah. I don't want to tell Hazel. Not right now. She'll feel guilty, and I just want her to enjoy this wedding and have fun. Bristol too. She's got a lot on her own plate, and I don't want to drag her into my moral dilemmas."

"Fair enough."

So that was it then. I had the Marlowe good girl stamp of approval to go forth and take naked pictures for Grant Stockton in exchange for keeping the bar out of the red and Hazel's wedding celebrations on track.

SEVEN

G RANT

I'M in a disgruntled mood today. I'd gotten less sleep than I wanted because of the event we had last night, and I'd woken up way too early and stared at the ceiling wondering what the fuck I was doing with Dakota. I glare at my phone, wondering if I should just tell her to forget everything.

I put her off last night. Told her I needed sleep because of how late it was and how long the day had been. It wasn't a lie, but I also wanted some time to reconsider my decision. It had been a rash one prompted by her tears. I couldn't stand to see her cry like that, knowing she works as hard as she does and that the new bar we opened is probably contributing to her problems just like she said. Everyone likes the pretty new thing. Some of her regulars will drift back after the shine wears off, but it may not be in time for her to right the ship.

She also wasn't wrong about this fucking wedding costing a small fortune. I had a veritable army descending on the hotel in a few weeks to put on what I have to assume is the biggest event Purgatory Falls has ever seen. Everyone in our extended family and Hazel's, at least a dozen of his teammates, and a handful each of friends, acquaintances, and business associates were all going to make their way to see the two of them get hitched again. Their first wedding had been modest, and Ramsey's insisting on making this one perfect for her with all the bells, whistles, and pre-wedding events.

So I can't blame Dakota for being overwhelmed. There's probably an avalanche of to-dos and expenses that she's struggling to shoulder while she plays maid of honor to Hazel's unhinged bride of the year. But the way she'd been trying to solve it was dangerous. The same way she tries to solve every problem she has—by herself with very little forethought to what happens if things go tits up. Or what she'll do if her gangster landlord finds out and leverages it as blackmail against the debts she owes him.

I feel a whisper of guilt trickle down my spine. I rarely feel anything. It's all business to me. But with her, I feel something less cold—call it obligation to her brother, a tinge of humanity in my blackened heart. As much as I'm desperate to teach her a lesson and make her learn it the hard way, there's a hint of reluctance on my part. Probably because when I stopped seething with rage, I started wondering if she could manage talking to me the same breathy way she did to those men, and I was curious if she'd be brave enough to send pictures if I forced her hand.

"You look deep in thought." Levi enters my office with the same stalking silence he always does and sits down across from me.

"I've got a big fucking problem on my hands."

"Dakota?" He smirks. We know each other too well after all these years working together.

I nod.

"The site's deleted, and I assume you reamed her ass out thoroughly over it. So what else is there to solve?" His brow furrows in question, and he pulls his glasses off to clean them with the edge of his shirt.

"She needs the money. The money I seized from her and then some."

"Ah. And you're thinking of loaning it to her because you always have a weak spot where your former ward is concerned?"

"I don't have a weak spot. I have an obligation to Jesse." I give Levi an unamused look. They weren't as close as we were, but Levi treated him like a brother too.

"I think you fulfilled that obligation a long time ago. What she does now isn't your problem."

"Well. In all the fucking mess that was yesterday, I made it my problem."

"How so?"

I take my pen and turn it over on the desk. I don't even know how to explain it. I already know the face he'll make when I tell him. He clears his throat and raises his brow in expectation.

"I told her there were other ways besides money she could pay me back."

Levi curses under his breath and shakes his head as he looks out the window. "I could have seen this one coming from a mile away."

"There's nothing to see," I snap, and his eyes return to me.

"You said yourself it's a problem."

"It's a problem because if I back out of it, she won't take it seriously. She'll go back to doing all this risky shit. Putting her life in danger. Talking to strangers like that online. Selling photos for their entertainment. No. Jesse would hate it. Not to mention, the wrong guy gets too attached to her? She'll end up some sick fuck's plaything."

"As opposed to what you're planning to do with her," he mutters sardonically.

"It's just to teach her a lesson. Make her send a couple of pictures. Force her into a corner or two. She'll break easily, and I'll let her off with the warning."

"What if she doesn't?"

I laugh at the thought of it. "She could barely speak after I suggested it. I don't think it's a question of if; it's just a question of how fast. She hates me, and it's torture to her that I'm sitting on all the leverage."

"I think it's a bad fucking idea. With everything going on right now? It's a huge distraction. At some point, she needs to make her own mistakes."

"I don't get distracted."

He gives me a silent skeptical look in response.

"You have another solution that doesn't make me look like I can't handle holding a line with her once I draw it?"

He sighs and shakes his head. "No. You've well and truly fucked yourself on this one."

He wasn't wrong there. It had been a tactical error, one I'd let a rare surge of emotions drive me into. That wouldn't be happening again.

"This stays between us."

"You think she'll keep quiet that she has the head of the Horsemen wrapped around her finger?" he muses, his eyes dancing with the thought.

"Funny." I level him with a stern look. "She wants to keep her business private, and I'm keen to let her do that."

He nods and then reluctantly eases back out of his chair. "You ready to go find out what our little brother needs?"

"One more discussion of wedding details, and I'm going to take off on a month-long vacation and come back when it's all over," I grumble as we make our way to the door.

———

A HALF HOUR LATER, we're at the bar with Ramsey, sipping our drinks, when he springs some surprise news on us. I'm not a fan of surprises on a good day, but this one I couldn't have imagined in a million years.

"Went in to finish out all the paperwork to wrap up my parole, and I overheard some of them talking about the newly appointed sheriff." Ramsey swirls the whisky around the stones.

"They finally find someone to replace old man Sheppard? I still can't fucking believe he went out that way." I raise my brow as I think back to the scandal that rocked the police department last year when he was indicted on drug and weapons charges.

"You're not gonna believe the name that floated down the hall from their conversation." Ramsey's eyes lift over the rim of his glass as he takes a sip.

"Fuck. Longmeyer didn't get promoted, did he? I don't need his brand of squeaky-clean bullshit," I grouch. He was one of the lieutenants who was always giving me shit, implying that someday he'd have my head for all the crimes I committed. Despite the fact he couldn't prove a damn thing.

"Jay Stockton." Ramsey drops it like the rock it is.

"Our Jay Stockton?" Levi's face drops as fast as my stomach.

"The very one."

"How the fuck is that possible?" Levi's brow furrows as he sits straighter in his chair.

"It's a political appointment until the next election. He could get it if he was kissing the right ass. Which is apparently what he's been doing since he left," I answer him absently. My mind is already rushing ahead to a list of possibilities, each one more dire than the next.

Jay had been part of the mess we found ourselves in last year—not immediately speaking—the double homicide and the arson and the whole rest of the ugly summer the three of us shared was ours alone. But the impetus behind it—the robbery gone wrong and the fact that we'd ended up with something someone very clearly wanted on the black market—that had been a gambit my uncle and my father had been running together. It was one they'd largely kept Levi and me out of the loop on. When I'd asked questions in the wake of my parents' deaths nearly six years ago, Uncle Jay had told me it was need-to-know only, and apparently, even as the new head of the Horsemen, I didn't need to know. He'd said it would needlessly complicate my life, and he could handle it on his own.

I hadn't trusted him then, and I certainly don't trust him now. On his way back to Purgatory Falls without a single word to his family? On the side of the law, no less. Something had me wary in every new layer of this information, and I needed to get to the bottom of it as soon as possible.

"When? Did they say when?" Levi immediately starts asking about the facts. He's usually more in a rush to unravel a problem than I am.

"Nah. No details. I just caught the tail end of a conversation. They didn't seem happy about it. Seemed to think he wasn't the right one for the job," Ramsey explains.

"Wonder why?" Levi rolls his eyes and shakes his head.

Corruption runs rampant on both sides of the law around

here, but it's more than a little odd for someone from our family to start swimming on the right side of it.

"Has he reached out to you yet?" Ramsey looks at me.

"No. Nothing. Still silence." It leaves an unsettled feeling in my gut. I turn my glass as I think through how to handle it. "We'll see if he decides to check in when he gets here. Until then, you'd better start keeping an eye on it." I look at Levi.

"Do I want to know what that means?" Ramsey looks between us. Ramsey's the youngest of all of us, and since he went from college straight to playing pro ball right around the time our parents died, he missed out on the family business. Last year dragged him all the way back in, and he's still trying to adjust to that circumstance. It doesn't help that his wife, for good reason after last year, wants him clear of it all.

"Probably not," Levi responds casually, watching as our server walks by. "I'll look into it though. Could make it work for us."

"Somehow I doubt that." I shake my head. "He might not cause trouble for us, but given his silence, I don't think he'll be inclined to help."

"Won't want to bring too much attention to the family name." Levi surmises.

"Let's at least give him a chance to reach out before we decide what he wants. I thought he and Dad were close?" Ramsey's the optimistic one. That's the thing when you don't have to be neck-deep in the family business—you can pretend that people aren't their worst selves.

"They were close out of necessity for the business. There wasn't any sort of real love lost between them. Especially when Uncle Creighton left everything to Dad and us. It set him off," I explain.

There'd been times when Jay played the uncle to us kids. We went fishing and camping a few times. He always came over to play cards with dad and there was the occasional summer barbecue. But the older we got, the less we saw of him.

"Any chance he's feeling remorse for the way he handled that now that he's on his own? Maybe he's hoping he can come crawling back to the family?" Ramsey asks.

"After all the silence, you mean?" Levi shakes his head. "I don't care if he shares our last name. I'll treat him like every new sheriff we've gotten. If anything, we should be more wary, given that he knows too much about our business model. With everything he's seen over the years..." Levi's eyes lift to mine as he trails off, concern etched across them.

"He won't. There's no way he wouldn't go down as collateral damage. And if there's one thing that man values, it's his own interests," I counter.

"Don't we all." Levi's practical nature comes through. "I'll look into it. See what I can find."

"Good. We'll monitor it. If anything comes of it, we can discuss what the next steps should be." I down the rest of my drink and slide the glass to the edge of the table.

"WELL, if that's settled, I've got the second thing I've gotta drop on you." Ramsey looks between us and swallows another sip of his drink before he motions to the server for a water.

"Which is?" Levi looks at him expectantly.

"If this is another special request for the wedding..." I narrow my eyes at my younger brother. I'd do just about anything for him, especially now that he's back in town, at least part-time when he's not playing, but the attention to detail for this wedding has reached official state-event levels.

"Not exactly a special request, but Hazel's decided she wants to do something special at the ranch in lieu of a wedding shower. Wants to do a couple of days and an overnight. Her family, mine, and the folks on the ranch if they want to come too."

"What exactly are we doing?" Levi looks as suspicious as I feel.

"Just sitting out by the fire, some games, good food... that kinda thing." Ramsey sits back in an awkward way that makes me feel like he's not telling the whole truth.

"What kind of games?" I press the issue.

He smirks and looks into the distance like he's thinking about her now. I have to suppress my own smile in return. It's been so fucking good to see my kid brother smile again, and his happiness is almost contagious. *Almost*.

"If I tell you, you won't come, and she'll have my ass for ruining it." He looks at me, his brow worried.

"Now you have to tell us," Levi chimes in.

"All right. But you're coming. If I have to drag you there kicking and fucking screaming. She's the happiest she's been in... well, forever, it feels like, and I'm not letting anyone ruin it."

"Fine." I nod and motion for him to continue explaining our fate.

"She wants to do what she's calling wedding party games. She wants to pair everyone off, do some games around the ranch—riding, roping, shooting—and have it be a competition."

"What's the prize?" Levi asks.

"She hasn't decided yet. She was mulling an island vacation or something like that."

"She thinks this is fun?" Levi's rarely amused, too serious for his own good, even by my standards.

"She thinks she's playing matchmaker." He grins.

"It's a losing bet if she thinks she can do that with us." I shake my head.

"Nah. She considers you two lost causes—confirmed bachelors—she put it. But she's determined now that she's happy
again; she wants her brothers to be too."

"Poor bastards," I mutter.

"As long as she keeps us out of it." Levi shrugs.

"She will, but you're the decoys. They'll be on to her if
she's too obvious. Which is why I have to make sure your asses
are there. I told her it was going to be a near impossible sell, and
she told me if I enjoy being in her bed every night, I'll make it
happen."

"You're whipped as fuck." Levi laughs.

"And enjoying every fucking second of it." Ramsey grins.

It sounds like fucking torture. But I don't want to let him
down—not when he's so happy and last year was such a
nightmare.

"We'll be there," I say, and Levi side-eyes me briefly but
doesn't say a word to the contrary.

"Thank you." Ramsey gives me a surprised look.

"Another round?" I raise my nearly empty glass.

"I should get home," Ramsey answers. "Don't want to keep
her waiting."

"And I've got research to start on our dear uncle." Levi
presses his lips together.

"All right. I've got emails to check and business to attend
to." I look down at my phone and see there's a message from
Dakota. I open it without thinking and nearly choke on my own
tongue. Levi and Ramsey's heads both snap up.

"That serious?" Ramsey starts to lean over my shoulder,
and I quickly press the lock screen while I try to catch my
breath.

"No, just neck-deep in things I need to take care of," I
manage to say, but his brow slants like he doesn't quite believe
me. "I've got the check. You two go on."

"You sure?" Ramsey taps his wallet.

"Positive. Have a good one. Tell the once and future wife I say hello."

"She'll be charmed."

"I aim to please."

He nods and says his goodbyes, and Levi follows suit. I sit still for a few minutes, staring into the abyss. Dakota has decided to deliver early today—and I wasn't lying when I said I was neck-deep because before I can stop myself, I open the photos to look again.

One of them is of her in lingerie, her legs spread as she sits on a table with the bottle of Scotch—my bottle of Scotch, to be precise. It's the one small consolation she's finally given me in the last few months, so I have something to drink when I visit the bar. It was a small concession from her to me after I brought back one of the bottles of champagne she likes on Valentine's Day, so it feels like a subtle peace offering on her part.

The next photo is more artistic, the side of her jaw and neck framed by a shadow that falls across her chest to where the bra she has on is starting to slip off. The straps are hanging limply off her shoulders, and her breasts are threatening to tumble over the edge of the lace. I note that she doesn't put her face in the photo, just like with the ones she posted on the site. I'll give her credit for that much.

I flip back to the first photo. No face there either, and her upper body is blurred because of the focus on the bottle and her legs. My eyes trace the silk ribbon that travels over her thigh and connects to the garter she has on. I can only see parts of it. The bottle blocks most of the view I want. Or would want. If it was a different woman. One I'm allowed to fantasize about.

But I'm already imagining running my hands up the insides of her thighs. Telling her to spread wider for me. Trying to decide which is the shot and which is the chaser.

Fuck.

I press the button to darken the screen and lay the phone flat on the table, closing my eyes to try to find my fucking reason. Clearly, I've lost it. I can see Jesse standing in front of me, threatening to gut me from stem to stern. He would drag me back to hell for even thinking it.

If I'm going to keep doing this with her, I'm going to have to face that reality every day. I'll have to look at myself in the mirror knowing full well I'm a bastard for even fantasizing about the idea even if I never act on it. Which I won't. *Ever.*

My phone buzzes quietly on the table, and I pick it up again like it's a fucking snake. Her name is emblazoned across the screen, and I swipe it open.

HARTFIELD:

> You have to tell me what you like besides Scotch and money if you want me to make good on the debt.

The devil on my shoulder and my dick are already working in concert, making a list of the things they want next. I rub my temples and drink the last of my whisky just as the server appears to pick up the empty glass.

"Rough day?" He gives me a sympathetic look.

"You could say that."

"Another?"

"Nah. I'm good. Thanks." I nod, and he takes off back to the bar.

I pick my phone up again and open the contact screen for Hartfield. I delete her name and replace it with "HELLFIRE." Apparently, I was going to need a constant reminder. My eyes drift back to her message when I close out the pop-up.

> We need to lay some ground rules.

EIGHT

D AKOTA

THE DEVIL:

We need to lay some ground rules.

I SEE the text pop up as I work to fill a couple of beer glasses with the IPA on tap. Not my favorite, but these guys drink it up like it's water, so who am I to argue? I roll my eyes at his text. If I thought this situation would make Daddy Grant disappear, I was wrong. He's back in full force.

I hand the beers off and tuck the cash in my apron after I thank them for the tips. My attention returns to my phone, and I run my teeth along my lower lip as I answer him.

> Rule number one should be that we don't tell anyone about any of this.

THE DEVIL:

> That's a given. It doesn't need to be a rule.

> And correction. I didn't mean we in the collaborative sense. I meant I'm setting the rules.

I roll my eyes at his declaration. Of course. He always has to be in charge. He leads, and the rest of us are simply meant to follow. Not that I've ever done it well. I'm pretty sure those brief months he had to put up with teenage me nearly broke him.

> You like setting rules then? I guess that makes sense. Your obsession with control is unmatched.

> I'll have to think about how to incorporate that into the content. I know you said you wanted me to beg.

> Apparently, you like being a sugar daddy when it suits you. Do you like being called Daddy? Or just Cowboy?

> Or maybe a hyphenate? Sugar-daddy Cowboy?

THE DEVIL:

> Jesus Christ, Hartfield.

> Do not under any circumstances call me Daddy or Cowboy. Sugar or otherwise.

> No cutesy nicknames. Period.

I break out into laughter, and Gemma eyes me from down the bar, raising a brow in question, and I just shake my head.

Is that rule number one?

Apparently, it needs to be.

What's number two, Cutesy Cowboy?

I can imagine him now, pinching the bridge of his nose and leaning back, dressed to perfection in one of his expensive suits, to give me that deadpanned look of disappointment. I can't help the roll of laughter that escapes as I move to the next customer.

"Okay, you have to tell me what's so funny." Gemma sidles up next to me as she grabs some cherry and lime to garnish the drink she's mixing.

"Just a guy I'm talking to. He's so uptight, and I drive him insane."

"In a good way or bad way?" Her brows knit together as she secures the slice of lime to the edge of the glass.

"That's the question. Both, maybe?"

"Hmm. Can't wait to hear the updates on this one." She grins and hustles off to deliver the drink.

THE DEVIL:

Stop. Or I'll put you on your knees and make you call me sir.

I feel the flush of excitement over my skin and the warmth of interest pool low. I don't hate the idea. Not even a little bit. But I'm not about to let him know. The man has enough aces up his sleeve. I don't need to give him any more by letting him know he might, on rare occasions, feature in a fantasy or two of mine.

> I'd rather be over your knees. You can slap
> my ass a few times while I recite the names
> I'm not allowed to call you.

The dots appear and disappear a couple of times, and I give up on getting a reply. Maybe I don't have to be nervous about any of this; maybe I've already ruined it before it ever got started.

An onslaught of customers makes their way in, and I get lost in the shuffle. I've almost finished the line when I turn to another customer, one with pretty deep-brown eyes and dimples. This one is much more my speed than the one I'm trading barbs over texts with.

"What can I get you, handsome?"

"Your number for starters." He grins and then looks up at the draft board. "And then whatever kind of wheat beer you've got on draft."

"I've got a Blue Moon or a new one from Breckenridge. Pick your poison."

"Breckenridge works."

"Coming right up."

"And the number?"

"You have to earn that." I wink at him and then move to start pouring the glass.

I look down, and my phone flashes again with a message. I hand the beer off and take his card for a tab. He compliments the head on my pour and makes a promise to earn his way into my phone before I can look at it again.

> THE DEVIL:
>
> Rule number two is that you don't fuck
> around while we're doing this.

> If you read my conversations, then you know I liked to joke with my clients.

> You need to find your sense of humor.

"You misunderstood." A deep voice greets me from the other side of the bar, and I startle before my eyes meet his. He looks prettier than usual tonight in a suit that's perfectly tailored to highlight his broad shoulders. I'm lost for words, and he's amused at the fact he's caught me off guard. "I meant there are no other numbers in your phone besides mine while we do this."

"That sounds like an overreach." I manage to find my voice again. "And besides... What if he'll let me call him Cowboy when I ride?" I give him a teasing grin, and I see the slightest hint of one on his lips, too, before he smothers it.

"He lets you ride, and it'll be his last rodeo before I break both of his legs." He leans on the bar. "How's that sound?"

"Sounds like you need a drink." I press my lips together and raise a brow.

He opens his mouth to respond, and I hold up my hand.

"Scotch neat. I know." I go to reach for the bottle, only to find it missing. "Shit. I left it upstairs."

I blush as I remember why it's still in my apartment—that he's seen the photos I took with it. I'm out of my depth on this new dynamic, and there's a sly grin that tugs at the corner of his mouth as he sees me floundering. The kind that's almost charming.

"Give me a Jack and Coke then."

"You're sure?"

"Positive."

I give him a skeptical look but pull out the glass anyway.

"What are you doing here?" I ask, keeping my focus on my pour.

"Thought I'd be on hand while we establish the rules. In case we need to iron out any details."

"Afraid I won't agree to them?" I risk a glance as I add the Coke.

"I don't think you have much choice."

"There's always a choice." I slide him the drink.

"Fair enough, but yours are pretty limited at the moment."

I have to disappear to take care of another customer who's waving me down, and I get caught in the rush of people pouring in for happy hour. But I hear my phone ding again and look up to see that he's finally rooted back in his usual seat.

THE DEVIL:

> Rule number three: I want delivery of assets every night by last call.

>> Rule number four: Don't call them assets.

> Isn't that what they are?

>> It's what I'm making use of, not what I'm creating.

>> Rule number five: You don't ever show them to anyone.

> I told you. I set the rules. Actual rule number four: We don't ever show them to anyone else.

>> Deal. But I mean it about the assets.

> You haven't given me a better term.

>> Something wrong with just plain old photos?

I look up from my phone behind the bar and raise my eyebrow at him. He matches it.

THE DEVIL:

It'll be more than photos you're delivering.
You were going for video and live tiers. You'll
need them if you want to work this debt off
before retirement-home age.

> I'm still hoping for a last-minute sugar daddy
> to save me from you.

Afraid the clock's run out on you for that. See
Rule Number Two.

> I haven't agreed to the rules yet.

You're still confused. You don't have to agree.
They're my rules to make. Yours to follow.
That's what happened when you got yourself
so deep in debt with the Horsemen.

> Maybe Levi will save me then.

Not a chance in hell.

> Would he let me call him Cowboy?

No.

> Daddy?

Hartfield. Look at me.

Do I look like a man who shares?

I glance up, and he looks positively devilish—living up to every single whispered rumor of his reputation from across the room. I don't respond to him; we just stay locked like that for full moments, staring at each other from opposite ends of the bar.

I'm in danger.

I realize it now. This side of him is so different than the one

I normally get. I'm not sure whether that's good or bad for me, but I know one thing for certain: I'm going to enjoy it while it lasts.

NINE

D AKOTA

THE NEXT DAY, I'm at the ranch helping Hazel set up for what she's deemed the "wedding games" this weekend. She's pairing everyone off and making them compete to win a prize in lieu of having a bridal shower. The girls and I had planned for some more traditional games and pink champagne, but we could adapt.

"I don't need more things. I just want more time with my friends and family, you know?" Hazel looks at me as we put together centerpieces for the tables. She's been worried about making every detail perfect to make Ramsey happy, and he's been worried about making sure every last thing is just the way she wants it. They're adorable, and I've nearly forgiven him for everything he did. Which makes me a little short on Stockton hate these days and a lot in danger of liking them—one in particular.

"I feel the same way. Less stuff. More time spent with the people we love. There's never enough of that."

"Exactly!" She finishes the last piece with a bouquet of wildflowers and slides it off to the side. "But I did have to invite his siblings, you know, to keep the peace around here. Family unity and all that." I can hear the uncertainty in her tone. She, more than anyone, knows my feelings about the family. She just doesn't happen to know about recent developments.

"Ah. Do you think they'll actually come?" My stomach flips at the thought of him being here, but I can't imagine Grant Stockton at a wedding shower.

"Aspen already RSVPed." Aspen is their one and only sister. She's quite a bit older than Ramsey, and I'd only met her once or twice.

"Do we like Aspen?"

"We love Aspen. She checked in on me even after the divorce—er, the original divorce-not-divorce, not the accidental real one." Hazel grimaces.

Hazel and Ramsey's story is a long one. One you'd have to hear from her to even begin to understand the mess those two got themselves into last year.

"Well, that's good. But Levi and Grant?" I try to sound nonchalant when I bring up his name. His being here this weekend would make this arrangement we've found ourselves in even trickier, and I'd like to know ahead of time.

"Who knows with them?" She looks up at me. "Will you be okay if Grant comes? I know the two of you have been getting along less and less."

"I'll be fine. He can stay on his side of the house, and I'll stay on mine." I grin at her, hoping she can't see anything on my face.

"Am I crazy to split everyone up like that? I just felt like it would be fun. Plus, it'll drive Ramsey insane to not be in the same bed as me for a weekend." She gives me a mischievous grin.

"I don't think you're crazy for splitting people up. It's like a giant slumber party. The guys can camp outside if they want to complain." I can't stop smiling when I look up at my best friend and I see the evil little grin on her face. She decided to have all the girls sleep in the bedrooms upstairs and the guys sleep downstairs, including her soon-to-be husband for the second time. "Keeping Ramsey at bay might be a little crazy."

"I'm counting on it. Because the second you all are gone." She bites her lower lip and stabs the floral foam with another round of greenery.

"I hope he uses a little more finesse than that." I laugh.

She bursts out laughing and shrugs. "Depends on his mood —and mine." The look of mischief returns to her face. "It's part of why I want to see what happens if we're separated for the weekend. We've been trying a new thing I've been loving though."

"What's that?" My brow furrows as I work to get the centerpiece into the glass jar.

"Free use."

"Free use?" I quirk a brow as I manhandle the floral foam into the glass.

"Just like it sounds. He can have me anytime he wants me, any way he wants me, without asking. Unless I say the safe word."

I blink. I could count the number of boyfriends I've had on one hand and how long we stayed together with even fewer fingers. They never live up to the promises they make at the start, and I won't settle for anything less than what I give in return. But that means that there really hasn't been the option for me to develop the sort of relationship Hazel and Ramsey have where they trust each other unequivocally, and it meant things like "free use" don't even exist in my vocabulary.

"So you're just... doing the laundry, bending over to pull something out of the dryer, and bam?" I ask, mulling over the idea in my head.

"Okay, *that* makes it sound not nearly as good as it is. He hasn't tried that particular one." She looks up at me with a distracted smile on her face. "But... Like the other day, he woke me up by going down on me for breakfast, and the other night, I was so frustrated running the software update at the inn that he just bent me over the front desk and railed me right there."

"With guests in the inn?"

"It was late."

"Where was Grace?" I blink. "I feel like you'd scandalize her for life."

"In the back doing inventory. She'd be fine. She's not as innocent as she looks." She dismisses my concern for her inn manager.

"She looks like a preacher's daughter." I give Hazel a skeptical look in return.

Hazel shakes her head and laughs. "She'd probably just turn around and walk back out and then high-five me later. Plus, the risk is part of the fun. Also, he had just come in from the field, so he had the whole cowboy thing going on. So fucking hot." Hazel nibbles her lower lip and stares into the distance.

I study my friend, thinking about everything that's changed recently. It had been a rough few years for her after he left, and while I was ready to put the man six feet under if she said the word, I'm happy they found their way back to each other. Ramsey has a soft side that Grant doesn't, one that's completely exposed when it comes to Hazel. The kind of love you dream about growing up—the kind some part of me still wishes I could find even if reality has made it feel impossible.

"I love you two together." I haven't seen her this happy since the day she told me he'd finally asked her to be his girlfriend in college.

"So do I. Now we just need to find you your Prince Charming."

"Easier said than done." I sigh as I go back to assembling flower arrangements.

"I have a few ideas." She wiggles her eyebrows but doesn't look up at me.

"I hate to even ask."

"Well, I wasn't planning to tell. Have to keep some things up my sleeve."

I was never much for surprises. They're rarely a good thing.

"That's ominous."

"Oh stop. You'll like this one." She flashes a bright smile as she waves the scissors in my direction.

"Is that a threat?" I joke, and she hands me another arrangement to stuff inside a mason jar.

"Maybe." She watches me for a moment. Long enough I start to feel a little self-conscious. "I mean, do you like being single? If you do, I don't want to interfere. I support you however you want to do things. I just want you to be happy."

"I... don't know what I want."

It's a lie. What I want right now is for Grant Stockton to have the same sort of appetite his younger brother does. I'm imagining him giving up his stern big-brother act for good, right along with the rules he set, and bending me over the desk in his office while he whispers dirty things in my ear. He'll never do it. It's one thing to play games over text in secret. Another if it's real.

"Dakota?" Hazel's looking at me confused.

"Hmm?"

"You seemed far away there for a second."

"Sorry. I just was thinking about what it must be like to be in the kind of relationship you and Ramsey have."

"Would you ever get married?" Hazel asks. It seems like such a far-off concept for me. I don't know that I've ever seriously considered it.

"Maybe someday? Hard to say when the men in my life have been... well... You've met them." I grimace a little as I think back to some of the guys I've given the time of day to. I had to learn my lessons the hard way. Grant was right about that much.

"You will." She gives me a sympathetic pat on the arm. "You just need to find the right guy. One who puts you first, and one who actually has his shit together enough to match your energy. Too many of them have been intimidated by your boss-bitch ways. We need someone who thinks that's your best quality."

I laugh. "Good luck to me with that. Trying to find a guy taller than me, likes my attitude, and doesn't suck in bed? I think we're looking for a unicorn."

"I mean... If I can find Ramsey."

"You think there's more than one in this tiny little town?" I give her a cynical look.

"Doubtful, but then I think anything is possible. Maybe we just need to import some for you. Or you know... if you go on more trips. If you visited me in Cincinnati more this year. Guarantee I could work magic. There are unicorns everywhere. Just saying." She's gotten very optimistic in her Ramsey-reunited world. She breaks into laughter when she sees my face. "Fine. Fine. I just want to see you more. You and Bristol and Marlowe need to come out more. Have girls' weekends with me and go to games. I miss you when I'm not here. And there are plenty of single guys in Cincinnati. Ones on the team even. You and Hayden seemed like you got along when he was here for New Year's Eve."

"We miss you, too, but I don't know if Hayden is my unicorn. Or if Cincinnati even has what I'm looking for."

"Maybe. Maybe not. You don't know until you try. You could come with us when the season starts." She hedges and gives me a sideways glance.

Maybe. Maybe I could run away and follow Hazel to Cincinnati for a while after they come back from their honeymoon. I might be able to escape this dangerous web that I'm willingly weaving with Grant. One I know only ends with disappointment.

Hayley and Gemma have been holding down the fort pretty well without me on nights like tonight. Getting away from the bar, truly getting away and not just being upstairs, would be huge for me to try to figure out the future.

But some small part of me keeps wishing I could find a unicorn closer to home.

TEN

GRANT

"THANKS FOR COMING." I greet the raven-haired woman I've come to call a close friend as I meet her in the hall.

"Of course. Much easier to discuss this in person than to try and talk in code over the phone. Essie and I had a pickup to do in the city anyway." She smiles at me as she follows me into the chess room. It's my own version of a SCIF. A place where I can oversee the bar and the casino floor but devoid of cameras and recording equipment. The perfect place for private meetings. I nod to the guard who stands outside the room to shut the door.

"Have a seat, please." I point to one of the overstuffed leather chairs. "Can I get you anything?"

"No, thank you. I just had breakfast at a little place in town. Hotcakes? So good."

"Ah, yeah. Marlowe's place. She's a good friend of my future sister-in-law."

"Sometimes I wish I lived in a small town. Some place where everyone knows everyone. A place where you all grew up together. It must be reassuring." A sentimental smile forms on Charlotte's lips.

"It's the opposite more times than you can imagine."

"Ah well. I guess the grass is always greener."

"I can't tell you how many times I've wished for the anonymity you get in a big city." I admit. I love Purgatory Falls. It's home. But we all crave what we can't have from time to time.

"Hudson has all of us set up with the best of both worlds. The penthouse in the city and then the country house. Not that we ever get to spend much time there. It's in the middle of nowhere though. None of the small-town charm. Just acres and acres of fields and forest." Charlotte's smile returns, and I see the way her eyes go distant as she's thinking about her men as she describes it.

"Good hunting and hiking, I imagine." I reflect her smile.

"If one had time for hobbies." She gives me a knowing look. "We all lead lives too busy to have much time for anything besides our work."

"Hazards of the job."

"It is beautiful though." She nods, and I sit down across from her, satisfied we've broken the ice with small talk.

"All right. Hit me with the plan."

"We've gone through all the authentication stages with the buyer, and it's clear they're very keen to get their hands on it. They outbid several other people on the market when they found it was finally up for auction after the presale exhibitions we did last year. I even had a friend try to drive the price up, and they continually bid well over market for it. So we're fairly certain it's them. Now it's just a matter of letting the relic lead us to them."

"Understood." I lean forward, steepling my hands and nodding along so she knows I'm following her. We put this plan in motion last year when it became clear that the man who tried to get close to Hazel back then, and had succeeded in deceiving her, was originally sent after her to get access to the ranch and property there. Given that he had also infiltrated the casino by getting a job on staff, one that he was hoping would eventually lead to vault access, Levi and I had immediately been suspicious that he was after the relic we owned.

Or rather, the relic we had stolen. Years ago, shortly before our parents were murdered, our father had agreed to do a job that involved obtaining a number of pieces of rare art and relics. He and our Uncle Jay had been nervous about every aspect of it, and Levi and I had assured our father at the time that we could pull it off without incident.

It had seemed easy. Levi would hack into the system, dismantle the security measures, and overlap the CCTV. The two of us would go in and take the items on the list and bring them home. An in-and-out job really. Our father had wanted to go with us, but he'd suffered a cardiac incident a few weeks before, and doctors were worried that any stress could lead to a heart attack or worse. I was worried for him and his stress levels, but practically, we had also discussed what a liability a medical incident like that could be in the moment—catastrophic.

Reluctantly, he had agreed to let Levi and me handle the job alone, so we'd set off to do just that—confident in the way only twenty-somethings who have never seen the worst of it could be. And then it had all gone to hell. Levi's work was over-ridden as soon as we got in the door, like someone else was waiting for his handiwork. The alarms had gone off, and the police were on their way when another group of masked men had entered the building. They'd held us at gunpoint and taken everything in our possession, barely escaping as the authorities arrived. Quick thinking and Levi having hidden one of the relics prior to going deeper into the building were the only things that had us leaving with our lives and anything at all to show for our efforts.

The incident rattled me so badly that I insisted on staying a couple of extra nights. There was no hurry to get home, and I wanted to hit up a few clubs. I needed alcohol to settle my nerves and sex to remind me I was still alive. Things I came to regret when I woke up, hungover with a woman in my bed, to a phone call telling me I needed to come home because my father and mother were dead. Murdered in cold blood on the porch. It had clearly been a hit, but the ransacked home and sloppiness of the murder convinced the cops that it was a burglary gone wrong. They believed the thieves had fled the country. Their only consolation to us was that they would report the incident up the chain where it was lost in a drawer and forgotten about.

We'd never gotten justice. At least not until last year when Ramsey came back home and helped unravel the murder of our parents. Those answers only led to more questions though. Like who sent us hunting down the relic in the first place, why they were so desperate to have it back, and who sent the Flanagans to our property to torture Hazel.

Charlotte, an expert in black-market art and smuggled antiquities, agreed to help us try to lure out the source of our troubles by putting the relic up on the market. We reasoned that if they were willing to kill and steal for it, they'd likely be willing to pay an exorbitant sum for it. Offering it on the market meant there was less of a chance of more thieves being sent to harass my brother's once and future wife—something he'd been outspoken on as an imperative.

"Will you hand it over to them directly?" I ask.

"No. These things are done through couriers. Usually, a system of them so no one person has too much information. I'll hand it off to the first designated courier later this week after they confirm they have it, and I confirm the money has been wired into the account they set up."

"And then?" My brows knit together. I want to know how we find out who the buyer is when everything involved in this plan feels like a house of cards.

"I have my sources listening in, but this particular train of couriers is one that's a mystery. I'm looking forward to answers myself. I'm hoping what we can't get from sources and educated guesses—meaning who is out on delivery and who's neatly tucked in their offices and gallery spaces this coming week—we can get from the device I've embedded in the case."

"That seems risky." My lips flatten as I worry what sorts of alarm bells a device could set off. If we'd get caught trying to pull this off.

"It's well disguised in the hygrometer. That's a temperature and humidity gauge. It's not uncommon to have them during transport to make sure none of the carriers are leaving it in the heat too long or anywhere with high humidity. I've worked with Levi to create one that's attached to a custom program he created. It'll log the temperature, humidity, elevation, and GPS coordinates every four hours or so. That'll ping back to a remote server and give us the data."

"That's clever. Will they question why it has something transmitting?"

"They shouldn't. It's not unheard of. I'll argue that since it's a courier service I'm unfamiliar with and a very rare and expensive item, I want evidence it isn't mishandled in transit. Since the price for loss on these sorts of items can be death or worse, the couriers shouldn't argue with that."

"But it could raise questions?" I want this plan to succeed. I need it. We all do.

"It could, and likely as soon as it arrives at its destination, it'll be separated from the gauge altogether. Maybe before, depending on how paranoid the buyer is."

"Fuck," I curse. I'm worried we're giving all of this up, material that could be evidence in my parents' murder, for nothing.

"Every plan has its risks. But I feel confident about this one," Charlotte reassures me. She's one of the most self-assured people I've ever met besides Hudson. It's why they make a good match.

"If you're sure."

"I am."

"And you're meeting with the courier personally?" I question the sanity of that. If the buyer was smart, they'd be trying to figure out who the seller was.

"Yes."

"That isn't dangerous? Hudson's not going to be furious, is he?"

"Calculated risk. Rowan and Essie will be with me. The two of them won't let anything go wrong."

"All right. I'm sorry to ask so many questions. I don't doubt you know what you're doing. I'm just..." The words fade on my lips.

"Nervous. I get it. I would be." She pauses and looks out one of the mirrored windows to the bar. "I am, too, really. This could lead back to the death of Hudson's grandparents if it is what we think it is—who we think it is."

Hudson's grandparents had died in a suspicious house fire around the same time as my parents. It had sent him on life-altering mission to find the culprits. We suspected the killers had been one in the same after last year's events and long hours of research on Charlotte's part.

"If it is who we think it is pulling the strings, we'll have all-out war on our hands." I scrub a hand over my mouth.

"A war Hudson will start." Her face falls, and she shakes her head.

"I'll be right there with him." I don't want war. But I need answers, and if answers lead to war, then I'll do what I have to.

"I know. That's what worries me."

"But we can't let it go on like this."

"And if it's not someone familiar behind the curtain?"

"I don't know what's worse. The devil we know or the one we don't." I lament our options. None of them are good. We sit in contemplative silence for a few moments, watching the tourists on the casino floor before Charlotte shifts in her seat.

"I should be going. Essie and I need to be back in Denver before tonight. Meetings and all of that," she announces.

"Essie came back to Purgatory Falls? I thought this was too backwater for her." Essie is Charlotte's personal bodyguard, a woman who could rip most men limb from limb. Even I wouldn't want to cross her unprepared.

"Hudson insists. Rowan and Finn don't even like me going to the grocery store without her if one of them won't be there."

"You do your own grocery shopping?" I tease her.

Hudson and Charlotte ran in very elite circles. The ones us backwater kind were rarely even invited to attend. Years ago, when the underground order of things had been decided, the Kellys, better known colloquially as the Gallowsmen for their ancestors' ability to narrowly avoid the gallows, had been the anointed ones. Years of being on the inside of the best homes and privy to society's secrets, they snaked their way into positions of power and prestige. Positions that included the well-connected East Coast upper crust where they connected the haves with the have-nots and the thieves and criminals with the wealthy parts of society that could afford their goods.

The Stocktons, or the wider association out west that the Stocktons came to lead—The Quiet Horsemen—were silent partners. Money launderers and facilitators, making sure that all of the money was washed back out through legitimate and some less-than-legitimate means—saloons, silver and mineral investments, ranching, and casinos among them. It's why Purgatory Falls was the perfect home and how it got its name— halfway between sin and salvation.

"I do occasionally have time to go grocery shopping, yes, and I prefer it. I still don't feel right having help for everything, given how I grew up." Charlotte shakes her head. You wouldn't know her humble beginnings given her current lifestyle—one I imagine she could earn herself even if Hudson hadn't been in love with her.

"There's no reason to make it difficult just for the sake of difficulty." I grin, thinking of Hudson worrying about her mulling around the grocery store.

"But challenge for the sake of challenge."

"Is the grocery store a challenge?"

"Have you ever been in a grocery checkout line the night before a snowstorm? It's a knife fight." She laughs as she stands.

"Can't say I've tried it, so I'll just have to believe you." I smile in return.

"All right. On that note, I guess I'm off then. We'll see you back here in a few weeks for the wedding, though, right?"

"Absolutely. You'll get to meet the entire dysfunctional family then."

"Wouldn't miss it for the world. And I can't wait to see your brother finally get his girl. They're so sweet together."

"We all can't wait for that. We might finally get some peace and quiet for a moment then." I walk Charlotte to the door, and she grins back at me.

"You next or Levi?"

"I think hell would need to develop a thick layer of ice first."

"Wilder things have happened."

"So they say."

"Be safe." She nods at me.

"You too. Careful on the drive back." I wave her off as she heads for the elevators and then return to the chess room.

I press my hand to the glass and lean over to look out on the casino floor. It's busy already, which is a good omen. I just hope that occupancy numbers and the busyness of my casino floor continue to be at the top of my priority list for the foreseeable future, rather than the number of men I have dying while fighting an unwinnable war in the streets.

ELEVEN

GRANT

I'M EXHAUSTED by the time I get up to my suite. I collapse on the couch with a bottle of water and the late-night snack I grabbed from the kitchen. I didn't even manage to eat dinner tonight, too busy entertaining guests, having meetings with my late-night staff, and checking off on some final orders and arrangements for Ramsey's wedding with all the guests coming in from out of town for it. All after the day I had handling business.

If I had more energy, I'd sink into the hot tub out on the patio to soak my tired body. I was on my feet all day, and the workout I did this morning in the gym was more brutal than usual. I can feel it every time I have to move my shoulders. I don't know how Ramsey keeps up. Or rather I do—it's his job, and he has staff on both sides of the country to keep him in shape and eating right, and probably a whole post-workout regimen on top of it. Not to mention the ten extra years his body has off mine. I'd give anything to be that young again and get to redo some of this—appreciate what I had when I had it. Speaking of young, my phone dings, and I see her name across the screen. Or rather, her nickname.

HELLFIRE:

> Any special requests? I opened today, and I just want to take a shower and climb into bed. But I don't want to be out of compliance with assets.

I smile at her sassiness.

> That makes two of us.

> Take your shower and text me when you get in bed.

> All right. If I don't fall asleep in there, I'll text you.

I slip my phone onto the table and take the last bite of my pita, downing the water before I make my way to the shower. I imagine Dakota doing the same in her apartment, slowly peeling her clothes off and letting them drop to the floor, turning the water on and letting it steam up the small tiled room. Her hands drifting over her body as she soaps herself up.

I can't stop the roll of images that flash through my mind. I can't unsee what she posted. I knew she was pretty—gorgeous even. I could tell that from the number of men who flocked to her side of the bar whenever she was working. But in my mind, she was always his kid sister. Someone I was supposed to watch over and keep safe. Forever stuck in time as an irresponsible eighteen-year-old with an attitude. Not someone that I could even remotely imagine as anything else.

Now, though... fuck. It's all I can see. The swell of her breasts and hips. Her hand following the curve of her stomach. The sound of her voice—that perfect, sweet husky quality it has, the full way she laughs when she teases me. I want every dirty fucking thing I can get from her, and I'm a sick fuck for pressing her into this situation. She already hates me enough, and I can't imagine this is helping any.

But I can't stop myself. Not yet. I'd have to though. We couldn't take this too far. It would be a disaster with all the ways the two of us are tangled up in each other's lives. But there's room to play before we get too close to that edge, and I don't plan to deny either of us that fun until I have to.

FORTY MINUTES LATER, I'm half-asleep, sprawled across my bed, when I hear my phone ding with a message, and I reach for it. It's not a text though. Just a picture of her spread out on her own bed, an arm drawn over her face, and damp hair spread out around her. The sheet is draped over her abdomen and falling between her thighs. But she doesn't bother covering her breasts, and her nipples are peaked from moving from the heat of the shower to the light breeze of the air conditioning.

> Falling asleep on me already?

HELLFIRE:
> I was hoping maybe you already were, but I didn't want to risk it.

> I was drifting off. Smartass.

> You still haven't told me enough to know what you want, so you're getting the basic package.

Nothing about her is basic. But I hate that I can't see her eyes and her gorgeous smile in these photos. I want all of her.

> You don't have to cover your face for me.

> Risk giving you more blackmail material?

> I have enough blackmail material to bury you already.

> Very reassuring.

> You asked what I wanted, and I want to see your face.

> Surprising. I always figured you for the nameless, faceless type.

> Plus, I thought it would make it less awkward for both of us.

> I went through all the stages of discomfort the other day when I found all your toys charging on the counter and everything on your computer. I think we're past that now.

> The toys too? Wow.

> Maybe kidnapping and death would have been easier.

> Don't joke.

> Is that what you like then? You have quite the collection.

The dots pop up and disappear several times while I smirk at my phone.

You're not gonna toy shame, are you? Those guys always end up being disappointing in bed.

No. Just curious.

You won't have to worry about that.

That confident?

That confident you'll never know the answer to whether I am or not. This stays behind a screen.

Is that another rule?

Another given.

Let me see your face.

A moment later, another picture comes through. It's one of her reflection in the mirror in her room. She's tangled up in the sheets and looking back over her shoulder at the mirror in profile as she holds the phone. She doesn't bother blocking her face this time.

She's fucking stunning. I understand why all these men were paying for an ounce of her attention. I'd sell my soul for her if I had one left.

HELLFIRE:

There. Two photos. One giving face. Anything else, boss?

No. You should go to sleep. You said you had a long day.

I'm awake now. Apparently sexting with your landlord does that.

Are we sexting?

I'm sending you naked photos, so I think yes.

Although it's very one-sided. I'm used to getting an avalanche of dick pics by now.

I've only ever sent one dick pic in my life, and it was on a dare.

A dare? Who?

My friend's mom.

What?!

It was college. We were drunk. She was hot, and I was going through a phase where I was into older women.

And you give those poor college boys shit.

I know what those poor college boys are up to.

So what happened?

She invited me over.

Did you go?

No. She was married, and my friend would have killed me if she cheated on his dad with me.

Have you ever had sex with a married woman?

Trying to get blackmail information on me?

Just trying to learn more about you. As long as we've known each other, there's still a lot I don't know.

You're better off that way.

I think you just like the air of mystique. Keeps people guessing. Scared about what they don't know.

Fear is a useful tool.

Does it frustrate you that I'm not scared of you then?

It frustrates me that you're not scared of anything.

There are things I'm scared of.

Tell me one.

Only if you tell me one.

Deal.

Dying alone. Everyone else has family— siblings, parents, spouses, children—the works. I've lost so much already, and I'm not sure if I'll ever have any to call my own.

Fuck. That one hurts. Seeing someone as strong as she is hurt over something we all take for granted. Like a fucking knife straight to the chest. Especially because I know I contributed to the loss.

If I don't die first, I'll be there.

Always.

I know we don't see eye to eye on a lot. But you're family to me.

HELLFIRE:

I know. Anytime I've really needed you, you've always come through.

I'm sorry for what I said the other day when we were fighting after the sink. You press every button I have, but I know you care underneath it all.

You don't have to be sorry. I know I'm not Jesse, nowhere fucking close.

Your turn.

Well, speaking of Jesse. That I can't keep my family safe. That I won't be there when I'm needed most.

It's already happened so many times that I feel sick most nights when I go to bed and think about it.

You do everything you can. You can't let the past haunt you. Jesse wouldn't want that. Neither would your parents.

Truth or dare?

TWELVE

D AKOTA

Truth or dare?

THE DEVIL:

That was an abrupt left turn. Are we in grade school again?

We've got to stop talking about sad stuff. We'll go to sleep depressed. And when I go to sleep that way, I wake up that way.

I have too much to do tomorrow as a bridesmaid to be sad.

Dare.

Send me a picture of you.

I'm getting ready for bed…

> So? I was in bed.

I WATCH the dots pop up and disappear for a moment.

THE DEVIL:

> Fine.

A minute later, a photo comes through, and my heart stops. I've only seen Grant shirtless a handful of times in my life, and almost all of them were when I was a teenager, and he still lived on the ranch. A mental image of him tossing hay bales off a truck while shirtless has lived in my mental vault since I was sixteen. But all of them were from a distance and never in a format I could save for safekeeping.

He's standing in what I assume is his bathroom. I'm realizing at this moment that I've never seen the inside of his home, either, even though he's been in mine dozens of times. Hundreds, really, if you count when Jesse owned it.

His shirt is off, and he's got low-slung, dark-gray sweatpants on. He's got a slew of tattoos running down his right arm and wrapping over his shoulder and teasing the edge of his neck. I'll have to study them later, see what secrets they hold, as I think I've only seen a few of them before. His abs are perfection, and his arms are perfectly defined. He's that perfect kind of fit where you know he works out plenty but not so much that he lives in the gym. His hair is mussed, and his hand is tucked behind his head as he takes the photo, a look of discontent on his face at the idea of capturing his late-night routine.

THE DEVIL:

> Truth or dare?

> Truth.

Do you actually get off talking to those men, or is it an act?

An act usually. The toys do the hard work.

There were times it wasn't?

Yes. But not because of them. Because I could check out enough to think about someone else instead.

Who do you think about?

Truth or dare?

Truth.

Who do you think about?

Unfair.

Unfair was you trying to get multiple truths out of me in a row.

Zac's mom.

All these years later, and you're still jacking off to Zac's mom?

You just said who. You didn't say when.

Truth or dare?

Truth.

Who do you think about?

A nameless and faceless man who I can trust to give me my fantasies.

It was technically true. I did my best not to let that name-less, faceless man with the perfect abs and the bossy attitude, who liked to set his Stetson to the side and roll up the sleeves on his dress shirt before he manhandled me, turn into anyone I knew. It's pure coincidence he also has icy blue eyes, thick dark hair that's graying at the temples, and a hint of a smirk that always taunts me.

> Truth or dare?

THE DEVIL:

> Truth. I feel like we could skip these and just say we're exchanging truths, you know.

> I'm just waiting for you to get brave enough to say dare again.

I start to ask him who he thought about the last time he got off, but I don't want to know who she was if she wasn't me, and I don't think I have good enough chances to risk it. For all I know, he wasn't even alone. So I ask a safer question.

> What were you imagining the last time you got off?

It takes him a minute to respond, and I'm half worried he fell asleep talking to me.

THE DEVIL:

> I was imagining a woman sitting on top of the bar for me, legs spread wide while I sat on the bar stool in front of her. Her fingers in my hair while she whimpered for me and rocked her hips against my face, begging for more.

"Fuck," I whisper out loud in the quiet room and bury my face in my pillow. My stomach flutters right along with my clit. He knows what he's doing.

THE DEVIL:

Truth or dare?

Truth.

What were you imagining the last time you got off?

I stare down at the screen, my heart skipping beats in my chest, and I sit up. I have to remind myself that the chances I ever have Grant Stockton on the other end of the phone in the middle of the night like this again are slim to none. So if I want to play this game, I have to act like I know what I'm doing.

A man waiting for me in the dark in my apartment before he kidnaps me and uses me however he wants. Tearing my panties off, bending me over while he wraps his hand around a fistful of my hair, and fucks me without asking.

The phone rings, and "THE DEVIL" flashes across the screen. I drop it onto the quilt and stare at it like it might bite me—or worse yet, manifest him out of thin air. As much as I think I might want the oldest Stockton brother, I don't know that I'd know what to do with him if I got him. I might finally be out of my depth, which is equal parts terrifying and exciting.

I pick the phone back up and answer it.

"First rule of texting is you don't call the person mid-texting. It's very unsettling."

"You don't *ever* let a fucking strange man treat you like that. You hear me? You didn't tell these guys that, did you?" His tone is furious.

Welp. Zaddy Grant is gone, and Daddy Grant is back. It was fun while it lasted.

"It's called a fantasy, *Daddy*." I try to stifle the laugh as I tease him, but it escapes anyway as I fall backward on the bed and roll my eyes at his inability to relax.

"Did you say that to any of those men?" His voice is rough, and if he wasn't angry with me, it'd be sexy. Now I wish he was here with me, whether I can handle him or not. He could handle me, all furious and sexy at the same time.

"No. I didn't say that to any of those men." I sigh.

"Good. Levi's still getting all their addresses and work information."

"What?!" I sit up again. This man is gonna give me a workout in bed, and not the good kind. "Leave those men alone. They expect privacy."

"I'm not going to do anything unless it becomes necessary."

"Those men are harmless. Just bored single guys looking for some attention when they're alone on the weekend. One of them volunteers at the local senior citizens center and another grows roses in his spare time."

"We'll see if we can corroborate any of that. I'd put money on all of it being bullshit lies to get off your screen and into your pants," he grumbles. "And don't call me Daddy."

"I mean, I'd call you Zaddy, but then you keep falling back into dad mode even when we're having a heated conversation. It's like you can't control yourself."

"The fuck is zaddy?"

"It's like... a sexy older guy."

He makes a guttural noise in his throat but ignores it to continue his rant instead.

"I'm just telling you, don't talk to men like that. They take you up on the offer, and I *will* be in control when I break their fucking bones."

"I wasn't talking to men like that. I was talking to *you* like that."

"You shouldn't."

"Why not? I trust you. It's not like you'd do it." I nibble my lower lip when the line goes silent.

"Don't bait me, Hellfire." He says it softly, so softly I almost can't hear the last word.

I raise my brows, and a smile spreads.

"What did you just call me?" I ask.

"Hellfire." He clears his throat. "It's your name on my phone."

I burst into laughter, and he groans as it sounds like he falls back onto his bed.

"Yes, please have a long laugh at my expense."

"No, no. It's just you're the devil on mine."

"The devil?" He sounds confused.

"On my phone. The contact. You're the devil." I try to stop the laughter, but a few more giggles tumble out.

"Not a very nice thing to call the guy who's been trying to help you."

"Is that what you call it?"

"A few selfish choices along the way, but generally speaking, I'd say that's what I've been doing. Yes."

"I know," I say quietly, letting the line fade back to silence. This one's more comfortable though. Too comfortable because my mind's wandering back to our earlier conversation. Thinking about him doing those things to me.

"I'd trust you to do it," I blurt out before I can stop myself.

"Help you?" He sounds confused.

"No. To be the guy waiting in the dark."

"That's good since I've already been him." There's a dark chuckle on his end of the line.

"Would you do it?"

"Do what?" He plays obtuse. He wants me to say the words so there's no misunderstanding my meaning.

"Take me. Use me." I hold my breath, and my heart feels like it's pounding in my ears while I wait for this answer.

"If we set ground rules. Safe words. I'd think about it."

I dig deep for the bravery I need to say the next thing.

"Then think about it and tell me what you'd do to me," I whisper.

THIRTEEN

G RANT

FUCK. Me.

My cock's hard, and I'm aching to run my hand over it for some relief. I'm exercising every last drop of self-control I have. My teeth are biting into my lower lip while I decide if I let myself have this with her. I want it, but there's no going back if I do. It's one thing for me to look at her pictures and tease her over text. Another thing to be telling her how I'd fuck her if she gave me free rein—confessing fantasies I've imagined her in a dozen times in the last week.

"This is a bad idea. Us doing this."

"We're already doing this. You're already talking to me in the middle of the night. Looking at nude photos of me on your phone and imagining what I'd taste like. It's too late to go back now. So tell me—" There's a pause and rustling on her end of the phone before she speaks again. "Tell me what you'd do."

"What are you doing?"

"Taking my panties off. They're getting wet," she muses. Her tone is teasing and sweet. One I rarely ever hear, let alone directed at me.

"Hartfield... Fuck..." I plead with her for mercy even though I know it's hopeless. She's ruthless when she sets her mind on something.

"Don't. Call me the nickname. You might hate them, but I like them. I like that you have one for me," she says so sincerely with a tone so tender. I'm imagining her spread out in front of me, naked and looking up at me like she wants me.

She's good at this. So fucking good at this. I don't know how I didn't notice it before, how easily she can just wrap you around her little finger and make you do what she wants.

"We can't do this, Hellfire." I slip my hand under the elastic and run my hand over my cock. I have to suppress the groan of relief. I need it to be her sassy fucking mouth, but I'd settle for anything right now.

"Tell me you're not getting hard just thinking about it, and we'll get off the phone and go to sleep like it never happened."

"You know I'm an excellent fucking liar. I do it for a living."

"So then lie to me and tell me you're not touching yourself right now."

"Fuck... I can't..." I give my greedy cock another pass, trying to sate the need to be deep inside her.

"Tell me how you'd use me then. You've already torn my panties off. Now what?"

"I'd ball them up and stuff them in your mouth so you wouldn't say something to make me feel like I have to bust someone else's face in. I'd need to concentrate if I'm kidnapping you. Fuck knows you won't make it easy."

She laughs softly through the phone, and the sound of it zips down my spine. Arguing with her has always given me a rush, like a shot of fucking adrenaline to my system. But this new thing we have where I make her laugh—amuse her? That's something else. Something I might be addicted to already.

"You can assume I'll try to be good for you in this particular instance."

"Then I'd grab the back of your neck and bend you over the table. Nudge your knees apart and spread you wide. You'd fight me for control like you always do when we dance, trying to take the lead even when you know your body wants to follow."

"I'd be desperate to have you inside me, and you'd be taking your time lecturing me."

"I know, Hellfire. You'd be grinding that ass up against me while I try to pin you down with one hand and undo my pants with the other. I'd have to take my belt off first and tie your hands behind your back so you'd have less leverage."

She doesn't answer me this time. There's just a soft whimper through the phone.

"How wet are you?"

"Soaking. I'm getting one of my toys. I want it to feel like it's you."

Fuck. I stroke my cock in a steady rhythm, just enough to build the need but not take me there too quickly. I want this to last. I want to hear her fall apart when I come.

"Use the blue one."

"You paid attention."

"Hard to forget."

"The blue one it is." I hear her walking through her bedroom back to her bed and the low hum in the background when she turns it on.

"Keep it on low and put it in nice and slow. Tease that clit of yours for me."

"Yes, Daddy." She murmurs the words more than speaks them, a little hitch in her breath as she slides it in.

I might be losing my hate for her arsenal of nicknames. I have to force myself to slow my own pace, too caught up in her sounds. I take a deep breath and close my eyes as I lean my head back against the pillow. I'm picturing her in front of me, wet and wanting, bent over and waiting for me.

"Fuck it's so good," she curses. "I bet you look sexy as hell with your hand wrapped around your cock. Tell me it is."

"It is." I nearly choke on my answer and clear my throat. I'll lose it if she keeps talking. "But remember you have panties in your mouth, yeah? I don't want to hear anything but moans and whimpers out of you unless I ask. Got it?"

"Mhmm," she responds eagerly.

"Where were we?" I'm honestly trying to remember because she has my head on a full fucking spin right now. Hearing the sound of her vibrator humming and how slick it is as she uses it is distracting whatever focus I have left. "Oh right, you were bent over, and I was testing to make sure you were wet for me. Fucking dripping it sounds like."

She curses under her breath, and I can tell she wants more.

"Turn it up. One setting. That's it."

A soft murmur of agreement comes from the other end of the line, and I give myself a little extra squeeze at the tip as precum leaks out. I'm out of fucking practice. It's been way too long since I've had regular sex, and almost as long since I've had any. Work has taken too much out of me the last year. Horsemen business keeping me up at all hours when the bar opening hasn't. All the family drama and the wedding. I forgot how fucking good it feels to just give in to something I want— someone I want.

"So wet and ready, I don't even need to tease you, do I? You just want me deep, in and out of that tight little cunt at the perfect angle, while I wrap my hand around your throat and tell you how good you feel. Spreading wider for me so I can take you deep. Fuck." I curse and lose my train of thought as I can feel the tension building up my spine and back down into my balls.

She starts to whimper on the other end of the line.

"What do you need?"

"Please tell me I can come. I'll be so good for you," she begs.

"If I let you come, I want pictures of your spent little body sprawled on the bed and you tasting yourself off your fingers since I can't do it for you."

"Yes. Anything you want," she agrees.

It's a sobering plea. One that reminds me I have to be careful with her.

"Come for me. I want to hear you though."

"Yes. Okay." She gives in immediately. "Oh my god. It's so fucking good. I'm almost there…" She's a mess of whimpers and moans then. Her breathing is stuttered until she finally gasps for air. "Oh fuck. Fucking hell… I can't…" Her voice fades, and I hear the vibrator grow louder and the sounds of her wetness as she fucks herself with it beyond her murmured curses.

"That's it. Fuck yourself for me like a good girl. Fuck… the way you sound, Hellfire."

"Oh fuck," she murmurs, and then I can hear her coming clearly by the way her breathing changes and the soft begging sounds she makes, pleading for the end of her torture.

I let go then, giving myself permission to come while I can still hear how good she sounds. It doesn't take much; I'm so close from listening to her that I careen over the edge a few moments later. Hot streams lash across my abdomen and over my hand. The phone falls to the side as I curse and groan through the last of it. Wishing it was her here with me.

"Fucking hell." I wipe my hand on my sweats.

They were headed for the laundry anyway, and I might need another shower. One I'll need to take quickly because between the exhaustion and the way this orgasm zaps the will from my body to do anything but lie here, I'm in danger of just collapsing in there. I pick the phone back up when I hear her say my name.

"You still there?" she asks.

"I'm still here. Dropped the phone." I realize I don't know what else to say.

I said what I meant. Things I hadn't been able to stop thinking about since we went racing across the line in the sand between us. I don't want to take it back, but I'm also not keen to say anything to fuck it up. The clarity of her orgasm might make the chances she bites rise again.

"That was... different," she says softly.

"No regrets confessing your secrets to your mortal enemy?" I joke, hoping it puts us closer to our usual footing.

"No. I'd do it again. Anytime." I can hear the smile in her voice.

"Watch what you offer up. I'll take until there's nothing left," I warn her. She has to know, even as strong and capable as she is, that I'm not good for her. Not good for anyone. At least not as anything but a bulwark against people worse than me. As dark as my heart might be, there are plenty out there that are merely voids.

"I don't hate the idea of that." There's a hint of trepidation in her tone.

"Then you need sleep. And so do I. Get some."

"After that, it's going to be easy." The amusement returns to her voice.

"Goodnight, Hellfire."

"Night, Devil."

I kill the call, and my head falls back on the pillow. I can't decide if I've lost my mind or if I'm a fucking genius for getting myself into this situation. I'll have to decide that when my brain is functioning again, but at least I'll sleep well tonight knowing for once I made her curse for the right reasons.

FOURTEEN

G RANT

"IT'S BEEN A MINUTE." I wrap my arms around my sister, Aspen, and she squeezes me tight.

"It has," she acknowledges, looking me over for any damage as she lets me go again. It's the kind of once-over our mother always gave us, and I can still see the echo of her in Aspen.

"Where's Ethan?" I ask, frowning as I don't see him anywhere nearby. Her husband isn't my favorite, but he is family. I hope he isn't already hiding out in a room on his phone.

"About that." She sighs and looks into the distance, tucking her hands into her back pockets.

I study her face for a moment. Underneath the fading smile and the perfect makeup and hair, she looks sad, tired even. I know her job keeps her busy, on the road almost as much as her husband is, but she swore up and down she was going to start slowing down and taking it easier.

"He fuck up?" They spend a lot of time away from each other, and if she told me that he cheated, I wouldn't even raise a brow. Pricks like him don't know loyalty the way we do.

"Something like that." She looks into the distance, and I can see whatever has her here alone has done a number on her.

"Is it a temporary sort of fuckup or the kind that sticks long-term?" I ask because she's always been a little too under-standing where her husband's concerned, especially because of their daughter.

"The latter. Attorneys are already involved, and I've got Fallon in counseling. She says she's fine, but you know teenagers." She shrugs.

"She's not coming to the wedding?" I look around for my niece.

"She's upstairs already, getting ready to go out to the barn. She was gushing over Hazel. You know how those two get along talking about horses." Aspen smiles up at the house.

"Well, at least she'll have a little escape while she's here. But what about you? Need me to snap some necks? Fix you a drink? Fix him one with a little extra ingredient? What's the occasion calling for?" I joke with my sister, hoping my threats at least cheer her up.

Aspen gives me an admonishing look. "It's not that kind of fuckup. It's for the best really. We've been growing apart for a long time now. Time was waiting on the perfect storm of events to finally capsize us. I just feel bad for Fallon. I wish we could have made it a couple more years until she was off to college before we changed everything on her."

"She'll survive. She's strong, and she's got you. Ethan was never good for much, anyway, with him always being on the road all the time. You both might be better off without him."

"It's not his fault. Life of a coach, you know."

"Not exactly, but I understand work being busy. That's why I've stayed clear of it all."

"You gonna ease into the retirement home alone? Get all the ladies there?" she teases me.

"You think I'll make it that long? I'm starting to feel doubtful." I smirk at her to let her know that I'm playing, but I sometimes wonder if I'll make it long enough to see all the hair on my head go silver in the mirror.

"The family business is weighing heavy these days?" It's her turn to frown at me. We've largely kept Aspen out of the family business. She was a lot like Ramsey, where she had other dreams and aspirations, ones that meant she had to leave Purgatory Falls.

I tilt my head to the side, squinting through the late-day sun. "Heavier than usual at the moment, but it comes with the territory."

"Well, you know I'm here if you need someone to talk to."

"Same goes for you, not that you'll ever take me up on it."

"I'll keep it in mind."

"You gonna stay out on the East Coast with Fallon?"

"Yes. We'll have to find a house. Ethan and I agreed we'd sell ours and split the money."

"You could come home, you know. You could teach at one of the colleges here in the state. We've got dozens of them."

"Yeah, but how many of them need a new archaeology professor?"

"What about the museums or one of the CRM firms?"

"You want me home that badly?" She smiles at me.

"I wouldn't hate it. Ramsey's back part-time, you know. Even while he finishes out that new contract of his. I'm sure he'd let you fix up one of the cabins on the property for the summer. Or you could come stay at the resort. I've got rooms we could convert for you and Fallon."

"Raising my daughter in a casino might cause the judge to question my custody agreement." She raises a brow at me.

"You already have one of those?" This was part of why I wanted her back home. She shares so little of her day-to-day life, and I worry about her. It's always just a quick text here or there giving me the highlights and focusing on Fallon's achievements.

"They're drawing one up. We're trying to keep this divorce as low-key as possible. Neither of us needs the disruption in our careers right now. I'm working on a book, and his hard work is finally paying off."

"You're too nice for your own good, you know. I hope you don't let the next one take advantage of that. You gotta find your inner asshole like the rest of us." I smirk at her.

"Don't worry. I have plans to find my inner bitch. But let's forget any talk about the next one. There's not gonna be a next one. If marriage has taught me anything, it's that I'm not cut out for it. Once Fallon is off to college, I'll have the house to myself, and I can figure out what I want to do with all my free time. I might try to publish another book. Some of the work I've been collaborating on has been fascinating. I'll have so much more time to be out in the field too. I'm actually kind of excited about it. I just hate to tell any of my friends. They all expect me to be pissed off or depressed, and I just... don't have it in me to feel anything right now, you know?"

"I get it. Trust me. I love my fuckin' freedom. I tried to talk Ramsey down from being shackled down again with the same ball and chain. But—" I laugh as Aspen punches me in the arm.

"Leave our baby brother alone. You know he's always had a bleeding heart for her. I love that they're back together again. It looks good on him." She juts her chin in his direction, where I can see Ramsey and Hazel making their way over from the inn, carrying some food and drinks. "The last time I saw him this happy was before Mom and Dad."

Fuck. I think that's the last time any of us looked that happy. Their death had left a pall over the whole family for years. Made it hard to celebrate anything. Between finally getting some closure for them last year and being able to pull our family back together on this ranch, it felt like maybe a page that had been frozen in time was finally turning for all of us.

"It's good to see him happy. Good to have him back. The only thing that would make it better is having you back." I press my point a little harder.

"The only thing that would make it better is seeing you and Levi go down hard the same way." She grins at me.

"You'd wish your fate on us?" I raise my brows at her ill will.

"Nah. You'd never be in this position. You'd never choose someone like Ethan. If you go down, well... Let's just say I'm excited to meet her and watch the fireworks." Aspen winks at me and then turns to greet our baby brother.

"Hey, sis! Did you have a good flight?" he asks, leaning into her hug even though his hands are full.

"I did. Hey, Hazel. Can I help with something?" Aspen asks, and I hold out my hands for the stuff Ramsey's carrying.

"I've got it." Dakota appears from behind the screen door. "You guys catch up! Can I get you anything to drink?" Dakota looks between the four of us.

"You're the sweetest. I think we're good." Hazel nods at Ramsey and then looks at Aspen. "Can we get you something?"

"You know. I'd love a Stockton Shandy."

"Hitting it hard already?" Ramsey gives her shit.

"I was told we're spending this week celebrating." She

holds out her hands palms up. "Just figured we might as well get started."

"Someone's going to have to tell me what's in a Stockton Shandy." Dakota looks at Hazel for help.

"I can show you, and we can put this stuff away," I say, nodding to the door.

"Okay." Dakota's eyes lift to meet mine and then look away just as quickly, her lashes fluttering like she's remembering our last phone conversation. And fuck... now so am I.

It's gonna be a long fucking weekend trying to pretend like I'm not already on fire where she's concerned.

FIFTEEN

D AKOTA

"LOOK WHO'S HERE." Hazel steps to the side of the doorframe, and a six-foot-three football player I last saw when I was in his lap on New Year's Eve walks through the door. She's talking to Ramsey, but her eyes drift to me, and she winks.

"No shit!" Ramsey shouts, making his way over to grab Hayden's hand and pull him in for a terse slap on the back.

"In the flesh." Hayden nods over Ramsey's shoulder at his other teammate, Cooper. "Thanks for keeping the secret."

"Come on in and have a seat." Ramsey nods back toward where we are, and Hayden's gaze falls on me. The smile on his face widens in an instant, and his eyes drift up my body and land on my face. His dimples are popping, and I bite my lower lip to keep from smiling any harder than I am.

I'm a little shocked he remembers me because he was very drunk on New Year's. So drunk that as much as I wanted to go back to his hotel room like he asked, I didn't feel like I should.

"Dakota..." My name is a gravelly command on his lips, and I stand to greet him. The man is tattooed sin and covered with dozens of bright red flags—the kind I'm drawn to like a moth to a flame. He hugs me, and I'm bathed in the scent of his cologne. "How have you been?"

But when he pulls me in tight, I can see over his shoulder. Two bright-blue eyes are burning a hole into the place where my fingers are running lightly over his traps as I greet him.

"I've been good. Didn't know you were coming." I put daylight between us, but his hand stays on my side, and his eyes rake their way over the outfit I have on. I dressed way too sexy for a friend's bridal shower, but then I knew someone whose attention I wanted would be here.

"Wouldn't miss it for the world. So good to see you again." His eyes meet mine for a brief moment before he leans in again, speaking only loud enough for me to hear. "When Hazel said you'd be here—haven't booked a flight faster in my life."

"Well, she kept that a secret, but it's a good surprise—so good to see you again."

I turn to look at my friend, and she's beaming at the two of us like it's Christmas morning. I realize what's happening. I feel the flush of the obvious setup rush up my cheeks. Hayden Warner is hot as hell, but this heat is because I feel like I'm in some fifth circle of it. It would be this weekend of all weekends that she decides to play matchmaker.

I have no easy way out either. Hayden is exactly my type. It's why I was in his lap, kissing him when the clock struck midnight at the start of this year. And why I continued to stay there, listening to him drunkenly tell me about the places he wished he could take me. A club he went to once in Aspen. A beach in Costa Rica. A place with the best pasta he's ever eaten in Italy. We'd had a whole relationship and gone on a world tour while we sat at my bar with our friends. But then we went our separate ways, and I never expected to hear from him again. Certainly not now when I'm otherwise...

What am I really? Grant and I have some kind of game going on. There's clearly attraction. But besides that, in black and white facts? He's just a client. One who pays well. One who I like pleasing. But not exactly the kind of thing you can build a future on.

But even as gorgeous as Hayden is, and as good of a kisser as I remember him being—even drunk, which makes me curious about what the sober version would be—he pales in comparison standing next to Grant.

Grant walks up with Ramsey to greet him, and I swear the temperature drops. His hand finally leaves my side as he turns to shake Grant's. Ramsey gives introductions to both of his brothers. Grant's in full business mode, his icy-blue eyes have melted into an ocean of cordiality, all the smiles and nods and friendly words of welcome. The devil is exceedingly charming when he wants to be. All calm waters on the surface, but I know underneath it all, he's seething while he tries to decipher the relationship between Hayden and me. One I'm not eager to explain, given we all have to spend the weekend together, and Grant's been very clear about his feelings on other men flirting in my general direction during this agreement.

My eyes ping back and forth as the two of them talk, trying to make sense of what this is going to mean for me and this weekend. I don't need to think too hard about it. Grant's a lot of things, but bossy and territorial are at the top of the list. Hazel pushing me into Hayden's lap again while Grant watches is going to be a mess of epic proportions. On the other side, I don't imagine many women tell Hayden no either. All while I try to play host to this party and keep Hazel happy.

I'm ready to go back to the bar and have another drink.

SIXTEEN

G RANT

I'M IN HELL. My own version of it. Where I've finally had the smallest taste of something I've unknowingly craved for years but have to watch it all slip away right in front of my eyes.

Our agreement has my feet rooted in the ground as I watch this fucking prick teammate of my younger brother's spin her around a makeshift dance floor. She's teaching everyone a new dance for the wedding, using him as an example. His hands are all over every inch of her body, like he's had them there before. And I just have to stand here and watch. All while everyone in the room cheers them on.

"Who the fuck is this guy again?" I ask quietly as I look at my younger brother. He introduced us earlier, but I was too busy trying to make sense of how he was so friendly with Dakota.

"Hayden. Plays for the Chaos with me. Good guy." Ramsey smiles as the prick's feet falter, and his hands slip a little lower on her ass. She laughs as he rights himself, but he doesn't bring his hands back up where they belong as he turns her around the makeshift dance floor. I take another sip of my drink. I might break a few of his fingers and see who's fucking laughing then.

"Good guy? Is he always so fucking handsy?" I glower at the way he's running his hand over her hip as he pulls her closer to him again.

"No, but he and Dakota hit it off on New Year's Eve." Ramsey's brow furrows.

"What do you mean hit it off?" I don't bother to cover my tone, and Ramsey's head snaps in my direction. He studies my face like he doesn't like what he sees.

"Why do you care?"

Fuck.

"You know why I care. She's his sister." I try to sound nonchalant but fail miserably when her fingers drift over his shoulder, and her lashes lift as she laughs at something else he says. This fucker must be a fucking comedian in his spare time.

"That tone doesn't sound like worry. It sounds like jealousy." Ramsey's already done the math. I can see it in his eyes.

"So what if it was?" I say flippantly, trying to throw him off.

"You got a hell of a big hole to try and climb out of. One you dug." He makes a low whistle. "I don't even know if there are ladders made for that."

"You managed it," I argue, pointing out that Hazel and Ramsey had spent a good portion of last year trying to make each other suffer—at least when they weren't eye fucking the hell out of each other in between.

"She liked me before she hated me."

I blow out a breath and take another sip of my drink. My eyes drift back to Dakota as he spins her awkwardly. She's a damn good dancer, and she's reining it all in for his benefit—working hard to make him look like he knows what he's doing. The way she's laughing so effortlessly as he whispers something in her ear has my teeth set on edge. I don't think she's ever laughed like that in my presence, proving Ramsey has a point. She's never been a fan of mine, minus one awkward moment when she turned eighteen.

"When you say they hit it off..." I have to focus on one problem at a time. Getting her to like me is one for a different day. Today is just making sure he doesn't make her forget I exist.

"I don't know the details..." Ramsey trails off.

"But?" I brace for whatever he's about to tell me.

"She was in his lap most of the night when she wasn't working. They were pretty heavy by midnight. Hazel and I left not long after." He shrugs like me not having more details isn't going to kill me. It's left to my imagination, and well...

I'm imagining her stripping down and climbing into bed with him. Thinking about her making all her perfect little sounds for him and him knowing all the minute details of her body that I do. I feel fucking sick. It's even worse when the song stops and Hazel catches Dakota, linking arms as they both giggle, and Dakota tells her something that makes her grin. Hazel talks animatedly with her, and I realize what this whole "wedding games" thing is: an elaborate ruse to push these two together. And fuck if it isn't working like a charm.

"Your wife seems to have ulterior motives at this event."

"I told you she had some plans."

"And she thinks what... these two fucked once when Dakota was drunk, and now they'll fall in love and Dakota can travel back and forth with her?"

"It's crossed her mind." Ramsey's eyes run over me like he's judging whether or not I'm going to be a problem for Hazel's scheme.

"No. No fucking way." I shake my head.

"I don't think you get a say in that." His tone stays calm, even as mine deteriorates.

"The fuck I don't. She's my—" I stop mid-sentence. I'd promised her we wouldn't tell anyone. Specifically Ramsey because he'd tell Hazel. I can't break that promise now. "She's my closest friend's sister. She's not running off with some fucking loser."

"He's my friend." Ramsey's demeanor shifts.

"Dakota's your friend too."

"She is, and I told you, I'm not worried. He's a good team-mate too—like a second family to me." My brother can't stand anyone attacking someone he cares about. He'd done prison time for it. But I'd do that and more for Dakota.

"He does anything to hurt her, you won't have to worry about him being on your team." I toss back the last of my drink and turn. I need off this floor. Out of this room. Or I'll do or say something I regret. "I need a refill."

"You need air. You want to figure things out with her, fair enough. But this isn't the way."

"Don't go running to tell your wife." I flash him a look of warning. He might have a point or five, but he's still my younger brother. I have ten years on him, and he damn well knows I don't ask much of him.

"There's nothing to tell. *Yet.*" His eyes search me one last time, like he's trying to figure out where the hell his real brother is and where I've come from. I couldn't tell him either. I'm as blindsided as anyone by the way I'm taking this development.

BY THE TIME the women have gone upstairs for their spa slumber party and the rest of us guys are wrapped around a table playing poker, I've worked myself up to being well and truly pissed. I've spent the entire night watching this prick put his hands all over Dakota, and now he's bidding up the table at poker. I've lost my patience with him. I shove all my chips in, raising the bet sky-high.

"Too rich for my blood." Bo folds his cards.

"Yeah, I'm skipping out on that." Anson follows suit.

Ramsey calls my bet, and it falls to Hayden again. He stares at his cards and then looks at the pile of chips, drawing out his decision while the rest of us wait. That's all we've been doing all night. Waiting to see what this asshole will do.

"Don't have to be afraid to fold. We don't mind if you run tail tucked," I mutter.

"What now?" He smirks, looking up at me. "Nobody's tail's tucked. I'm just trying to play smart. Not let my mood affect how I play."

"My mood doesn't affect my play. My hand does. Might be hard to know what yours looks like when you got them all over her ass though."

"You got a problem with me?" His smile fades as he looks at me over his cards.

"Nah, no problem. We've all gotten a little too drunk and tried to hit way out of our league before. Can't blame you for trying."

"Seems like you're a little nervous. The way you're throwing money around like it'll buy what you can't earn. That an old cowboy thing? You think she's into that, or you think maybe she finally found something she really likes?" His smirk returns, and I'm ready to take his jaw clean off his face.

"I think what she likes is someone who knows how to treat her with respect instead of trying to throw cheap lines and even cheaper moves at her the second she walks into a room. She's got a dozen of you to pick from at the bar on any given night."

"I'm going to get a beer outside. Want to join me?" Ramsey looks at me pointedly, and I push back from the table, the legs of the chair dragging loud enough to underscore my point.

I follow my baby brother silently. I know he wants to lecture me in private. He'd never give me the disrespect of undermining me in public, but we're about to have it out, nevertheless. Ramsey keeps the ceremony alive by grabbing two beers out of the fridge on our way to the back porch, popping the tops off them before he swings the screen door open and holds it for me to follow. He shoves one at my chest and eyes me carefully.

"You're my older brother, so I'm not gonna tell you what to do. But I am going to point out that this whole wedding week is very important to me, and I don't want my wife to have to come downstairs because a brawl has broken out in her home."

"You should tell your friend that he needs to watch his mouth and his hands then."

"He hasn't said or done anything disrespectful to Dakota. At least not unless she was yours in some way, and last I checked, that wasn't the case. Has that changed in the last few hours?"

"No."

"Then maybe let her decide what she is and isn't comfortable with."

"That guy isn't right for her."

"She seemed to think so the last time she saw him. Hazel, who's almost as protective as you when it comes to her, likes the two of them together. Says they're a good fit. You got a reason to say they aren't besides jealousy?"

"I'm not jealous," I snap. "Never been jealous a day in my fucking life, and I sure as shit didn't start today."

"That's not the way it looks to everyone else in that room. You're not gonna have to worry about *me* telling Hazel because her brothers can see it plain as fucking day."

I take a swig of beer and lean on the railing. I've been stupid, letting things flare my temper like that. Worrying about every little fucking thing like some jealous fucking idiot. He's right, and I fucking hate it when that happens.

"If you want her, why don't you tell her that?"

"Because I shouldn't fucking want her, Ramsey. She's my best friend's kid sister."

"She's not a kid anymore."

"Doesn't matter. I was her guardian. I swore I'd watch over her, and I'm pretty fucking sure he didn't mean while I was buried inside her."

"You've slept together?" Ramsey sounds surprised.

"No. I haven't touched her." It was technically true. I've imagined it. Promised to do it. Thought about it thousands of times at this point. But I haven't followed through. Yet.

"How does she feel about you?"

"I don't know. We don't talk about feelings."

"Maybe you should start. Whatever is going on between you two that doesn't involve feelings or touching seems to have you all twisted up."

"I can't. It's... too complicated." My heart drops to my gut because I know what I should do. I just have to bring myself to do the right thing. "Is he really a good guy?" I take another draw of my beer to wipe the bad taste out of my mouth created by even asking that question.

"He is. Mostly has his shit together. As much as any of us do. Doesn't fuck around a lot. Spends a lot of time with a charity in town. Has our backs on the field and off it."

"You'd let him near Aspen?"

"Aspen would tear him to pieces, but I'd trust him with her. Yeah."

It's not the answer I want, but Ramsey wouldn't lie to me.

"Fine... I'll stay out of the way."

"That's not what I'm telling you to do. I'm just telling you not to rip the guy's head off and to talk to her if you feel some kind of way about her being with someone else."

"It's none of my business who she's with or what she does."

A loud, rumbling laugh rips out of Ramsey's chest, and he nearly spills his beer. It takes him a full minute to recover enough to stand straight and look at me.

"A full fucking quarter of your personality is worrying about what that girl does and when."

"Because I've been trying to keep her safe."

"Is that what you've been doing that's got you like this?"

"I thought it was..." I shake my head. Now I'm wondering if it might be me she needs to be kept safe from.

We stand there for a long time in silence, staring out at the night sky while we both drink our beers. Until Ramsey finally breaks the silence.

"I've never seen you like this."

I take the last sip of my beer and stare at the empty bottle.

"I've never felt like this." It's more honesty than I want to give. More than I'd give to Levi or Aspen on this particular subject. Levi would warn me off and tell me to keep my head in the game. Aspen would go buck fucking wild with the information that a woman caught my interest and be planning a future where I hang up my hat and fill my life with family photos and PTA meetings. But Ramsey knows what it's like. He's right in the thick of it now with a woman who isn't all that different.

"Talk to her."

"And tell her what?" I look over at him. "I know I've been your guardian and I made you fucking hate my guts, but uh... I think maybe I've had a change of heart. How do you feel about an aging asshole who runs a casino and a criminal empire?"

"I think there are better ways of putting it."

"She's better off with your friend. She's always liked athletes, and he probably comes with a lot less baggage. Starting with the fact he didn't get her brother killed."

"You don't think she deserves to know? Doesn't she have a choice in the matter?"

"What choice? That's not a fucking choice. It's wrong. I shouldn't even be thinking about her like that."

"If Hazel would give me a second chance..."

"You two were obsessed with each other from the start. You said it yourself."

"I wasn't, or rather I was, but only after I stopped seeing her as Bo's little sister. It's not that far off from the two of you."

"It didn't take you ten years to wake up and realize she was there all along."

"No. It took me finding her in my teammate's room, half undressed on his bed. Nearly fucking killed me. I don't recommend waiting that long."

"Yeah, well he better not even fucking try it while he's here. If he wants to fuck her he can fly her back to Cincinnati and do it there."

Suddenly, I hear a throat clear, and I look up to see Dakota standing on the steps.

"Excuse me. I just need to take these upstairs." Dakota holds up a case of hard seltzer, and her eyes slice over to me. My heart plummets six feet under my feet.

"Wait." I step to the side and block more of her path.

"I can take them for you," Ramsey offers, playing the good brother.

"You can't go upstairs," Dakota protests.

"I'll holler up to Hazel or text her first. I won't break her rules. I promise."

"I—" She looks between the two of us, clearly not wanting to give me the time of day. But when her eyes land on Ramsey, something softens in her gaze, and she holds out the case for him. I glance back over my shoulder, but whatever passed between them, I can't decipher it.

"I'll get this straight up," Ramsey promises and abandons us on the deck.

When I hear the screen door shut, I look back to her and see her eyes swarming with skepticism and distrust.

"I don't know how much you heard, but—" I start, but she cuts me off.

"Enough to remind me of where we stand with each other."

"It's not what it sounded like."

"It sounded like I should tell him yes when he asks what my final decision is on that trip to Cincinnati this summer. He said I could fly there first, see where he lives, and then we could take a trip somewhere. Anywhere I want before he has to be back for camp."

I slide my tongue down the inside of my cheek and look into the distance.

"Is that what you want?" I swallow my pride and fuck if it doesn't taste bitter.

"Since when does what I want factor into anything where you're concerned?"

"Since I'm asking."

"Very romantic of you to do it now when you're feeling threatened," she bites back, and I can see the look on her face, realizing that she's said too much.

"I'm not the romantic sort, and I'm not feeling threatened. I'm just looking for clarity."

"Clarity on what?" Her tone is impatient.

"Do the two of you have something going on? Something that *is* romantic?" I look at her, and she avoids my gaze.

"So what if we did?"

"Then you'd be breaking rules you agreed to."

"It would predate our rules. It started on New Year's Eve."

"So you knowingly entered into our agreement when you had a boyfriend."

"He's not a boyfriend."

"Paramour. Plaything. Whatever you fuckin' want to call him." I step closer to her, and she takes a step back. "And you didn't tell me at the time. Not when you took pictures for me. Not when you were teasing me about your fantasies. And sure as fuck not on the phone the other night."

"Keep your voice down," she hisses.

"Why? Worried your guy's going to find out all the dirty little things you do for me in your spare time?"

SEVENTEEN

D AKOTA

"YOU SAID you wouldn't tell anyone. That we *shouldn't* tell anyone." I take another step back, and my ass hits the railing of the deck as he closes in on me. My eyes search his for some sign of reassurance, but I'm not getting any. He looks wild, like his mind is somewhere ten steps ahead of me while I struggle to catch up.

He leans in, his lips so close to the shell of my ear that I can feel his breath dance down my neck, a soft derisive chuckle coming from his chest before he speaks.

"Oh, I won't tell a fucking soul." His hands ghost their way over my hips and then slide in until his thumbs meet at my navel. "You're gonna do that for me."

He moves to unbutton my pants, and his lips are at my throat a moment later. It's not a soft exploration but a desperate claiming. His tongue laves over my pulse point, and his teeth scrape against my skin as I writhe underneath him. It's too many sensations at once and not enough all at the same time. My hands go to his chest. I tell myself I need to stop him. That we're feet away from everyone we know, and he's not going to hold back if someone asks what's going on. I'm not sure if he'll even give me an opportunity to speak. But I don't want him to stop. Grant Stockton's hands are finally on me. His mouth is at my throat, and his hand is slowly teasing the edge of my waistband.

"Tell him to come save you from the one you hate so much. You can do that, can't you?" he whispers as he pulls down the zipper of my shorts.

"Grant..." I breathe out his name. I don't know what else to say.

"Scream his name. Tell him to save you," he instructs as he turns me around and presses me against the railing, my back to his front, his lips at my ear. "That's what you wanted. You were gonna have a sugar daddy save you from me, right? He'd be perfect for it. Could take you away from this fucked-up little town with all that football money. All that fame would keep you safe from me. You and Hazel could sit in the box together every Sunday like two pretty little wives." His fingers ease under the waistband of my panties, and he nips at my throat.

I can't think. Can't breathe. My whole body's on edge, just waiting for him to make his next move—silently begging him to do it. It's wrong though. So fucking wrong. Hazel would be hurt. Hayden would be confused.

"Anyone could walk out here right now." I try to talk sense into him, but he's not listening.

"That's what you want, right?" His fingers creep lower. "Someone to put a stop to all this. Save you from me. Why don't you call for him?"

"You know why," I whisper back.

"I have my fucking suspicions. You were so quick to comply with my orders, so willing to follow my rules. So eager to please me and give me what I wanted." His fingers ease their way down, just on the cusp of teasing my clit.

"Grant, please..." I lean into his touch, and my ass brushes his cock through his jeans. He's hard and thick against me, and I want to beg him to fuck me. Just put us both out of our misery and take until we're both exhausted on the floor.

"Tell me what I want to hear. Tell me why you agreed to all of this, and I'll give you what you want," he taunts me.

"I don't want to be saved. I want you," I whimper, so afraid to even speak the words out loud that I hold my breath in the wake of them. At least until he delves down and brushes my clit with his fingers, spreading them so that he gently teases either side, skimming the edges of my piercing. It's all too much and not enough at the same time. His hand freezes mid-motion.

"What is *this?*" His voice is rough.

"A piercing."

"A piercing?" He repeats my statement as a question.

"Yes." I breathe the word more than speak it as his fingers slip over it, searching the borders and teasing me in the process.

"Holy fuck," he mutters against my skin, his tone distracted and fascinated all at once. "I bet it looks fucking pretty. I want pictures next time you're alone."

"Okay," I agree easily.

"Does it make this feel better?"

"You've never been with a woman who's pierced?" I'm surprised. Given that he has a decade on me and looks the way he does, I figured he'd had every variety.

"Can't say I have." There's amusement and curiosity in his tone as his fingers toy with me, and I roll my hips forward for more.

"I could be your first for something then," I whisper, smiling to myself. "If you'd just give in and fuck me."

"You want me to fuck you here on this porch, where anyone could see?" He's dubious that I'd go through with it. But hell, I think I would. If it meant having him, finally, I don't think I'd care if half our friends and family were witnesses to it. Those would be their therapy bills, not mine. Because all my mind would be focused on is that I finally got under his skin enough to make him cave.

"I don't care who sees. Them. Anyone. You could fuck me live on the app. I just need it."

"Fuck... You're so raw and desperate. Deprived of the attention you need. I know. But I'm here now." He scoops me up and pulls me over to a bench at the side of the house, depositing me in front of him. He finishes unbuttoning my shorts and slides them down my thighs along with my panties but pauses above my knees. "Spread for me. I want to see it now."

"Anyone could—" I look toward the back porch.

"You said you didn't care, and neither do I. Show me," he demands.

I spread further and reveal the piercing on my clit. The moonlight catches it, and it glints in the light.

"Fuck. Look how wet and swollen you are for me." He leans forward and runs his thumb over the piercing, and I let out a soft whimper. "That thing is so fucking sexy. *You're* so fucking sexy." His eyes rake over me with renewed interest, and I roll my lip between my teeth as he studies me. "Play with yourself and show me how you use it."

My heart skips a beat at the request. But the fact that he's fascinated with how it brings me pleasure, praising me instead of asking the boring and borderline stupid questions I normally get from men about whether or not it hurt, and if I was wet when they pierced me, has me doing whatever he asks. I start to tease myself with my fingertips, nudging the piercing gently back and forth as I do to help build the tension in the sensitive nerve endings there. My breathing gets heavier, and he watches me with bated breath.

"You're so goddamn gorgeous I can barely stand it. It's one thing in the pictures... on the phone. But in person, Hellfire... Fuck me. I don't deserve to watch."

"I want you to watch. I need you to finish me. I want your hands on me when I come," I say, teasing my fingers over my clit and dipping down lower to nudge my opening with the tips of them. I need him. Badly.

It's been too long, and all the taunting and teasing we do with each other has me on the absolute edge. I'm too wary to tell him quite that bluntly though. If I stop too long to consider what I'm doing and where—*who* I'm doing it with—I'll probably melt into a puddle on the floor. But as it stands, I'm holding my own, and he likes it.

"I'll give you my hands when you need them. But I need a taste. I haven't been able to stop thinking about it since the other night."

I hold my fingers out, and he shakes his head and nods back down.

"Soak them. I want the taste of you branded on my tongue for the rest of the night so I can remember what I get, and he never will."

I do as he asks, running my fingers through my wetness and dipping them inside until they're coated, offering them up again. He wraps his hand around my wrist and pulls them deep into his mouth, practically swallowing them up as his tongue wraps around them, delving between them and around, tickling the pads of my fingers with the tip of his tongue as I try not to squirm. My eyes are locked on him, watching him like he's starved until his lashes finally lift, and he catches me doing it. He sucks on the tips of them and then laves his tongue over every square inch. Lapping up every drop like he's giving me a preview of what I'll get someday.

"If you're good, and I earn it, I'm gonna spend a night on my knees worshipping your pretty little cunt and sucking on this jeweled clit until you have to beg me to stop from how exhausted you are."

"I'll be good."

"Then let's hope I earn it." He pats his lap. "But for now, come here. I have to settle for what I can take from you tonight."

I turn to sit, but the shorts around my thighs restrict my movement as I try to make space in his lap. He grabs them and strips them off over my boots. Tossing them and my panties on the bench next to us before he pulls me into his lap, my back to his front. He uses his boots to kick my feet wider, exposing me for anyone who might walk by to see. The sensation of his jeans, the rough cotton and metal grommets and buttons against my bare ass has me nibbling my lower lip. I feel dirty in the best way, and I can hardly believe whose hands are on me.

"Look how pretty you are like this in my lap, spread and glittering for me in the moonlight. So fucking gorgeous." His fingers start to work me over again, and I roll my hips to add to the building friction. I don't miss how hard and thick he is underneath my ass, and I work to center myself on his cock as I writhe beneath his touch. I'm just hoping he's getting the smallest taste of his own medicine.

"You fight dirty." He growls against my throat and rakes his teeth over my skin.

I buck forward at the sensation, and his fingers slide inside me, working their way in and out as I rock my hips against his hand. His thumb toys with my clit, and it doesn't take long for him to have me worked up to the edge of my orgasm. He slows his movement down to a snail's pace, his fingers sliding effortlessly from how wet I am for him. I lay my head back against his shoulder, taking in a deep breath only to hear how ragged his is.

"You're gonna make me come in my fucking pants if you keep up like that," he warns.

"Good." I can't hide the amusement in my voice.

"Not good if I have to walk into the house like that for everyone to know."

My excitement for the idea of making him fall apart like that for me dims at the thought of the awkwardness.

"I'd clean it up. Get you another set of pants," I offer. "Tell them a bear ran off with the other set." A laugh tumbles out of my chest at the idea of their expressions with that explanation.

"You've got the smartest fucking mouth I've ever known. You know that?"

"I know. That's why you like it. You'd love it if you knew what else I could do with it."

"Fuck me." He nips at my neck again and then pulls me tighter to his body before he slides his hand around my throat and whispers in my ear, "I'm gonna fuck this tight little cunt with my fingers while you sit perfectly fucking still, or I won't let you come at all."

"You wouldn't."

"Don't test me," he threatens, picking up his pace. His fingers work me deeper, and he alternates between the heel of his hand and circling my clit with his thumb, speeding up his pace. His fingers curl, and he's relentless, the tension building in my nerves until I can barely stand it. I feel like I might burst apart at the seams from how desperate I am to come. I can't hold still any longer, and my hips roll up of their own volition, despite him wrapping a leg around mine to try to still me.

"Goddamn, Hellfire. We're gonna work on that. You're

gonna learn to listen. But fuck it. I don't care tonight. Grind down on me. See if you can take us both there like this."

His words, along with his relentless pace, are apparently all I need. I come hard, too hard for my own good because I feel the release—one more intense than I've ever had before. I can't stop myself. I slide over his cock as he fucks me with his fingers, hitting me at just the perfect angle as I bite my tongue to try to stifle my moan, and he bites my neck. I suspect he loses himself in the process. I can feel the wetness as it seeps through his jeans. Except... my upper thighs are wet, and so is his hand as he pulls it away. Wetter than it should be, even given how good that was.

"Oh shit," I curse, immediately shocked and ready to scramble away. But he holds me tight. I've heard about this like it was an urban legend. Bristol has bragged about it happening to her twice with a guy she met last year. But I've never done it before.

"Hellfire... fuck. You're just full of surprises."

"I'm sorry." I feel the heat rise in my cheeks.

"Don't apologize."

"I've never... That's never happened before."

He plants kisses up my neck as his ragged breathing slows right alongside mine, nipping at my neck in intervals and finally sucking one long permanent kiss into my flesh.

"That's fucking perfect. Then we're both getting each other's firsts tonight." He whispers in a low, rough tone that could honestly make me come again if I had a moment to focus.

"You're not mortified?" I ask as his grip on me loosens. "Because I am."

"Look at me," he instructs, and I crane my neck to meet his eyes. "Don't be. Honestly. It's hot as fuck." His hand runs over my thigh, and he gently squeezes it in reassurance. "The only problem is now I'm gonna be tempted to challenge myself every single time," he murmurs against my shoulder. We sit like that for a minute before reality starts to sink in, and I realize I'm half naked, and we're both soaked.

I stand and grab my underwear and shorts, toeing out of my boots to put them back on, and then look over him with a smirk. Even with the black jeans and the low light of the moon, his whole lap is wet. I press my hand to my lips as a smile forms.

"Bonus is you don't know if it's all you or me too."

"That's unfair. You have to tell me. That was my own little challenge."

"You like guys who come in their pants?" He gives me a skeptical look. "That turns you on?"

"Um... fuck yes. Especially someone like you. Do you know how good you'd have to be to make a guy like Grant 'The Devil' Stockton come in his pants?" I tease him in a whisper, worried again about our proximity to the house.

"Woman, I think you might be confused about who the devil is in that scenario if you're trying to bring men down like that," he muses, half a smile on his face despite the scolding look his brow is giving me.

"I don't think you realize how hot it is."

He gives me another skeptical look, but then his attention returns to his pants.

"Either way, this probably isn't a good look going back into the house."

"Hold on." I hold up my hand as I put my boots back on. I duck around the corner and grab one of the beers out of the cooler that sits on the deck, thankful when it's a twist top because I don't have a bottle opener, and we don't have time to waste. When I round back to the other side of the house, he's already standing, and I toss the beer at him. It splatters across his shirt and pants in wild fashion, creating a Pollock-like stain down his front and making him reek of hops.

"Fuck me!" He shakes his hand and looks up at me like I've lost my mind for a moment before he recognizes my plan for what it is. "Smart ass."

"So you keep saying." I grin at him. "Just blame it on me. Tell them I was clumsy when we were both trying to get in the door. My hands were full, I wouldn't take help, and you got the short end of the stick."

"You're too clever for your own good sometimes." His lashes lift, and he studies me like he's amused. But there's something else there too, something I can't quite read in the way he takes me in now.

"Only when required."

"I know," he answers without missing a beat, smiling at me. "All right. Let's make a commotion on the way back in. It won't be hard for any of them to believe you dropped beer on me."

EIGHTEEN

DAKOTA

WHEN I STUMBLE into the kitchen in the morning, the pale light of the sun is just streaming in and casting long shadows. So long, in fact, that I miss the man sitting at the kitchen counter before it's too late. Hayden.

"Morning, sunshine." He grins at me.

"Morning," I say softly, edging my way around the counter. This time of day might as well be the dead of night for how often I see it. But I couldn't sleep. Not after last night with Grant. I just keep replaying it over and over in my head. So it's coffee and an early call time this morning. I might be able to whip up something for everyone for breakfast.

I wince as the sunlight hits my eyes. Or maybe just some freshly squeezed orange juice. We'll start small and see if Hazel made any plans with Kit, the inn's chef, for breakfast. I need coffee first if I'm going to be functional though.

"I got the espresso fired up if you want one." He nods toward the fancy machine Hazel has tucked away on one side of the kitchen.

"I wouldn't even know where to start. I leave the fancy stuff to my friend at her shop when I want it."

"Let me make you one then. You look like you need it." His eyes drift over me with concern but his smile doesn't fade.

"Ouch." I laugh, but I nod when he picks a big mug off the shelf and holds it up for me.

"Rough night?" he asks as he starts his ministrations on the machine.

"You could call it that. What are you doing up so early?" I raise my brow as I watch him move so deftly you'd think he worked part-time as a barista when he wasn't playing football.

"Stayed up with the guys playing a couple of rounds of poker. Had more drinks than I'm used to, especially at this altitude. So after about a gallon of water, I decided to have a little Irish hangover cure." He taps the bottle of Irish cream on the counter.

"Ah. Sensible." I nod as I pull out the oranges and a knife so I can start slicing them open.

"Do you want some in yours?"

"I think I'm okay. Just some juice and coffee, a little toast. I'll be good as new." I offer up a small smile, and he studies me.

"So this..." His fingers slip gently over the side of my neck. "Was obtained while you were sober?"

Panic wells in my gut, and I turn toward the glass where I can see my reflection. It's not as clear as a mirror, but I don't need it to be because the bruise is a bright purple. I instinctively cover it with my hand, and I feel the heat flush all the way down to my chest. Grant haunts me that way no matter where I am. His eyes follow the trail of bright red, and he smirks.

"Now I *know* I wasn't drunk enough to give you that and forget." His brow quirks up, and his eyes slip over me in question.

"I..." I stop no sooner than I start, staring at the floor.

I don't even know how to explain it. My fingers drift over it again, and I feel the echo of Grant's lips on my skin. When I look up, I expect judgment and an accusation in Hayden's eyes, but he's just grinning as he takes another sip of his coffee.

"You?" His other brow joins the first as he tilts his head to the side in patient expectation.

"It's complicated."

"Ah. I know complicated." He takes another slow draw off the drink and then looks up at me again. "Let me guess, he saw me with my hands all over you yesterday and didn't like that very much."

I frown at how transparent we are and worry if everyone in this place knows that something's up with us. His smirk just widens as the steam from his coffee wafts up and curls around it.

"To put it mildly."

"And I'm guessing the fact he didn't stop me outright means that whatever you two have going on is secret?"

I nod.

"Yeah... I'm all too familiar with that particular brand of situation."

"And yet you're here." I give him a playfully accusatory look.

"Trying real fucking hard to be reformed." He pours the espresso for me, pointing and adding the extras as I nod my head to them before he hands me the drink.

"I see." I roll my lip between my teeth and lean forward on my elbows, cup in hand, as I study him. "She married?"

"Not exactly, but she's as off-limits as they come. She doesn't even really like me, if I'm being honest. She just likes what I can do for her." The smirk reappears on his face, and he looks out the window. In the distance, I can see Kell taking some folks from the inn on an early morning trail ride.

"Hmm." I nod. Sounds like me. No wonder we hit it off on New Year's Eve. "That makes two of us familiar with that particular brand of *situation,* as you put it."

"Ah well, then we can commiserate and share tips." His smile is back, and it's a brilliant boyish sort that would melt my panties off in about two seconds if someone else didn't have ironclad control over them.

We hear voices trailing down the hall, the sounds of other people in the house waking up, and he turns back to me.

"How do you want to play this then?" he asks. I furrow my brows, and he continues, "Do you want me to back off or turn up the heat a little for his benefit? I can take care of myself if he gets a little punchy."

"If he gets a little punchy, we'll have bigger problems. But don't back off. Hazel's heart is dead set on this idea. I think she thinks we'll fall in love this weekend, have a whirlwind wedding, and I can live part-time in Cincinnati with her."

"What size ring? We can really get under his skin." He chuckles as a mischievous look crosses his face, and I shake my head laughing.

"We can't tease her like that though. She'd never forgive me. I just want to keep her happy for the weekend."

"She wouldn't be happy about the real guy?"

"I have no idea how she'll react, but I don't think it's what she needs to hear right now."

"All right. I got some tamer ideas. You have to take a picture in my lap later, though, so I can post it and see if my situation is still paying any attention."

"You've got a deal." I nod. The least I can do is help the guy out some.

"You better run and get some makeup or something on your neck, unless you want me to take credit for it."

"If I can't cover it up, would you?" I give him a pleading look.

"I got you." He winks, and whoever she is—she's lucky.

"Thank you. And for the coffee." I hold up the cup. "It's delicious." Incredibly lucky.

NINETEEN

GRANT

LEVI and I are sitting alone on the back of a couple of carts watching the competition taking place. Everyone's paired up today to compete in Hazel's wedding games for an all-inclusive resort vacation at the same couples-only place Hazel and Ramsey are headed to after the wedding. She's not even trying to be subtle about how she's paired them off either because she's got all her friends paired up with her brothers, with the exception of Dakota, who she's stuck with Hayden yet again.

Two of Hazel's other college friends, conveniently for us the two we were supposed to be paired with, missed their flights last night and didn't make it to town in time to get here. I'm not complaining because I'd much rather watch the competition from a distance than be involved, and it means I can keep an eye on where this asshole puts his hands.

I glare at the way Hayden helps line her up for her next shot. She's probably twice the shot he is, just like she was twice the dancer. But she lets him show her the ropes anyway, and it fucking digs at my temper.

I pop a piece of gum in my mouth just as Dakota giggles and leans into Hayden as they practice another round on the targets. Despite our discussion last night, she's playing coy and flirting with the damn football player who can't seem to take his eyes off her. But she's still got a bandana scarf wrapped around her neck, tied in a pretty little knot to cover up the marks I left there. Ones I might have to make more of if he keeps touching her hips and whispering in her ear as they rack up points in the target practice portion of the games.

"I NEED A FAVOR." Anson pulls me aside halfway through the day.

"What's that?" I rip my attention away from her and look him over.

Anson is Hazel's oldest brother and, therefore, soon-to-be family again. He's a lot more than that, though, as we frequently do business together. He owns a construction company, which makes him a convenient partner for all kinds of legal and less-than-legal business dealings.

"Bristol desperately wants to win this thing, and we're only a few points behind Dakota and Hayden. But lord knows I'm shit at horseshoes, and Bristol's already convinced she'll lose to Dakota when they play their 'Who Knows Hazel Best' game." Anson shakes his head, a combination of worry and annoyance written all over his face.

"They're all pretty close, aren't they? I'm sure she knows her well enough." I shield my eyes from the sun as I study him.

"I don't know. All I know is she's worried, and I'm trying to help."

"Guess you better beat them in this next scavenger hunt then."

"You want Hayden and Dakota going off on a romantic vacation together? 'Cause that's where this is headed," Anson warns me.

"Why would I care what she does with her free time? If it makes her happy." I shrug halfheartedly, and Anson breaks out into slow, stuttered laughter. Levi, for his part, stays quiet and looks between us.

"You think I believe that after your outburst at poker last night? The way you were drilling him at cards. I don't fucking think so."

"I just don't like people like him who think they're God's gift to the world. She deserves more respect."

"Uh-huh. Which is why you're following them around and watching her like a hawk instead of inside with the A/C and a cold drink." He eyes me like I'm a bad liar. "Just admit you don't want her near him, and let's figure out what we're going to do."

"Since when are you so concerned with Bristol?" I turn to look at him and raise a skeptical eyebrow, ready to change the subject.

"She takes care of my kid. She takes care of his grandma. She works hard. She deserves a vacation somewhere nice and a chance to get away."

"You remember the part where it's a romantic one?"

"A vacation's a vacation. It is what you make of it. Leave the details to me," he grumbles, and I shake my head laughing but stop short when I realize we might just be in the same boat. Two confirmed bachelors, me lifelong and him once again after the death of his wife. We have no business even trying, but I feel for him.

"So what's your plan?"

"You up for starting another fight with him? Put him in a bad mood and send him back inside?"

"Nah. Ramsey's already warned me off."

"Dakota then... You think you can distract her?"

"She doesn't listen to me; how do you think I'll get her to do anything I say? Not to mention she's managing the event." She's running herself ragged playing hostess. She's barely slept or sat down the last few days, and it shows on her face today, even if everyone else is having too much fun to notice it. She needs a break. Food. Water. The fact that he can't even see that has me irritated all over again.

"All right. Figured I'd try." Anson frowns at the way Dakota racks up ten more points on the board as Hazel cheers her on.

"Nah. I got an idea. Just leave it to me." I feel for him and I'm worried for her. I can at least give it a shot.

"Want to fill me in?"

"You're better off not knowing. Plausible deniability and all."

"Fair enough."

"HOW MUCH DO YOU LOVE ME?" I ask Aspen when I finally find her and manage to wrangle her away from our baby brother and Hazel.

"A lot." She eyes me apprehensively. "Why do you look like that? What are you up to?"

"I need your help. Just a little favor."

She gives me a skeptical look and crosses her arms over her chest.

"What kind of help?" My sister grew up in the same family as the rest of us, but she's a lot like our mother was, more than happy to pretend we were a normal family instead of what we really are. That doesn't stop her from being constantly suspicious.

"Nothing of the illegal variety. Just a little tipping of the scales for a guy who needs the help."

"And let me guess, you're the guy."

"Nah. Hazel's brother is the main target." I nod in Anson's direction. Despite Bristol's sideline cheering and support, he appears to be losing the round of horseshoes he's currently involved in. "I might reap a little side benefit though."

"I see." She looks me over like she's trying to figure out what I'm not telling her. "What do you need?"

"I'm gonna make Dakota disappear for a little bit. She needs a break. She's working herself to the bone trying to keep everyone happy and make this all fun for Hazel. But she needs food, water, and out of the sun. You know?"

"And you're going to take care of her? Won't she bite your head off for that?" The skepticism returns.

"She might bite a little bit. Nothing I can't take."

"I don't see how Anson benefits from this." Her brow lifts.

"Dakota's gonna miss a round or so of the game. Give Anson and Bristol a chance to catch up. He really wants to win the vacation for her."

"Couldn't he just buy it for her?"

"She'd never take it. She's too proud. All four of those girls have to do every damn thing themselves." I tilt my head to the side as I look back at my sister. "You'd know something about that."

My sister's lips flatline, and her eyebrow hikes impossibly higher at my mild criticism. Probably not my best timing given I'm asking for her help.

"You'd be doing a lot of favors all around," I plead with her.

"I'm just trying to figure out how this helps you. It must someway."

I shrug, but she must see something on my face because hers suddenly morphs into recognition.

"You don't approve of that guy she's with this weekend. Do you?"

"Didn't say that."

"You don't have to." She looks to where the two of them are standing together and then back at me—something dancing behind her eyes I don't love.

"Can't I just be worried about her? And yes, maybe a little annoyed he's not doing a better job watching out for her."

"You remember you're not actually related, right?" She gives me another quirk of her eyebrow. I'm half jealous of all she can communicate with that one little arch but annoyed she won't stop picking at a stone I'd rather not overturn right now.

"Again. Can we quit busting my balls over this and talk about logistics, assuming you're agreeing?" I grouse.

"What do you need from me?" She relents.

"Just when you see she's gone, explain that she had a headache from all the sun, and she went to take a rest for a while but didn't want anyone distracted. Make sure that the last part is clear with Hazel, or she'll go after her, trying to take care of her. Then Dakota will stress she's ruining it."

"Keep Hazel busy. Make things run smoothly. Dakota's got a headache. Got it." Aspen's eyes run over me, still trying to make sense of my motivations.

"They've got horseshoes now. Then a scavenger hunt and a game of who knows Hazel best. I'll bring Dakota back when that's over. You can text me."

"It'll be odd for Dakota not to be at that."

"Just say she didn't think it would be fair. Easy."

"I'm not good at the lying stuff, remember?"

"I know. It's like you and Ramsey don't even belong in this family." I smirk. "But thank you. Anson would thank you himself, and Dakota, too, really."

"I don't know if I'm doing anyone but you a favor."

"Maybe not. But I'm your favorite, remember?" I smirk, and she rolls her eyes.

"Fine. When is this all going down?"

"I'll snatch her when they start the scavenger hunt."

"All right. Good luck." She nods her agreement, and I hurry off to fill Levi in on the plan. No fucking way can I tell Ramsey because he'll blurt something to Hazel and ruin it all, but someone else needs to know what's going on to help keep things going.

TWENTY

D AKOTA

I HEAR the sound of hooves as I make my way across the pasture to the patch of woods where the creek runs through. I'm lagging behind everyone else, trying to make sure the last event is cleaned up and the next one is ready with the rest of the staff. Kit, Grace, Kellan, and Elliot, the full-time ranch and inn staff, all bowed out of the competition portion of the day to help with the events but still planned to join us later for dinner and the campfire portion of the evening. Hazel lamented that they didn't want to participate, but I'm grateful for any and all help I can get keeping things running smoothly.

I turn to see who's riding out, wondering if Kell is trying to catch up to tell us we forgot something. My phone only works intermittently depending on where we are on the ranch. Whoever's riding looks the part, cowboy hat and Wranglers, as he bears down on me. No sooner I squint and cover my eyes against the sun, I realize it's not Kell at all. It's Grant. The broad shoulders and the signature black hat are a dead give-away. I've rarely seen him ride, even though he's probably better than most of the people on this ranch, so I stop to take in the sight.

It's a mistake because as he gets close, I see him reach for something at his side—rope. It's a blur of motion then. He pulls it out and winds it up in the air as he races toward me. I'm a clueless ball of confusion as he ropes me, pulling it tight and circling me as he draws it even tighter. He yanks on the rope, and I'm forced to walk toward him as a devilish smirk forms on his lips under the shade of his hat.

"What the hell are you doing?" I snap as I feel the rope rub against my arms through my shirt, bits of fray coming loose and floating through the air.

I might find the man attractive. He might provide a lot of entertainment and orgasms, but I still feel like throttling him on occasion. One of them being now.

"Kidnapping you."

"This isn't a good time. I'm already behind and have to catch up with the rest of them."

"They'll be all right without you for a little bit."

"Hayden won't be. I'm his partner. And if anyone needs anything..." I give him an impatient look, struggling against the rope to try to shake it loose off my arms.

He tugs, and I stumble forward, my eyes snapping up to meet his, and a sardonic chuckle rumbles from his chest.

"Before I was anything else, I was one of the best ropers in the state of Colorado, Hellfire. Levi and I used to spend several days a week out here practicing with the cattle when we still had 'em. I wouldn't fight it."

My eyes drift over him as I try to decide whether he's

telling the truth or not, and he looks even more amused when he realizes what I'm doing.

"Don't make me prove it." He tugs on the rope again, slow and steady, and I'm forced to walk toward him.

"Is your goal to irritate me?" I glare up at him. I've barely slept or eaten today. I probably need water, too, given the headache I'm starting to develop. So needless to say, I'm cranky and not as amused as I might be under other circumstances.

"Nah. My goal is to kidnap you."

"Don't be ridiculous." Whatever I said about orgasms and entertainment, I take back. The man's timing sucks. "I told you. I have things to do."

"And I told you, as long as you're in debt to me, you follow my rules." He says it in a low tone, leaning over and glancing back at the woods to make sure no one's near the tree line to see or hear us.

"This isn't cute." I glare at him.

"Neither is this attitude you've got going on." He hops down off his horse and approaches me.

"Hurry up and take it off," I grouch, wiggling my shoulders under the rope, trying to crane my arms enough to pull at it.

He yanks it hard, pulling me to his chest, and puts his hand under my chin, forcing me to look up at him.

"You don't tell me what to do, Hellfire. You listen, and you obey. Got it?"

My eyebrows slam down, and I open my mouth to let him have it, but his thumb presses to my lips.

"Think real carefully about what you say next and the fact that you've been trying my patience all day with your boy out there." He holds my gaze steady, and his icy-blue eyes look brilliant in this light. His thumb sweeps back and forth across my lips. "Now. We're gonna walk back to the house, and you're gonna be good for me, aren't you?"

I narrow my eyes, but I don't disagree with him. I have no idea what he's up to, but I do know that arguing with him is futile at this point. I can't get out of this rope without his help, and I have very little energy to keep arguing. But it doesn't stop me from one last burst of defiance.

"I have zero intention of being anything for you. You don't own me just because you're helping me."

Before I know what's happening, I'm being manhandled. The rope's being wound around me twice more, and then I'm being hauled up off my feet and onto the back of the horse. He throws me across the saddle like I'm a bag of potatoes.

"Asshole! I can't believe you—" I start to shout but lower my volume when I remember I don't actually want anyone running out here to find me like this. It would be way too much to explain, and he'd be happy to make the story much more colorful for them.

His hand comes down swift on my ass. Not enough to truly hurt, but enough that it leaves a stinging reminder in its wake.

"Call me another name, Hellfire. See what happens when we get back to the house."

"Nothing's happening when we get back to the house other than me marching right back out here to find Hayden and telling him I'm going to Cincinnati with him. You think you control everything, but you don't." I feel ridiculous arguing with him from this position as the horse starts to slowly walk us back to the house.

"I don't think I control everything, but I definitely control you at the moment. And right now, you're being an ungrateful little brat. So I'm going to treat you like one until you give me a reason to stop."

"This is uncomfortable. At least let me sit right in the saddle," I grumble.

He sees reason in that, pausing to help me get situated but refusing to loosen any of the binds as we ride back to the house.

"Someone is going to see me like this and think you've lost your mind," I complain as we get closer.

"Someone is going to see you like this and congratulate me for doing the thing they wish they could, darlin'." He looks up at me, smirking and shaking his head before his focus is back on the path ahead of us.

I press my lips together and glare at the back of his hat. This man is going to make me commit murder. One moment, I can't get enough of him, and the next, I want to choke him out in the dirt. I thought maybe, maybe after a few moments of intimacy between us, he'd finally treat me with some respect, but apparently, that's too much to ask. Daddy Grant can't let go of the reins, literally or figuratively.

I glance around as we get onto the path to the barn, hoping like hell no one is around to see me like this. I can only imagine what they'll whisper about, and it's not like he gives a single solitary damn that he's embarrassing me.

He makes quick work of getting me down and his horse back into his stall. He ties the rope to one of the cross ties in the aisle of the barn so I can't run off, and I glare at him wordlessly. I'm done speaking to him. He can have silence for the rest of the damn day. Maybe the week. In fact, every picture I send him will probably just be my middle finger with my blurred body behind it. If I send him any pictures at all.

He looks at me, his eyes drifting over my body and my face before his lips draw up on one side.

"Plotting my murder?" he asks casually.

I press my lips tighter and look away. I hate his mind-reading abilities more than almost anything else about him.

"Ah. The silent treatment. That ain't punishment though. I

get to look at you all tied up like this and not have it spoiled with you calling me names."

I take a deep breath and let it out slowly as he closes the distance between us. I'm trying to remember the exercise my therapist taught me for moments like this. I'm too distracted by him though. Backlit from the open barn door, with his cowboy hat and a wry grin, he's so different from the man that runs the casino—closer to the younger version I crushed on so hard. He leans in, tilting his head and putting his cheek against mine.

"I could fuck you like this you know. All pretty and tied up in knots. I bet I could make you talk for me."

My defiance falters as I imagine finally having his hands all over me the way I wish he would. Him using me the way he sees fit. Even through my frustration and anger, it still holds appeal. I look over at him, catching his eyes from the corner of mine.

"You like the idea of that, don't you? I thought so." He unhooks the rope from the cross tie, occasionally looking up to make eye contact again as he does it. "I'm gonna take these ropes off you so Kit doesn't chase me down with a skillet, but you're gonna listen to me if you ever want any of those things I've told you I could do for you."

He winds the rope around his arm, a thing that's remarkably sexy as I watch his forearm flex with the movement. He hangs it up and turns back to me. I stretch my limbs, noting the way it's marked my shirt. It was one of my favorites.

"How will I explain that?" I blurt the question before I can remember I'm not speaking. Fighting him was always a losing battle.

"Don't worry about it." He shakes his head. "We're gonna take you inside and get you a change of clothes anyway."

"What are we doing here?" I frown up at the ranch house. I

can't imagine his plan is anything too nefarious, but I'm still wary.

"You'll see." He nods in front of us. "Lead the way."

I take a tentative step, briefly wondering if I could outrun him all the way back out to the woods. But like he can read my mind, his hand darts out, grabbing me around the waist and pulling me tight against his chest.

"Don't even think about it. You're exhausted, and you'll drop halfway there in that sun. I'll be fucking furious. You don't want that. I promise," he threatens.

TWENTY-ONE

D AKOTA

I LET my shoulders fall in defeat, putting one foot in front of the other as I walk toward the main house. I feel ridiculous. Like I'm letting Hazel and everyone down. That whatever I've done wrong attracted enough of his attention that he feels like he has to intercede. By the time I get inside the house and take off my boots, I feel like collapsing into a pile on the couch. The cool breeze on my overly heated skin is a relief, even if I don't want to admit it.

"Come on." He looks at me, a hint of pity in his eyes as he reads my expression and takes my hand. He leads me to the kitchen and pats one of the stools at the island counter. "Sit."

I do as I'm told. The lure of modern conveniences like chairs and A/C is too much for me to fight right now. Maybe after a few minutes. I lean over, pressing my arms to the cool quartz counter. He makes his way around the kitchen, grabbing a glass and filling it with water from the fridge before he slides it in front of me.

"Drink," he commands. "But not too fast." He points at it and then me before he heads to the fridge again.

I take a sip and then a few gulps while his back is turned before I set the glass down again. The cool water feels good on my tongue and my parched throat. Yelling rules and directions to everyone all day has nearly stolen my voice. Even worse than the bar does.

"What are you doing?" I ask, my voice husky from tightness in my vocal cords, and I clear my throat.

"Making you a plate." He pulls out various leftovers from earlier in the day, fruit and mini sandwiches along with a couple of appetizers, and arranges them on a piece of the Stockton family stoneware. The set Ramsey's mother had handed down to Hazel when they got married the first time. He sets it down on the counter with a napkin and fork. "You're gonna eat and drink this while I watch. No running off." He reaches down and snatches my phone from my pocket. "No taking calls. No texting. Nothing."

"They'll notice I'm gone any minute and be worried."

"Aspen's got it under control, and Levi's helping her."

"You roped your siblings in on this?"

"They do what I say when they know I need the help."

I frown at the fact that several people dropped what they were doing just so I could eat a snack.

"This is silly," I protest while I take a bite.

"What's silly is you not making time to eat or drink while you run yourself ragged. It's hot out there. I hope you at least put sunscreen on this morning," he grumbles as he takes the stool next to me and turns it toward mine before he sits.

"Okay, *Dad*," I grouch, popping another strawberry into my mouth.

"I thought it was Daddy?" He smirks when I risk a glance over at him.

"You only get Daddy when you're being good to me." I shift my eyes back to my food and nip off a bite of my sandwich like it's his head.

"I'm good to you all the time, sweetheart. You just sometimes like to do things that aren't good for you."

"This again." I sigh. "I've told you. I can take care of myself."

"I know you can. But sometimes you don't have to." He takes a strawberry and dips it into some of the sweet fruit dip he piled on the plate and holds it out for me. I go to reach for it, but he grabs my wrist and presses it to my lips. I look between him and the fruit and take a bite. "See? Not so hard," he remarks as I chew the bite slowly, studying his face.

"Torture," I say as I take the second bite, and he drops the stem to the plate along with my wrist. I'm not about to admit it, but the surge of carbs into my system does seem to be helping my brain function properly again. I don't feel like I'm on the verge of tears and ready to snap a man's neck all at the same time. "Is this your thing then? Bossing women around and telling them when to eat and what to do?" It's more curiosity than admonishment at this point, and I do my best to make sure he hears it in my tone.

"Nah. I don't care what women do. You're grown and entitled to your choices," he says, dipping another strawberry in the fruit dip and bringing it to his tongue. "But I care what belongs to me is well taken care of. Especially when I spend a lot of time and energy trying to make things right." He gives me a pointed look.

"And you decide what that looks like?"

"Only when you stop making smart decisions and start putting yourself needlessly in harm's way. Then I might step in from time to time." He states it bluntly. "Last I checked, you were reaping a whole lot of benefits from my interference, without many downsides."

"Dealing with you isn't a downside?" I tease him, letting the smile break on my lips for him to see as he studies my face.

He smirks and looks down at the counter for a moment before his lashes lift and his eyes meet mine again, holding me with a steady gaze. "Not by the way your body reacts to me. The way your cheeks flush... Fuck. That's my favorite part, honestly, because you don't blush for anything."

I can feel the heat of another flush rising up my neck at the accusation, and I'm keen to get out of his line of sight before it happens. I don't want to have to watch that self-satisfied grin grow on his face. I grab the plate and go to stand to take it to the sink, but he stops me, his palm on my wrist.

"Finish the last strawberry." He nods to what's left on my plate. I take it and dunk it into the remaining dip before I pop it into my mouth, biting off the stem and putting it back on the plate. He takes the plate from me and walks it back to the sink, washing it off and tucking it into the dishwasher with the rest of the dishes waiting their turn. He still respects the house like his mama will turn up any minute, and it's another one for the list of things I like about him.

"Thank you," I say softly while his back's turned. "I was hungrier than I thought."

"Looked like you were gonna collapse out there."

"You could have just told me to eat. Or brought me a snack. I'm not sure it required a kidnapping."

"Oh yeah. That part was for me." He leans back against the counter, his arms braced on either side of him. "And Anson." The new surge of energy has me imagining things we could do in this house before everyone gets back. Until my brain catches up on the "Anson" part of his statement, and I frown.

"Anson?" I ask, trying to figure out how he fits into this puzzle.

A smile spreads on his face. "I think he's sweet on Bristol. Or at least has a weak spot for her, despite what he says. He wants her to win that vacation, and you and your new boyfriend are being ruthless out there today."

"Oh shoot. I wasn't even thinking about that. Hayden and I are just both... competitive, I guess." I stumble over my words. It was competitiveness, but I also felt like I needed to prove a point. One I'm regretting a little now that I'm sitting here with the less ego-driven and more thoughtful side of this man.

"I noticed how *competitive* you two were being." Grant raises a brow.

"He knows." I decide to admit defeat.

"How?"

"Because I didn't have these covered early this morning when we ran into each other in the kitchen." I untie the bandana I'd tied around my neck and let it drop, revealing the marks left on my skin.

He grins at his handiwork, propelling himself off the edge of the counter behind him and leaning over the island to get a closer look. His grin only gets wider as his thumb brushes softly over my skin.

"Good. That's what he gets for touching you." But then his brows knit together. "He got a death wish today, then?"

"He has his own... complication. He's just trying to make it look like he's moved on. Taking some photos and videos for socials," I explain.

"Ah." He nods his understanding. "I guess I won't snap his neck then."

"I heard you tried to last night at poker."

He rolls his eyes to the side. "Everyone's exaggerating the reality."

"Your temper is pretty frightening."

"You've never seen my temper." He shakes his head. "Not the real one."

"I only get the irritation?"

"You only get the concern." He stands straight again. "Speaking of. Drink the rest of the water. I'd tell you to take a nap, but I'm sure you'll fight me on it."

"I'm better now. If I grab a Coke or an energy drink, I'll be all right." I grab one from the fridge drawer and crack it open, wandering over to the island and leaning back on it next to him. "One of the best riders and ropers in the state, huh?"

He scrubs a hand over his face like he regrets mentioning it. "It was a long time ago."

"How long ago? Because imagining you as some rough and tumble cowboy..." I smile and let my eyes fall over him. As gorgeous as this man is in a three-piece, this dressed down version of him is doing things for me a suit never could. I can only imagine how many hearts he broke.

"Before I came to terms with reality, I wanted to be a bronc rider. Wanted to do the rodeo circuit and earn my money that way, away from all this. Thought I was gonna make a million dollars and ride off into the sunset with some cute barrel racer. All the naïve, romantic ideals you have when you're young enough to still believe in them."

I blink at him as I try to picture him in that scenario. "This sounds like an entirely different man than the one I know."

"Because I wasn't a man. I was a kid." He turns his back toward me and pulls down the collar at the back of his shirt to reveal the start of a tattoo. I reach up and tug it down further and see the words *Born to Ride* inscribed on his skin in faded black ink. "Mom about died when she saw it, and my dad took the time to explain to me what I was really born to do."

I trace my fingers over the ink, and it feels like a rare glimpse beyond his walls. One I'm grateful for.

"Well, judging by today, you would have been amazing at it. Selfishly, I'm a little glad you didn't get the wraparound porch and sunset with the barrel racer though." I say the words quietly as my fingers brush up the back of his neck, and I circle to his front, setting my drink down on the counter in the process.

He looks at me warily, but I slowly put a hand to his chest, and he doesn't stop me. I raise onto my tiptoes, kissing the side of his cheek, the roughness of his short beard against my lips.

"Thank you. I'm sorry for what I said when I was hangry."

"You're forgiven." His voice is low and deep, and my hand slips down his chest.

"Anything I can do to make up for it?" I give him my best sorry-I-was-a brat, doe-eyed look, and his lips move to speak when the screen door squeals on its hinges. We both move to separate ourselves, and he straightens his shirt as we look up to see his sister standing there. Her eyes dart between us, but she doesn't say a word.

"They're on their way back up." She looks at Grant and then turns to me. "Is your headache improved, or would you like me to play hostess until dinner?" Her words are plain, but I don't miss the way she watches me like a hawk.

"I'm good. Just having some Coke to get my energy back up." I hold the can up like it's a plausible defense for whatever part of that she saw or heard.

"I'll get out of your hair and go check on my brothers." Grant grabs his hat off the hook where he left it and tears out the door like I've singed his clothes.

Aspen is silent for a moment, like she's waiting for him to

get out of earshot, and then she looks up at me, studying me quietly and glancing back at the door where Grant's disappeared.

"What you two do is none of my business. You're a grown woman, and he's getting the silver highlights to show for all his time—however young he might still think he is." She smiles a little to herself before she continues. "But you need to know underneath all those thick layers of armor is a very broken man, with a big heart that's barely held together by fraying threads. Because he's let anyone and everyone take a stab if it meant protecting the rest of this family and yours." She turns back to meet my eyes, the amusement in hers gone, and the bright green reflecting the sunlight pouring in from the window when she speaks again. "You're one of the few he might let reach under it all, and if he does, and you do anything other than help hold it together..." She shakes her head and makes a clicking sound with her tongue. "I'll make sure he's not the only one bleeding out from it. Do we understand each other?"

"We do." I nod, coming to the fast realization that the Stockton women are every bit as terrifying as the men when they want to be.

"Wonderful." She smiles brightly and tucks her long, dark-brown, braided hair back over her shoulder. "Hazel said we could start getting drinks ready for dinner and let Kit know that she and Grace can bring it over from the inn. Do you know where the chafing dishes are?"

TWENTY-TWO

G RANT

"IT'S in a home in Denver. Expensive neighborhood. We're looking into who owns it, but it's behind a shell corporation," Hudson says as soon as he sits down across from me at the chessboard. He'd just gotten into the state this morning and hurried down to meet with me to let me know the latest news in person.

"A shell?" My brows knit together.

"Clearly trying to keep a low profile. The bid was paid for by another shell corporation."

"Guaranteed then that it's someone on our side of the law." I look up at him, and he nods. No one doing business above board would be working through that many different companies.

"Occasionally, there are legitimate collectors who bid in

those auctions. I'm one of them, and I try to keep my privacy as well for obvious reasons."

"But I wouldn't exactly call you above board either."

Hudson's past is as checkered as mine, and he isn't keeping it a secret from anyone. But he has enough legal business interests in Cincinnati and abroad that it makes sense to at least present the air of legitimacy. I work to maintain similar optics. Plausible deniability keeps my lawyers happy in the event anything ever goes sideways.

"No. I think it's almost certain our John Doe is a bad actor. We'll have to have someone go up and surveil the house, see what they can garner from the comings and goings. Have Levi dig a little deeper into the paperwork and see if he can turn anything up. Bonus points if he can hack into the security system. The one they have is robust."

"Might be able to get someone in on a maintenance call or a routine gas line check. Plant a bug or two."

"We'll have to work quickly. They haven't discovered the tracker yet. It's still logging. But it's been in the same place for days. If it gets turned off, there's no telling where it goes or how they might cover their tracks."

"I'll get one of my guys on it. Make sure it's on the top of Levi's priority list. Other than this wedding, I've cleared my schedule."

"Not the best timing for a wedding." Hudson frowns, but it fades into a small smirk. "But I am happy for your brother. Getting to know him and his wife better in Cincinnati has been good. It's hard to make friends you can trust." He makes another move on the board. "Not like you don't know that."

"Hard to keep friends when you're constantly burying them at chess." I can already tell he's cornering me.

"Yes, well, don't throw me over before we find out who this is. Or before the wedding. Charlotte's excited about the dancing and the food. It's all she can talk about this week. She's also interested to know if you're bringing a date." He looks up at me with a curious expression on his face. "I think we all are."

"I'm in the wedding party. They're making us sit at those big banquet tables up front like we're on display. Their first wedding was pretty small, given they were both still in college. They both want all the pageantry this time." I shake my head.

"The whole performance is part of the fun, you know."

"It'll be more fun when it's over."

"Not a party person?"

"Not particularly. But it's Ramsey. So I want him to enjoy himself, and then I want to get down to the business of finding out who this fucker is and what he wants."

"Agreed." Hudson nods.

"Any guesses on who it is?" I raise a brow.

"Could be anyone. Art collector. Art dealer. Could be someone who has a buyer in mind. Something darker or with a more criminal element. Might meet an exchange they're looking for. Could even be a clergy member or someone religious wanting personal possession of it. The true believers who think it has healing abilities. Whoever it is, they have a lot of money to spend."

"We still think our problems are one in the same?"

"It still seems the most likely." Hudson studies the board, hands steepled as he considers his options.

"This feels worse than gambling."

"This game or that one?" Hudson looks up at me, amused.

"Both. When I gamble, I know where I stand. The house always wins. When I play you, I always think I've got some small chance of finally beating you. That game? I always think I'll win. Because the good guy always does, right? Except we forget for every story where we're the hero, there are two more where we're the villain."

Hudson tilts his head and moves a bishop. "Truer words..."

There's a knock at the door, and we both look up.

"Open!" I call out, letting my security know they're free to let whoever it is in. You can't make it down the hallway outside this room without vetting from my team.

I'm expecting Levi, but when the door opens, it's Dakota. She's come prepared to make me lose my fucking breath, too, because she's in a knockout sundress. A short one that flares at the bottom and swings around her thighs as she walks toward us. The top is deceptively prim because it covers everything and barely shows any cleavage, but it's so tight it shows the outline of both her breasts and the way the cool air in this room is highlighting them. She smirks at me as she walks toward me, like she knows exactly what I'm thinking as my eyes rake down over her thighs to her boots.

I hear Hudson chuckle under his breath at the way I'm staring, but I don't even have the will to tear my eyes off her long enough to shoot him a glare.

"I see you've finally found your vice," he murmurs quietly before she gets close enough to hear.

"You're early" is the way I manage to greet her.

"I thought you appreciated punctuality."

"He does." Hudson's amusement is growing by the second. "I can make myself scarce."

Dakota's eyes finally find him, and I don't like the way they stutter over his form, shining brighter when her blue-green eyes meet his.

"Hello. I'm sorry. I don't mean to be rude. He doesn't always like me meeting his colleagues. Prefers to maintain their privacy." Dakota's prim greeting meets with Hudson's approval as he smiles back at her.

"I do enjoy my privacy, so I'll let you have yours. At the very least, it looks like he'll need it to regain his speech."

Hudson stands as I scowl at him, and to add insult to injury, he makes another move on the board. One that has me danger-ously close to losing.

"Well, it was lovely to meet you, whoever you are." She flashes a coy smile, the kind she always uses on customers at the bar.

"You as well." He grins wider and nods to both of us. "See you later, friend."

"Later." I nod in return to him, not missing the subtle shake of his head at my predicament.

Once the door is closed, my attention is back on the woman in the dress. Except her eyes are still on the door. I feel the subtle rise of jealousy up my spine as she sits in his seat and runs her fingers over the arm of the chair, like she's tracing where he's been before her gaze returns to me, a soft look of appreciation on her face.

TWENTY-THREE

D AKOTA

"WHO WAS THAT?" I ask as I sit down in the stranger's seat. My eyes follow the path he took to the door.

"Hudson Kelly. You can pick your jaw up off the ground."

"Is he single?" I tease. I don't really mean it, but I love the little flare of jealousy in his eyes as he looks me over.

"He is not, and he's absolutely obsessed with her. So obsessed he's willing to share if it means keeping her."

"Willing to share?" I raise a brow. That didn't look like a man who needed or wanted to share.

"She has him and two others."

"Two? A man like that and two more? I need to meet this woman." My jaw drops as I stare at the door. Maybe she can teach me a thing or two.

"I've met Charlotte, and trust me, she needs all three." He smirks, and I sit up straighter.

"Does she now? Is she that pretty?" I ask, trying not to let the inquiry sound as jealous as it feels.

"She's gorgeous, incredibly smart, and dangerous as fuck." His tone has reverence to it I don't miss.

Envy flares in my chest with the way he describes her. She sounds like exactly the kind of woman Grant would fall for if such a thing was even possible.

"Does she give lessons?" I run my fingers over the crown on the queen's head.

Grant laughs as he sits back in the chair, studying the chessboard in front of him.

"I wish. We could all learn a thing or two from her."

"You still have more to learn, even at your advanced age?" I run my teeth over my lower lip as I grab one of the chess pieces and move it forward on the board.

"Always." He makes the next move.

"You and Hudson play chess together?" I follow suit.

"I like to play chess with people I'm in business with." He tilts his head and makes another move.

"I would've thought you'd do something more in line with your hobbies. Playing cards or riding." Seeing him the other day confirmed my suspicions. Hazel mentioned in passing while we were out riding that Grant has horses on the ranch again, now that she and Ramsey are back together.

"Most of these guys wouldn't know what to do with a horse, and playing cards usually makes them want to put money on the table to sate their ego. You don't want any more money or pride on the line than you already have when you're doing business. Besides, how someone plays chess tells you a whole lot about how their mind works. Who they are as a person." Grant's brow furrows as he studies what's left of the board.

"What kind of business do you do with him?" I ask absently, studying the board and finally picking a piece. It's been a long time—too long—since I learned to play, and I forget nearly all the rules. I'm just waiting for him to call me out on it.

"The most important kind." He moves again on the board but dodges my question.

"What does he do for a living?"

"He exists."

"What does that mean?"

"He's rich—filthy fucking rich."

"Richer than you?"

"Richer than me." He looks up at me, studying my face for a moment before his eyes return to the board. "And getting richer by the day."

"Not satisfied with being *filthy* rich?"

"It's not the money he's after. It's the power. Being a prince isn't enough. He wants to be king if it means he can crush the people who hurt his family," Grant says absently as he watches me make the next move.

"But you don't?"

"No. I don't. All that stuff they say is true—heavy is the head that wears the crown. Not to mention all that pomp and circumstance. I'd much rather be lurking in the shadows where no one expects me." He holds up the knight. "A dark horse."

"But the king needs his horse."

He turns the chess piece over in his hand. "We need each other."

"Why?" I ask, and something flickers over his face before he returns his attention to the board.

"Checkmate." He smirks as his lashes lift, and his eyes meet mine.

"I haven't played in a long time." I offer up a weak defense.

"You should play more. You've got good instincts, just too

hasty in some of the plays you make. Watch the board more. Watch how your opponent plays. You want to be thinking about what they'll do next, not what you'll do."

"You could teach me. Get some practice in yourself." I hold up his knight in my hand.

"I do need practice, but I'm not a great teacher. Levi would be better than I am for that."

"I'm sure you're perfectly adequate," I tease, and he smiles at that. "We could play for stakes to make it interesting."

"What kind of stakes are you offering?"

"Favors. Little ones at first and then work our way up to bigger ones once I remember how to play." I round the little table and stand between him and the chessboard.

"Do I get a favor for winning this one?" he asks, and his eyes follow the movement as I turn the figurine over in the palm of my hand.

"Depends on what it is and if that means you're agreeing."

"Do I owe you favors if you win?" His lashes lift as his eyes work their way up my body.

"Seems fair, doesn't it?"

"I don't care about playing fair. I care about getting what I want."

"But I do," I argue.

He sighs and leans back in his chair, considering my proposal.

"Do we know the favors ahead of time?" he asks thoughtfully.

"I mean, the first one is going to be an introduction to Charlotte. I need to find out how to get three men at the same time and make one a gorgeous billionaire."

"You get one gorgeous billionaire, or you get three men. You don't get both." There's a firm edge to his voice.

"She did," I argue with him, even though there's no real heat in it, and he knows it.

"She has a man with a stag kink and the patience of a saint. You don't share that luxury."

"What luxury do I have then?" I point the knight at his chest.

"I wouldn't call it luxury." His eyes follow the movement.

"Fine... what kinks do I get to entertain then?"

He gives me a skeptical look, like he's not keen to answer.

"You have to tell me some. You already know a few of mine. You practically have a list. It's fair," I fire back.

"I don't recall this list. Remind me."

"If I tell you, you have to tell me."

"You'll just use them against me."

"*For* you," I counter. "Do we have a deal or not?"

"Fine. We have a deal. Tell me."

"Making a man come in his pants. Hot as hell under the right circumstances."

"Which circumstances are those again?"

"Making you come like that is hot under any of them." I grin brightly, and he shakes his head but amusement dances behind his blue eyes.

"Noted. Next?"

"Being tied up. Even though I was cranky at the time, I can't stop thinking about it."

"As I said... I don't mind that one at all." He smirks.

"Nicknames. Especially when you call me them."

"Definitely noted that one already. Can't say I'll ever get used to it, but if it makes you happy, then I'm happy to do it."

"The whole deal with the devil thing we have going on. It really backfired on you because the idea of being forced to do all these sexy little photos and videos for you... I actually like it. I'll never admit that in public, and if you'd asked me, I would have said hell no. Never. Especially not with Grant Stockton." I run my fingers over his tie. "But I like you telling me what to do. How to do it. Giving over control to you. I'm not sure if that's a separate one but that too."

His brow pushes higher. "If you had told me that Dakota Hartfield likes to cede control anywhere..."

"It feels good with you. Like I can let go for that little bit of time." I spin the knight in my palm. "And the way you react to it... You got softer." I look up at him. "It makes it feel safe."

"You're always safe with me. You know more than anything that's my priority." His tone shifts back to business.

"I know." I nod, and then I give him an expectant look. "Now... your turn. I've been asking for weeks."

"I think you might have given me a daddy kink. It wasn't something I liked before, but fuck... the way you call me it... I shouldn't though. It's fucked up." He shakes his head.

I can't help the grin, but I try to smother it anyway. He clocks it, and his lips flatline in admonishment.

"What?" I say defensively. "It's just... kind of a thing for me too now. Again, I would have hated it with any other guy. But with you..." I trail off before I say something shockingly vulgar. "Anyway—what else?"

"Watching you touch yourself. Playing with your toys. Knowing you're thinking of me while you do it. Doing what I tell you while you do it."

"I figured that one." I smirk.

"Yeah, but I've just started to realize some things that I didn't before," he muses.

"Like?" The smirk fades to a questioning smile, and I raise a brow.

"Like." He stands and snatches me up. He carries me to the far side of the room where there's a bar stretched across the back wall. He lifts me on top of it, and his hands fall over my thighs. I wore this dress for him, a little summer sundress I thought would get his attention, and his eyes track over the frilled hemline as his fingers tease me there, pushing it higher.

"When you did this at the bar, I thought you were trying to humiliate me in front of everyone—that *that* was maybe your kink with all those guys. But now I realize why you did it." His eyes trace over my skin as he speaks.

"Why was I doing it?" I ask, setting the knight down on the bar next to me and leaning back on my palms to watch him.

He reaches over the bar, grabbing a bottle and a fresh glass. He pours a couple of fingers of whisky, sets it down on my other side, and then sinks back onto the stool to look up at me again. A devilish grin spreads over his face.

"Did you wear panties?"

"No. You told me not to." I watch him carefully, trying to get some read on him besides the fact that he's up to no good.

"Perfect. Spread wider for me. Like you did at the bar."

"I had shorts on then." I hesitate.

"There's no one but me watching now." I look around the room because I know he has security throughout the hotel. "No cameras in here. This is for private meetings only. I wouldn't let anyone else see."

I spread wider, and he pushes my dress up my thighs to give him a better view.

"We might not get along well on any other front, but on this part, we're a match made in hell. The way you like being watched, and I like watching. Touch yourself for me." His eyes meet mine with the dare, and I slip my hand between my legs to do what he's asking.

"I like watching too."

"I know you do. But you like watching me watch you even more. You like having my attention however you can get it. Don't you?" His hands go to the inside of my knees and nudge them farther apart. "You can have every man's attention in the bar, but if it's not mine, it's not good enough."

"I don't know. That one with the curly red hair and the sweet drawl. He wasn't bad. I bet he would have been eager." I'm only joking with him, and he knows it. He still makes an unimpressed grunt and sinks lower on the stool to watch me as my fingers tease over my clit.

"How many guys do you think spend their nights fantasizing about you?"

"After a night at the bar? I don't know. Not many. I imagine most of those guys go home with someone."

"Someone they're wishing was you, and if it's not, the next night they're tugging on their little dicks imagining you spitting into their mouths. Dozens I bet. And that's before we even get to your subscriber list. I bet there's one of them getting off right now on their break at work imagining the sounds you make."

"I think you're exaggerating, but I like the way jealousy sounds on you." I taunt him as I slip two fingers inside and close my eyes, imagining they're his. I need his hands on me, but I'm too interested to see where this fantasy of his is headed.

"I was. I would be." His eyes are glued to my hand, watching how wet I'm getting, and his tongue slides over his lower lip. I'd kill to have him take a taste of me right now. Watching him watch me is like a drug. "But then I figured it out."

"What's that?" I ask softly, distracted by the way the tension in my nerves pools lower and lower with each pass of my fingers.

"They imagine you. But you? You imagine me." His eyes dart up to meet mine. "I'm the guy who crawls into your head every night. The one you imagine with his hands all over your body, whispering his wicked, fucked-up thoughts in your ear. I'm the one you need. Because you don't want to be some guy's fantasy on a pedestal, you want someone to be the real deal. You crave it—hate fucked, tied down, and used up. The way I tried to push you over the edge with my demands, the rope, the orders, all the things I thought might set you straight, but you *like* it."

I scoff, but I can't bring myself to argue with him. Just listening to him say it has me getting wetter by the second.

"Answer me," he demands.

"Yes." It's a breathless confession, but truth all the same.

"And I'm the only one you think has a chance in hell of living up to your needs." He points out the obvious for his own satisfaction.

"So fuck me and put me out of my misery. Put yourself out of *your* misery. You're not saving all those photos out of the goodness of your heart to save me from myself. You want them." I hold his gaze with my own and watch the war play out behind the blue depths.

TWENTY-FOUR

G RANT

I'VE NEVER BEEN MORE TEMPTED in my life. The only thing that stops me in this moment is that I want to edge the fuck out of her. I want her so desperate for my cock when I finally fuck her that nothing else on earth will come close. All my other concerns, the part of my brain that thinks critically, has fucking left the building. I'm just thankful I still have a razor-thin margin of control when I need it. Enough to show her how tight I can hold the reins for both of us.

"No."

She lets out a soft frustrated sigh and closes her eyes, her hand dropping from its work between her thighs, glistening and wet from the way she's been working herself up for me.

"But don't worry, sweetheart. We're not gonna waste a drop." I take up her hand and kiss her fingertips. "You're gonna imagine we're still in your bar, with all your college boys watching you come the way you need it. You're gonna finish yourself off on my tongue."

Her eyes open again and slip down to watch me as I make a tentative swipe of my tongue over her clit. I grab her thigh and prop her leg over my shoulder so I have better access. Her lips curl at the corner with anticipation, and I take another long lick of her, teasing her clit and tracing over her piercing before I work my way down again.

"I wish they could all watch you do this." She moans softly as I start to work her over with my tongue. "Especially all those girls who look at you like they want to fuck you right there in the bar. Imagine how jealous they'd be right now." Her fingers explore my scalp, weaving between the strands of my hair as she rocks her hips up to meet my mouth.

"They'd be so disappointed to have to go home with one of those boys instead of you," she continues, and I love the way she sounds when she talks like this. Her voice has a honey-like quality to it—thick and just that little bit raspy.

I suck gently on her clit, and there's a series of soft curses and gasps.

"If I'd known you could use your tongue like this..." Her voice fades to a soft moan, and her fingers drift down the back of my head to my neck, where her nails scrape slowly over my skin. "Fuck, you eat like one of those desperate cowboys who's been out on the trail too long."

I smirk as I pull away, glancing up at her before pressing a kiss to her perfect little clit. I slip two fingers inside her. She coats them easily, so fucking wet and perfect for me.

"I need more. I want you," she begs.

I almost comply. The urge to just take her right here on the floor is so strong it's very nearly painful. But neither of us is ready for that yet—what it would mean if I finally claimed her the way I want.

If she needs more, though, I can give her that. I grab the knight off the bar next to her and drag it over her, teasing her clit before I slip it inside her. There's a gasp at the intrusion, and she looks down, flushing when she realizes that I'm fucking her with the chess piece. I work it in and out with my fingers at a steady rhythm, and her skin flushes with heat.

"That full enough for you?"

"You're a tease, not nearly as good as your dick would be," she muses.

I lean over and suck on her, my tongue working over the jewelry and massaging her clit in the process. She squirms against my face, clearly desperate for more, and my fingers bite down into the flesh of her thighs. I come up for air to tell her what to do.

"Fuck my face, Hellfire."

Her fingers drag through my hair, and she uses it like an anchor, tightening her grip as she rolls her hips. She uses all of me. My tongue, my lips, my teeth. I bring her closer and closer to the edge as she soaks my beard.

"That's right. Use me. Imagine all those guys are watching, and you're showing them how much you like being fucked like this," I murmur as I look up to watch her face and catch my breath. I tease her again with my tongue, and she writhes against it.

"Fuck," she curses and readjusts her grip on my hair. "I'm gonna come. I'm so close already."

Her nails prick at my scalp, and I know it's my cue to stop. I tear away from her, her grip so tight she nearly takes a chunk of my hair with it, and I take my knight with me as I sit back on the stool, letting her leg drop to the bar again.

"What the fuck?" Her eyes pop open, and she stares at me in confusion.

"You gotta earn the last bit, Hellfire." I smirk at her

"Grant, please." She gives me a desperate look—one I've been dying to see.

"Begging's a good start." I take the knight and swirl it in the glass of whisky, watching her wetness mix with the amber liquid before I toss it to the side. "But I want you to tell me who owns you."

"You do, Grant. Please. You know you do."

"Open your mouth," I say before I knock back half the drink, keeping it in my mouth as I step up on the ledge, and I grab her jaw. She complies, and I hold her in place while I spit it in her mouth. Her eyes go wide, and then she swallows, her throat bobbing with the motion. Then I wrap my hand around it so I can feel it slide down her throat. "Can't wait until I can feel my cock here, watch you take all of me. You'd like that, wouldn't you?"

She nods, and I watch her lids fall. "Yes, I think about it when I fuck myself."

She's lost in it now, just the way I want her.

"Spread your legs wide for me like a good girl, and lick that drop off your lips before it falls to the floor. You're too good to waste like that." She does as I ask, scooting to the edge, her tongue darting out to save the amber drop before it slips off.

I reach down and tease her clit with the pads of my fingers. Giving her the softest brush of friction, she moans and gasps, rocking her hips and cursing.

"Please, Daddy. Put me out of my misery," she begs again, and I hold up the glass to show her the last of our drink and then throw it back. She opens for me, and I spit it into her mouth, letting her swallow it down and smirking before I give her what she needs.

I slap her clit hard and fast, and she cries out. Her pussy quivers with the impact. I watch it pink up for me before I slap it a second time for good measure.

"Holy shit," she curses through her teeth. "Fuck. Oh my god."

I lean over and wrap my lips around her clit to suck the last bit of her wetness into my mouth before I slip my tongue down to tease her entrance. It gives her one final flood of sensation as she rides out her orgasm, rocking her hips against my face like she can hardly stand to let go of me before I pull away.

"What the fuck was that?" Her breathing's still heavy, and her lids are half-shuttered as she looks me over when I sit back on the stool in front of her.

"You all right there, Cowgirl?" I smirk at her. I take inventory of the damage I've done to her and her pretty pink pussy. She doesn't even try to cover herself, just watches me watching her. She likes me looking, even in the aftermath. We were fucking made for each other.

"No, that was..." She shakes her head and licks her lips. "You really are the fucking devil, you know."

"I know." I lean over the bar and pour myself a shot, downing it to help clear my mind. Because I still desperately want to fuck her, and my cock is straining against my zipper as I try to take steady breaths and count to ten. I offer her one but she shakes her head.

"Let me return the favor... please." Her eyes fall to the front of my pants. It's not like I can lie and say I'm good.

"It's okay."

"You just said you wanted to fuck my mouth." She gives me a skeptical look.

"I do. But I like the torture, Hellfire. It feels like I'm paying for my sins before I indulge in them."

"You need to put us both out of our misery soon, or I'll be

doing the kidnapping." She grins, a small laugh tumbling out of her.

"You gonna tie me up, Hellfire?" I bend over and kiss her knee, meeting her eyes as I do it.

"If you make me."

I kiss her other knee as her fingers slip through my hair, gently brushing it back where it's fallen over my forehead.

"Come on. Let's go find a room and get you cleaned up. Then I'll take you down for some dinner." I hold out my hand, and she slips hers into it as she hops down from the bar.

TWENTY-FIVE

D AKOTA

IT'S a busy Friday night at the bar, and as happy as I am about it, the crush of college students pouring in to get Sinner's Showers is starting to make the locals get antsy. I watch as some of my regulars scoot farther into the corner of the bar, scowling as another group of girls stumbles to one side of the dance floor.

I make a slicing motion across my throat at Hayley and Gemma from across the bar, nodding to the group of girls. We've got to start cutting people off sooner if they're going to cause problems for my usual crowd. I want more business, but not at the expense of what's always made this place a great little dive bar.

I look up, and another guy is hoisting his girlfriend in the air next to my red neon sign, the one that reads Bad Decisions/Good Nights on the wall, so they can take photos. I raise a brow at that still life before I'm taking another fifty dollars to prep a Sinner's Shower.

"Waiver. Read it. Sign it." I pass it across the table and check his eyes to make sure he's sober enough to understand what he's signing.

"Got it." He nods.

He takes his time reading it and then signs it, snapping a photo with his phone when he thinks I'm not looking. I don't like the looks of that. But maybe he's just a record keeper. Someone who wants to make sure he has a copy of everything digitally somewhere. But in my experience, those types are usually litigious.

When I walk back over with the shot and the water, I line them up beside the paper he signed.

"ID?" I ask because two can play this game.

He frowns at me and hooks his thumb over his shoulder. "They ID'd me at the door."

"I need to see if the signatures match," I shout over the music and tap on the paper. I don't usually check. I assume people are being forthcoming, and technically, people can sign a giant X instead of their name if they want to. But I just want extra information on this guy in case he turns out to be as slimy as I think he is.

He gives me an irritated look but reaches for his back pocket anyway. Instead of a wallet, he pulls out a police badge. I raise a brow at him.

"That's not an ID," I state the obvious.

"Your patrons can't sign a waiver allowing you to hit them when they're inebriated."

"You're not inebriated."

"You assume, but you have no way of knowing for sure without testing."

"Does anyone have that ability when they sign a document?

Do you think all those doctor's offices and government agencies do a sobriety check before people agree to sign on the line?" I argue.

"You serve alcohol. The burden is higher for you."

"So what are you suggesting I do?" I don't think this guy has answers. I think he just has a lot of bullshit complaints.

"That you stop serving these shots."

"I'll send that suggestion on to my lawyer." I flash him a bright smile, one he doesn't like, judging by the way his brows drop like a hammer.

"Ma'am, you could be credibly accused of assault."

"Based on what? I haven't heard a single person in here complain." I feel my temper rising. "Should we ask them?"

"You'll cease selling the shots immediately, or I'll be forced to arrest you."

"Again, based on what? I haven't heard a single person in here object." I jump up on the table of the bar and look around. "Anyone in here want to complain about their Sinner's Shower? Worried that I gave them a love pat that was a little too much for their liking?" I yell out, and patrons start to turn around.

"Ma'am, get down off the bar," the plainclothes cop yells to me from my knee level.

Hoots and hollers start to echo across the bar.

"It's my bar. I've given myself permission to do so, and don't worry, I've concluded I'm sufficiently sober."

"You're breaking health codes by standing on the bar."

"I'll wipe it down."

"All right, ma'am." He grabs my leg and jerks, nearly toppling me, and the crowd starts to surge toward us.

"Let her fucking go!" One guy shouts.

"Hey, man! Not cool." Another admonishes.

"You heard her! It's her bar!" They all start bellowing at him, but it doesn't stop him from pulling on my leg.

"You're under arrest, and if you don't come down, I'll add resisting arrest to your list of charges."

"Let go of me!" I swat at his hand. "You're hurting me! I'll get down on my own."

"Get off of her, you fucking asshole!" Hayley shoots down to my end of the bar and starts pointing at the cop.

Suddenly, the room is filled with them. Three more cops emerge out of nowhere and start threatening the crowd that's getting rowdy on my behalf.

"Get down here, or you're going to get more people arrested. I don't think that's what you want."

"Everybody get the fuck out! Drinks down! Let's go!" one of the other cops yells.

I start to slowly climb down from the top of the bar, but he grabs my ankle and yanks, which has me tumbling off the edge to the floor. The corner of the bar and the stool hit my leg, scraping me down my thigh, and my knees hit the hard wood of the floor.

"Holy shit!" I curse at the pain, rubbing each knee as I try to stand.

"Hey! Don't treat her like that!" Gemma calls from behind the bar and gives me a sympathetic look.

"This is insane. You're hurting her. I'm calling 911!" Hayley joins in the reprimand.

"I am 911," The officer laughs at her.

"Don't be a fucking pig! She didn't do anything!" one of the guys the cop is ushering out yells just as he takes an open-palm shove to the chest and starts to trip backward.

I don't have time to see if he falls because my own personal problem yanks me to my feet by jerking my upper arm and shoulder with zero care for the fact that I've just fallen. He won't stop shoving me around either, and he pushes me into the bar as he twists my arms behind me. My yelps of pain don't even slow him down.

The way the cops quickly usher everyone out has me suspicious. Like they were all just sitting around lying in wait to close me down. If it wasn't the cops or recent history, I'd assume it was Grant trying to teach me a lesson. But he'd never involve the police, and he sure as hell wouldn't let a strange man handle me like this.

So now I'm stuck wondering who would be harassing me like this. Morton's and Cowboy's, two other bars down the street, were jealous of the crowds I pulled some nights, but certainly not enough to go after me like this. I don't have a lot of enemies. At least ones who would go to these lengths. At most, they'd sign me up for some catalogs and newsletters I didn't want.

"Does it need to be so tight?" I grouch when my wrists feel like they've been crunched between the cuffs.

"Shut up, and let's get out to the car so I can read you your rights." He tugs on my arm and drags me toward him, shuffling us both across to the door.

I look back at Hayley, who has a helpless look on her face.

"What can I do?" she calls after me.

"Call Grant. Or Hazel if he doesn't answer. Whoever you can get a hold of," I call back to her.

As he walks me to the car and I watch the crowd flood out onto the streets, dispersing to other bars and back to their cars, I curse my luck. It would be the first night I start doing well again that creates a problem like this for me.

TWO HOURS LATER, once I've been read my rights, driven across town, and booked into the local jail, I see a familiar face. Grant.

He's furious. It's written all over his face, and I'm not sure if I even want to get up and walk over to him. I'm not ready for a lecture about how I never should have done those shots, how he warned me, how he told me exactly what he knew the cops would tell me if I kept it up, or how I've made my bed and now I've got to lie in it. Mostly because I've already spent the last one hundred and twenty minutes doing just that, then trying not to cry over it, then lamenting that I'm dressed in shorts and a lace corset when the entire room is a freezing cold concrete box, and then restarting the cycle of self-loathing. I'm going to need to talk to my doctor about upping my antidepressant and anxiety meds whenever I manage to get out of here. Maybe find a new therapist. Because clearly, I'm fucking up left and right.

Tears start to form in my eyes when they buzz the door open for me, but Grant doesn't say a word. He just stoically escorts me through the corridors and out the double doors to the parking lot where my truck is waiting. That's when they nearly fall. I'm grateful to see Jesse's old pickup. I just wish he was here.

If it wasn't the middle of the night, I'd take it tearing down a backroad with the music turned up to a hundred while I screamed the words at the top of my lungs. I could use the escape. But I'm pretty sure that would just lead me right back here, and I'm in enough trouble already.

Grant opens the door when we get there and holds his hand out to help me climb into the passenger seat. The silence is killing me by the time he rounds the front of the car and gets in.

"Aren't you going to say anything? Say I told you so?" I ask as I run my fingers along the edge of the worn door panel.

"The only thing I'm planning to do is put my lawyers on every single one of those fucking cops for the way they handled you. The way that fucker grabbed you off the bar; he'll be lucky if I don't fucking tear his throat out tonight myself." His tone is low and lethal as he pulls out of the parking lot.

"Wait. Who told you what he did? Hayley?" I sniffle, trying not to let any tears fall. "I'm sorry she called you. I didn't know who else to call besides you or Hazel."

"She didn't call me. My brother did."

"Ramsey?"

"Levi."

"Levi?" I feel like we're beating around a bush here.

"Levi saw what happened and called me. I came as soon as I could, but they insisted on drawing every last damn step of your release out like it was a fucking ceremony."

"How? He wasn't at the bar. Are there videos? Did someone post them?" I'm so confused, and now I'm worried the bar will be at the center of a notorious social media scandal.

"I have cameras in the bar." He says it nonchalantly, but it hits me like a ton of bricks.

"You have cameras in the bar?" I swivel myself to face him, and my jaw drops. I knew he took his role a little too seriously, but literally keeping an eye on me remotely was a bridge too far. Even as upset as I am about everything else, maybe worse for it.

"Yes, I have cameras in the bar." He glances over at me like he's clocking my reaction. "Don't look at me like that. You wouldn't get security, so I had to make sure someone was covering things."

"Who is someone?"

"They're wired to the main security room at the Avarice. My staff watches them."

"Your staff watches me every day?"

"Every night, technically."

"Oh my god! It is not the time for exacting language." I huff in irritation.

"Before you get too far into your self-righteous indignation there, think for a moment about the fact that that footage is probably exactly what's going to save you in this scenario. They can toss the body cam footage, take him at his word. But they can't get rid of the recording we have."

The man has a point. Not to mention I might still be sitting in the jail cell right now if it wasn't for the footage. But I still wish he'd been transparent about it.

"You still could have told me."

"So you could tamper with them or take them down? No, thank you."

"I can run my business how I see fit."

"When it's well and truly yours, and I don't own the building, then yes, you can. I'll gladly step out of the way."

"Fat chance of that happening when I can barely stay in the black and these fucking cops are running out my clientele on one of the busiest nights of the year so far. I'm going to have a reputation for bullshit cop raids, and everyone will go to Cowboy's or the Avarice instead." I stare out the window, watching the world roll past as he starts down the main road.

"I'll take care of the cops."

"They want me to drop the Sinner's Showers. He basically said all the things you did. So, you can tell me you told me so. I'd like to get that part out of the way."

"Seems like you've got those bases covered on your own. We'll run everything by my lawyers and see what they say. And before you argue, I know you had a lawyer look at it, but mine are a different brand of lawyer, and they can help refine it until it's impenetrable. They can also help us figure out how to tell these cops to go fuck themselves for the harassment."

"You're not mad at me?"

"Why would I be mad at you? That was no reason to arrest you. The whole thing—that many cops. Feels like a stunt. You have anyone pissed at you?"

"Not besides you, no."

He half grunts and half laughs at that. Tilting his head as he takes the corner.

"Well, I didn't raid your bar."

"I know."

"But it might be about me." The words are as much a realization for him as they are a statement to me. "Fuck."

"What?"

"Nothing. Just some things are going on behind the scenes with the business. I'll need to talk to some people."

"If it involves me, shouldn't I know about it?"

"If it does, yes. I'll have to see what I can find out."

"Where are we headed anyways?" My brows knit together as he takes another turn that doesn't seem like we're headed back to my apartment.

"Does Vendetta have enough food and water for the night?"

"Yes..." I trail off. I gave her extra before I started my shift since I figured it would be a later night than usual.

"Good. We're heading to my place then."

My heart and brain go to war with each other over that information. My heart is doing tumbles over itself with excitement that I finally get to see where this man lives. That he trusts me enough to let me in. But my brain is reminding me that I'm on the verge of a crash out, and I don't want to have it in front of him. We're still in the whole need-to-be-sexy phase of this. Well, it's not even a relationship. It's an agreement that's on shaky ground since I didn't even deliver on my side of the bargain today. But no matter the circumstances on that front, I definitely can't be falling apart in front of this man.

"I don't know if that's a good idea. I'm tired, and I'll probably fall asleep the second I walk inside the door."

He flashes me a sideways glance. "I'm not expecting anything if that's what you're worried about. You can go straight to bed if you want, and I have an extra bedroom if that would make you more comfortable."

Maybe I could make that work. Hide from him long enough that he can't see... but I doubt that. He'll have eyes on me like a hawk. There's probably a camera in every room of his apartment so he can make sure nothing he doesn't know about is happening under his watch.

I think I need the crash out—the long self-pitying cry that I'll now have an arrest on my record and possibly charges I'll need to fight. My eyes start to well up again at the prospect of jail time or a large fine that will bankrupt me. As if I'm not nearly there already.

"No. I know you can be a gentleman. It's just that..." My voice wavers, and I have to pause to continue. His eyes flash over to me again, and I can feel them like a heavy weight as he watches my reaction. He can hear it in my voice and see it in the way I rock back into the seat. "Honestly, I've been on the verge of tears for hours. I just didn't want any of those assholes to see me cry. But I was planning to curl up at the bottom of my shower when I got home and cry until I was tired enough to sleep. I need to let it out, or I'm going to combust. I'm sure that sounds pathetic—"

"It doesn't sound pathetic. If it makes you feel better, you can cry anywhere you want for as long as you want at my place. I just want to know you're somewhere safe tonight. Make sure that they can't give you a hard time again in the morning. Know you have someone to protect you. Give me that?" He glances over at me.

"You think they'll come back?" Panic rises in my throat.

One night I could handle, if this was going to be a multi-day event, well, I don't know if I can hold tight that long.

"I don't know. But I don't want to risk it. Give me a chance to look into some things first, and then we'll get you home, okay?"

"I'm sorry for dragging you out here in the middle of the night." The tears start to roll down my cheeks, half relief and half exhaustion.

"You know as well as I do that we're both up at these hours. It's fine. More than fine. I'm just happy I could be there to get you." He reaches over and gently places his hand on my thigh.

"Thank you." I run my palm over the backs of his knuckles.

He pulls my hand up to his mouth and kisses it softly, keeping his eyes on the road, and then lets it fall to the center console, still squeezing tight. He drives the rest of the way like that, in the quiet of the night. Letting me have my peace while still making sure I know he's there. Things like this are what are going to break me. The man might not be the best with words or with saying all the things I'd like to hear. But he does all the right things to show that he cares and always shows up when I need him the most.

TWENTY-SIX

G RANT

WHEN I GET Dakota back to my place, through the back
entrance and up the private elevator to the floor where the
residences are, she seems hesitant to even enter. She hovers at
the entrance, pulling her boots off slowly as she strikes a
quick glance around the place when she thinks I'm not
watching. My place looks fancier than it is. All dark walls
and flooring, drenched with muted golden light and dimmed
at this hour because I can't stand a flood of neon white light
when I've been in the bar or on the casino floor most of
the day.

The blackout drapes are drawn, or she'd see the massive
floor-to-ceiling view of the mountains and the surrounding
woods. This place is one of my favorite things in the world. My
own little fortress in the treetops, safe in the quiet and solitude.

A place where I can escape and almost feel human again for a few hours.

I rarely let anyone up here, and almost never anyone who isn't family. The Kellys are the only exception to that rule. But she's as close as it gets to family, even if it's not true blood that links us. Not to mention, this is the only place I trust that I can keep her safe besides the ranch, and it's too late to drive over there and wake them at this hour to get to one of the cabins. That could wait for the morning, if we need it.

"If you give me your clothes, I can put them in the wash and give you a T-shirt and some sweats to put on for the night."

"You have a washer in here?" She looks skeptical.

"Technically, yes. But I was just going to have house-keeping come get them to wash and deliver back in a couple hours."

"That would be nice. I feel disgusting from... everything." She sighs.

Her shoulders slump, and I can tell she's emotionally exhausted as well as physically. The cops who did this to her are going to pay. What I saw on the camera footage had my blood boiling, and I'm already plotting how I'm going to make their lives miserable. But I'm doing my best to keep the desire to slit throats and smash bones to myself right now and focusing on making sure she feels better in this moment.

"Let's get you cleaned up. I can get you some towels."

I motion for her to follow me, and we make our way to the guest bathroom. I flip on only the necessary lights, as I'm not trying to blind either of us in the middle of the night, before I grab some towels out of the linen closet and put them out for her.

"All right. Here." I turn on the hot water in the shower. "That should get the hot water coming pretty quickly. Benefits of living in a hotel. I'll go get you some clothes to change into."

"Thank you." She's already stripping out of the shorts she has on, and it draws my attention to her leg where I can see the giant scrape and the bruises already forming on her knees. I kneel down for a better look, gently running my palms over her skin.

"He shouldn't have done that to you."

"It's fine. I was mouthing off." She shakes her head.

"Don't blame yourself. You were asking questions. That doesn't give him any fucking right to manhandle you. A guy does that to a woman in any other situation, his ass would be in jail or worse." I run my thumb lightly over the blooming bruise on her right knee and look up at her. "I'm sorry I wasn't there."

"You're a little bit busy with other things. I don't expect you to be my personal bodyguard, Grant."

"No, but I can get you one. We're putting security in your bar. Starting tomorrow. I'll give you a couple of guys. They won't let them treat you like that."

"Your security is going to override the cops?" She gives me a skeptical look.

"They'll make them think twice before they knock women around and give me names if they do." I kiss the tops of her knees before I stand again.

"I don't like the look in your eyes. Don't do anything about this on my behalf. I'll get my lawyer to deal with it."

"My lawyers are already on it. They knew it was my family when they touched you, and they knew it was my property when they went in there. They knew exactly what they were doing, and I'm not going to stand by and let them think they can do it again."

"Grant." She reaches out and puts her hand on my shoulder. "Please. It's not worth going to war with the cops over. You told me it was a stupid idea to be doing those shots, and I didn't listen. I wanted the money and the exposure the bar got with it.

I should have listened. These are the consequences. I'm sure I'll get a slap on the wrist and have to pull them from the menu. I'll make a formal complaint about the cop."

"You make a formal complaint about that cop, and he'll just find you after hours and make you pay for it. He already has a reputation for coloring outside the lines of his job. The fact that they sent him was a message."

"A message about what?" She looks confused.

"I don't know yet. I only have suspicions. But I'm going to find out tomorrow." I grit my teeth at the thought of having to go and find my uncle. Apparently, he isn't going to be ignored.

"Just be careful. I don't want you getting into something because of me. I'm fine." Her fingers slip down my forearm, and my eyes are drawn to the red marks on her wrists where the cuffs pinched her skin.

"I'll be as careful as the situation dictates." It's the best I can promise. "Now, get in the shower so we can get you to bed. Just set the clothes on the counter here, and I'll swap them out for clean ones."

"Yes, sir." She gives me a soft smile, and her eyes drift over my face for a minute before she speaks again. "Thank you for this and for getting me tonight."

"Of course. That's what I'm here for." I pull myself away because if I stay a minute longer, I worry I'll do and say things I'll regret.

TWENTY-SEVEN

G RANT

JACK AND SAM, two of my security team who work for the Horsemen, follow me up the narrow walkway to the back of Officer Spencer's house. Levi already did the research and asked around, confirming that he works the night shift and that the white Camaro we passed in the drive is his. He's also divorced, and she has custody of the kids, so we don't have to worry about any other family disturbing our meeting this morning.

We walk up the aging steps of his back deck, and I nod for Sam to make his way around to the master bedroom window. It's half-open, letting in the cool morning air, and I want him ready in case we have to choose an alternate entry point. Then I rap my knuckles on the back door.

Sam confirms the sound of movement in the master

bedroom with a nod, and Jack presses his body up against the side of the house so he's out of view as I hear footsteps through the house. A disheveled mop of hair presses against the glass of one of the windows, peering out at me, and then I hear the sound of his footfalls approaching the door. It opens a moment later, and he answers with a sneer.

"What the fuck do you want? Do you know what time it is?" he bitches immediately, and we're already off to a bad start.

"Not a very polite way to answer the door to company." I make a disapproving sound at the back of my throat.

"I got better ones." He pulls his hand from behind the door frame and waves a gun back and forth before he narrows in on me, his eyes squinting in the sunlight.

Jack doesn't hesitate, reaching around to grab his wrist and bend it over the frame. It forces him to drop the gun, and it clatters to the ground. He goes to reach for Jack with his free hand, and I catch it, making him stumble out the door and onto the deck with both of us. He grunts and struggles, his bare feet searching for purchase before Jack kicks his legs out from under him. He stumbles face-first onto the deck, smashing into it with his nose as we yank his arms back behind him.

"Fuck you!! Who the fuck do you think you are?" he curses as blood smears on the deck from his face, and he fights the pressure we exert on his shoulder blades. It's a useless attempt to buy time as Jack's knee goes into his spine and mine goes to the back of his neck.

Sam arrives just in time to put the cuffs on his wrists, which are crossed behind his back, and pin his ankles with a booted foot.

"Trying to shoot us when we merely knock on the door sounds a lot like unlawful use of force, Michael. The kind of thing that I might answer with force to protect my life." I grind the heel of my boot into the back of his neck. "Especially when you come on my property and rough up women. Are you that pathetic, you little prick? You have to toss women around and beat them up to feel like a man?"

"I don't know what the fuck you're talking about." He grits out the words, clearly feeling the pain that we're doling out.

"You can't remember last night? Harassing some poor woman at a bar?"

"That slut who's spitting whiskey for attention? She deserved what she had coming. Dumb fucking cunt wouldn't listen."

"Nah, Michael. I think you're confused. You're the dumb cunt not listening."

Jack and Sam roll him over for me, and I kick him hard in the balls, making him curl up into the fetal position as his face turns bright red, and he rocks back and forth. It takes him a minute to respond, cursing under his breath and telling me to go fuck myself before he can form real words again. But he hasn't learned his lesson. He starts over again.

"You fucking asshole. All this for that bitch? You know she's probably been run through by half the men in that bar."

"Wrong fucking answer." I shake my head. "I don't think you're learning your lesson here, Michael. We need less talking and more listening. But maybe I can help you with that."

I strike him hard in his windpipe. He wheezes and gasps for air. Trying and failing to grasp his throat with his hands as he tries to wiggle them out of the cuffs behind his back.

"Oh damn. I'm fucking sorry. Did that make it hard to breathe?" I taunt him.

"Fuck you." He sputters, rolling over to his side, but he quits mouthing off, blood still trickling down his face from his nose.

"I want to be very clear that you don't touch women like that ever, but you especially don't touch women in my town that way. My family, my property, my friends, my fucking barista—I don't fucking care. I see it, and I will bring it back to you ten fucking fold. Do you hear me?" I crouch down to his level, making sure he can hear every word.

"Fuck you." It's a raspy whisper now, and he spits out a mouthful of blood. Apparently, his vocabulary is limited.

I hold out my hand for the expandable baton Sam's pulled out of its case. He hands it to me, and it makes a beautiful sound as I shake it to its full length. Spencer's eyes go to the weapon. One I'm positive he and his ilk are familiar with.

"But since it seems like a calm exchange of ideas isn't your strong suit, I figure I better give you a more permanent lesson in what I mean. A little more violent since that's your communication style." I grin at him before I stand and draw the weapon back. "You bruise her knees, I fucking break yours." I crack it down hard—once on his left and again on his right. The bone-crushing sound it makes is one of the more satisfying ones I've heard in my life. He screams bloody murder, and Jack shoves a towel into his mouth to silence him. This house is off a country road, and I don't see any close neighbors, but one can never be too cautious.

"And if you scrape her leg dragging her off a counter? Well..." I pull the switchblade out of my suit pocket and knock the blade loose from her sheath. "Then I'm going to carve that same line into your flesh as a reminder to be more careful the next time." I stab him just above his knee and drag the blade up his thigh, careful not to cut too deep. He screams then, muffled by the rag Jack presses tight. Tears stream from the corners of his eyes, and his whole chest is racked with sobs from the pain I've exacted.

I watch him writhe in agony for a moment, committing the scene to memory. It's only a hint of the satisfaction I want for what he did to her, for any confidence he might have stolen or any humiliation he might have inflicted, but it'll have to do since I can't kill him.

"Now, I'm going to go talk to your boss and let him know you're gonna need some time off from work to heal because we all got a little jumpy when you pulled a gun on us. I'll let the two of you work out whether that's a paid leave or not, so long as I never see you step foot on my property again." I wipe my blade off on his clothes and tuck it back into my pocket. "And before you think of doing anything rash, remember I don't give a fuck about that badge and there are much *much* worse things than death."

MY UNCLE'S office tries to play coy about where he is until I repeat my last name like it's a demand, and they finally locate him for me. He leaves me waiting for a good twenty minutes before he lets me in, which is his boy's loss considering he's the one bleeding and broken on the deck.

"Good morning, Grant. It's been a while." He points to the seats across from his desk where we can sit down without five hundred pounds of wood between us. I don't know that it would be my choice if I were him, but if he wants to act like we're family again—I can play that game.

"Morning, Uncle. It has been a bit since we've gotten to chat like this. I appreciate you making time in your schedule."

"Of course. Anything for one of Jacob's sons." He smiles wide like he truly cares. I wonder if he ever did. All those holidays when we were kids. All those late nights playing cards and drinking beer with my father. Camping trips. I can't imagine up and disappearing on Ramsey or Levi's kids if they ever needed me, and the same goes for my niece, Fallon. I'd do anything I could to help. "To what do I owe the pleasure today?"

"Well, a bit of unpleasant business first. One of your boys got a little wild at my bar in Purgatory Falls."

"The Avarice?"

"Seven Sins."

"I thought that was owned by the Hartfields?"

"The business, yes. The building is mine."

"Ah, I see."

"And you know how we are in this family. Very sensitive about the way people treat things that belong to us."

"I'm aware of that sentiment."

"So you'll understand my disappointment. Did you send them?"

"Send cops to the bar?" His brows knit together in confusion, and it's unfortunate I don't know him well enough anymore to determine whether or not it's fake. "I can't say that I did. They might have been in the area. I've asked them to crack down on some of the rowdiness after hours. We keep getting a lot of reports about out-of-towners making a mess of the place and running the locals out of the places they love. Doesn't seem like a good model for the future."

"Ah well. They took that mandate a little too far. One of your guys roughed up one of the women, the owner actually, and I don't care for men who put their hands on women. Badge or no badge."

"I don't blame you there. I'd do the same." It's a warning as much as it is an agreement.

"I'm glad we see eye to eye because on the way over, I made a little pit stop to chat with one of your officers. Unfortunately, when I knocked on the door, he pulled a gun on me, and well... you know Colorado law better than anyone." I lean back in the chair and give him a pointed look.

"He still breathing?"

"He was when I left him, but I imagine he'll need a little help and a couple of weeks' leave to really process our discussion."

"I see."

"Truly hoping he takes it to heart. I'd hate to fucking hear he put his hands on another woman. Particularly someone I hold in such high esteem." I stare at my uncle and wait for his reaction. I'm a betting man, but there's always a risk when you run with a hand like this one.

"I'll make sure he gets it. Did you say the officer's name?"

"Spencer, I believe it was."

He pulls out his phone and fires off a text before he returns his attention to our conversation.

"We'll get him some help, and I'll see to it that he's not in a position to bother any women any time soon."

"Glad to hear it."

"Was there anything else you needed?" He lifts a gray brow in expectation.

"I wanted to make sure you knew you were invited to the wedding. It's coming up pretty fast, but we didn't know you'd be in town until recently. We'd love to have you there. Figure we could get caught up. You could bring a date."

"I'd love to come. I've missed out on so much over the last few years. It would be great to catch up and be there for Ramsey. I know he must miss my brother. The two of them were so close." He fakes another smile.

It's an underhanded jab on his part to work that last bit in. It was never lost on anyone that Ramsey was the baby and the favorite, but I also never let that change the way I felt about my father. Ramsey was easy to love, and I wasn't. He was going to go off and play football, and I was going to stay and protect this family. My father needed me to be a legacy, not lovable.

"He does. Quite a bit. I know he'd be happy to see you. Levi and Aspen too."

"Ah, the whole family is coming then?" He seems a little surprised at that information.

"Yes. Your great niece as well. She's nearly in college. It's hard to believe."

"Well, I'm looking forward to it then. I'll give you my number, and you can send me the details." He pulls a card out from his pocket.

"Hopefully, you'll have the time off with the new position and all."

"I'll make time for family." His smile widens.

"Well then, I'll let you go in the meantime. Let you get back to your work, and I can get back to mine. Less interference for us both in the future."

"Let's hope." He walks me to the door, and we exchange one last set of goodbyes before I head back off to check in on Dakota.

TWENTY-EIGHT

D AKOTA

"CAN you do my eyeshadow for me? The smokey look you always do?" Hazel rolls her bottom lip and gives me doe eyes. We're all in her suite at the Avarice, getting ready to go down for dinner. I've planned the whole night. Dinner in the restaurant, drinks in the bar, some lap dancing lessons, and then some gambling to round out the evening. Grant was kind enough to give me a limitless tab to treat all the girls tonight as long as I promise not to raise too much hell.

"Of course," I easily agree, and Hazel slides her eyeshadow palette and a case of brushes in my direction. Bristol and I have always been her go-to makeover team. In fact, she pretty much insisted that Bristol does her makeup tomorrow for the wedding, and we spent hours going over looks the last few weeks.

"Have you decided when you're going on vacation yet?" Hazel glances over at Bristol before she lowers her lashes so I can apply the first sweep of shadow over her lids. Bristol and Anson took first place in the games at Hazel's pre-wedding party and won the trip we'd all been chasing. But it means that she and her former brother-in-law are set to go to a romantic couples-only resort on an island.

"No. Not yet. Anson told me I could go alone if I want, but I feel guilty. He did so much to help us win." She sighs as she applies a coat of mascara in the mirror. "Plus, it's a couples resort. Will they even let me in without someone else?"

"I don't think so," Hazel mumbles, trying not to move, as I continue my work.

"Right, so see? I feel like he should go, but he's been so cagey when I've tried to nail him down on a date." She slips the wand back into the tube and turns her head from side to side, surveying her work.

"You know how he is," Hazel adds. "If it's not work or family, he doesn't leave the house. Do you want me to talk to him?"

I sweep the brush back over the shadow palette, but I look over at Bristol to see her deep in thought for a moment before she shakes her head.

"No. I don't want him to feel pressured. Plus, I have no idea who will watch Ford while we're gone. He'd drive Mama crazy if she didn't have help, and I can't do that to her. Not for a whole week," Bristol laments.

Ford is Anson and Bristol's sister's son. When her sister died, Anson became a shell of his former self, and Bristol stepped in to support him. She's helped raise Ford since he was little, but that, combined with taking care of her own business and her mother, has left her with very little time for fun. They both need a vacation.

"Depending on the timing, we could take him for a few days," Hazel volunteers. "He could come stay on the ranch. Spend some time fishing and hiking. Ramsey and Bo would probably take him camping if he wants."

"I could take him for a few days too!" Marlowe chimes in. "Does he have any interest in learning to make French pastries?"

"I mean, the way that boy is eating, he needs to learn to cook for himself, period. I'm not ready for a full-fledged teenage boy. He's going to be so much damn trouble, and I don't think Anson knows what's about to hit him," Bristol says as I finish up the smokey shadow on Hazel's left eye. We all burst into laughter because while Anson is private and reserved, his son is anything but. That combined with his dad's looks means Anson can pretty much kiss his peace and quiet goodbye until Ford heads to college.

"All right. Look in the mirror and see if you like that before I add the eyeliner for you. You should do the mascara yourself." I give Hazel a hand mirror.

"Or I've got lashes and glue if you want." Marlowe waves a pack of them in the air.

"Lashes, please," Hazel answers as she blinks and lowers her eyes to look at my work. "I wish I had half your talent." She grins up at me.

"Glad you like it." I return the smile and pull the eyeliner out. I draw a thick line along her upper lashes while she waits patiently. "By the way, I put hangover kits in everyone's room. Water. Headache medicine. Drinks with electrolytes. Make sure you use them before bed!"

"Yes, Mom," Marlowe teases me.

"I had one sent to Ramsey's room for you, too, just in case," I muse as I finish Hazel's other eye.

"I won't be in Ramsey's room. He can survive one more

night." Hazel's determined to make him sleep alone the night before the wedding.

"You're torturing that poor man." Marlowe shakes her head but then grins. "I love it."

"He's going to tear that gorgeous dress to shreds," I warn her.

"I know. That's why I'm switching to the shorter one at the reception." Hazel taps her temple as I step away.

"Smart." Bristol nods at our friend's forethought. "I love that dress too much to see it in pieces. It needs to be framed."

"I love yours." Hazel touches the edge of Bristol's hemline. "All of yours really. We need to get pictures tonight!"

"We also need to get pregaming." Marlowe pulls out a flask. "We have questionable decisions to make, ladies."

"Big plans?" I raise a brow at her.

"I need to break this little dry spell I've been on." Marlowe downs a shot's worth of alcohol and passes it on while she grimaces from the burn.

"I'm supportive of this." Hazel takes one, hands the flask to me, and then turns to Marlowe for help with her lashes.

"I think we could all use the end of a dry spell tonight." I down a shot and hand the rest to Bristol.

"You didn't take that insanely hot man to bed?" Bristol raises a brow at me over Hayden.

"He's too much trouble for me." I hedge my bets. Hazel has backed off the idea since the wedding game night, but we haven't exactly discussed me crushing her hopes and dreams yet.

"Isn't that the point?" she asks.

"She likes more trouble than that," Marlowe mumbles as she works on Hazel's lashes, glancing at me with a mischievous look dancing behind her eyes.

"Wait... what does she know that we don't?" Bristol's still grimacing as she slides the flask back to Hazel.

"There's nothing to know." I shake my head, lying through my teeth. I plan to tell my girls everything after this weekend because I'm in way too deep with the devil, and I need perspective. He can stay anonymous, but I'm desperate for advice.

I want this evening and tomorrow to be about Hazel. After that, it'll be time to figure out what the hell the two of us are doing and if there's a future beyond sexting. Tonight, though, I at least plan to finally get the man in bed.

TWENTY-NINE

G RANT

WHEN RAMSEY, Levi, and I walk into the private room we reserved for the bachelorette party, they're in the middle of enjoying a demonstration from a stripper. But not some guy in a police outfit or a cowboy hat and assless chaps, no. These women decided they'd rather learn to give lap dances themselves and so all five of them, my sister included—God fucking help me—are bent over in front of chairs wiggling their asses at their imaginary clients.

"Bend like this and give him or her a nice preview." The tiny woman, whose thick blonde hair overwhelms her stature, explains as she slowly rises back into a standing position. "Then stand and turn around. You have two choices, depending on the seating height and how comfortable you are. You can stand like this, one leg on either side of their thighs, or you can climb into their lap. If you've got a chair like this, I highly recommend reaching over their shoulder and using the back to help steady yourself and keep your balance. Use it like you would a headboard at home, okay?" She grins at them, and they all follow suit.

"Holy fuck." Ramsey's jaw drops next to me as he watches his once and future wife wiggle her ass and then start to dry hump the chair. "I'm not going to make it to the wedding night. This is unfair as fuck."

"I think I would have preferred male strippers," I mutter as I watch Dakota roll her lip between her teeth as she follows the motion with her hips.

"Fuck that. I don't want some guy's sweaty junk in her face," Ramsey grouches, tearing his eyes off Hazel and looking at me. "And I don't need you beating someone bloody because one of them flirted with Dakota."

"Well, now we have to watch our sister learn to strip." I wave my hand in her general direction while trying not to watch too closely.

"Let her have her fun. She needs her confidence back with everything going on." Levi adds his two cents.

"Well, maybe you can send Hayden her way instead of after Dakota if he's such a great guy." I shrug. Ramsey shoots me an unamused look before we're caught.

"Can we help you?" the blonde woman asks, her brow skeptical of our presence in her private session.

"It's the groom and his brothers," Bristol announces as she finishes her practice session.

"Oh, perfect! You can help them practice some of the moves we've been working on." The blonde woman claps her hands together.

"Happy to volunteer." Ramsey practically runs to be Hazel's practice session.

The blonde looks at Levi and me.

"I actually need to go make sure all the stuff is set up for the whisky tasting before the Briggs brothers get here," Levi announces.

"Fucking traitor," I mumble under my breath.

"Like you won't enjoy it." He smirks before he disappears back out the door.

"Sure. I can help." I make my way slowly into the room.

The lights are down low, and Dakota looks like a fucking smoke show in the dress she has on. She always looks sexy regardless of what she's wearing, but her bar outfits are as much functional as anything else. Mostly jeans and shorts. Besides the sundress the other day, I've rarely seen her in one, and I had been secretly looking forward to getting to see her in the brides-maid's dress tomorrow.

"Come here, Casino Cowboy." Dakota pats the chair she was practicing with and grins at me. I don't miss the way Marlowe and Bristol both snap to attention when I make my way over to her. Their eyes follow me with skepticism and suspicion, but they don't say anything when I sit down. The silent threat that I better be supportive without getting handsy still lies heavy.

"All right. Guess that leaves us three. We can practice together," Marlowe announces, clapping her hands together.

"I can be practice too," The blonde woman walks over and sits in the chair in front of Aspen before she pulls her phone out, and music starts to play over the speakers. "All right, ladies, let's go through the steps from the top."

I can still hear her voice over the music, but all my attention is on Dakota as she bends over in front of me. Her skirt is pulling up her thighs and teasing at the edges of her cheeks. She sways her hips back and forth before she straightens back up slowly.

"Not too much different from what I teach at the bar, I guess," she says softly as she turns around and places her hands on my shoulders per the instructor's orders.

"You start teaching country stripping instead of swing when I wasn't looking?" I raise a skeptical brow.

I get a swift pass of her blue-green eyes before she lifts them to the ceiling. She lowers herself into my lap, though, her hand going to the back of the chair like her instructor told her to as she starts to grind over me.

"Did you hire strippers for the bachelor party?" she asks absently.

"So Hazel could rip me in two because one of them touched Ramsey? No thanks."

"That's too bad for you. You look stressed. Like you could use some relaxation."

"I'm not worried. I have a woman who sends me photos every night before I go to sleep. Sometimes, if I'm lucky, she calls to tell me all the filthy things she wants to do to me. And if I earn it, she shows me what she wants me to do to her," I whisper, making sure that her friends can't hear me over the low thud of the music.

"I'm glad you found someone so supportive of your needs." A wry smile forms on her lips. "I need someone like that tonight."

"Yeah?" I ask. I don't have better words when she's grinding over my cock while I get harder by the second as everyone else we know, and don't want to find out about our little indiscretion, is sitting a few feet away from us. "You need something tonight, Hellfire?"

"It's been a stressful week with the wedding prep and the issues at the bar, and I still have all my maid of honor responsibilities tomorrow night. I just need someone to take the edge off. Blank my mind out, and let me switch off for a little bit. You know?"

"Is this someone Jim or Jack tonight? Maybe Johnny?" I smirk.

"Smartass." She grins at me before her eyes take on a devilish glint, dancing with mirth as she leans in, dragging the heat of her cunt straight over my cock. It soaks in as she whispers in my ear, "His name doesn't matter. I'll call him whatever he wants me to call him tonight. Let him have me whatever way he wants. As long as he finally stops teasing and takes."

"He sounds like a lucky man," I choke out.

The alarm bells are all going off. Telling me to get the fuck out of here. Telling me her entire hit squad is right here in the room with us, ready to bury me if I look at her wrong. But I can't be bothered to stop, and my hand ghosts up the side of her thigh as I shift my hips and let her have a better angle. Her tongue teases along the edge of my earlobe, and her nails slip into the hair at the nape of my neck as she grinds down on me.

"I'm going to be such a good girl for him. So fucking good he won't even believe it's me on my knees for him."

"Hellfire..." I say it like a warning for both of us.

"Yes?" She says it in the sweetest tone, her big blue-green doe eyes shifting to mine like she's just waiting to be told how to please me. And fuck me. I'm not built for this. I want her so badly, even when I know I shouldn't.

"You don't want that. Not really. You'll end up with rug burn over the bruises on your knees and a second set of marks on your neck when the first ones are just now fading enough that you can cover them with makeup. Can't have that before the wedding."

There's a little growl of irritation in her throat, and she nips at my neck before she whispers in my ear.

"I could find a Jim or a Jack or a Johnny, you know. Maybe

all three." It's an empty threat, but I can tell she's frustrated that I keep putting her off.

"You wouldn't dare."

I just need a little longer. If we can figure out who has the relic, who is behind everything, I'll be able to plan for the future. I might be able to find a way to keep everyone safe and turn this business more legitimate. Create a world where I could be something more for her than just a guardian. But I need those answers first, and I haven't found a way to tell her yet.

"I'm starting to think you need a push." Her eyes search mine. "I don't know what else you're waiting for."

"We need to talk first."

"All we do is talk." She sighs softly as she pulls away from me, and I hear the disappointment in her voice.

"All right, ladies. That was a good practice session for lap dances. Time to take a quick spin on the poles." The blonde stands and claps her hands together, pointing to the portable poles she's set up on the far side of the room. "We're not gonna do anything too advanced, but I can at least show you a few basics to get you started. Gentlemen, I think this will work better if the women have some time to themselves again."

I hear Ramsey grumble to my right, and I'm not thrilled about standing up right now either. But at least the lights are dim, and we can sneak out the side door.

"I'll find you later tonight." I run my fingers down the back of her forearm, risking getting caught to make sure she knows I mean it.

"Have fun with your whisky tasting." She flashes a bright smile, one meant for everyone else in the room, that stabs me in the chest.

THIRTY

D AKOTA

WE DOWN ANOTHER round of blowjob shots with our hands tucked behind our backs, one Marlowe manages to down faster than the rest of us much to everyone's surprise.

"We did them in college a lot." She looks at us defensively as the bartender hands us another round of vodka tonics to sip on while we decide what activity we're doing next.

"Y'all, I don't know how late I'm going to make it." Hazel sips her drink daintily. "It's been such a fun week, but I need to get some beauty rest before tomorrow. The makeup and hair people are coming at nine in the morning."

"Good lord. I thought the point of having the wedding at night was we didn't have to get up as early." Bristol shoots her a look of dismay.

"I know, but we still have all the pictures to take, and they said that was going to take two hours."

"You're lucky I love you so much." Bristol flashes her a disgruntled look but then wraps her arm around her shoulders and squeezes.

"I love you too. All of you. And I'm so glad we get to be sisters again." Hazel looks up at Aspen, and she smiles.

"Me too. I missed you keeping my baby brother in line. I always kinda hoped you two would find your way back to each other again." Aspen's eyes light with tenderness, and she reaches out and pats the back of Hazel's hand.

My phone rings then, jarring us all out of the sweet moment.

"I'm sorry!" I apologize, rooting through my purse until I pull out my phone and see Hayley's name across the screen. I left her in charge of the bar tonight, and she wouldn't call unless it was important. "Shit. I have to take this. I'll be right back. I'm sorry."

"No worries." Hazel gives me a sympathetic look. She thanked me a million times today, wanting me to know how much she appreciated everything I've done.

"Hey! Hold on. I'm in the bar, and it's loud in here. Let me step outside so I can hear," I say before I get through the doors and out onto the patio. "Okay. Everything okay?"

"No." Hayley sounds like she's choking back tears. "The cops came back, and this time, they were worse. Knocking bottles over, roughing up patrons." She sniffs back another sob, and I feel my heart bottom out into my stomach. "They're saying they're closing down the bar until further notice. They have something that looks official from the health department, and I don't know what to do. I'm so sorry to bother you. I know it's Hazel's big day tomorrow, and you all are out. I feel terrible, but I was scared not to tell you."

"It's okay. It's okay. It's not your fault. They're being assholes. You can't do anything about that. Are you safe? Are the rest of the girls safe?" I ask.

"Yeah. Grant's security guy was here and threatened them with everything in the book. But they still didn't stop. He made sure they didn't touch any of us though."

"All right. Just make sure everyone is okay. I'm coming, all right? I'll be right there." As I'm saying the last words, I see Grant on a mission, headed straight for me. His security must have called and given him a heads-up. "Just give me a few minutes to get a ride and get over there."

"Okay. You don't need to rush. I'll stay here until you get back." I hear a murmur of a voice in the background. "Jack said he's going to stay with me so don't worry, okay?"

"Okay. I'm so sorry this happened to you, Hayley. Please don't blame yourself, okay?"

"I'll try. See you in a bit."

"See you soon," I say and then disconnect the call. Grant's eyes are blazing with fury.

"I assume that's your staff telling you what's going on." He looks at my phone.

"I assume your security told you."

"I know you're going to want to go over there, so we'll go together. I'll have one of my guys drive us since we've both had drinks."

I nod. "I can't believe they're doing this. She said they're shutting down the bar altogether. That there was something official."

"Yeah. Jack gave me a heads-up about it. They've got a laundry list of stupid little fucking details. They don't normally shut people down over them, but my guess is that Officer Spencer has a friend in the health department. Don't worry. We'll get it handled."

"I still need to go and see the place. She said they broke things, and I'm just worried about her. She was so upset. I hate that this happened tonight." It's one of the many reasons I hate taking time off.

"Jack's there with her. She'll be okay. But I agree. Let's go take a look and make sure."

"All right. Let me just tell Hazel I have to leave for a bit."

WE'RE PULLING up to the bar in record time. His driver didn't waste any getting us over here, and this time of night, there wasn't a ton of traffic to compete with in a small town like Purgatory Falls. Hazel was understanding and even told me not to worry about coming back. But I left everything at the hotel that I needed for the night and tomorrow since I planned to stay at the Avarice. I'm more worried about the fact that I'm going to have giant bags under my eyes by the time everything is said and done.

When we walk in and Hayley sees me, she starts crying, running over and wrapping her arms around me.

"I sent everyone else home except for Gemma and Addy. I needed someone to help me clean up all the broken glass."

I look over and see Gemma and Addy with a giant trash can and a broom and pan. It's full of glass, and I walk over to peer inside the bag. It's nearly half-full.

"That many?" I gasp.

"Those motherfuckers," Grant curses under his breath.

"They said some of them had fruit flies inside, and they had to destroy it so we didn't serve it that way. But they were lying. They were just making up excuses to make a mess. They did it in front of patrons, too, as they were throwing people out. They kept saying how dirty it was—"

I press my hand to my heart, and tears start to form in my eyes. I kept it together on the drive over, and Grant let me have my silence when he asked if I was okay. I needed to think. To meditate on staying calm because letting these motherfuckers have my peace when they didn't deserve an ounce of my attention is not a thing I'm willing to cede. But knowing they denigrated this place like that, the place my parents left to my brother, and my brother left to me when he died—the place I worked so damn hard to keep up and make a second home and an escape for the people of Purgatory Falls is crushing my heart.

"I'm sorry. I shouldn't tell you all this. I didn't mean to upset you; I just can't believe it. Especially after the other day." Hayley rubs my back as she talks, and I shake my head.

"It's okay. It's what happened. I just hate that I wasn't here."

"I think they knew you wouldn't be here, honestly. They didn't even ask to speak with management or anything. They just slammed that paper on the bar and started running people out and smashing things."

"Everyone in this town knows the wedding is tomorrow and that you're busy with it. They did it on purpose, waiting until tonight." Grant's voice still has a lethal undertone to it. I know he'll make this all right for both of our sakes. I at least know that much, and it's keeping me on my feet right now. I take a deep breath and clear my head.

"All right. You should go home, Hayley. Gemma and Addy, you guys too. Please. I just want you all to get some sleep. And you too, Jack, is that your name?" I look at him.

"That's my name. Yes..." He looks at Grant instead of me for permission on whether or not he can leave.

"Do a perimeter check. Lock the doors. Set any outside alarms and lights. Make sure they're all gone and no one's sitting outside. Get the girls to their cars and on their way home safe. I'll meet you back at the Avarice for a debrief when we're done here." Grant nods to Jack, and he jerks his chin in understanding.

"I'm sorry again." Hayley looks remorsefully around the room. "Any help you need getting it fixed back up, you just call me, okay?"

"Same for us. We're here for you, girl." Addy pats me on the arm, her brown eyes two pools of sympathy. I was lucky I had staff like this.

"I'm so sorry this happened to you all on your shift. You're both okay too, right?" I look Addy and Gemma over. "No one got cut on glass or anything?"

"We're good." Gemma nods.

"Nothing we couldn't handle," Addy assures me.

"Thank you. And again, I'm so sorry. I'll keep you posted on when we're reopening and what's going on. Don't worry about your paychecks. I'll make sure you get a check for any missed work, okay?" I make the promise knowing full well I don't have the money, but I'll find it. At worst, I'm more in debt to Grant.

I SIT at the bar on one of the stools after they've left, and Jack reassures Grant that everything is locked up tight. I'm staring at the mess they've made of the back wall. An array of liquors and glasses that I've always been proud of is now a mess of missing pieces and bottles. I glance at the sign they've stuck on the door. The one that says I'm closed for violations I know don't exist.

But people won't believe that. They'll believe whatever the

paper says. Whatever the cops say is true. Rumors will run around town about the kind of establishment I run, and while the good ones will be there to say all the nice things about me and my girls, the assholes will say they've always liked Cowboy's better. That it's cleaner, and this place has always been a dive bar. The absolute cunts will say they prefer the Avarice's bar over mine. A nameless high-end monument to marble and gold, luxury and lush menus, and plush seating. Everything this bar isn't. Everything I'm not.

Polar opposites. Just like the man who owns it and me. My depression and anxiety are talking loudly when I shouldn't be listening to them. Telling me I'm a loser no one really wants. Not Grant. Not Hayden. Not any man. Because I'm the cheap bottom-shelf whiskey that gets broken when someone decides it's not good enough.

Dread sets in when I think about all my interactions with Grant through that lens. I start wondering if it's the real reason he didn't want to take me up to a room tonight. That he doesn't want to lead me on to thinking this is anything more than what we are. That this deal we have isn't the sexy fun I've made it out to be, but some cheap agreement that kept him entertained. I'm spiraling, and I know it, but I can't stop my brain from telling me all the things I don't want to hear. By the time Grant comes back to where I'm sitting, I'm ready to break all over the floor myself.

"You doing okay?" He gives me a sympathetic look. One that feels like pity in the neon light.

"You said we needed to talk."

He winces and looks around the bar. "You want to do that now? I don't think that's a good idea. It's late and—"

"We're alone. I've got nothing better to do. I'm not going to go back and crash Hazel's bachelorette with this mood. I won't be able to sleep. You've made it clear you won't touch me, which is the only other thing besides more alcohol that might improve this night. So I want to know why you won't. Why you won't let me touch you either." I sound bitter to my own ears.

My eyes drift over him. He looks like sin tonight. Gorgeous in a black zipped hoodie that fits him perfectly under a suit jacket that probably costs more than the bar makes in a month. The black cowboy hat was left in the car with the driver, but the black snakeskin cowboy boots with the steel tips set off the whole outfit. He looks every bit as expensive as he is.

"Dakota..." He so rarely says my name, my real first name, that I know this isn't going to end well.

"Don't sugarcoat it. Just tell me the truth. I need to hear it. I need you to crush my heart so that I can stop thinking about you. I need you to tell me it was all just a game, some amusement for you while you were bored so I can get on with my real life once I've finished paying you off. We should probably talk about that too. How many more naked photos and videos you need to feel satisfied that you've well and truly rubbed my nose in what a desperate whore I am for selling myself."

"Don't you dare fucking call yourself that." His temper snaps, and his nostrils flare.

"Wasn't that what this was? You teaching me a lesson. Showing me what would happen to me if I kept doing what I was doing. Selling pictures of myself. Spitting whiskey into men's mouths. And look. I've lost my bar. My reputation's in the trash. And I'm some man's plaything. Just like you predicted."

"I wanted to teach you a lesson because I wanted to protect you from people who could hurt you. I didn't want to see it happen to you. That was the last fucking thing on earth I wanted."

"And yet... here I am."

"If you want out of our deal, I'll call the debt settled. Most of it was for the wedding anyway, and it's my baby brother. I should be helping cover the costs as the head of the family."

"What happened to holding me to it?"

"I don't want it if this is how it makes you feel. If this is how you see yourself. That was never what I wanted."

"Then why did you want it?"

"Because I..." He scrubs a hand over his mouth and sinks onto the barstool next to mine. "You've always been important to me. I've always cared about you. Fuck. I enjoyed our little hateful banter routine. That you weren't scared of me, and you'd tell me the truth to my face without sugarcoating it."

"But you never saw me the way I saw you. I was always a little girl to you. One who didn't learn her lesson the first time. Naïve and silly."

"I didn't give you the respect you deserved. You're right. I think part of me didn't want to see you as anything other than the kid who I looked after when your brother died. That kept things simple between us. Made all the lines clear as day for me, and I could stay far away from them. Have zero interest in crossing them, or at least tell myself that was the case. But then..."

"But then you saw pictures of me naked, and I seemed like an easy toy to play with."

"No. You're not easy, and you're not a toy. But I... I saw you differently, yes. It started before that. Last year when we danced that one night. Valentine's Day when we had our little truce. When we got into that argument in your apartment when I tried to fix the sink. I realized you're not her anymore. You're not the girl who needs my protection. You're all grown up, and you have your own life and your own dreams. You can take care of yourself, and you don't need me. And then I thought about a life without you in it anymore. I realized how much I cared about you. How empty it would be without you. Not you—the kid sister, and me—the poor substitute for Jesse. But you as a friend... not that you could label us that, exactly but..." He sighs and takes a breath. "I was just getting used to figuring out how we might be able to be friends, and then I saw those pictures, and fuck..."

I raise my brow. This wasn't what I expected him to say. It's throwing me completely off guard, and I'm too tongue-tied to even think of what to say in response now.

"I realized I wasn't seeing you as a friend. But I couldn't reconcile what I thought I was seeing you as with who I am. I don't fall for women. And I'm not saying that as some sort of hardass who thinks he's above it. I'm saying that as someone who just... isn't wired that way. I look at Ramsey, and I wish I could have it, but I don't see how I get from where I am to anywhere else.

"But I couldn't just let you go either. The idea of you with some other guy suddenly had me in fucking knots. Hearing you talk to those other men like that? The way I saw you with Hayden."

"So why not just tell me that?"

"I promised Jesse I'd keep you safe. That I wouldn't let anything happen to you—including me and the Horsemen. Whatever it took, you were gonna know what it was like to be happy and have the things that made you happy. You weren't gonna have to worry like Jesse did or put yourself in danger." Grant's eyes go glassy, and his teeth saw their way over his lower lip like he's trying to focus. "If he hadn't been so fucking proud I would have just given him the money. So when you needed it, I didn't want history to repeat itself. I didn't want you to be too proud to let me help you and let someone else take a bite out of you while you were exposed. I figured it was better if it was me."

"But then I liked it—you liked it," I think out loud.

He nods. His eyes go distant even as he stares at the bar.

"He'd kill me if he was here. I'd be the last man on earth he'd want touching you. Looking at you like I have been. The things I've said to you? If he heard them, if he can hear them now. He's turning in his grave, wishing he could put me down next to him."

"He wouldn't touch a single hair on your head because I wouldn't let him. I have a protective side, too, you know. I worry about you. I worry that you'll keep doing what you're doing, and you will end up next to him. I can't lose you. You're the closest thing I have left to family. The one person who I know has my back no matter how much I fuck up."

"The girls have your back."

"They do. I know that. But they don't just love me. They like me... I'm one of their favorite people. If Hazel had to go to a deserted island and could only take one person, she might struggle to pick me or Ramsey, you know? She'd pick him because she's madly in love with him, and he's her person. But she'd have to think about it because I'm her other person." I laugh through some of the tears falling down my cheeks. "You can't stand me. Everything I say and do irritates you, and you still show up. That's a different kind of love."

"You don't irritate me; you just test my limits sometimes. As long as it's in my power, I will always be here. Always have your back. I promise." He gives me a soft smile, one that goes all the way to his eyes, and that little hint of vulnerability on his part melts away any hardness I have left where he's concerned.

"I know you will." I'm fighting the rest of my tears back as hard as I can so I can say the next part without falling apart because I need to hear him say it so I can move on. "But you need to be honest with me about why you don't want to take things further with me. You've got to tell me so I can stop imagining this thing between us ends in something other than heartache. The more time we spend talking and playing this game, the more I think I can climb over all those walls you have up, and I need you to shatter the illusion for me while I can still take it."

THIRTY-ONE

G RANT

MY HEART IS about to fracture in my goddamn chest, listening to her pour hers out on the floor in front of me. Knowing I don't have a single fucking good answer to any of the questions she's asking. Knowing I don't even have the guts to push her away like I should. Because we're both in the deep end now.

"I won't take things further with you because I'm still working through my own feelings and my own guilt about it. I know he's not here. I know you're a grown ass woman who can make her own decisions, but I also know how I'd feel about someone like me getting anywhere near my sister. I know how Jesse would feel about me getting near you. It feels like I'd be breaking my promise to him."

"He's not here. *I am.* I get to say who does and doesn't get near me. I don't need my brother's permission, and neither do you. I know you loved him, and I know you want to honor his memory, but this isn't that. He knew then like he would now that you're a good man. He wouldn't have been friends with you otherwise. He made some mistakes, but he had a good compass when it came to the people he loved. And he wanted the people he loved happy."

"But that leads me to the next part, which is..." I take a deep breath, looking up to the ceiling for a moment and then back at the bar. "There's a lot you don't know. A lot of things that happened last year, things that have been escalating again since my parents' deaths. It's why Hudson and Charlotte have been here, why I've been traveling back and forth to Cincinnati. We're on the edge of getting more information, the kind I'm hoping lets me know what my future looks like. How grim it might be. Because regardless of how Jesse would feel"—I swallow hard, and my eyes rise to meet hers—"I would never forgive myself if I let something happen to you. If something happened to you because of me, the way it did with him. I couldn't live with myself."

"You can't control everything, Grant. It's not possible. You can't stop every bad thing in the world by force of will. Bad things will happen. To me. To everyone you care about. As long as you're there for them... that's what matters. You keep pushing people away because you can't control them. That breeds resentment."

"This is more than just me wanting control. This is about the danger I pose to anyone who touches me. All this stuff with the cops. All the stuff going on with Hudson. My uncle being back in town... I already have a target on my back, and I'm worried it's getting bigger by the day. If they find out that you're... If they know how much I care about you, what I'd do to protect you—they'll use that against both of us, and you'll be the one who suffers for it. It'd rip me to fucking shreds. I wouldn't be thinking straight, and I can't protect you or my family or all the people who depend on me if I can't think straight."

"But what is life if you can't enjoy it? What is life if you don't have someone who loves you? Protects you? Sleeps next to you at night and knows you inside and out? What kind of life is that for you, Grant?"

"It's the life I agreed to. It's the life I signed up for years ago when I promised my father I'd keep this family safe. It's the only way Ramsey and Aspen and Fallon and fuck, hopefully someday Levi, get to have the lives they want."

"So that's it then. There's no other option?" She sounds resigned, and as much as I want her to respect it, I feel as hopeless as she does when she says it out loud.

"If this project that Hudson and I have going goes well, there's a chance I might be able to change some things for the better. It'll take time, but I'm hoping that someday I'll get to a point where I don't live in fucking terror of you or my family getting hurt. But right now, I don't know the basics yet, and I can't move forward without it. Once the wedding's over, I should be able to put my attention back on the problem."

"I see. So what about our arrangement then? From the outside, from someone who wants to hurt you or me, how is it functionally different from something more?"

"Because we've kept it a secret. Not a very good one, given how my brother and everyone keep seeing through it. So it needs to have an expiration date. Fuck. It should have never happened in the first place. It's why when I thought you might have feelings for Hayden, part of me—a very small bitter part of me—was relieved. I thought maybe you could get away from here. Move somewhere else where you'd still have Hazel in your life and have someone who could keep you safe. One of my brothers still knowing you're all right. I could have found a way to be at peace with that."

"I don't want Hayden. I don't want anyone else but you. Do you want someone else?"

"No. No one compares to you, Hellfire. Not a single solitary soul on this earth, or under it, comes close."

"Okay..." There are tears in her eyes, but she nods her agreement. "Then we end it tonight. Until you know more and we can know if there's a future or not. Then we can both think clearly again."

I reach out and grab her hand, stroking my fingers along the inside of her palm. I can't take my eyes off her, let alone walk away from her. I'm so fucking twisted up inside. So angry with myself for letting either of us have a taste of this that I feel like I should never let myself have another taste of her again. Resolve I've barely started to form before she tests it.

"But stay the night. After the way this week has gone and tonight, I have to be back with my game face on tomorrow, but tonight, I don't want to be alone."

"Dakota..." I protest weakly because I can't say no to her. Not when I hear the sincerity in her voice.

"I'll keep my hands to myself. Just a platonic sleepover. You're my emotional support person to help me deal with all the stress."

Like hell would it be platonic. I'll be thinking about fucking her all night. But I don't want to leave her alone when she needs someone. Not after everything she's been dealing with and the stress of tomorrow looming. She watches me, and she can tell I'm caving.

"Think about it. You'd have to call your driver to come get you. We'd have to wait. There'd be the whole drive over to the Avarice, getting back to our rooms, checking on all our friends and explaining what happened, then showers and bed." She makes a compelling case. "Here, we just take our showers and then bed."

"The showers and bed part are exactly what makes me nervous."

"Nervous? A big bad man like you with someone as harmless as me?" She bats her eyelashes playfully, and I shake my head as I roll my eyes.

"Nothing about you is harmless, darlin'."

"Fine. But I'll be good tonight. I promise." She looks at me sweetly, taking my hand and tugging me toward the stairs.

"Fuck. All right," I concede, following her up the stairs even though I know I'm probably making a mistake.

THIRTY-TWO

D AKOTA

I FEEL a weight off my shoulders knowing he's staying the night. I want him, and it's going to be damn near impossible to keep my hands to myself, but I'm going to do my best. I wasn't lying when I said I needed him. The last thing I want tonight is to be alone—in this apartment or in a hotel room. I don't want to think about what might never be with him. I don't want to think about my troubles with the bar. I definitely don't want to be trying to recite my maid of honor speech in my head at three in the morning because I'm worried I'm going to mess it up. I need him there to help me forget all of that.

When we get inside the apartment, Vendetta rushes us, jumping up on the table so I can pet her. Her eyes dart warily to Grant. She's never been a big fan of outsiders, but the fact she's not hissing at him or disappearing to a corner the minute she sees him is promising. He's always been kind to her, but I've never thought of Grant as a cat person. If anything, he's a Rottweiler or a Dobermann sort.

"I can just sleep on the couch." Grant takes his suit jacket off and hangs it on the back of one of the chairs before he holds out his hand for Vendetta to inspect. She nudges her head against his palm and purrs. I bite my tongue to keep from making a comment and raise my brow at him.

"That couch wasn't made for a six-four man to sleep on. You can sleep in the bed." When he gives me a skeptical look, I return it. "We're adults. I can make a pillow wall if you need it."

"I'm good."

"You can shower in this bathroom, and I'll shower in mine. I'll just get you some towels." The hallway bath shower is a little bit bigger than mine, and it was the one Jesse had always used since he'd given me the master suite in the apartment growing up.

I disappear into my room while Vendetta keeps him entertained, returning with a stack of towels and an extra bottle of body wash.

"There's shampoo and conditioner in there. The good stuff because that's where I do my hair treatments. You'll have to settle for smelling like key lime though. Unless you want peaches or pineapple."

He smirks. "Key lime works."

"All right. I'll meet you back in bed." I wink at him.

"Don't do that."

"Do what?"

"You know what you're doing."

"Okay, Cowboy. If you say so." I smirk and then turn around to head for the bathroom before I halt in my tracks. "One last thing... did you want a last set of pictures tonight?" I glance back over my shoulder at him.

I can see him thinking through the consequences, and he shakes his head. "Better not."

AS I FINISH up my shower, I glance down at my vibrator that's sitting on the edge of the tub. If I'm going to be as good as I promised for him, I'll need to take care of myself first. I've barely turned it on when there's a light rap of his knuckles against the bathroom door, and I freeze in the shower. I swear this man reads my mind.

"Yes?" I call out.

I expected him to talk to me through the door, but instead, I can hear him open it and step in. In the small space between the wall and the shower curtain, I can see him in the mirror, wearing nothing but his boxer briefs, and it's not helping my self-control.

I try and fail to turn the vibrator off, my finger slipping off the button. I'm worried I'm going to come while he's in here or that he'll hear the low hum of it. Usually, I wouldn't care, but it feels embarrassing to admit I'm this desperate for him that I have to take the edge off my nerves. Thankfully, he starts talking, and I'm hoping between that and the water he can't hear.

"My eyes are closed, but I was just wondering if you have a —" He stops mid-sentence and clears his throat. "Are you... do you have a—" he stumbles over his words, and honestly, Grant Stockton lost for words in my bathroom in his underwear is simultaneously the cutest and hottest thing I've ever experienced in my life. At least until he rips back the curtain and glares at me.

I jump back and hide the vibrator behind my back. Don't ask me why. It's not like he doesn't know. I'm just working on instinct at this moment.

"If you want me to be good, then I have to make sure I can be," I say defensively as his eyes drift over me. He holds out his hand, and when I hesitate, his lashes lower, and his eyes narrow. I place the vibrator in his hand, and he exchanges it for a towel.

"Get out here."

"You can't be mad at me for this! I'm doing what you wanted."

"You know, I thought about it when I was in the shower. Getting off with the smell of your key lime soap and shampoo all around me. But then I thought, no... I shouldn't. It won't live up to what I really want, and if she's being good, I can hold it together for one night."

"I never said it was living up to what I want. I just thought it would take the edge off so I could sleep next to you and stay on my side of the pillow fortress." I towel myself angrily.

He's only half listening, though, because he's opening my drawers methodically until he lands on the one that holds the rest of my toys. I assume he's going to put this one back, but instead, he starts looking through them.

"What are you doing?"

"Deciding which ones I want you to use."

"Excuse me?"

"You already started it, so we're going to finish it. But we're doing it my way. Not with you cheating behind a curtain."

"I wasn't cheating!" I huff, tossing the towel over the bar to dry.

I watch as he pulls out a small anal vibrator and sets it alongside the regular one I'd been using in the shower, smirking to himself before he grabs a bottle of lube and lays it out next to them. Then his brow shoots up at something in the drawer. He pulls out another, holding the bendable one up and looking at me with curiosity.

"It bends so I can switch it up, front to back," I explain.

"Interesting," he mutters, and my skin heats at the way his eyes rake over my body like he's imagining it.

"If you get to use one on me, I get to use one on you."

"I'm not making deals here, Hellfire."

"But I am," I argue. "I was going to be good, but if you're going to start crossing lines, then I think it's only fair."

"I don't play fair, and you weren't being good." He tilts his head. "I play dirty, and after that little stunt... It's gonna be real fucking dirty. I don't even know if I'll let you come. I might just torture you until you fall asleep from exhaustion."

"You could do that... or you could give in and let yourself have something you want too." I hold up the anal vibrator. "Think how good this would feel buzzing inside you while I suck your cock. How hard you'd come."

His brow goes higher, but I see the way his eyes spark with interest.

"Don't tell me you've never tried it."

"Can't say I have."

"Oh... you're missing out."

"Now you're just trying to distract me."

I reach into the drawer and pull out the smallest one I own. "I have a smaller one. Perfect for beginners." I roll my lip between my teeth as I watch him consider it. "I'll let you torture me as long as you want if you try it for me."

His nostrils flare, and his eyes widen at that. His hand wraps around my throat, and the other slips down over my naked form.

"You don't let me do anything. I tell you what to do, and you listen." He practically growls the words, and the sound of his gravelly voice is like fire down my spine. I've hit a nerve with my attempt to bargain, and his fingers dig into my flesh as he turns me around to face the mirror. "Do you understand?" he asks me, his eyes meeting mine in the mirror.

I nod, nibbling my lip nervously as I take the sight of us in.

"What's your safe word?" He kisses my neck and shifts my hair forward. Drops of water bead off the ends of my hair and run down over my nipple, making it peak under the cold.

"My safe word?" I ask, the question clear in my tone. It's hard to imagine the protective man I usually know pushing my limits.

"You've got me worked up and greedy to hear you beg. It's not a good combination for you."

"Avarice."

He frowns.

"That's my safe word."

"Interesting choice."

"Just making sure you have to think about me every time you see it." I grin at him in the mirror, and he nips at my neck.

"Always trying to find a way to manage me."

"It's worked well for me so far, hasn't it?" I sass him again, and this time, his hand slips around the side of my throat as he kisses his way down the other side and over my shoulder. I rock back against him, rubbing my ass over his dick through the cotton of his boxers. His hand coasts over my hip, and he grabs my ass cheek, squeezing a handful as he watches me in the mirror.

"We'll see if you're saying that in a few minutes," he threatens, taking the bendable vibrator from the table and turning it on. He hands it to me.

"Show me how you fuck yourself with it," he instructs.

I take it from him and let the head of it brush over my clit. "You don't want to fuck me like this? I'm already nice and wet from thinking about you fucking me in the shower."

His hand runs down over my forearm, and he puts his palm

over my knuckles, guiding me and the toy downward and then pushing it slowly inside. I close my eyes as the mild vibration starts bringing my nerve endings back to life from the abrupt ending he gave them a few minutes ago. He uses the pads of his fingers to press the other end of the vibrator against my clit, bending it close so that it gives a soft vibration to my piercing.

"Fuck me," I curse.

"You're the most gorgeous woman I've ever seen, Hellfire. When I close my eyes and dream of all the perfect things I could ask for... it's you. These perfect hips. These full tits. This ass that's so sweetly shaped. A perfect fucking handful." His fingertips trace all the parts of my body, and he squeezes my other cheek for good measure. Then his hand slips up between them, a finger teasing my entrance. "You like being full, don't you? All these toys for it."

"Yes, sometimes." I rock the toy in and out to give myself a taste of what I need—what I really want from him. "Sometimes, it feels better that way. I can pretend to be Charlotte." I smirk, knowing damn well he's going to wipe it off my face, but I can't stop myself.

He reaches down and grabs my wrist, stopping the motion and pulling the toy out of me slowly. He sets it back on the counter, a low guttural sound releasing from his throat when he sees how wet it is already.

"You better not be imagining you're anyone but you right now in this moment. Because you're gonna want to remember everything I do to you." He picks up the first anal vibrator he pulled out of the drawer. It's a rainbow metallic color with a little heart-shaped jewel at the flared base. He douses it in lube and puts some on his fingers. He slips them back between my cheeks, massaging me gently with it, taking his time teasing me before he starts to slowly push the toy in.

"Hmm..." I make a soft humming noise, breathing out as he slips it in.

"Fuck. Look how pretty you look with that. I don't think there's a single part of you that isn't gorgeous," he comments as he reaches for the vibrator I'd been using.

He reaches around and presses it against my clit, turning it on to a low setting that has me running my teeth over my lower lip. My hips rock back of their own volition, searching for his cock.

"All I need now is you inside me." I lift my lashes to meet his eyes. "You could fill me all the way up, Daddy."

"Trust me, when I finally fuck you, you'll be so full of me, I'll be leaking out of you for days."

"Do it. I want you so bad I can barely stand it anymore."

"It's not that easy." He kisses his way over my shoulder and across to the other shoulder, all the while teasing my clit and then taking it away again. Over and over until I feel like I might scream.

"It is that easy. You just pull these down." I reach back and slip my fingertips under his waistband. I'm desperate for a glimpse of his cock. He looks big, feels big. I just want to stop guessing and know for a fact that he's been the one I've always needed. I tug slowly, and he lets me, his eyes following the movement in the mirror.

The head of his cock strains against the elastic for a moment and then finally slips free of it. And fuck if it isn't perfect. I let out a soft cry of approval, and his brow arches up at me.

"I can't help it. Look at you..." I whisper as I wrap my hand around him.

"Fuck." He presses his forehead to the back of my neck and kisses me softly. "I've needed this."

"I know, Cowboy. I can take care of you. Just put me to work." I start to stroke him slowly.

"You're playing with fire touching me like this. You're gonna bait me into breaking our rules."

"I don't care about rules."

"We need them. It's the only thing that keeps you..." The words fade on his lips as I grip him a little tighter.

"Keeps me?" I ask.

"Keeps you safe." He slips the vibrator back inside me, and I let out a soft moan. The feeling of being full and having him in the palm of my hand is the best I've felt in a long time. But I can still think of a few things I'd like better.

"You gave me a safe word. If I need it, I'll use it." I breathe the words more than say them because I'm lost in how good it all feels. "So tell me what you need from me. Tell me what part of me you want to fuck first, and it's yours."

"I can't fuck you. I do, and it's over," he insists, and he pulls away from my hand. "There were ground rules for a reason."

"Stop trying to be noble with your rules," I snipe at him, and his eyes snap up and meet mine in the mirror, the blues there fading to a near black the longer I talk. "I don't want your good-boy act. I want the man who takes what he wants. I want the dark side."

"Get on your knees," he growls.

Fucking *finally*. I hit them hard. Even with the fluffy bath rug under my feet, I can feel the impact. I've been waiting for this—dying for it. When I look up at him and see his determination, I have to suppress a smile. As his fingers slip through my wet hair, tightening in the roots, and he nudges his dick against my lips I know I'm finally getting what I want.

"Open and let me see that wicked little tongue of yours," he grinds out, and I do as he asks. He slides his cock over it, the tip almost hitting the back of my throat. He slips it back out and back in again, taking it a little deeper on the next pass and again on the next as my eyes water with the effort. "This what you want? Me using you like I own you?"

I blink my yes. "Fuck... you should see how stunning you look. Taking my cock down that pretty pink throat. Keeps you from telling me what to do when your mouth is full like this, doesn't it?"

I hum a soft yes.

"Close your mouth and suck like it's your job."

THIRTY-THREE

GRANT

I'M HAVING AN OUT-OF-BODY EXPERIENCE. I must be because Dakota's mouth is wrapped around my cock, and her tongue is every bit as good as she promised it would be. I don't deserve it. I don't deserve her on her knees like this for me. But she begged me. Taunted me until I lost my temper and fell right into her trap. My inability to say no to her is going to be a long-term fucking problem if I can't get a grip.

She slips back slowly, taking me shallower, and her tongue plays over the tip as she mixes it with soft, sucking deeper passes, and whatever's left of my brain is shutting off and instinct is taking over. Telling me to fuck her throat and every single part of her until I've marked it all as mine. She teases her clit with her vibrator and rocks it deeper inside as she fucks me with her mouth, her hips grinding down chasing her own orgasm as she tries to suck me dry.

"That feel good?" I ask. "Grinding that little cunt down on your toy?"

Her tongue swirls around the tip of my cock before she pulls back and takes a breath.

"Feels as good as you taste." She laps up a drop of precum with her tongue, and I can't help running my knuckles down her cheek. She's so eager to please. I feel like I must be dying and living out one final fantasy before everything goes black. But I can tell she needs more from me, and I want this to be every bit as good for her. I owe her that much, at least.

"What do you need?"

"Your cock would solve everything." She gives me a sly grin. "But if that's off the table, then more vibration would help." Her eyes meet mine for permission, and I can't refuse her when she looks at me like that. I just want to be in control of it right now—her pleasure and her focus.

"Up," I command her and hold out my hand to help her stand. I run my hands down the sides of her body, taking in how soft her skin is and how perfect every curve of her body feels, before I grab her hips and turn her to face the counter, her back to my front. I want this experience from every angle, want to feel her come apart under my hands and watch it on her face at the same time.

"Fuckkkk," she curses as I turn up the vibration a notch. The mirror serves as the perfect window to her thoughts as she leans over on the counter. She's giving in to the sensations while I stand behind her and gently stroke my hand over her ass, admiring the little heart shape of the toy she still has there. "It's torture," she mutters into the counter.

"Good. You deserve it for being such a brat." I run my other hand down the length of her spine. "We were supposed to be in bed with a pillow fort between us, and now look at what we've done." Except I can't even force regret into my tone; I'm glad for every moment of this.

Her lashes lift, and she studies me in the mirror, her eyes drifting over my form, standing at her back.

"We could do better," she mutters as her gaze lands heavy on my cock. "You could put us both out of our misery."

I should say no, should try to be the one who slows us down because she's set on us both leaping over a cliff tonight—one we might not survive. But I'm lost in her, and every argument she makes is chipping away at my resolve.

"The lube's right there. You could take the heart out and slip right in," she taunts me.

I run my tongue along the inside of my cheek and slowly shake my head. For all the good it does, because even I can see in the reflection how desperate I am for her. So fucking tempted to take what I've wanted for what feels like forever now. I could let her have this. Give her these things she wants, at least, even if I can't give her everything. I'm only tormenting us both right now.

"I want to see this one in you." I run my fingers gently over the double-ended, bendable vibrator before I pull the heart-shaped plug I have in her now out slowly. I reach forward to grab the lube, leaning over her, and my cock brushes against her soft skin. I mutter a curse, and she seizes the opportunity, pushing back, and the warmth of her slipping over the head of my cock is too much. I squeeze the bottle and close my eyes, trying to count backward and take control of the situation.

Ten. I could do this. Nine. I really could. Tease and torture but not give in fully. Eight.

"I want *you* in me," she demands.

Fuck. I've forgotten where I was. Seven? I'm too busy imagining how tight she'll feel, how good it'll be to know it's me and not a toy making her fall apart like this.

"That private school Jesse made me go to my last year said it doesn't count this way." She licks her lips and runs her teeth over the lower one in a way that has me dying to kiss her. "In case you need an excuse to ease your conscience."

She knows exactly what she's doing. These few short months have given her everything she needs to find my Achilles', or maybe she's been studying for years just waiting for the opportunity. I raise a brow at her but stay silent. Still at number seven and moving very fucking slowly down to six and then five as I go to put the lube on the other end of the vibrator. But I pause, letting it dribble down in between her cheeks instead. I start teasing her with my fingers, slowly circling tighter and tighter, while I watch her face contort with anticipation and pleasure in the mirror.

She rocks back against my hand, murmuring a soft curse and letting me stretch her. Before I know what I'm doing, I'm coating the head of my cock in lube and lining myself up with her. Her eyes meet mine in the reflection and then rake down my body. I can't remember what number I was on. Fuck, I can't remember my own name right now.

"Fuck me, Daddy. Please. I need it." It's a soft plea, one that severs whatever resolve I had left.

Before I can think, I'm easing inside her, listening to her muted whimpers as she slowly moves her hips back and forth and bites down on her lush lower lip. I let her take control, taking as much of me as she wants as slowly as she wants. I'm just trying to breathe through it because she's so tight and so fucking sexy; I worry I might never breathe again if I don't focus.

"Oh my god." She closes her eyes as she moans and leans over the counter for purchase, her palm running desperately over the surface and gripping the edge.

"Thought I was the devil."

"Right now, you're both." She opens her eyes again to meet mine. "You've got me so full." She starts to move, rolling her hips to test the feel of me while she counters with the vibrator, the one she has slipping slowly in and out of her until it's glistening with how wet she's getting.

"That's my girl. Fuck that tight little cunt for me." I grab her hips and start to fuck her, slowly at first, but she urges me on. I can tell she only needs a little more to take her over the edge. "Spit on your fingers and work that clit for me. I want to see how far we can push you before your body gives in."

She follows my instructions without question, using her free hand to start teasing her clit. The jewelry glints from the movement, and I grin at the soft gasp that leaves her lips.

"I'm gonna come fast like this. It's too good. I'm sorry." She apologizes between moans and whimpers, and I'm thankful as fuck because I can't take it either. The tight feel of her around my cock as the vibrator mercilessly punishes us both, torturing me through the thin barrier, the sounds she's making, knowing every inch of her is mine now. It's all too much.

I don't have enough willpower for this. I take her a little slower, trying to draw it out for both of us, but then she mutters a soft final plea for more—one I deliver on—and I can feel her lose control. She grips me tighter, and her whole body shivers like waves on a lake as she comes apart, saying my name like it's deliverance. It's more than enough to take me with her, and the sight of it all reflected back to us in the mirror has me swearing through my own release.

"That's my girl. You're being so fucking good for me, Hellfire. Taking me so well like this." I watch mesmerized as I pump her full, and I start to drip out of her. "Oh fuck... look at me leaking out of you."

There's another whispered obscenity on her part, and she pulls the vibrator free, collapsing forward and leaving just me as I lose the last of myself inside her. I pull out of her slowly, obsessed with the way she's covered in me—my sweat, my come —as I run a palm over her ass cheek.

"You're fucking gorgeous, but right now... Fuck me. I don't think I've ever seen anything this beautiful, sweetheart," I whisper.

"You're not bad yourself, Cowboy." She turns around, and the way she studies me, every inch of my skin feels like it's on fire. Like I didn't just claim her, but she took some part of me with her in the process. She leans past me to turn on the hot water. "I'll get us some more towels, but we'll have to shower together this time. We're pushing the limits of the water heater."

I nod my agreement because I don't have better words right now. I'm still processing what I've done. What we've done. I already know how this night ends now. But it feels like she's finally in control.

When she comes back, she takes inventory and smiles at the chaos she's created.

"Get in." She nods to the shower, and she presses softly on my chest and plants a kiss on my jaw before I follow her instruction.

She steps in behind me and pours soap into my palms, but instead of putting it on my own skin, I put it on hers. I'm still craving more of her, and I spend my time lathering up her shoulders and chest, moving slowly over her breasts and ribs and down over her abdomen. Then around her hips and over her back and ass, slipping between her cheeks to clean the mess I made of her. She moves just as slowly and allows my ministrations, lifting each leg, one at a time, so I can get her thighs and behind her knees. I kneel down to reach her ankles and toes, and she gives me one foot at a time so I can work over every inch of skin.

She follows my pattern, pouring the soap into her hands and washing every inch of my body. She pauses at all the parts she likes, not saying a word but admiring them all the same— my arms and my ass seem to get extra attention, and I smirk when she kisses the tip of my cock as it starts to come to life again from her touch. When she comes back to standing, she looks up at me, and there's a question in her eyes, one I only have a single answer for.

I run my fingers through her hair, threading them until I have a tight grip and tilting her head back so she's forced to hold my gaze. I'm scared to tell her the next part. Terrified that now she's had some of what she thought she wanted, she'll realize that I'm not any of what she made me out to be in her head all this time. But I'm in the habit of doing things that fucking terrify me, and now one of them is confessing the truth to her.

"I want every part of you. Your mind. Your heart. I'm gonna earn them all. It's gonna take time, though, and you're gonna have to be patient with me while I learn to trust myself with them. I have to figure out how I can balance how much I don't deserve you with how much I need you. That's probably gonna take a lifetime and then some, and I don't know if either of us is ready for it." I hold her blues with mine, worried I'm gonna get both our hearts broken in the process, but I can see the way her eyes soften with the words. The quiet way she relaxes into my arms.

"I'm ready to start whenever you are," she whispers back.

"Thank fuck because I don't think I can wait any longer." I grin before I kiss her.

She wraps her arms around me and pulls me close, her fingers searching over my skin as desperately as my tongue tangles with hers. We've both needed this way too long. The touch of someone who sees us for who we really are, all the ugly flaws and doubts and worries, and loves us for exactly those reasons.

A feeling we get to enjoy for all of five seconds before the water turns ice cold.

"Fuck this!" I shout, pulling her out of the spray of the water and shielding her with my body until I can turn it off. When I turn around, her arms are wrapped over her chest, and she looks frozen.

"Oops," she chatters, laughter bubbling through. "Got a little too carried away."

I help her out of the tub and hand her a towel. We make quick work of drying ourselves off, and then I scoop her up, carrying her back to the bed and laying her down in the middle of it. I climb on after her, and she wraps her legs around my hips as I start to kiss my way over her chest, pausing to flick my tongue over one of her nipples on the way to her throat.

"Think you could fuck me again?" she asks, amusement and admiration seeping through her tone in a way that melts away whatever ice was left.

"Yeah." I slip my cock through her wetness, teasing it over her clit as she rolls her hips. "I think I might be able to help with that." I grin at her. "Condom?" I ask when I realize I don't have one on me. It was part of my say-no-to-her reinforcement plan, but clearly, it's out the fucking window now.

"There's one in the drawer, but I'm on birth control. I'm good if you are."

"I'm good," I reply softly.

"Do I get the sweet cowboy or the rough gangster this time?"

"Which do you want?" I ask, studying her face as she looks up at me.

THIRTY-FOUR

D AKOTA

IT'S NOT AN EASY DECISION. I love them both equally.

"Can the gangster wrap his hand around my throat again while the cowboy tells me how pretty my eyes are and calls me sweetheart?" My fingertips draw circles over his shoulders as I cradle his cock between my thighs. He's growing harder by the second, and I'm dying to have him inside me.

He laughs, a full genuine one that I haven't heard often. Definitely not much in the last few years with all the stress he's been under, and my heart swells a little in my chest that I'm the cause. That I might be his soft place to land after all.

"Yeah, sweetheart. I've got you." He kisses his way up my neck, pausing at my earlobe to nip it gently before he speaks again, lower this time. The kind of thick, graveled, throaty tone that travels all the way to my clit. "But just know I'm claiming this last part of you, and then you're all fucking mine. There's no way back after this. You understand? You ever think you want another one of your college boys up here? This is your last chance to run."

"I'm pretty sure you've ruined me for all other men, Cowboy." If I'm being really honest, no other man has ever lived up to him in my head.

"Good. 'Cause I think you've had me ruined for all other women for a long time. Longer than I want to admit." He makes the confession, the kind that feels like he's pulled back more of the curtain than he planned.

My heart skips a full beat in my chest as his lips press against mine. The idea that this man might want me as much as I've wanted him feels like the perfect kind of whisky burn, the kind that seeps into your chest and wraps around your soul. For his part, he kisses me like it's his last night on earth, each one more heated than the last, and I melt under his touch. My hips rise to meet his, and I tease the tip of his cock over my clit.

"Fuck me," he curses softly, and his lips make their way up my jaw. "Your body feels like fucking sin. I can't believe how perfect you are." He takes me slowly, easing in inch by inch like he knows I need this to last. I want every single memory of the way this man claimed me for himself. I need it like oxygen. "And every perfect inch is mine."

He bites down on my neck, and I arch up into it. I love this man's obsession with marking my skin, the way he needs to leave visible marks showing that I belong to him. I need it after how long it took for us to get here.

My fingers drift down his side and over his back and ass. The fact that I get to touch every part of him the way I want, that it's mine to take as I please.

I wrap my leg around him as he starts to fuck me harder. He pulls back so he can look at me, and his lashes lower. He looks lost in his thoughts as his knuckle drags down over my lips and chin, making its way over my throat until he wraps his hand around my neck.

"Say my name, the one you use when you don't think I can hear you. I want to feel it vibrate against your throat when you moan it." He rolls his lower lip between his teeth as I lift my chin for him to rub his thumb down the column of my neck.

"Devil," I whisper, and he starts to fuck me harder.

"There we go. That's my girl. So perfect. Taking my cock like it belongs to you," he mutters as I wrap my leg tighter and raise my hips to meet his strokes. "You can take more, can't you? You can take all of me fast and hard like this because you were made for it. Made for me."

"Fuck..." I gasp as he takes on a pace that hits me nearly perfectly every time. Each stroke takes me closer to the cliff he's ready to push me off. "You're so fucking evil. It's unfair how fucking good you are at that."

He grips me tighter, bringing me nearly to the edge. "Fuck me. How wet you get... The way you soak my cock. That's what's unfair."

I dig my teeth into my lower lip as I start to come, the pleasure blooming like tiny sparks that spread as embers would, melding into one another until they're explosions through every nerve ending in my body. It's better than anything he's given me before this, somehow more perfect and more overwhelming because of the way he's looking at me right now—like he's in awe of me, of us.

He leans down, pressing his cheek to mine, and I swear I'm on the verge of a second crest, one he takes me over as I hear him whimper softly on the edge of his own orgasm. Grant Stockton whimpering because he's about to come? That sound is going to live in infamy.

"Oh fuck. I'm gonna come again." I murmur the words

against his ear, and it takes him with me as he starts to groan his release. I can't stop the flood of praise that comes out of me as I come a second time. "That's right. Fuck me full of you, Cowboy. You feel so fucking good." His breathing is heavy and hard, and every stroke of his cock feels like he's marking me again and again. "Fill me up until you're leaking down my thighs. I need it. I need *you*."

He collapses a moment later, his head hanging low and his lips lazily kissing a circle over my shoulder. He's quiet as he rolls off to my side and catches his breath, staring at the ceiling until his eyes shutter.

"Hellfire..." My nickname is a slow breath on his lips. "I know I gave you a hard time, but whatever that just was... the filthy way you talk. I think I just found a new thing I like."

I giggle at his honesty; the pure, unfiltered way he speaks feels like we've finally pushed through whatever wall was between us. I roll over onto my stomach and kiss my way up his arm, resting my head on his shoulder. His arm wraps around me, and he kisses the top of my head.

"If I wasn't ruined before, that definitely sealed it," he murmurs against my hair, and I close my eyes.

I'm finally the thing I never thought I'd ever be. A feeling I thought was out of reach, given the number of times I've tried to find it and failed. I can't bring myself to say the words out loud yet, but they're echoing through my chest all the same.

THIRTY-FIVE

G RANT

"WHERE ARE YOU GOING?" I wake up to the sight of her wiggling into her jean shorts. "I was gonna get at least another couple of rounds out of you this morning." I wrap my hand around the back of her thigh, and she smiles down at me. I glance at the clock; it's still early. We have to be back at the hotel by eight, but we've got time.

"I need my morning coffee, or I'll turn into a praying mantis and rip your head off." She grabs an old Johnny Cash shirt off the back of her chair in the corner of the room and pulls it over her head. "It won't take long, and I'll be right back in bed."

"Well... that's fair. At least let me go get it for you then. You got some in the house?" I sit up.

"No, I always go over to Marlowe's. I was just gonna sneak over and get one. Do you want one?"

"I'll get it. You just stay naked in this bed." I slip out from under the sheets and grab my jeans, putting them on while I nod back to her side of the bed.

"If you walk over to Hotcakes with your bed head and the clothes you had on last night, word is gonna get back to Marlowe before we do." She looks at me skeptically, her eyes falling over my appearance. "If Mrs. McDaniel sees you, the whole town is gonna know."

"Fuck 'em. They're gonna know soon enough." I wink at her and pull my shirt on as I watch her sink back onto the bed.

"But last night you said..." Her brows draw together.

"That was before we both said a lot of other things, sweetheart." I lean over and kiss her cheek. "How do you like your coffee?"

"At this hour, black as midnight."

"Any sugar?" I ask, and she nods. "How much?"

"If you tell Emma it's for me. She knows."

"All right. Back in a minute." I head out the door and down the stairs before she can fight me anymore. But a second later, I hear the door to her apartment and the pattering of her feet down the hall after me.

"Grant!"

"Yeah, Hellfire?"

"A couple of croissants with some jam too? I'll need the energy." She gives me a teasing grin, and I'm half tempted to run back up the stairs to kiss it off her face. But then I remember the threat of violence without coffee and think better of it.

"You got it." I smirk.

I don't think I've been this excited to still be alive when I wake up in the morning in years. I haven't been this fucking excited for breakfast in... well... ever.

But then I feel it—the slightest rumble under my feet

before the searing blast of hot air. A fraction of a second and my whole world is ripped apart.

WHEN I COME TO, I feel like I've been hit by a truck. The room is spinning, and it's hot. So fucking hot I can barely get a breath in. I blink once, twice. Trying to sit up and get my bearings. I'm trying to remember where I am. How I got here. Everything fucking hurts from my skull down to my ankles, and I realize I've landed against the bar, knocking bar stools over and hitting my head on the wooden wall beneath it. I groan as I try to get to my knees. If I can just get some momentum, I can stand up.

Everything comes rushing back to me, and my head snaps to the bottom of the stairs where I'd been standing. She'd been at the top of it. Except I have no idea where the blast came from and if she was closer to it than me. If it's blown the whole second story off the building or taken out that entire side.

"Fuuuuck," I roar as I push myself up, trying and failing to ignore the pain ripping through my body.

I'm running on adrenaline now, taking in the devastation around me as I make my way to her. There's fire burning heavy and thick with smoke. A crater in the ground just a few feet away where more flames lick their way up from the basement. It's an inferno down there. All the bottles of liquor and beer fueling it into a whirlwind of flames that's being fed by the wind blowing in from the shattered windows. It looks like hell has opened up under our feet, and we don't have much time until we go up in flames with it. I have to find her.

I get to the bottom of the stairs, and I can see her. She's collapsed halfway down the steps, a pile of limp limbs, her eyes closed and blood running from the top of her head and hair, dripping its way down her arm to where her hand dangles over the last step. My heart folds in on itself, and I race to her side, shouting her name over and over again.

"Dakota! Dakota!" I cough and sputter, covering my mouth with the sleeve of my shirt as I rush to her. She doesn't answer, and I drop to my knees on the step when I get to her side. She has to be okay. She has to be breathing. I hold my hand over her mouth and nostrils, and I can still feel air. I stare at her for a moment and see her chest rise and fall with shallow breaths.

My mind floods with an overwhelming sense of guilt. She's here because of me. If she dies, it'll be my fault. My own greed and selfishness for wanting to have her for myself has gotten us here. If I hadn't stayed the night, she would be at the hotel safe and sound tucked into the sheets and ready for the wedding today.

Fucking hell. I can't do this now. Right now, I have to act.

"Dakota. I need you to wake up, sweetheart. We have to get out of here." I plead with her gently, running my hand over her arm and shaking her harder when she doesn't respond. I bend down further and yell her name into her ear as I shake her again. "Dakota!"

There's a soft groan from her, followed by a racking cough as her eyes open. She blinks hard and then moves to sit up quickly, crying out in pain in the process. But she's moving, and she's awake. I could cry I'm so fucking happy to see her coughing like this because it means she's breathing.

"We've got to get out of here. There's a bad fire, and the smoke is gonna choke us out. Can you walk, or do you need me to carry you?" I ask.

She moves to stand and falters. I put my arms underneath her shoulder to help give her some support.

"I got you. Just lean on me, and we'll get you out of here," I promise her. The door to the back lot isn't far, only about fifteen feet from here. She halts suddenly, though, and looks back at the stairs and then to me. She opens her mouth to speak and sputters again, pointing up the stairs as tears form in her eyes, and then I realize what she wants.

"Okay, sweetheart. Let me get you to the door, and I'll go get Vendetta."

"No. She might not... for you..." She coughs again, the words fading on her lips. I know she's warning me that Vendetta might not come for me, but I'm not about to take her up with me.

"You're in no shape to get up those stairs. You'll get hurt worse, and I need you safe. Please," I beg her, but she shakes her head.

"I'll stay here. I'll wait then," she insists.

"Fuck me, sweetheart. Okay. Fine. Fine. Here." I rip part of my shirt off and tear the fabric in two, giving her a piece of it. "Cover your mouth. Try not to breathe in too much smoke. Get lower to the ground. If it gets bad, promise me you'll crawl outside."

She nods her agreement, and I cover my mouth and lumber up the steps as fast as I can, doing my best to shut out the pain. The smoke is already getting thicker up here, and given where the explosion happened and the way it blew out the windows, I don't have high hopes for finding Vendetta. But I can't let her down. She loves that cat to pieces, and she's had her since she was a kid. I wiggle the handle but it's locked. Or maybe just wedged shut. I kick at the door, thankful for once that she has one of those old-school doors that's made of MDF. It only takes three swift kicks before it collapses, and I'm inside.

"Vendetta!" I call out, searching the room with my eyes as I hurry from the living room to her bedroom. I check the bathroom and the small spare bedroom she has, but she's nowhere to be found. The cat is skittish on a good day, and I can't imagine an explosion has helped.

I run back to her room, pulling up the skirt and looking under the bed. Vendetta always used to hide under her bed at the ranch. It's worth a shot.

She has a dozen shoe boxes under here and a big box with photos and a photo album. One of them I know has most of her family photos in it. I yank it out and toss it up on the bed. I can at least save that for her.

"Vendetta!" I call for the cat again, choking on the thickening gray plume as I inhale too much smoke with that breath.

Fuck it. I'm going to have to try the one thing I haven't yet. I let out a desperate meow, one that sounds as tortured as I feel right now. I can't go down there and tell her I don't have her cat. She'll come up here and try to find her herself, and we'll all die here together. If I drag her out without the cat that's been by her side for more than a decade, she'll never forgive me. A racked and frustrated groan leaves my chest and then, like fucking magic, I see two bright green eyes at the far side of the bed watching me. I could scream for joy that I've at least found her alive, but it doesn't mean I'll get her to come with me.

"Vendetta, you come here you little fucking brat before you get us all fucking killed," I grumble under my breath. She does the opposite, though, pulling her paws back from my reach and curling up against the wall.

"Fine. We'll do this the hard way." I glare at her through the smoke and shadows.

I pull the album back down to the floor, and then I flip the mattress, moving fast to snatch her up while she's disoriented by the movement. She screams, hissing and swatting and biting as I pull her from the dusty rubble under the bed. She draws blood, marking my whole forearm as she struggles. But I have her.

I take a deep breath and look around for something to put her in. I'm too scared she'll jump out of my arms, and I can't carry her and the album and Dakota. I see a gym bag. The kind that has vents on the sides.

"You're gonna have to forgive me for this." I stuff Vendetta inside along with the album and zip it shut. A screeching meow echoes against the walls, and her green eyes look neon as she glares at me through the vent. I sling the bag over my shoulder, and I take off, racing down the stairs.

"She's inside. Angry but alive. Let's go!" I call to Dakota, but she doesn't answer. She's slumped on the floor unconscious and even bloodier than she was when I left her. "Oh god, Hellfire. Fuck. I knew I should have made you go outside. Please. Please stick with me. You can't leave me now. Not now, sweetheart." I pick up her limp body in my arms, and I hurry for the door, a loud protest from Vendetta at the rough ride, and my heart cracking wide open when we reach the light of the morning sun. Her hair is soaked in blood, and the cut across her forehead is deep. I can't tell how deep from all the mess, but I know it's not good. Not paired with the way she can't stay conscious. I should have taken her out when I had the chance.

I collapse to my knees as we hit the blacktop and lay her down gently. I check her mouth and chest again and see that her shallow breathing is still there. I take a deep breath of the fresh air myself as I reach into my pocket for my phone and pull it out, dialing Levi immediately. Too worried to call 911 with all the harassment she's received. Another cough racks my chest as I wait, and I press my hand to hers, wanting to make sure I can still feel the rise and fall of it.

"Just hang on. Stay with me, sweetheart. I've got you."

"Grant?" Levi's confused voice comes through the line.

"Come to Seven Sins. It just exploded. Bring security."

"Holy fuck..." His words fade with the shock. "Be right there."

I want to get them both somewhere safe. Vendetta somewhere Dakota won't worry about her, and Dakota to a hospital to be evaluated. Right now, I sure as fuck don't trust calling 911, and I'm desperately wishing I'd driven myself.

Minutes pass, and it feels like hours as we wait for someone to come get us. I feel exposed and anxious as I wait. It's the worst fucking feeling in the world just staring at her hopelessly. No amount of money or power or fear I've instilled in the people in this town can save her for me. Nothing I have, no skill, no chip to call in is going to keep her alive for me. It's just up to fate now, and I feel so sick and helpless I can barely breathe.

I want to scream for someone to help, but the alley is dead at this hour of the morning, and at the back of the building, there's no one to see or hear us. I can hear the wail of a siren in the distance though. Someone overheard the explosion and called 911. Fuck, the patrons at Hotcakes had a front row seat for the explosion. The last thing I want to do is deal with cops who are about to show up or have them try to convince me to let her go with the EMTs. I briefly consider breaking into one of the cars and taking off to the hospital that way.

"Grant!" I hear a familiar voice and look to see Levi there with the car.

"Thank fuck. We've got to get her to a hospital. She's lost a lot of blood from her head. She can't stay conscious," I say as he jumps out to help me load her and Vendetta into the back seat. I slide in next to her, holding her up.

He speeds off, glancing up at me in the rearview. "You want to discuss it now or later?"

"Explosion. Came from the basement. Could only be a gas leak or a bomb. I lean toward bomb with the way it ripped the place apart. Too many coincidences, considering they just cleared the place out tonight too." I explain the thoughts that have already been running through my head.

"You think it's the cops or them again?"

"No idea. Doesn't feel like an accident though."

"She get hit by something, or?"

"Blown off the stairs. I found her collapsed halfway down them. There's too much blood, and it's too dark for me to see. We just need an emergency room, fast." I look down at her and press my fingers to her pulse point. She still has one, but she's fading fast.

Levi runs three lights as he speeds his way onto the highway. The small hospital is two more exits from here, and I'm just hoping we get her there in time.

"We're almost there, Dakota. Just hang on. Okay? Vendetta and I need you. So you gotta fight, sweetheart." I squeeze her hand and kiss her temple. I hold my ear to her lips to listen to her breathing, and the whisper of breath in response threatens to take me under. The thought of her not making it has me ready to lose my goddamn mind. My first priority is finding a doctor who's going to save her life whatever the cost, but then I'm going to take another when I find whoever did this.

THIRTY-SIX

G RANT

"FUCK ME," I curse as Levi shows me the bombs that were rigged to blow in the belly of the Avarice's bar. All in the champagne cases we ordered for the wedding. "They planned to kill all of us."

"The ones at Seven Sins went off early." Levi surveys the evidence.

"Didn't realize they were taking the 'All Stocktons Must Die' so fucking seriously." I run a hand through my hair, and I can feel it sticking up in every direction under my fingers.

None of us have slept. I haven't even showered. I'm still covered in blood and ash from the bar.

Once I knew Dakota was safe in the hospital, out of danger with her head wound, and with Hazel and Ramsey at her side, I came straight here to help Levi. When the fire department put out the fire, they told him they suspected it was an explosion somewhere in the liquor storage room that had blown the place apart. It set off alarm bells for Levi when I mentioned the champagne I'd given Dakota, and he found this when he investigated. Luckily, he knew a guy who was EOD out of Ft. Carson—who owed us a favor and his silence. But now I'm staring at a dozen diffused bombs and wondering who could hate us so much they'd want to kill our family. We had enemies, sure, but I'd never imagined it was enough to turn a whole wedding bloody.

"Have you told Hudson yet?"

"No. I only told him about Seven Sins. Let him know the wedding is off. Fuck. What about all the guests?" I suddenly think about all the things Dakota will ask about when she has a moment to breathe again. The guests, the food, the staff—all of it will cause her to panic if I don't make sure we take care of it first.

"Aspen has it under control. She helped Bristol and Marlowe work with Hazel's brothers to let the guest list know the wedding is postponed. Then she worked with the hotel staff to make sure everyone would still get some dinner and cake delivered to their rooms."

"I'd forgotten how nice it is to have our sister around."

"Think we can get her to move back home now that Ethan's gonna be out of the picture? She can take over this shit, and we can take a vacation." Levi smirks.

I laugh, needing it after the day I've had. "Somehow, I doubt it. But fuck, after today..."

"We need to bring Hudson in on this. If this is all related to the relic and whoever wanted it..."

"He could be a target as much as us," I acknowledge.

Levi presses his lips together and raises his brows.

I pull my phone out of my pocket only to see that I have several missed calls and texts from him.

H.K.:

Call me as soon as you see this. It's urgent.

"Well fuck, he's already been trying to get a hold of me," I explain to Levi before I hit the call button.

"Where are you?" Hudson answers the phone with a question.

"Downstairs at the bar. Are you still here in the hotel?"

"Yes. I'm coming down. Meet me in the chess room?"

"See you there."

"I CAN'T FIND the shell corporation that owns the bidder account. But I found the one that owns the house. It took my guy several layers deep, but he found one of the owners."

"Someone we know?" I'm guessing by the disturbed look on Hudson's face that it isn't a good answer.

"This room—it's compartmentalized from the rest of the place?" Hudson asks. I've never seen him strung this tight in the entirety of our business dealings.

"Yes."

"Do you have your phone on you?" he asks quietly.

I nod. I usually don't bring it into this room, but I needed to know if anything happened with Dakota. He shakes his head and then mimics me turning it off. I do as he asks, and Levi follows suit. We place them in a box on the far side of the room, and Hudson grabs a piece of paper and a pen from the book-shelf before walking us to the far corner. He scrawls across it quickly and then holds it out for us.

ABBOTT SCHAEFER

I stare at it blankly for a moment before I can even begin to process what I'm seeing—what it means. The Governor of Colorado owns the home where the relic came to rest after we sold it, which likely means he was the one who bought it. Which could mean he's the one who sent us after it all those years ago, and the same one who burned down the Kellys' ancestral home trying to cover up the theft of the second relic.

He also would have been the one who appointed the new sheriff—my uncle. The same one who ran the police department that was harassing Dakota. The same man who would have known exactly where and what to target in this building because I gave him all the details when I invited him.

"Fuckkkkk." I roar the word, and Levi falls back against the wall in shock as he has the same realization. Hudson takes a lighter out of his pocket and sets the paper on fire, tossing it into the wastebasket as we all watch it turn to ash.

It feels like a metaphor for my entire life right now.

"I didn't think he was that far gone," he mutters under his breath.

"Nothing's safe here if this is what we're up against. Nothing and *no one*." My mind immediately goes to Dakota, Hazel, and Ramsey at the hospital. "I have to get back to them. Make sure they're safe and take them somewhere we've got more security."

"The hotel's not safe. Not after knowing this and the bombs. It could be anyone on staff who helped him." Levi keeps his voice low.

"The bombs?" Hudson asks in a surprised whisper.

"They rigged the whole wedding—the reception room would have been full of bombs disguised as champagne bottles. They were going to kill everyone who attended," I explain.

"Two birds, one stone." Levi shifts his finger between the two of us, and Hudson's face falls.

"Rowan's with Charlotte now. But we should get everyone out of this hotel. There's no telling what they'll do now that they know the wedding's been postponed. If they figure out that we've discovered them..." Hudson trails off.

"I agree. We need to get our family off the streets. But there's one family member in particular I'd like to have in a room alone right now." I grit out the words, surveying the floor of the bar. Full of people who are completely clueless to how close we all came to being dead.

"We'll get him. But let's get our family rounded up and safe first. The ranch?" Levi looks to me to confirm his suggestion.

"The ranch. Do we know what security we can trust?"

"The usual inner circle. We'll get them on the ranch, and we'll lock down all the gates. I have drones we can put up to help patrol who's going on and off the property, and we updated all the cameras last year after the incident with the Flanagans." Levi's already putting a plan into action.

"Do it. I'll go to the hospital if she's not discharged yet and make sure we're all on the same page. Can you get Aspen read in on things?" I ask, and Levi nods. Then I turn to Hudson. "You, Charlotte, and Rowan should come too. It'll be safer there than here until we get to the bottom of the whole situation. We had our security team run an inspection on the whole building after we found the champagne situation, but there's always the chance we could have missed something. I'd like to do another round first."

"Always a chance that they'll try to strike again while the iron's hot, and we're still disoriented." Hudson gives me a worried look.

"Agreed. So you'll come?"

"If you'll have us. We can squeeze in wherever there's

room. I just want to get through the night to get the jet ready and send Charlotte back to Cincinnati. Rowan or I can stay with you to help work out a solution."

"I'm sure Hazel can get you a couple rooms at the inn."

I'm almost positive there isn't a solution to a problem of this magnitude, but I was grateful as fuck he was willing to help pretend there was for a little while longer while I figure out how to keep my family safe.

"Hazel and Ramsey might want to head back to Cincinnati too. The Chaos start training camp soon, and it's probably a hell of a lot safer than being here for them anyway." Hudson makes a good point. I nod along with his assessment and make one of my own. I can't bring myself to say it yet, but if Hazel and Ramsey go back, Dakota should go with them.

THIRTY-SEVEN

D AKOTA

THE NEXT DAY, after a night of observation and Hazel hovering over me the entire time, I'm finally allowed to leave in the afternoon. I have a mild concussion, and the wounds to my head had needed stitched. Because of the blood and the concussion, they wanted to keep me for the night and run a few more tests, making sure that they hadn't missed anything before they released me back to the wild. I was anxious to leave and find out what was going on with Seven Sins and with Grant.

Grant stayed with me for as long as he could at the hospital. But his phone hadn't stopped silently buzzing in his pocket, and each time, the news seemed more dire than the last, judging by the look on his face—not that he shared anything with me. He was too concerned about my stress levels while I was recovering. I finally told him to stop worrying about me and go do what he needed to. When Hazel arrived with Ramsey, they eventually convinced him to get a shower and deal with business at home.

"I feel awful that you're having to take care of me. You should be on your honeymoon." I look at Hazel as she and Ramsey help me get out of the truck and into the ranch house.

"Don't feel awful. I don't want to be anywhere else right now. The wedding and the honeymoon are just getting moved to a new date. Right now, family is the priority." Hazel smiles at me as she links our arms, and we walk up the steps together.

"Well, I love you for everything. I really can find somewhere else to stay if you all want to have the place to yourselves." I feel guilty because I know Hazel made Ramsey wait all week, and the last thing he probably wants is me monopolizing all her time.

"You can find a place when you're feeling better and have a chance to recover. You've been through a lot in the last twenty-four hours. Let's focus on you first, okay?" Hazel gives me a meaningful look, and I lean my head against her shoulder.

"I don't know what I'd do without you." There aren't good words for friends like her, the kind who take care of you through thick and thin—best friend doesn't begin to cover it.

"I don't know what I'd do without *you*. I was so scared when I heard, and then I just kept thinking about how chaotic the last month has been. You've been busting your ass for a month helping me get everything together, and now this. The world isn't fucking fair, that's for sure." She leads me into a guest room, and I look around at what I recognize as Grant's old bedroom. "Now there's a bathroom off this room that's all yours, and I brought some of my clothes in here for you so you have something to change into out of this. I got some basics for you at the store—bras, underwear, pajamas, a few T-shirts, and jeans. That stuff's in the wash now, and I'll have it for you in a couple of hours. The toiletries and suitcase you had at the Avarice are being sent over too."

"I need to get food for Vendetta and get my prescriptions refilled." I sigh. There was such a long list of things I'd need to replace. I feel tears sting my eyes just thinking about it. "I have to get my car from the Avarice."

"Ramsey'll bring it over later. Don't worry about that. I already got some food for Vendetta. I don't know if it's up to her bougie tastes, but I grabbed some cream and treats, too, so she won't go hungry. Can you call stuff in to the pharmacy in the city? We can run down if they've got it in stock." Hazel reassures me.

"Yes. Thank you. You're the best, honestly. I'm just so overwhelmed with how many things I have to think about."

"I think being overwhelmed is allowed, given the circumstances. I would be too. But we got you. Anything you need, we'll get it figured out. I didn't want to get you anything too fancy clothes-wise because I figure you want to pick that stuff out yourself. I just wanted to get you through the week first."

"Thank you. Truly. Are you leaving? I heard you guys talking."

"Grant wants us all out of town. He thinks there's something nefarious behind all this. That it wasn't an accident. That's all I know right now." She sighs and sits down on the bed next to me. "Ramsey needs to be back in Cincinnati by late next week. I'd planned to go with him to get him settled after the honeymoon and then come back here for a bit. I've got everything I need there already, so there's no reason I can't go, but... I don't want you here alone. You and Vendetta should probably pack up and come stay with us. I know that's a lot of change in a few days, but..." Hazel's brow creases with worry as she looks me over.

"I'll talk to Grant. If he's staying, I'd rather stay here.

Maybe I can stay with Bristol or Marlowe." I run my hand over the quilt on the bed absently.

"No, if you stay, you can stay right here. Even if we go, the house is yours. I don't want to leave you here alone though. Feels like a bad idea."

"I won't be alone. The girls are here." I needed to call Marlowe and Bristol and let them know I'm okay. I'm sure Hazel already has, but I know they'll want to hear from me since I told them not to bother coming to the hospital today when I found out I was leaving.

"I mean, on the ranch. If it's as dangerous as Grant let on. Dakota, there's a lot you don't know about this family. There's a lot I can't tell you because you're better off not knowing. But I don't want your association with us to end up with anything worse than what's already happened. You could have died in that explosion, and if it turns out not to be an accident—" Hazel's tone turns more serious.

"You don't think it was an accident then?"

"I don't know. But... the fire at the barn last year wasn't, and neither were a lot of other things that went wrong over the years. I don't know what Grant has told you yet, but, it's bad."

"I mean. I was suspicious about some of it." We exchange awkward glances. I know she probably can't tell me the family secrets. As close as Grant and I have gotten, as much as these people feel like family to me, they're not. I can understand wanting to keep some things quiet.

"Like I said, it's better if you don't know all the dirty details. I'd rather let Grant share things with you. But I couldn't live with myself if something else happened. I think you'd be better off coming back with us to Cincinnati. You could stay with me, and we could come back here together. Give yourself some time to recover and plan what you want to do next. I'd say Hayden's there too, but it feels like maybe that ship has sailed."

She gives me a questioning look, and I know what she's asking without saying the words.

"You could just ask, you know."

"Okay. Well, I know he could have had other reasons to be there, but it was awfully early in the morning, and the way he was panicking about you being hurt at the hospital... I'm kind of making some assumptions. You can tell me they're the wrong ones."

"No. You're right to assume, but I don't know what we are. Or if we're anything. Things have been different between us this last year, and then it started escalating. Last night was the first time we actually slept together. Feels like a pretty bad sign when the whole place explodes the next morning." I laugh even though the tears are still threatening to fall again. Yesterday morning I'd been the happiest I can remember being in a long time. Today feels impossibly bleak in comparison, and I don't think I've even fully comprehended all the consequences yet.

"If he's anything like his brother, that just kind of happens. Usually not quite so literally though." Hazel laughs and nudges me gently.

"It's been fast and intense the last few weeks, but it felt natural like... Everything just led us here." I sigh. "I don't know that he feels that way. In fact, I think after this morning, he probably feels like it was all a giant mistake. Especially given how he feels about Jesse and the past and all that."

"How do you feel?" She gives me a thoughtful look, her eyes searching mine.

"It was... it felt *right* with him. For the first time in a long time —maybe ever. We just get each other in a way that I don't think is possible with anyone else. He knows me in a way I've never been able to let anyone else in. But... I feel like he's gonna break my heart one way or the other. I'm not stupid. I know who he is. I know a man like him isn't the kind you make a boyfriend out of. He's not made of the right kind of material. Hell, he's not even Ramsey material." My lips twist to the side as I try not to cry again. "But I can't stop hoping it works out somehow. Is that crazy?" The tears come anyway, and Hazel wraps her arms around me.

"I don't think it's wrong to hope. Not at all. Honestly, I think he loves you in his own way. He's just bad at showing it sometimes. Even with his own family. And the history you two have—it's obvious he cares about you deeply, Dakota."

"I know he cares. That's all I need to know right now," I say softly, hugging her back. "I'm just scared he's going to push me away after all this, and other than you and the girls, he's the person I need right now. You know?"

"I know." She brushes my hair out of my face. "Just be careful with your heart, okay? Don't let him break you because you gave more than he deserved. I don't want to have to fight him."

"I won't make you fight him." I laugh.

"Good, because he did kinda squash his curmudgeon-ness for me and put up with a lot of my bullshit leading up to this wedding. But I'd cut him in a second if I thought he hurt you deliberately."

"I know you would." I offer her half a smile, and she rubs her hand over my back. "Speaking of. What are you doing about the wedding? Is there anything I need to do? I can help now that I'm out."

"Absolutely not. Bristol, Marlowe, and Aspen put my brothers to work, and between them all, they called the whole guest list and got it all handled. Delayed until further notice. Ramsey's already talked about a quick trip to Vegas this week or a courthouse in Cincinnati. That's how our friends did it, but I'd rather wait and see. I still think we might be able to sneak in a wedding somewhere before the season. Just nothing quite so fancy like he wanted."

"I'm so sorry, Hazel. I hate this for you. You two deserve the big wedding and the big fancy honeymoon. Could you still do that at least?" I squeeze her hand.

"We were able to get our money back. So I don't know. I suppose we could still go if Ramsey wants to at some point. But again, with everything going on... I don't think he could relax and enjoy it. I definitely couldn't, but I'd try to make the best of it if it would help him get ready for the season." She lets out her own long sigh.

"I mean it, if there's anything I can do. I'll just be sitting around until I find out what insurance will cover and what the fire department has to say about causes. I can be put to work!"

"I love you for that, but I'm thinking we just eat some of the wedding food and cake. I don't know about you, but I could stand to drown myself in some buttercream frosting right about now."

"That sounds perfect." I grin at her.

"All right. Get yourself a shower and whatever else you need, and I'll meet you back out in the living room in a bit. I'm gonna check on a few things, and then we can relax. Sound good?" Hazel smiles at me, and I hug her one more time.

"I don't know what I'd do without you."

"Same." She squeezes me tight and then leaves me to my thoughts, closing the door in her wake.

THIRTY-EIGHT

D AKOTA

WHEN GRANT SHOWS up at the ranch house looking downtrodden and somber, I do my best to give him and his brother space. He goes into the study and talks to Ramsey for a long time while Hazel and I sit out on the couch eating cake. I've lost the plot of whatever we're watching because my mind's already racing with worries over what Grant's found out. What it will mean for him and his family, and for us—if there even is an us now.

He was good to me at the hospital, sitting by my side and holding my hand while we waited for all the test results. But I know he got at least one phone call from Levi that didn't go well. He came back into the room rattled even though he played it off like it was nothing. After Hazel and Ramsey convinced him to leave, it had been radio silence, not a text or a call, but I know it's because he hasn't had a moment's peace today and likely didn't get much, if any, sleep last night. As soon as he's out of his meeting with Ramsey, I plan to turn the tables on him and insist he sit down and eat. Get some rest. Try to give himself a break.

He doesn't argue much when I do—too tired to protest, I guess. He sits down at the table while I reheat one of the meals Kit brought over for us. I watch as Ramsey nods for Hazel to follow him up the stairs, and she gives me a sympathetic look before she disappears. The kind that says she knows what it's like to have to deal with a Stockton brother in this condition. It won't be an easy conversation.

"I'm sorry about leaving the hospital before you were ready to go. If I could have stayed with you, I would have. You know that, right?" He apologizes before anything else, and it makes my heart ache that he feels like he has to.

"I know." I shake my head and smile at him. "I'm not upset. I know Levi needed you, and I know you wouldn't have left if it wasn't important. You don't have to explain. But is everything okay?" It's a silly question. I know it's not. I'm just trying to ease into this conversation as slowly as I can.

"You have to go with them back to Cincinnati." He says it like an order, and I bristle.

It's not the same easy back and forth we had before the explosion. It's the old cold and calculating tone he used when he thought I was misbehaving and needed to be put back in line. I expected a backslide; I knew that the explosion and the escalation of violence would make him go back to holding the line on how dangerous he was for me. I was prepared for that and ready to let him take time to come around, but I didn't expect him to try to send me across the country.

"What am I going to do in Cincinnati? I've got nothing there," I dispute calmly, hoping I can get him to see reason.

"Hazel and Ramsey will be there. Charlotte will be there. Most importantly, it's far away from the clusterfuck here. You could have died yesterday, Dakota." His eyes pierce mine with a look of remorse.

"I can't impose on Hazel and Ramsey right now. They're still reeling from the canceled wedding and honeymoon. They have their own challenges at the moment, and I don't think they want me in their house like a third wheel. I feel awkward enough being in their way here." I keep my voice even, doing my best not to turn this into an argument.

"You're not in their way. They love you and just want to be sure you're okay. If you don't want to stay with them, you can stay with Charlotte. I'd rather you stay at the Kellys' residence anyway. It's a fortress, and there's no chance of you being a third wheel there." There's a hint of levity in his last statement but not enough to distract either of us from the seriousness of the conversation.

"I barely know them. It would be every bit as awkward, just in a different way." Hudson and Charlotte seemed genuine when I'd spent time with them over the last week, but there's a difference between liking new acquaintances and moving in with them.

"They're good people. I've suggested Ramsey and Hazel stay there too. With him being gone at practices and camp all hours of the day, Hazel would be better off somewhere with more security."

"I want to stay here at the ranch. You have all this security swarming the grounds." I point out the window as another security truck passes down the road in front of the house. "It's as safe as anywhere." I set his dinner in front of him.

"There won't be anyone here to stay with you when Hazel and Ramsey leave. Ramsey has to be back at camp, and there's no way in hell he'll let Hazel stay back without him."

"I've lived alone all my adult life. It won't be any different." I sit down across from him at the table, trying and hoping he can remember that as much as I've learned to appreciate his help, I don't need it.

"Minus the fact that someone could sneak onto this property and into the ranch house and kill you in the middle of the night—or worse." His face clouds with the thought.

"They could have done that in my apartment. You don't think that's a fear every single woman in existence lives with in the back of her mind every night of her life?"

"I'm saying the chances the fear becomes reality are infinitely fucking higher at the moment." He loses his patience, putting his fork back down on the table even though he's barely had a taste of the food.

"So stay with me." I can tell he wasn't expecting that argument when his brow furrows, and he shakes his head.

"That's a bad idea."

"Nowhere safer I could be than with you. You'd do a lot more for me than some random security guard in Ohio would. And it would help my anxiety to know you were okay."

"I'm not okay. I'm neck-deep in a war I inherited, and I don't even know who all the players are on the board. They tried to kill my entire family and Hudson's, along with our friends, and I didn't even see it coming. *Nothing* is okay right now." It's a rare moment of vulnerability for him to admit he doesn't have all the answers. I soften my tone when I speak again because I want him to know above all, I'm here for him.

"Then all the more reason I want to be here. You need someone who can be there for you too. You don't have to do all this alone." I reach out and put my hand on his forearm, and I'm relieved when he doesn't pull away from me.

I know the accident ripped open old wounds for him. I know it dragged up every fear he has, and I can't blame him for it. But I'm scared he'll push me away in the process and never let me back in. My leaving will only make it that much easier for him to wall himself off again.

"I have Levi. I have Hudson. People who can help me deal with the problem. You're not in a position to do that, and I don't want you to be. I want you clear of this entire fucking mess. I want you somewhere safe. I can't take a second time like yesterday morning. Holding you with you bleeding like that and not answering me. I thought I'd gotten you killed too." His hand comes up and covers mine, and his eyes search for under-standing. I can't give him the easy agreement he wants, but I know fighting him might just make him shut down more. The last thing he needs is an argument about feelings when he's just trying to survive and make sure the rest of us do as well, so I do my best to temper my response.

"If you're asking me, I'd rather be here by your side rather than get the news in Cincinnati via a phone call. You're worried for your family—so am I. You're the closest thing I have to family. You can't ask me to just walk away from that, knowing all the risks you're taking on, and just hope there's something left whenever I come back. Please don't ask that of me."

"I can't do my job if I have to worry about you, Hellfire. I can't. I can't think straight if I'm always thinking about you."

"Then stop thinking about me and start trusting me to be able to make decisions for myself. You've got security on the ranch. It's just as safe as Hudson's, given that they're after him too. Here, at least you can check in on me, you can know I'm close by, and I can check on you."

"Dakota..." My name is a curse ripping out of his throat like a desperate plea. "You don't understand. It's not safe. It's not the same."

"Then make me understand. Tell me. If you can trust your

brothers and Hudson—you can trust me." I hold my ground even though I know I'm risking a bigger fight.

He drops his hold on me and leans back, straightening his spine for a moment before his shoulders slump. I see him give in. He scrubs a hand through his hair, mussing it as he looks into the distance before he turns back to me, a dire look on his face.

"It's the fucking governor and the sheriff behind the bombings—my uncle tried to kill us. A person who knows every dirty fucking secret this family has going back generations and a man who has the power to make all of this, all of us, disappear with a few quick strokes of his pen. A long prison term or death by cop. That's what I'm up against. It's a death sentence either way. There isn't a way out. You stay and get caught up in it somehow, it's a death sentence for you too. I can't live with that."

We sit in silence, staring at each other as I soak the information in. I see now why he didn't tell me. Just knowing that little bit is probably a liability. One he doesn't take lightly as he tilts his head down, and I can see the agony wavering behind the deep pools of blue.

He looks defeated, the cracks from all the weight of this on his shoulders starting to show through the facade of confidence. I know inside he's desperate for some way to control the situation and put everything back to rights, make sure no one sees the house of cards start to teeter on the table. I just want him to know he's not alone.

"You're sure it's your uncle?" This family's loyalty was unshakeable.

"Yes. Levi found the evidence and looked through the security footage. We were able to figure out which employees were handling deliveries that day, and Levi took one aside. He explained everything. He didn't even realize he was being used.

Completely distraught about it. He was a longtime employee and thought he was doing a favor for my uncle. He knew him back in the day, and my uncle told him it was a surprise for us to have that champagne. No idea there were bombs inside." He grimaces. "One hell of a fucking surprise to try to kill what's left of your family."

"That's fucked." We could have all been dead on Hazel's wedding day. I feel my stomach tumble with the information. Another realization hits me hard. "And that's why the explosion happened at Seven Sins. How you know already that it wasn't a gas leak. You sent the champagne over as a gift." The pieces fall together finally. Grant knew the champagne for the wedding was a favorite of mine too, and as a sweet gesture, he'd sent a few cases over as a gift earlier this week. We'd stored them in the cellar for safekeeping when they arrived without opening them.

"Yeah." The hard facade threatens to fall. "This is what I meant when I said I'm a danger to you even when I don't mean to be, even when I shouldn't be. An innocent fucking thing like that could have gotten you killed because someone wants *me* dead. You see now?"

"You can't help that someone you trusted—your family, for god's sake—tried to do this to you. You went on the same instinct anyone would have. There's no way you could have known or stopped that, Grant. You can't take that guilt on your shoulders. I don't blame you." I try to help him see that some things are out of his control, the same way they are for all of us, but I can tell from the set of his shoulders that he's not buying what I'm saying. He's already laying the bricks of the wall back down, one by one.

"Whether you blame me or not, it's my fault. It's just the facts of the matter." He shakes his head, turning to look out the window and blinking rapidly to stop the tears. "And my instincts are shot to shit. Too fucking distracted to make the right decisions." The last bit sounds like he's repeating something someone told him, and if I find out who, I might cut them myself.

"This will get better; it just feels like it won't right now. I know. I feel the same way about Seven Sins."

"I'm sorry. Fuck. Here I am rambling on about my shit, and I don't even stop to tell you how sorry I am about that. I'm so fucked up right now, Dakota. I'm sorry."

"You don't have to apologize. I know you've got a lot on your plate." I pat his hand again, wishing it was magic that could cure his worries. "I'm here if you need me. Your siblings are here. You don't have to do this alone."

He nods and stays silent for a moment before he speaks again.

"I thought having Ramsey back... Seeing Aspen. Fuck even Hazel coming back into the fold. I thought it would feel the way it used to, but nothing's the same. The peace never fucking lasts. Just feels like I'm constantly scrambling to try to stop time and keep everyone safe for long enough to enjoy a week, a day, an hour." His tone is laced with regret and worry.

"You take a lot of that weight on your shoulders, and you've got to learn to share it with the rest of us who want to help. You can't control everything, Grant."

He presses his lips together and makes a soft grunt of acknowledgment just as the front door opens. I hear voices in the hall, Hazel and Ramsey, along with Levi and Aspen, and someone younger. Aspen comes around the corner to find us sitting at the kitchen table.

"Sorry if we're interrupting. Levi's getting ready to take Fallon and me to the airport, and I wanted to say one last good-bye," Aspen interrupts.

"Where's Fallon?" Grant's concern skyrockets when he

doesn't immediately see his niece. All those frayed edges Aspen warned me about are coming undone.

"She's going with Hazel out to the barn. She wanted to say bye to the horses."

Grant smiles in return and stands to hug his sister. "All right. Tell her I hope her college trips go well, and if she wants a horse for her eighteenth all she has to do is ask."

"I'll be sure to tell her that." Aspen hugs him a little tighter before she says, "We'll have to think about the horse." She laughs and smiles at him, clearly trying to lift his spirits, but her smile fades to worry. "I'll miss you."

"I'm sorry you're leaving like this," Grant apologizes, and I can hear the pain in his voice.

"I'm sorry it's come to this. You know I'd stay if it wasn't for Fallon." Aspen's face falls as she looks over her oldest brother. I imagine she sees the same cracks I can.

"I wouldn't let you. I want you all as far away from here as you can get." Grant shakes his head as he lets go of her.

"I told her the same," Levi interjects.

"It was good to see you again, Dakota." Aspen holds her arms out, and I stand quickly to hug her.

"You too," I agree, giving her a quick squeeze.

"Let me walk you out to the car so I can say goodbye to Fallon," Grant offers, and Aspen nods her agreement.

"I'll meet you all out there in a few." Levi nods them off, and the way he waits, I can tell he wants to talk to me.

"Grant told me about the incident at the Avarice. I'm so sorry you're having to deal with all of this," I say quietly.

Levi shrugs. "We're used to it. That's life. One fucking thing after another, and then you die."

"I just wish they could have had their wedding. Given your family a chance to celebrate something."

"Me too, but once we get through this, we'll celebrate.

Maybe even more than before once we've taken care of business." Levi pulls his glasses off, brushing the edge of his shirt over the lens and then returning them to their place.

The man was a mashup of contradictions. Tall and muscular with glasses and intricately designed patterns of tattoos, wise and patient, but with a temper that rivaled both of his brothers' combined. He's the kind of man you'd love to meet in a bookshop cafe and sip an iced espresso with while you read together in the middle of the day, and the last man you'd want to meet in a dark alley at night.

I don't want to be on his bad side, but I worry I will be if he thinks I'm causing his brother any more distractions or stress. Which is where I think this conversation is headed.

"We can cut the small talk. If there's something you want to say..." I offer because I'd rather just rip the Band-aid off.

He straightens his glasses, pushing them back on the bridge of his nose, and leans against the doorframe. He surveys me for a moment like he's underestimated me and wants to reassess how he approaches the conversation.

"Can we skip the sugarcoating too? I'd like to just talk freely, as two people who care about him and this family."

"You can." I stand a little straighter, glad at least that he respects the fact I don't need my hand held to discuss the issue at hand.

"He's going to tell you that you need to leave if he hasn't already. And you're going to be tempted to argue with him. I know how stubborn you both are and how much the two of you enjoy fighting as foreplay—but you need to do what he's asking. If you love him, you won't fight him on this."

"We're discussing it," I say tersely, feeling off-kilter by Levi pressing the point so hard.

"There's nothing to discuss. You're a walking, talking distraction for him. One he can't afford. Not right now. It could cost him his life—or yours or someone else in this family, which would be as much a death sentence as anything, given the way it would wreck him."

"He explained the seriousness of the situation, but he also needs someone who can support him. His mental state is exactly why I don't want to leave," I argue because Levi strikes me as someone who's every bit as hard as his brother but without the soft underbelly. He needs someone like Levi at his side, and I'm glad he has him, but he needs the other side of the coin too.

"His mental state is why you have to leave. You can support him from a safe distance, just like our siblings, where he knows you're out of their reach and behind lines they can't cross. Part of being strong in this situation is doing the thing you don't want to do because it's the right thing, Dakota. The right thing for him. The right thing for you. I'm not trying to be cruel or unfeeling. If you make each other happy—I want that for him. But you both have to survive this for there to be a future, and that only happens if you let him make choices with a clear head."

"I'll take it into consideration." I say the words like I mean them because as much as I hate it, the things he's saying make sense.

"That's all I ask." He nods and heads outside, looking back with a sympathetic glance one last time before the door closes, and I feel the tears start to stain my cheeks again.

I know Levi is right. It's the reason all of his siblings who aren't part of whatever they're planning are leaving like this. They're not running scared. They're leaving so that he has as many options on the table as he can get. So he can gamble freely without having to worry about what he could lose. I just worry that without someone here to remind him how much he's needed, he'll be willing to gamble everything away to save us.

THIRTY-NINE

G RANT

"LISTEN. While we wait for Fallon, I need to tell you something. I did a lot of thinking during this trip, and between things with Ethan falling apart and how much Fallon loves it out here, along with how much I miss you all... I met with a colleague in Highland State's archaeology department, and she was excited about the projects I've been working on. There's a chance something might open, and if it does, I'm thinking about moving back," Aspen announces quietly as we get out on the porch of the family home. My eyes meet hers, and she must see the fear-stricken look in them because she presses her hand to my shoulder reassuringly. "Not now. Not until you've dealt with whatever this is that has you so worried. But once things have settled."

"I can't guarantee it'll ever be settled. As much as I want

you back here..." I'd wanted us all back in Purgatory Falls for so long, it hurts to try and deter her now.

"I think you need me back here. I think this family needs to be back together again. Us all splitting up to the winds... I think our parents would hate it."

"I think our parents would want us to do whatever kept us safe. I know it's what Dad would have wanted, especially for you." I give her a pointed look. Aspen had always been the book smart one, off getting her doctorate while Levi and I were running bets and Ramsey was running the field. Our parents had always wanted her as far away from the chaos as possible.

"Yeah, well, they always underestimated how much I could take care of myself."

"I know you can. Fuck. You might have to if this doesn't end well. You know they'll need you if it goes that way. Ramsey's just finally getting his life back together after everything, and Levi. Well, if he makes it out and I don't, he'll be set on revenge. You know how he can be when he gets a singular focus. It's an obsession for him. You'll have to rein him back in, make him focus on something else." I stare off across the ranch. I hate having this conversation, but it needs to be said.

"I hope I don't even have to think about that. I can't imagine this family, this town... None of it works without you." Aspen looks at me thoughtfully. "I know you loved Dad, but you're twice the man he was. I hope you know that. Smarter. More capable. More driven in ways he couldn't even fathom. What you've done with the Avarice? How you've held this all together while we all ran off to have our fun? It's not fair. Most people would collapse under all the weight of it, and you made it look easy."

"I appreciate the deathbed flattery, sis." I smirk at her, trying to deflect because I can't take a compliment to save my fucking life, and my sister is so direct about the way she gives them.

"It's not flattery. It's truth. And here's some more for you. If you get through this, put a ring on that girl's finger and give yourself the time off you deserve. Spend some of your life doing what you want instead of what you think everyone else needs. The whole thing is gonna pass you by, and you're gonna wish you had that time back. Money, success, power. None of it gives back the time you've missed with people you love." Aspen gives me a sympathetic look.

"I don't know that she wants a ring. I think once she's over the shock and has some distance from this, she's gonna realize she lost everything she loved because of me and hate me for it. I wouldn't blame her if she did." I lean on the porch railing, staring down at the wildflowers Hazel's planted.

"The only thing she loves that she'll be mad about losing because of you—is *you*. Don't be that guy, Grant. Don't be the one who thinks he knows better than she does. Don't fall on your sword because you think it's noble and break both your hearts in the process."

"If I have to break her heart once so she doesn't have to have it broken over and over again when I fail her, I'll gladly do it the once. I just want her happy. Her life has been nothing but misery and struggle, and she's the last person on earth who deserves it. Her heart is so fucking pure, so fucking good that I don't even know what she sees in me." I shake my head as I look back at Aspen.

"Herself." Aspen looks at me like I'm clueless. "She sees herself in you, and you see yourself in her. It's part of the reason you fight so hard to protect her."

Such a simple statement. Such an obvious truth. And it hits me like a freight train.

"Mom! You ready?" Fallon calls, interrupting my thoughts.

"Come give your uncle a hug!" Aspen replies, and she comes running up the stairs, throwing her arms around me. I hug her back, still too shell-shocked to do anything but squeeze her in return as I look at Aspen over the top of her head. Aspen raises a single arched brow, and a small knowing smile tugs at the corner of her mouth. The same one our mother used to use when she knew she was right.

"I'll text you when we get back in town. Love you." Aspen hugs me one last time when Fallon lets go and then follows her down the steps.

"Have a safe flight!" I call after the two of them as they get into the waiting car.

I stand on the porch for longer than I should, staring out at the mountains past the fields, just wishing I could grab Dakota from inside the house, take two of the horses, and ride until we were lost and stay there forever.

FORTY

G RANT

"DO you remember the last time we were in this room together?" she whispers through the dark. We've been lying here silently awake for at least a half hour. We're in some sort of self-imposed purgatory tonight where neither of us can find the right words, and I'm too afraid to touch her for fear of making her head worse while she's recovering, or worse yet, begging her not to leave tomorrow when I've barely gotten her to agree to it in the first place.

"I thought we silently agreed to never talk about that again," I whisper back.

We're in my old bedroom, the one I stayed in while she lived with my parents when Jesse left me in charge of his estate and her until she went off to college. I had no business trying to look after anyone but me in the wake of his death. I was a mess.

Blaming myself. Drinking heavily. Wishing I could go back in time and take the bullets instead of him. But I was doing my best to make sure she was financially secure while my mom helped her make it through the day-to-day.

"We did..." She turns over to look at me through the darkness. We said our goodnights and laid down to go to sleep, but the tension in the room had been building as a million unspoken things passed between us in the quiet. "But it's all I can think about right now."

"Did you ever forgive me?" I ask because, at the time, she was furious. She barely spoke to me for a year afterward.

"When I was old enough to realize you did the right thing, even if it hurt my feelings." She shifts in the bed, and the moonlight catches the side of her face. "You've always been like that though. Doing the right thing even when it hurts, I mean."

"Guess I got that going for me at least." I chuckle. "Now that we're old enough, I can tell you it wasn't easy."

It was the week after her eighteenth birthday, and she'd come home drunk. She found out that her boyfriend had cheated on her, getting a blow job from another girl she'd considered a friend in the back of his truck after she'd told him she wasn't in the mood for sex. She'd fallen into a deep depression after Jesse's death the same way I had, and all the psychologists and antidepressants in the world hadn't stopped her from coming home every night to cry in her room. Nothing I said or did, nothing I bought for her, no amount of distractions or bargaining could fill the void he left.

"You made it seem easy with the way you told me no. You practically climbed the wall to get away from me." There's a soft laugh from her, but at the time, it had only been tears. "And then you moved out the next day." The laugh disappears, and the quiet of the ranch at night returns.

"I'm sorry I fucked that up." I'd put the incident in a black box and had done my best to forget it ever happened. We'd both silently agreed to never bring it up. At least until now.

"You didn't fuck it up. You did the right thing, and that speech you gave me in the mirror. I still think about it."

"I don't even remember what I said; I just remember I didn't want you to cry anymore. Felt like all I did back then was drink, and all you did was cry, and neither of us knew how to make it stop." I turn on my side to get a better look at her.

"I think he'd always kept us both grounded, and we just kind of... came unraveled without him." Her eyes search mine in the pale light. "You stood behind me and made me look in the mirror while you told me that Graham was a moron, and I was better than that—letting him get to me. You told me the best thing I could do was stop giving boys who didn't deserve me my time and stop giving men who were too jaded to appreciate me my attention. You made me repeat it back to you. Then you said that the right guy would wait until I was ready again." She smiles in the darkness, rolling her lower lip between her teeth. "You muttered something about how you didn't even know how he could look at anyone else given how gorgeous I was."

"Sounds like I was drunk, but not terrible wisdom."

"You were drunk... I'm sorry I put you in that position," she apologizes quietly.

When she'd gotten home from drinking with her friends that night, instead of going to her own bedroom, she'd come into mine, claiming she couldn't sleep. She crawled on top of me and kissed her way down my neck while I was still half awake and then cradled my cock with her palm while she begged to give me a blow job. I fully woke up just in time to see her strip out of her clothes and realize what the fuck was going to happen if I didn't stop it. My heart had nearly exploded out of my chest in my race to get her off me and keep her from doing something we'd both regret.

"I was a shitty fucking guardian."

"You had your own grief you were working through, and your mom was so good to me. I still think about her pancakes."

"Her pancakes were fucking amazing." I smile, remembering her making them in the kitchen on Saturday mornings, smothering them in butter and pure maple syrup. "Hazel still has the family cookbook. You should see if they're in there someday."

"Someday." She reaches out and brushes her fingertips down my arm. "And you weren't a shitty guardian. Honestly, that speech alone probably saved me from a couple of bad relationships."

"You still dated a couple of guys whose jaws I would have loved to crush under my boot for the shit they said." I roll my eyes and shake my head.

"Did you really threaten Chris's life?" she asks. "You said you didn't, but he swore that you put him in a chokehold and told him you'd rip off his balls and let him bleed out that way."

"I might have done that." I laugh as I remember the look on his face. He embarrassed her once at the bar, being a loud dick and talking about her like she was his property to play with.

"I defended you!" She punches my shoulder lightly.

I open my mouth to say something, but there's a loud feminine moan from above us, and I hear the sound of the bed rocking against the wall. We stare at each other in the dark, and then Dakota descends into giggles.

"I guess he finally convinced her to end the dry spell since they postponed the wedding," she giggles in amusement.

"What dry spell? I didn't think those two went a day without fucking."

"She put him on time-out the week before the wedding. Said she wanted the wedding night to be extra special."

"Fuck... no wonder he was so cranky all week." I laugh a little too loud, and Dakota's eyes widen. She covers my mouth with one hand and presses her finger to hers.

"Shhh. If we can hear them. They can hear us," she warns.

The bangs of the bed against the wall start to take on a rhythmic quality, and I hear the sound of Ramsey's sharp, demanding voice, but I can't make out the words. There's another moan, and a series of soft begging sounds out of Hazel. It fills the air around us, and the tension we managed to dissolve talking about our past is back in full force. Maybe even thicker for it.

"It's kind of hot... Hearing them, I mean." Dakota's eyes search mine, and her tongue slides slowly over her lower lip, wetting it and making it glisten in the low light.

"If I forget who they are." I shrug, but I've forgotten anything but her. I'm just imagining the sounds Dakota makes for me now, and fuck if I don't want them. "We should go to sleep. We both have a long day tomorrow."

Their sounds have quieted, and I'm hoping it means they only needed a quick fuck before they fell asleep. Can't blame my brother if she really made him wait. I don't know how long I'm gonna survive without Dakota now that I've had a taste of her.

"You're right." She lets out a soft sigh and turns over, facing the window, giving me her back. "Goodnight, Grant."

"Goodnight, Dakota," I answer, closing my eyes and resettling myself on the pillow.

I'm drifting off, trying to think about anything else other than sex right now. No matter how much I might want it, I'm worried about her head injury.

"Oh fuck... yes... Right there. Ramsey, please." Hazel's begging pierces through the night.

Dakota doesn't say a word, but I can tell she's awake, and she shifts on the pillow.

"Cowboy," she whispers.

"The doctor said no vigorous activity for at least a week," I protest immediately because otherwise, I'm going to give in.

There's a frustrated sigh on her part. One that creeps through my mind and down to my cock telling me where there's a will there's a way.

"That's the other thing they don't warn you about when your whole house burns down—it takes your toys too," she mutters under her breath.

"I'm sorry," I say softly.

"If you were truly sorry, you'd fuck me." She scoots back, and her ass brushes over my cock and then nestles up against me. I might have my own head injury soon, an aneurysm from trying to resist her.

"We could go slow," she adds in a whisper.

"I'm trying to look out for your health," I grumble back.

There's another loud groan from upstairs, this time from Ramsey, and the sound of him permeates the room. I see her shoulder move, and the covers shift subtly in front of me.

"What are you doing?" My tone is harsh even to my own ears, but I hear the sounds of her fingers slipping through her wetness.

"Getting off to the sounds your brother's making if you don't do something about it soon," she answers, and I can see the wicked little smile forming on her lips as she looks back at me over her shoulder.

"The fuck you will." I make quick work of my sweats and boxer briefs, and then I grab her panties, wrenching them down her thighs. I slip inside her easily a moment later, a groan ripping from my chest when I feel how wet she is. "That better fucking be for me."

"It is." She lets out a muted cry as I start to fuck her slowly. "The way you talked to me in that mirror that day is one of my most reliable fantasies. It just ends a little differently in my head than it did in real life."

"Hellfire, fuck." I pull the collar of the T-shirt she wore to bed to the side so I can kiss the crook of her neck as I ease in and out of her at a tortured pace. "You can't tell me things like that. It gives me fucked-up thoughts."

"So I shouldn't tell you that I used to get off after our arguments, imagining you hate fucking me up against the wall?"

"I thought that was a given. That's my favorite fantasy." I grin against her neck as I go to kiss her again.

"You feel good like this. I needed this after everything," she murmurs quietly as she rubs a circle over her clit and lets out a soft gasp.

"I needed this too," I whisper back, sucking a small mark onto her neck as my hand slides over the soft skin of her stomach. "Something about you makes the rest of the world fade away."

"Same," she sighs as I shift to a new angle. She adjusts her position, which lets me take her deeper, and I run my hand over her hip and down her thigh.

"How does your fantasy end in your head?" I ask. "Because I want to know them all. Give them to you." I dot kisses down the curve of her spine and over the top of her shoulder blade.

"You bend me over the bed and take me, fast and hard, like you can't control yourself while you tell me what a good girl I am for taking your cock."

"You *are* good, you know. Underneath all the fight. You're so fucking good I don't know if I'm worthy of it."

"Honestly, Cowboy..." she starts, the words faltered by her

gasps as she gets close. "You're the best man I've ever known in my life." Her voice fades into a soft cry as I hit her just right.

"That's right. Come for me, work that perfect little clit for me while I fuck you full." I bury my face in her neck, groaning as I come inside her and listen to her soft murmured curses as she comes all over my cock. "Fuck... That's my girl. Just like that." She rocks back against me, and we both fall into a quiet silence as I wrap my arms around her, and she leans into me.

"I don't know if you're a devil or an angel sometimes," she breaks the silence after a few minutes.

"For you? Both." I smirk and kiss the side of her cheek. "Let's get you cleaned up." I stand and hold my hand out for hers. If I ever needed a reason to live, her happy, sated smile as she stumbles out of bed and into my arms would be it.

FORTY-ONE

D AKOTA

THE NEXT MORNING, in the wee hours when we've both barely had coffee, and I've got Vendetta and the few belongings I have left packed and ready to head to the airport, we stand in the kitchen to say our goodbyes. His face is pained, and his eyes shift to the floor again as he nervously palms his cowboy hat. The man from last night is gone, and he's doing his best to be all business this morning.

I can tell he's trying to gather words together, and I know it's not his strong suit to say how he feels, especially when it comes to emotions in the bright light of day. So I wait patiently, doing my own mental inventory of my feelings. One where I try to tell myself not to blurt anything out or beg him not to do what we both know he has to. I can't ask him to ignore his obligations for me, and I can't cry. Not now.

He pulls a key out of his pocket and holds it up before he presses it into my palm.

"This is the key to a safety deposit box down in Colorado Springs, the bank on Tejon Street. It's yours."

"Mine?" I take the key, my brows knitting together as I try to figure out how I could have a safety deposit box I didn't know about.

"It's in your name, but I've been a key holder. I opened it after Jesse died." He takes a breath, and his eyes raise to meet mine. "There's just under a million dollars in it. It's yours either way, okay? But if something happens, you take it and run."

"I can't take your money, Grant." I hold the key back out to him.

"It's not my money. It's yours." He presses it back into my palm and closes my fingers over it.

"Mine? How can it be mine? Did Jesse leave it?" I can't imagine I wouldn't have seen that in the paperwork. Grant reluctantly let me help go through all of it.

"It's all the rent from the bar. I've been putting it in there. I needed it somewhere safe, so if anything ever happened with me... RICO or something, they couldn't touch it."

I'm struggling hard with the promise I made to myself not to cry. He sees how glassy my eyes look, and he turns away, running his teeth over his lower lip and glancing down at the floor.

"Now don't cry on me. I know you hated me for making you pay the rent, but I just wanted you to have something for yourself. I knew you wouldn't take handouts or help. But I wanted you to be able to buy your own bar or your own house when the time came. I was gonna give it to you when you got married or on your thirtieth birthday, whichever came first. But I might not make it to see those, and if Levi goes with me, no one else will know to give it to you, so..." He trails off.

"Thank you," I blurt out as the tears start to roll down my cheeks, and I jump the man, wrapping my arms around him as he teeters and struggles to keep us both upright. So much for being the stoic support he needs right now. But his arms close around me, and he holds me tight as he kisses the top of my head in return. "I wish I had better words than that." I have three I'd like to say, but they're the same three I don't know if I need to say. The ones that always feel like a silent exchange with him, and I worry if I whisper them out loud, it could be like a butterfly effect that sets our whole world spinning off. So I keep them silent, like we always do, when I hug him one last time.

"You don't have to thank me, Hellfire. You just stay safe, okay? I hope I see you on the other side of this." He looks down at me, sincerity burning through the ice to make his eyes two deep pools of glassy blue that I'm melting into.

"I wish you could tell me more. What your plan is or how I'll know when you're safe." I wipe away the tears from my cheeks, cursing myself for falling apart the exact way I told myself I wouldn't. I'm desperate for some sort of reassurance that I'll have his arms around me again. That we'll have another heated fight about something ridiculous, and then he'll end up back in my bed at the end of the night. But it's all promises he can't keep.

"There is no plan. Just a play we have to make and hope it turns out. Just assume I'm all right unless you hear otherwise. Okay?"

"I'll try." It'll be impossible. My mind will race with the worst possibilities, but I don't want to give him trouble this morning. I want to do what we both need to keep him safe.

"Charlotte and Hazel will keep you so distracted you won't have time to think about it." He forces a smile, and I do my best to return it. If that's the lie he has to tell himself to get through this, I'm not going to shatter it. Like Levi said, the best way I can support him is by being strong and doing the things I don't want to do. Things like getting in the car and onto an airplane and flying away.

"You ready?" Hazel appears with a carry-on at the foot of the steps, and Ramsey's just a few steps behind her with a duffel and a tired, sad look on his face as he sees his brother.

"We're ready." I gesture to Vendetta in her carrier at my feet.

"I got her for you if you want?" Ramsey points to the carrier, and I nod.

"Have a safe one." Grant looks to Ramsey, and he reaches over to give him a swift hug and a firm pat on the back.

"You too, brother." Ramsey grabs the back of Grant's neck and brings them forehead to forehead, whispering something I can't hear. There's another stoic nod of Grant's before they part. Hazel follows with a solemn sign of support to Grant before she and Ramsey disappear out the door.

"Guess I'd better go." I look up to Grant, and the look on his face nearly breaks my heart, but I force a small smile. "Be careful."

"Be safe, Hellfire." He pulls me in for one last hug, kissing my temple in the process, and it takes everything I have in me to let go and walk out the door.

FORTY-TWO

G RANT

WHEN JAY ARRIVES at the Avarice, I feel the buzz of nerves down my spine. This has to go flawlessly, or we'll all end up in prison for the rest of our lives—or worse. Hudson and Rowan are on call, a few short meters away in case we need them, but Levi and I are meeting him alone to keep suspicions down. He pulls his aviators off as he walks into the back entrance where he's parked, and he tucks them into his pocket before he flashes a brilliantly fake smile at us.

"Hot as hell out there today. How are y'all holdin' up?" he remarks on his way in, nodding at Levi before turning his attention to me.

"As good as it can be, considering the past weekend. Ramsey and Hazel are obviously disappointed, and the staff at

Seven Sins are having a hell of a time, given the circumstances there."

"Right. Can't believe it's a total fucking loss. Fire department's still on that one. Investigating the cause of it. The fire chief still thinks it could be a burst gas line. You know those old buildings... lot of maintenance and upkeep. Not as nice as this place." He chatters on as he follows us down the hall. "They're still sorting through the rubble but making progress."

"I assume they'll let us know when they've got a final finding?" I ask because the communication has been nearly nonexistent, given that I'm the property owner and Dakota owned most of what was inside. Then again, it's not exactly surprising with what I know now.

"Of course. I'll keep you updated as I know more. They just had that house fire up on Elk Landing, and that's been a fucking doozy of a mess too. Guess this whole town's going to hell in a handbasket."

"Certainly seems that way," Levi mutters under his breath, and I shoot him a look behind Jay's shoulder.

"So you boys got something you want me to look at?" Jay asks as we step onto the elevator.

"Yeah. There were a couple of things that were out of place, and with everything going on, we can't be too cautious. Figured you were the best person to look into it," I explain.

We'd invited him over under false pretenses, telling him we were unable to find something in our vault and that the log codes had been off for a period of time last month. That combined with some strange gaps in the entries in the security system this past week had us wondering if we had a problem on our hands.

"You guys don't have internal security?" He lifts a brow.

"We do, but we want to explore all possibilities and get your input," I answer as we ride the elevator down to the vault floor in sub-basement four. Running a casino meant having a fortress underground, particularly when that casino was a money-laundering facility and housed a fuckton of black-market cash at any given moment.

"Can't dismiss the possibility of an inside job right now." Levi looks over my uncle. His underhanded jabs, teasing too closely to the truth. I'm half worried my brother is going to kill him before we get off the elevator. We both have tempers, but Levi's is less practiced and more unhinged than mine, particularly when the offense is to something he holds dear—like this family.

"That'd be a real fucking problem for you boys. You gotta shore up leaks like that. Your dad and I had a couple back in our day. Not a fucking thing I wish on anyone." His eyes go distant for a moment, and I swear it's remorse I can see there. Given that we can't know anything for sure now, like whether or not he was part of the machinations that killed my parents, I have a hard time trusting any emotion on his face. For all I know, it's for show.

"You ever regret leaving the family business behind?" Levi asks, studying him.

"Not a day in my life. Only regret is not leaving it sooner. If I thought you two would listen to me, I'd tell you to pack it up and move somewhere you could forget you were ever a Stockton."

Which begs the question of why the man would return, but asking that would open a Pandora's box I'm not ready for yet. Not while a gun and half a dozen other weapons are strapped to his body and backup is a short phone call away. If I could tell my younger self something, it would be not to get into a life-or-death fight with family. But there's not much I can do about it as it stands.

"Well, hopefully, someday we can all have a quiet retirement." I offer up half a smile as we get off the elevator.

"Someday," he echoes.

We have to pass through several locked doors sealed by triple verification, badge, code, and biometrics. He does the courtesy of looking away, but we're trusting he doesn't have any sort of recording device on. Once we get to the vault, it's one final series of locks and challenges to prove our ability to have access.

"Do you have any idea how the vault could have been breached? How many employees have access to it?" he questions.

"A dozen not counting us," Levi lies. It's less than that, but we don't want to give him additional data points he could use against us if this doesn't go our way.

"Any that would have an interest in stealing from you? Disgruntled? Anyone who's left?" He presses on.

"We've had a few employees who have left, but not who we could point a finger at though. One of them retired, and the other had a wife who took a job across the country. The others who departed didn't have this level of access," I explain after Levi opens the vault, and we step inside.

"All right. So tell me what's missing then." He turns around in the vault, taking everything in, from the stacks of money to the lockboxes and shelves that contain valuables and art. We were a veritable underground bank, not just for our family but for friends and associates as well. Not to mention the cash that passed through the casino, legitimately and illegitimately alike, but that's in a different vault.

"If you look down here, you'll see the empty shelf." Levi distracts Jay while I step back toward the door. Jay follows, peering at the place he points toward. "Yep, just a little further down here."

Jay takes another step and misses the drop down in the floor. It was a constant hazard, but in this case, it was a benefit.

"What the fuck!" he shouts as he falls face first. He hits the ground hard. His hands and knees take the brunt of it. He groans loudly in pain as he tries to turn over. The man isn't exactly young anymore, and his knees struggle to bear his weight as he tries to get up.

Levi and I take the opportunity to step outside the door. I press the lock, and the doors start to shut, but it feels like an eternity until it closes. I watch him start to stand up slowly, dusting himself off, and turning around to see why we're not helping just as it seals.

The look of betrayal on his face is searing. The same look I'm sure I made when I realized it had to have been him who helped set up the bombs. He runs at the door, slamming his hand against it to try to open it again and desperately pounding the interior button.

"That won't work." Levi hits the intercom and opens a line of communication between us.

"What the fuck are you two boys doing?" he snarls at us.

"What are we doing? How about we start with what the fuck you've been doing." Levi's furious. I place a hand on his shoulder, trying to get him to find his center. This wouldn't work if we lead with too much emotion.

"I have no idea what you're talking about." He lies.

"We *know*. We know you worked with a staff member who trusted your last name to bring in the champagne crates. The ones you intercepted and swapped out. The ones you put bombs in. You tried to kill your whole fucking family and then some, at your nephew's wedding," I add. "Can you imagine what Dad would fucking say if he was here?"

"Dad wouldn't say anything to a corpse." Levi sneers. "That's what you'd be if he was here and knew you tried to kill his youngest. His grandkid? Takes a special kind of fucked up to do what you did."

"Says who? Some staff member? Of course he'd pin it on another family member. He wants to set us against each other. You can't believe every fucking thing someone tells you."

"We have a very limited amount of time on our hands. Let's not play games or lie to one another," I say, exhausted already that this is his play.

"You want the truth? Then let me out of this fucking cage." He slams his palm against the door again.

"So you can finish the job you started?" Levi laughs. "Do we look fucking stupid to you?"

"You look dumb as fuck holding a sheriff hostage. You know how that ends? With both of you in prison."

"Don't worry. We don't plan to hold you long." I shake my head. "Just long enough for you to tell us answers."

He presses his lips together in a flat line and raises his gun at the glass.

"I wouldn't do that," Levi warns. "There's a chance it'll ricochet and kill you."

He lowers the gun, and a desperate look crosses his face before he looks back toward the door. "What the fuck do you want from me? If you're gonna kill me then be men and come in here and do it yourselves, you fuckin' pussies."

"We want information. We want to know who you're working with," I demand.

"I told you—" he starts, and there's a sudden clicking sound and the sound of the air being sucked out.

"That's the oxygen leaving the room. Part of the fire suppression system." Levi's lost his patience already, skipping ahead to Plan B. "You've got until it runs out to tell us. Ask me if I care if you live or die after what you did."

"You're gonna kill a sheriff?" Even he knows he deserves death for this kind of betrayal.

"You're wasting your breath and our time." I shake my head and cross my arms over my chest while I wait. "We know about the governor. We know the stakes. You need to convince us that your life is worth saving right now, and the sand is running out on you."

"Fucking hell." He shakes his head, turning around for a moment like he'll find a solution somewhere in the vault to get him out. "Fine. Fuck... The governor put me up to it. He'll kill me just for telling you. But he has his sights on my daughter and her mother. I can't let anything happen to them. He found me earlier this year, and he put me up to all this. Told me he'd kill me for the way things went down years ago if I didn't find a way to make it right. I told him to fucking go ahead and do it. That I didn't want any more of that fucking life. I was retired and living in peace."

"You mean hiding out in a hole like the scared piece of shit you are," Levi interjects, and I shoot him a look. We need as much information as we can get before this clock runs out.

"Call it what you like. Live this life as long as I have, watch all your brothers die, and then tell me what you want to do with the time you've got left." He looks to Levi through the glass and then shifts his attention back to me. "I didn't want to kill any of you. You're family to me, but you're not innocent. My daughter? Her mom? They've never hurt a fucking soul. They don't know anything about this life or what we've done. They don't deserve it."

"Lots of fucking people that would have been in that room were innocent. Dozens and dozens of them who were just there to see a wedding."

"But they're not all my kin. I couldn't live with myself if he hurt my girl or her mom."

"So you were supposed to kill us all to save their lives. What else? We need something useful. A reason not to let you die in there. What does he want from us? What did he want all those years ago?" I press him on the essentials.

"It's a long fucking story. Too long to explain with the time you're giving me right now," he counters.

"Then buy yourself some. Give me a reason not to kill you right now," Levi demands.

Jay scrubs a hand over his face and looks to the ceiling. "I don't think he has everything he needs yet. I could try to get more details from him. Give you information."

"How do you know he doesn't have everything?" I raise a brow.

"It's been his plan for years. It was his plan before your dad died. He was going to bring us all in on it. Claimed he'd be so wealthy and so powerful that we could all have whatever we wanted. That we could leave this life behind us for good. That's what your dad and I wanted—out. Your dad knew more than I did." Jay starts to cough, making it obvious the air is getting thinner behind the doors.

"Why not tell us?"

"He's a very fucking dangerous man. He's related to powerful fucking people. Unstoppable people. If anything went wrong…"

"Like it did." Levi points out the apparent.

"Then our lives were all at risk. Look at your parents. Look at us now, killing each other." There's another long coughing fit. "Just give me a chance to explain. We can figure something out. I just have to make sure my daughter's safe. She's your cousin. She's family." He pleads with us. "Or if you're going to kill me, at least let me tell you how to find her. You can't let him kill her for my fucking wrongs."

"How come no one ever knew about her?" Levi asks impatiently.

"Her mom and I didn't last. She didn't tell me about the kid until she was older. When I tracked her down, after everything went to hell, I found out I was a dad. Blew my fucking world up."

Levi and I look to each other, me silently asking him if he thinks it's possible and him nodding but then holding his hands out in frustration.

He's right. We can't trust that he won't try to kill us. He did it once. He could do it again. He's said he'll do as much for his daughter. He realizes the conversation we're having, the decision we're making for him, and his shoulders slump.

"Her name is Skylar Wilson. She's from a farming town in Illinois, but she's attending college. The name is on a card in my wallet, along with her address. Her mom's name is Tracey Wilson. I don't know if he's watching them or if he's taken them. He told me if I contacted either of them, he'd kill them. So I can't know for sure. Please tell me you'll look for them. Make sure they're okay. Once he finds out I'm gone, and I can't help with you two, he'll have no reason not to kill them."

"I don't make any fucking promises," Levi mutters.

"I'll do my best. If she's a Stockton, then she deserves our help." I give Levi a sideways glance.

"Just know. I loved your dad, and I love you boys and your sister. It was an impossible fucking decision to make. I just tried to spare the innocent one." He shakes his head, and my blood runs cold as he falls to his knees, grabbing for his throat as another coughing fit overtakes him.

"Aspen's daughter is innocent. Ramsey's friends are innocent. Hazel's family is fucking innocent!" Levi roars, slamming his fist against the glass, saying the things I'm trying hard to be too calm to say out loud.

Jay gives us a desperate, twisted look, a mix of remorse and pain, before he collapses forward, gasping for air one last time. Then he goes limp.

I imagine myself in the same position on that floor. If I had to choose a wife or a daughter's life over the rest of my family. I don't know what I'd do. I'd probably go mad trying to make a plan to save them all. I slam the button to open the vault with my fist, and the heavy metal door slowly starts to creep open. Hopefully, not so slowly that we can't make it in time.

"What the fuck are you doing?" Levi looks at me like I've lost my mind.

"Saving him. A dead sheriff on our hands is more than we need. We know he's got a reason to want to live. If we can find a way to work with him, it's better for both of us." I look back at Levi. "Not to mention he's right. At the end of the fucking day, he's family."

"What stops him from killing us the second he wakes up?"

"We strip him of his weapons, and you zip-tie him. We'll get him to a room, and we'll talk sense into him. It's our only real shot. Why let this fucking governor tear this whole fucking family to shreds when we could go after him together?" I reason with Levi. He's not in the habit of questioning me, but he hesitates before he steps forward.

"If this goes wrong..." Levi doesn't finish the sentence. He doesn't have to. I already know all the ways it could go wrong and the consequences.

"We'll be dead. If it goes right, we have a chance in hell of getting out of this alive."

"Fuck." Levi rips out a curse and storms in with me. I strip him of his gun, dumping the magazine and tossing it out of his reach while Levi works to zip-tie his hands just as he's coming to. He struggles against us as I pat him down for other weapons, taking away his baton and his phone and walkie. He writhes on the ground, trying to get out of our grasp, but Levi works fast, and he's still struggling to catch his breath.

Levi moves from his hands to his feet, zip-tying them in rapid order and then dragging him to the far side of the room.

"We have you on tape telling us everything. We could take it to the governor or the nightly news," I explain as he gasps again, desperate for oxygen back in his lungs. "Or you can stay fucking calm, and we can chat. Your choice."

He closes his eyes, coughing again, and then barely whispers the word, "Calm."

"You got it. Let's go." Levi grabs one of his arms, and I grab the other.

We still need to work quickly. If he goes missing for too long, it will set off alarm bells with the rest of the cops under his watch and likely with the governor too. I can imagine he told them where he was going, knowing full well in his conscience he was the responsible one.

So now, time is an enemy for all of us, and I just have to hope we can find enough common ground to make this work. I don't know if it's better or worse to have this small sliver of hope in what's felt like certain darkness.

FORTY-THREE

G RANT

WE GET Jay into a room and have him secured in a chair across from us. Levi's still not ready to untie him, and Jay's livid about being held in these conditions, but we're not killing each other, and overall, that's an improvement for this family.

"Did you kill our parents?" Levi asks.

"No. You think I could kill my brother?" Jay glares at him.

"You were ready to kill us."

"With bombs that he provided, not with a gun at close range."

"'Cause you're a fucking coward." Levi sneers.

"Says the boy who's got me tied to a chair while we have a conversation," he snaps back.

"We'll untie you as soon as we've established some common ground. Like the fact we're in a mutually assured destruction kinda situation now, Uncle. We know your daughter and your lady's name, plus where they live." I remind him of his predicament. The man's already grown used to giving the orders instead of taking them.

"I gave you that information to save them, not to threaten them." His lips press together in a hard line.

"I'd love to. I don't want to see anyone else in this family or anyone they hold dear at risk of losing their lives. That's my goal. I need it to be yours too. You think we can come to an agreement on that?" I grab a bottle of water from the fridge in the room and screw the cap off.

"I never wanted any harm to come to either of you. I meant what I said. It was an impossible situation. He was going to try to kill you regardless. This way, I might have been able to save them from the same fate."

"Good. So we can agree going forward the only way any of us win is if we all win. Right?" I ask, passing him the bottle and cutting one of his hands free so he can lift it.

He drinks it down so fast he sputters a little before he nods. "We're agreed on that."

"Glad to hear it." I watch him take another sip. "Now tell us what we don't know."

"I don't know much about what you do know, so it's hard to say what you don't."

"Tell us why you and our father agreed to steal this relic in the first place," Levi instructs him, constantly watching where he puts his hands and how he moves. He has zero interest in trust, but we're going to have to learn to make it work.

"Abbott approached us years ago. Before he even started putting his plan in motion. He wanted these relics, said it was the key to getting something he needed. That the kind of money and power it would bring if he did would change his life, and in exchange, he'd change ours."

"Well, it definitely changed lives," Levi mutters.

"It was supposed to get us both out of this life. Give our family a fresh start. We could start over, settle old debts, and take things legitimate if we wanted," Jay continues to explain.

"I don't recall Dad ever wanting to go legit. He never mentioned it to me." I raise a brow.

"We didn't have any real guarantees on that front. I think your dad just hoped he could hold true to his promises. Obviously, he didn't." He takes another sip, clearing his throat. "But now he has the relic. I don't know how he got it, but he has the second one that you were meant to steal. All these years, he thought you had it. I did too. Your dad said you boys had done all right despite the botched robbery and the chaos. I thought when you took me to the vault, you were going to tell me that someone had stolen it."

"Is that why he wants us dead because he thinks we had it?" I ask because, even if I'm trying to trust him, I'm not giving my hand away. I need those aces for later.

"In part. Mostly he wants you dead because he ordered his people to go after your dad, and you all won't let sleeping dogs lie."

"I don't know many people who would let their parents' execution be written off into a cold-case file." Levi looks our uncle over with disdain.

"I don't blame you. I'm just telling you the way he looks at it. If you were ever able to prove that he was a party to their murder, he'd lose everything. But right now, there's no weapon, no motive, not anything to connect the two that he doesn't have control over. The only hitch is the people who helped carry it out have disappeared, and he's furious he can't find them."

"And the relic would only further connect the dots," Levi adds helpfully, glancing over at me.

Jay nods and looks back and forth between us slowly,

waiting for us to move the negotiations forward. I'm stuck in my head, processing exactly how fucked we are.

Abbott doesn't know that we've already taken care of his witnesses for him. A thing I would've avoided if possible, but my youngest brother's rage and trauma had conspired to make other decisions for us. We've also handed over the relic via the black market, the only thing that might have been evidence as a motive, and the chances we ever find a murder weapon are damn near impossible. The only silver lining is the fact that we sold the relic on the black market, and it led us to him. It at least makes it look like the Flanagans had taken the goods and run, selling the item on the market as a means to make their money and get away from Abbott in the process.

"But you could link him too." I look at my uncle.

"We all could, together with what we know. Not enough to take it to a prosecutor. Not without more evidence or more witnesses. It would be our word against his, and he has an untarnished reputation and the support of half the state of Colorado. Not to mention all his connections in Washington and the corrupt underbelly that's supported his rise thus far." Jay's brow creases with doubt. "Trust me. I've thought about it."

Levi looks at me. "He has a half dozen billionaires who supported his last run. Ones who are still advising him. The kind who make it look like he's gunning for the presidency after he finishes this term."

"Do you know how many relics he needs? More than two, I assume if he's still out there looking." I ask because I can't worry about the future. I can only worry about right now.

"I always heard him talk about three. I don't know if it was only three or if that's just where he started." Jay shrugs.

"Where do the relics lead? Why does he want them?" I ask because I still can't make sense of it. Other than the historical or cultural value, there was nothing particularly special about it. According to Charlotte, the price was inflated because of the buyer, not because of its actual value. So why the willingness to do anything to get them?

"I don't know more than what I've told you right now." Jay shrugs.

Levi gives him a skeptical look in return, irritated that we're not getting more answers and instead coming up with a bigger list of problems than we started with.

"I don't fucking know. I'd tell you if I knew. I've already fucking told you enough to get me killed three times over," Jay snaps at Levi, his face growing red with the force of his words.

"Do you know what they have in common?" Levi asks.

"Not a damn clue."

"Helpful." Levi looks at me. "So all we know after all this is that he wants relics. He's still looking for at least one. He wants us dead, and he put our own uncle up to killing us to make it happen. Oh, and he has a daughter we didn't know existed whose life is more important than dozens of ours."

"Lev..." I say his name like a warning because antagonizing our uncle won't help our cause.

"One who needs your help. She's your family too, and she's fucking innocent in all of this." Jay glares at Levi and then turns to me. "This doesn't work if you're not gonna help her."

"This works because if you don't help us, we'll make sure that she never gets any help. From anyone," Levi threatens.

"Are you fucking hearing this?" My uncle looks to me to diffuse the situation.

"He's right. It's mutually assured destruction. We don't have trust anymore. Not after you tried to kill us. All we know is that you value her life over ours. So all we can trust is that you'll do whatever you can to protect her, exactly like you said."

"What happened to common ground?"

"The common ground is that you don't want anything to

happen to us, and neither do we. We both need to slow your boss down to make sure of it." I explain the facts like I see them. They're not pretty but they're all we've got.

"He's not my boss. I'm as much a victim in this as any of you. He would have killed me if he didn't think there was something I could do for him. He might still when he finds out I don't have a backup plan to deal with you."

"And yet we didn't try to set off bombs to kill you and everyone you love." Levi's tone is cutting.

"Just tell him there was something faulty with the bombs. The first one went off early, right? I assume the one at Seven Sins was meant to go off at the same time as the rest?" I offer a solution.

"It was, and it wasn't meant to be at the bar at all. I didn't realize you were going to move some of the champagne." Regret clouds his face.

My stomach churns. In trying to do something thoughtful for Dakota, I'd nearly killed her. But I couldn't think about that now.

"So tell him the triggers were faulty. Or the wires. One went off early, and the rest didn't."

"And then what? He might buy that. He'll be furious, but at least it's the truth. Then he'll want to know what my plan is." Jay looks between us for answers.

"You just tell him you need time and that the bomb at the bar put us on high alert, so it'll be difficult for you to get to us for a while. He'll have to have patience. He's waited all these years; you'd think he could wait a few more months."

"He didn't have the relic before. He has it now. The only thing he was worried about was killing you before he knew where it was."

"Then do what's necessary to convince him. This is your

problem. Not ours. You want your daughter alive; you'll figure out a solution to deal with him," Levi says bluntly.

"And talk to him soon. I don't want him sending backup down here to make more problems for us." I add.

"I'll do my best. But I'm one person." I don't like the doubt I see on Jay's face.

"One fucking person who runs law enforcement for this whole fucking county. I think you can come up with some temporary solutions," Levi snaps.

My uncle starts to wind up to say something more, but I cut him off before he can speak.

"He's right. You can do this. You've been out of the game for a while, but you know the rules; you know the strategy. Make it happen. Our dad would have counted on you, and I'm hoping we can, even if you've made a few mistakes along the way."

"I'll do whatever I can." He looks remorseful enough in the moment, and I hope he holds true to his word.

I agree with my brother's assessment. We've got to put our energy into moving forward. That means finding out what these relics are for and how we find the one he doesn't have his hands on yet. Because if all he needs are three, our time might be running out faster than we hoped.

FORTY-FOUR

D AKOTA

"ALL RIGHT. I can't stand seeing you mope around here anymore," Charlotte announces as she finds me in her breakfast room, hunched over with my coffee, doom scrolling the morning away with Vendetta in my lap. I look up from the latest dumpster fire on social media to see her looming over the table like a force to be reckoned with. I'm not sure Charlotte owns jeans or old T-shirts. Everything she wears looks freshly pressed and perfectly tailored, and every day, she puts on a new pair of unique heels. Today's are four-inch stilettos with pointed toes and jeweled snakes that wrap around her ankles. I need to figure out how to take her style and meld it with my lazy cowgirl aesthetic because just looking at her is intimidating, and those are the vibes I need for the fresh future I've been planning. When I'm not worrying about Grant that is.

"It's not moping. Just worrying."

"If you're going to stay with him, you'll spend every day of the rest of your life worrying like this. You've got to learn to compartmentalize and remind yourself that he's where he is for a reason. He didn't amass all that power and all that wealth because he didn't know what he was doing." Charlotte lectures me, and it's a fair point. "Besides, we've got our own work to do—I got word we need to figure something out for them."

"Somehow, I doubt I was included in the dream team." I laugh because otherwise, I'll cry. I feel so useless when everyone else here seems to have a purpose. Mine was the bar and my staff, creating a place for locals to come and have community, but now I've got nothing, and it's hitting me hard.

"I'm including you on the team. It'll get your mind off things, and I could use a fresh perspective."

"What do we need fresh perspective on?" Hazel's in from a run on the trail on Charlotte's property. Her hair is tied up, and her face is sweaty and red from the exertion. She'd decided to stay here with me, in part to keep me company and in part because of Ramsey's own feelings about her being alone at home. Beatrix, Hazel's friend who was in Colorado for all the wedding festivities and subsequent mess, has been keeping us both company and trying to cheer us up since we got here. Hazel pours them each a giant glass from a pitcher of fruit-infused water.

"Me too." Finn, one of Charlotte's men, has suddenly appeared from his own workout, and he pushes another glass in front of Hazel.

"The relic that we discussed last year and the one I found. We need to find out if there are any others like them." Charlotte casts a sideways glance at Beatrix. "Is she vetted?"

The question is directed at Hazel, but Beatrix shifts her

attention to Charlotte when she realizes she's the one being talked about.

"I've signed NDAs with Finn and Ramsey as their PR rep for their brands, and Hazel and I have our own agreement because of the project we're working on. Do you need me to add an addendum?"

"This is a separate project. I work as their art consultant, and this industry is very protective of its insider information," Charlotte responds without missing a beat.

"Understood." Beatrix nods. "But if I can ask a question?"

"You can ask." Charlotte raises a brow in question. I suspect she has little intention of answering.

"Did you say relics? Like the kind from saints and things?"

"Yes," Charlotte answers easily.

"My sister-in-law specializes in medieval art and hagiographies. If you need someone, I'm happy to put you in touch with her. She'll be in town this week while we're shopping for... dresses." Beatrix hesitates because she's planning her own wedding and is worried it's a sensitive subject.

"I'd appreciate that." Charlotte's face softens and half a smile appears.

"I'm still invited, right? You're not gonna ice me out from dress shopping because you're worried about me being sad?" Hazel eyes Beatrix as she chugs her water.

"As long as you're up for it, I want you there." Beatrix looks at Hazel sincerely and then turns to me. "You're welcome to come too if you need a field trip. But I should get home. I need to prepare for a meeting with a potential new client this afternoon. Hazel, let me know your thoughts on those new plans I sent over to you."

"I'll look over them with Ramsey tonight. But we'll probably want to run them by the siblings, too, and well, you know..." Hazel trails off. She had plans for expanding the inn's footprint at the ranch, but now everything's in disarray until we get it sorted.

"We can wait a while. No problem at all." Beatrix gives Hazel a thoughtful smile and then turns to Charlotte. "Your property is gorgeous. Thanks for letting me run, and I'll send that contact info to Hazel for you."

"Nice to meet you." Charlotte waves her off and then turns her attention back to me. "All right. Let's get down in my office and see what we can research in the meantime."

"If you two are working, I'll catch up later. I've got to get ready and then run to the store. Text me if you need anything." Hazel waves at us and takes off.

"Want me to order dinner in tonight?" Finn asks from the corner of the room, nearly forgotten as the rest of us plot to help Hudson and Grant.

"That would be appreciated. Maybe one of those family meals from one of the Italian places?" Charlotte's eyes fall over Finn.

"Hudson's gonna start getting jealous if you don't order from Kelly's." Kelly's is the steakhouse Hudson owns in town. Hazel had explained to me on the flight over that it's where she had met Charlotte and Hudson for the first time.

"Hudson's not here, so who's going to tell him?" Something silent passes between them. "Besides, he'll just decide he needs to buy the Italian place or start his own. I wouldn't hate that."

"He doesn't need another project." Finn rolls his eyes and puts his glass in the sink before he comes over and kisses Charlotte on the cheek. "I'll take care of dinner. Let me know if you need anything else."

I watch Finn disappear, and then I stand to join Charlotte, dropping my coffee mug in the sink alongside the other glasses.

"You're honestly my idol, you know that?" I grin at her as we walk down the hall.

Charlotte presses her lips together and shakes her head. "Trust me. In theory, it sounds good, but in practice, it's a lot of household politics and negotiations."

"Can I ask a question?"

"You can ask." She looks ahead as we walk. It's her favorite phrase. The woman is nothing if not cagey in her answers, but I'm hoping eventually she'll warm up to me and share some of her secrets. Hudson and Grant seem to be so much alike in so many ways, and I'm happy to eat up any advice she wants to give.

"Does it ever get easier? Or are they always hypocrites about the risk-taking?"

"Hudson's always hated the risks I take, but he's learned to accept that this is who I am. In the same way that I've had to accept it about him and Rowan. If I thought about every single thing they did, I'd die of worry, and I have way too many things I need to do in life to die yet."

"Well, we have that in common." I grin at her.

"Then it's a good day to start focusing on what you want."

"I want to help with this."

"Perfect." She flashes a bright smile and ushers me into her office.

It's massive and filled floor to ceiling with stuffed bookshelves and large tables with art and manuscripts sprawled over the surfaces. I feel like I've just entered a secret lair, and I'm wondering how I got from pouring shots to working next to one of the smartest women I've ever met. Apparently, there's a silver lining to all of this misery.

FORTY-FIVE

G RANT

"I'VE BEEN DOING a deep dive into his family, his businesses, all his connections, and I think I might have a lead on something." Levi comes into my office looking like he's been up half the night when, in reality, it's probably been the entirety of it.

"All right." I motion for him to have a seat before he falls over.

"You see these family photos here." Levi taps the screen, showing me an image of the governor and his grown children. "This is Abbott with his family. His wife, his two sons, and his daughter."

"She goes off to college after this photo is taken. Starts studying at VSU, and her major when she goes there is art history."

"Interesting." I nod as I lean forward to get a better look at the photos he's swiping through.

"The first couple of years, she's clearly coming home, and she's in the family pictures. She's there for all the big ones—Thanksgiving, Christmas, Election Day. She's at her mother's side, helping hit the fairs with her dad and then again talking to female voting blocks. But then..." He flips through another dozen images. "She suddenly disappears. Not just from the holidays but from everything. It seems like she's never coming home from college. Or at least she's not in the photos."

"Maybe she just got camera shy? Or did she die?" I ask, wondering which of the two extremes it might be.

"I went to the school's records, and she disappeared from them about six years ago. The same period of time when she's no longer in the photos is the same time when she stops attending college. I thought death, too, but there's no record of her death in any of the systems. And there's an absentee ballot. She's voting in absentia, claiming citizenship status, but it looks like she's out of the country. Sure enough, there's a passport she picks up a little bit before that period where she disappears."

"Okay..."

"But she always votes absentee when Abbott's running. The last time was last year."

"I guess every vote counts," I mutter, staring at the evidence Levi has gathered.

"So I wondered if maybe she started taking classes overseas, joined a study abroad program, or something like that. Couldn't find any record of it though. Dug deeper into her social media and saw she also stopped posting. At least on her original accounts. But a couple of her close friends from college started posting their likes onto a new account shortly after her originals went dark."

"I worry about your ability to dig these things up sometimes. You're frightening, truly." I shoot my brother a sidelong glance.

"I'll take that as a compliment." He gives me an amused look before he returns to his explanation. "The new account has a nondescript name, no details in the bio, and the person who takes the photos never shows their face. It's just pictures of the countryside—rapeseed fields, rolling hills with some farms in the distance, and then suddenly mountains. One or two photos of a city street in Europe with no signs or anything to indicate a language or location. But it was enough that I could start triangulating the photos to narrow down where it was. Enough hint of the architecture that I could guess where to start, and then a matter of finding these fields with those views of the mountains—the Alps actually."

"And?"

"The fields are in the southern part of Germany. The city streets are Salzburg and Munich."

"You think she's at a college there?" I ask.

"I think she's up to something there. The timing is just before he asks Dad and Jay to go after the other relic for him. Right around the same time as the Kelly house fire. She goes to a place that's riddled with churches and abbeys and monasteries. Got to be thousands of relics. What are the chances that's coincidence?"

"But she's never reappeared in the photos, so she's never come home."

"My guess? She hasn't found what she's looking for, or whatever it is he's sent her to look for." Levi taps the screen as he looks to me.

"In six years?" I give him a skeptical look. "What sort of study abroad program never lets you go home? It doesn't make sense."

"I know. I'm not done yet. Charlotte and her set are trying

to narrow down the relic situation. I'm hoping that between the two of us, we can figure it out. But I'm wondering if I shouldn't fly over there." He looks to me for my thoughts.

"Right now? I'd rather not lose you. I'd really like to go see Dakota, and I don't want to leave this place unattended." I circle my finger around the room. "I don't think we can both be gone at the same time."

"Are you gonna bring her back?" he asks.

"I was thinking I should, once we get a report back from Jay on his meeting with the governor." I rock back in my seat. "Speaking of, how's that surveillance going?"

While we interrogated him, Levi installed spyware on his phone, and we also put one of our guys on detail as well. I want to believe what he told me, but trust requires consistent, reliable behavior, and we need a record of that first.

"Good so far. Nothing off that I've seen. Just his usual routine. He set up the meeting with the governor like he said he would. The governor was furious, as expected, but seemed to understand that some of this was out of his control. They meet tomorrow, and then I'll meet him here. Easier that way since he's supposed to be watching us as part of his deal with the governor."

"Well, that's promising. I'll be interested to hear his report back." I'll take any good news I can get.

"Agreed."

"If I fly out to Cincinnati after that, assuming it goes well, would you object? Hudson and Rowan are going back to be with Charlotte tomorrow night. Try to help her with some of the research, and Hudson's needed to approve some projects he has in the city. I could catch a ride with them."

"Fine by me. With the increased security measures, I feel much better than I have in years. I still want to talk to you about hiring that MC. We need some muscle who's not afraid to bend some rules. Their connections with other MCs in the state and outside of it... They'd be valuable. We should discuss it again." Levi leans back in his chair.

"I want to be easing out of this, not getting deeper."

"Sometimes, you have to dig the hole to the other side. It's easier than trying to climb back out." He offers up some of his brand of wisdom.

"Seems like that's becoming a metaphor for everything in my life."

"But go to Cincinnati. Bring her back. You won't be settled until you do."

"I just want to be sure they won't see her as a target." I have to live with the regret of what happened with Seven Sins, but I won't let it happen again.

"Jay swears he didn't report her name up the chain. Didn't want to see anyone innocent get hurt in the process. He just thought if he could distract you, you'd be too preoccupied to notice what else was happening. I wouldn't tell you to bring her back if I wasn't confident."

"Well, it worked, obviously."

"It won't the next time. But you need to make sure whatever she decides to do next, it's something with a little less public exposure." It's a fair point. One I've already considered.

"I have an idea. It would keep her in-house. I just don't know how she'll feel about it." I glance out the window because as much as I love the idea, she might hate it. "Did he fire that piece of shit that cut up her legs?"

"He put him on administrative leave. Said he's trying to find a place to transfer him to."

"Should transfer him to the fucking ground. He's a repeat offender. Not with Dakota, but with some other poor woman who doesn't deserve it. I want eyes on him, wherever he goes."

"You got it."

"All right. Get back to your research. I want to get to the bottom of this so we can breathe easier if things go well tomorrow. But get some sleep in there first, would you?"

He nods and dips out the door, leaving me alone at my desk. We're not out of the woods yet. Far from it. But that sliver of light in the canopy is slowly turning into a meadow full of it, and I'll take whatever reprieve we can get.

FORTY-SIX

D AKOTA

BY THE NEXT DAY, and with some help from Beatrix's sister-in-law, Harper, we've narrowed down a few different relics we think could be related to the other two. We also received word back that Grant has arranged a truce of sorts, and Hudson and Rowan are headed back to Cincinnati this week. Grant apparently sent a package express mail because, shortly after dinner, Charlotte's butler delivers it to my room with a card attached to the top.

I open it, and there's handwriting I easily recognize as Grant's.

MISSING YOU. THOUGHT THESE COULD KEEP YOU
COMPANY UNTIL I CAN BRING YOU HOME. THEN WE
CAN TRY THEM TOGETHER.

I reread it three more times to make sure I read it correctly. I'd given him the space and quiet Levi suggested, even when I worried it'd be the end of us. I was afraid to hope, but absence must make the heart grow fonder after all. I slice open the tape and open up the box to find it filled to the brim with new toys, replacements for the ones I lost in the explosion, and a few new ones too.

> I got your package.
>
> Thank you.

I hold my phone to my chest, waiting for his response. Hoping this means the man from before is slowly coming back to me.

THE DEVIL:

Did you like it?

I figured you needed replacements.

> You assume I haven't gotten them already.

I hope we're talking about toys. With Charlotte's influence, I can't know for sure.

> Good question. I've seen some of Finn's teammates, and I think I have a newfound appreciation for hockey.

Glad to hear it.

But we both know none of them could handle you as well as me.

> True.

I saw there were a few his and hers options. Does that mean you're open to some of my ideas?

I figure I owe you after everything I've put you through.

You don't owe me anything.

I'm the one who owes you, remember?

Not anymore. I figure after all this, we can wipe all the slates clean.

That said, I wouldn't say no to a picture or two tonight.

I might be able to arrange that.

But I want one in return.

Think I can do that for you.

There's a knock at the door, and I call for them to open it. Charlotte eases it open, and her eyebrow shoots up at the bright grin on my face and the box of toys in front of me.

"Do I want to ask?" She laughs, scanning the contents.

"He sent me a gift. I think he's worried you'll be a bad influence," I muse.

"I'll have to reassure him I've kept you well away from the hockey team, but I can't say for sure if Hazel's let you near the football players."

"Maybe I should tell him I'm going to watch training camp. Then he might hurry up and get his ass out here." I glance down at my phone when it lights with another message.

"Are you ready to go back to work? I found some more things while I was searching through a few of my older books."

"Yes. I need to tell you about something I discovered earlier. Let me just finish talking to him, and I'll be right there."

"Oh. I can't wait to hear. See you down there." Her eyes light with the information before she takes off, quietly closing the door behind her.

THE DEVIL:

> I should be up to my place by nine.

> > Turning in early in your old age?

> > That's eleven for me. Kinda late here, but I'll make it work. Maybe Charlotte will let me sleep in tomorrow.

> > Speaking of... I'm off to help Charlotte with research.

> Ha. Who's complaining about the time now?

> Any luck? You two getting along?

> > We think we might be on to something, and we might have some help.

> > I love her.

> > When will you be out here?

> As soon as I can. I'll explain more tonight.

> > Talk to you then.

I send him a kissy face emoji and then tuck my phone back into my pocket before I take off to help Charlotte.

I TAKE a seat at the large research table across from Charlotte. She's got dozens of books spread out across the table and a laptop open in front of her as she looks back and forth between the page and screen.

"Did you find anything else out?" I ask as I skim the page she's inspecting.

"Yes. That contact of Beatrix's was helpful. She had some

resources I hadn't thought of and volunteered her help with anything else we might need."

"Oh good. That's reassuring. While I was working out this morning, I had a thought. Instead of my usual podcast, I did a search to see if the governor had done any—and he had. Quite a few, so I listened to one while I was working out and another when I was making lunch. They were both the kind where a group of guys sit around and shoot the shit, talking like they've got all the secrets to the universe."

"I'm familiar." She smirks at the way I roll my eyes.

"Anyway, he did a couple of them, and in one of them, they were talking about getting your DNA tested and ancestry stuff. He mentioned that he was a descendant of Charlemagne. They all got excited about it, and he went all in on his connection to him and how he thinks his DNA affects the way he thinks. I know I've heard the name before in history class—is it possible that it has a connection?"

Charlotte sits back, looking up to the ceiling like she's sorting through the card catalog in her brain for information as she taps her manicured finger to her chin. Her eyes narrow, and she starts typing quickly into the computer before she looks back up at me.

"That's what I thought. He was never beatified," she murmurs as she scrolls down. "But he was considered. Lost out for all the murdering it looks like, but there's a reliquary with his arm bone in it, another with his head. I'll have to look deeper into this. I think it's a good lead though." She looks up and smiles at me.

"Happy to contribute something." I offer up half a smile. I just want to help Grant and the rest of them solve this. If they know his motivations, they might be able to find a way to get ahead and stop him or at least leverage it against him.

"You should keep digging on it too. See what you can find—

any other references the governor makes to things like that and any other information we can find about his ancestry. These bones are in Germany, in Aachen to be exact. It's on the other side of the country from where Levi was looking, but I think we're getting warmer."

"All right. Do you have anything on your shelves?" I look to the massive wall of bookcases.

"I don't think so, but check the database. You can use that laptop over there."

"Perfect. Thank you!"

The two of us spend the rest of the evening pouring over all the information we can find, making notes and creating what looks like a murder board out of one of her walls, connecting all the bits of information we have and pinning them up to try to see if we can make sense of the picture it paints. When ten rolls around, I excuse myself to go upstairs. I want to take a quick shower, change into some cute pajamas, and get ready for my chat with Grant. It feels like it's been an eternity since we saw each other last. I don't want to look tired and frazzled and make him worry. So we say our goodnights, and she continues on without me.

FORTY-SEVEN

D AKOTA

WHEN I GET INTO BED, he's already sent a couple of photos to me. One of him in the mirror half-naked coming out of the shower, and another with his belt undone and his pants partially unzipped. I nibble my lip while I try to think of something to send in return, finally settling on a photo of me with my shirt partially pulled up over my breasts and another of my legs stretched out across the bed. I figure we'll start tame and work our way up from there.

> Long day?

THE DEVIL:

> So fucking long. Making progress though. So I suppose it's worth it.

> Good.

I can't wait to see you again.

I miss you, Cowboy.

I miss you too.

You get dinner and a shower after work?

Yes. Both.

And their maid service put fresh sheets on the bed and sprayed the comforter with some sort of magic lavender spray that makes me feel so relaxed. My head hits the pillow, and I fall asleep. I need to find out what it is so I can get some.

Sounds like you might just drift off to sleep now.

I could, but I'd rather talk to you first.

Unless you have other plans.

Or if you like me asleep.

Fuck, if I was there... I'd have a few.

That another kink of yours, Hellfire? It sounds fun.

Then again, everything you come up with does.

Might be something to try.

What would you do if you were here?

Can't stop thinking about the way you looked tied up in that rope for me.

I want you tied up like that again while you wear one of your dresses for me, or maybe those tiny little shorts you like to wear behind the bar. Peeling those off you could be fun.

> Too bad you're not here.

> I have PJ shorts on now and pink lace panties I just bought underneath.

Send me a picture.

I snap one and send it off. Then I grab one of my toys out of my nightstand and turn the light off. I'm in the far wing of the house, away from their bedrooms, so I don't have to worry about privacy, but I'd still rather have the light off in case anyone wanders down this way.

THE DEVIL:

Fuck. You're gorgeous.

> I'm in desperate need of some toy time. Want to talk me through it?

I'm in public right now. Late meeting. I hope it's over soon. They needed me to sit in, so I can't talk.

But I can text you through it. That work?

He sends me a little devil emoji, and I grin at my phone.

> It'll have to do for now. Call me later though?

As soon as I can.

> Tell me what to do, Daddy.

I return the devil emoji, and I can just imagine his face right now. Here's hoping he makes it through his meeting and can still stand at the end.

THE DEVIL:

> Take the shorts and panties off. I want you naked from the waist down.

> Then turn over on your stomach.

> Did you pick a toy from the ones I sent you?

I do as he asks, tossing my clothes in a pile next to me and pulling a pillow under my hips and another under my chin before I grab my phone again.

> Done.

> The small blue clit vibrator.

> Fucking perfect. We're gonna tease that clit until you can't take it anymore.

> You don't come until I say. I don't care how close you get. Got it?

> Got it.

This man is going to torture me within an inch of my life. I can already tell.

> Turn it on. Low and slow. I want you to tease yourself until you're nice and wet for me.

> Fuck. It feels good. This one's stronger than my last one.

> The lowest setting. Or else.

> Yes, Daddy.

I turn it down a notch from where I started, down to the lowest setting, and I let it softly vibrate between my thighs. I barely let it touch me, allowing the sensation in my nerves to build slowly and steadily.

> Getting wet for me?

> Yes.

> Feels so empty though. Can I use my fingers?

> No. Not until you're in danger of soaking those new sheets.

> Play with your nipples for me. Use the vibrator on them over your shirt.

I follow his instructions, raising up on my knees for a moment to get access. I squeeze the pillow between my legs, grinding down as the teasing sensation in my nipples heightens everything I'm feeling. The phone flashes with a message from him, and I pick it up with my free hand.

> Better?

> Like torture. I need fucked. Badly.

> I know you do.

> Slip those fingers down between your legs for me. Tease your clit.

I set the phone down again, using the vibrator in my left hand and my fingers on my right. I brush the pads of my fingers over my clit, and I let out a soft moan. Completely lost in the moment and imagining he's here watching me. I let out another sigh before I remember that I'm not in my own home. I hold my breath, and I run my teeth over my lip, trying to convince myself that there's no way anyone heard me.

The phone flashes with another message, and I pick it up.

THE DEVIL:

And?

> Getting closer. I just moaned without thinking, though, and now I'm worried they'll hear me.

> Well, half worried and kind of turned on.

> What if they listen to me like we listened to Ramsey and Hazel?

They're not exactly shy, sweetheart.

Do whatever feels good. They'd probably get off on it.

You better be moaning my fucking name though.

> I am.

> Can I use the vibrator again?

Yes. You can turn it on and count to ten. Then turn it off.

But you cannot come. Got it?

> Got it.

I do as he asks of me, lying back down on my stomach before I slip it back between my legs and take my time counting to ten like I'm wringing every possible millisecond out of the experience. I sigh loudly into the pillow when I have to turn it off again. It's torture, and if it was just me, I'd be letting myself ride this little vibrator over the edge. But even when he's not here, I'm trying to be good for him.

I reach for the phone, and it nearly falls on the floor. I have to stretch to catch it, and the brush of my clit over the pillow is enough to get me to let out a soft cry. I bite into my lower lip, trying to force myself not to rock my hips over the pillow again. I swipe the text box open.

> You're torturing me.

> You need to give me permission to come.

THE DEVIL:

> We'll see.

> Soaking yet? Test yourself for me with your fingers.

I reach down with my free hand, and I barely have to brush my fingers over my skin to feel how wet I am. Everything is slick and swollen and dying for more friction.

> Soaking.

> Desperate.

> Please let me come.

THE DEVIL:

> You can wait.

> Three more seconds with the vibrator. Please?

> No.

I rock my hips forward over the pillow under my hips and let out a soft gasp. It's torment and relief at the same time. I'm so close, and it gives me the slightest hint of something I need but not enough to free me from the torture.

"I don't remember saying anything about putting a pillow between your legs." His voice is thick and graveled.

I nearly jump out of my skin. Turning over and scrambling up the bed even though I know it's him. Even in the dark, I can make out his shoulders and that jawline. His blue eyes catch a glint of the light, and he looks terrifying.

"Grant," I whisper. "How the fuck—"

His hand goes over my mouth.

"Not Grant, sweetheart. The devil. The one who's about to tie you up and have you every way he wants to punish you for disobeying the rules."

My throat bobs on the hard swallow I make, and he sees it, his tongue darting out and licking a trail up my neck. It sends goosebumps down my body in its wake. I've never been so turned on in my life.

"Your safe word?" He pulls his hand away from my mouth to give me the opportunity to say it.

"Avarice," I reply softly.

"You need it, you use it. Understood?"

"Yes."

"Lie back down on your stomach," he orders, and I do as he asks. He grabs a second pillow and shoves it under my hips. His fingers trace a line down my spine and between my cheeks, curving down until he can test how wet I am. He slips two of them inside me, and I rock back against them, seeking some kind of relief.

"Don't move," he demands.

"Please. I'm so fucking desperate to come," I beg as I press my face into the pillow.

He kneels on the bed behind me, and his hands come up to palm my ass cheeks, grabbing a handful and squeezing hard. I hear the sound of his breathing as he works his belt loose and pulls his zipper down. The sound of his clothing sliding over his skin is like music to my ears.

"You don't know desperate until you have to ride home

from the airport in a car full of men while your girl sends you half-naked pictures and tells you how much she wants you to fuck her."

"Your girl?" I ask, surprised he uses it so freely. It just sends another wave of want through my body to hear it.

He leans down over me, grabbing a fistful of my hair and forces me to arch my back as he pulls. His cock slips between my cheeks, teasing my ass before he nudges my entrance, hesitating for half a second before he slams into me. I cry out his name, and his hand wraps around my hip, holding me steady as he takes me hard and fast.

"Feels like you're mine right now, doesn't it? The way this cunt's clinging to my cock for dear fucking life."

"Yes."

"Yes, Daddy," he demands.

"Yes, Daddy." I repeat it back to him.

"That's my girl." He says it with admiration in his voice, and his thumb swipes back and forth over my hip. "Listen to how fucking wet you are for me. So fucking perfect and ready. Turns you on to get fucked by a stranger in the dark, doesn't it?"

"Yes, Daddy." I'm so close to coming; I can taste it.

"You want to come for me?" he asks like he can hear my thoughts.

"So much. I need you. Please," I plead with him, reaching for my toy like a request.

"Turn it on, and hand it to me."

I do as he asks, and he slips it between my legs.

"Oh fuck!" I cry out, starting to moan as he turns it up.

"I want to hear you. Let the whole fucking house hear you come all over my cock while I fuck you full. I want them to know this cunt's full of me when we go back out there."

I'm already a mess. Moaning and cursing, so getting a little louder for him isn't a stretch. It feels like I need it after the day I had and then him giving me this fantasy on top of it. My brain can barely process that it's really him and not some overactive specter of my imagination.

He groans out his own release, and I can feel him coming inside me, hot and heavy. When he pulls out, it drips down my thighs, and he stays kneeling, watching it for a moment before his fingers slip up the inside of my thigh. He catches it with his fingertips and slips them back inside me.

"Fuck me. I'll never get over the sight of me leaking out of you like that," he murmurs before he collapses next to me on the bed.

I climb on top of him, wrapping my arms around him and burying my head under his chin.

"You're really here."

"Fuck, I hope so. Otherwise, I'll have to kill whoever just fucked you like that." He laughs and kisses the top of my head. "I missed you so damn much, Hellfire."

"I missed you. But also, what the fuck was that? Not telling me you were coming!" I pull back and glare at him in admonition.

"Couldn't give you your fantasy if you knew I was coming. Also, you're a little cheat. Fucking that pillow when you know you weren't supposed to."

"You didn't say I couldn't," I muse.

It's his turn to glare, but it melts almost immediately, and he cranes his neck to kiss me.

"You survived."

"I survived," he confirms. "We still have a long road ahead of us, but there's a truce in place, and I wanted to come bring my girl home."

"Your girl." I kiss my way up his neck. "I like the sound of that."

"Get used to it," he murmurs, and then his lips crash against mine as we tumble back against the sheets again.

FORTY-EIGHT

G RANT

THE NEXT MORNING, we're up early for a quick debriefing before we take off for Colorado again. As much as a night away has felt like a fleeting vacation, I'm eager to be back home where I can keep an eye on everything. But in addition to picking up Dakota, I also want to be able to hear everything she and Charlotte have been doing research-wise. By midmorning, we're all wrapped around their massive dining room table, a half dozen laptops and twice as many books open to various points of research.

"Thanks to Dakota's bright idea to listen to podcasts that Abbott has done, we discovered he has a bit of an obsession with Charlemagne. He seems to bring him up a lot and has mentioned that he's looked into his ancestry. He thinks he's a direct descendant based on his research, and he's spoken quite a bit about the way he altered Europe during the Middle Ages.

"I started chasing that as a lead, and we were able to narrow down that both the relics he has in his possession right now, the one from the Kelly family and the one you obtained for him, are related to Charlemagne. They're all things he would have carried with him or on him. The reliquary you had, which predates the period of his life, is purported to contain the blood of a saint. The ampule necklace the Kellys had in their collection was created from materials that would have been contemporary to that time. The design features can practically be pinpointed to a region where he lived for several years while he was fighting border wars along his eastern front," Charlotte explains.

"We're talking to a hagiographer Beatrix knows. It's her sister-in-law, actually, who lives in Seattle. She's working her contacts to see if they can establish any records for provenance on the Kelly relic," Dakota adds, and I struggle to contain my surprise at the easy way she talks about the research. Dakota's always been clever, but I wouldn't have thought this kind of investigation was something she'd be this excited about.

"Don't look so surprised," Charlotte admonishes me. "She's a quick learner, and she's been incredibly helpful."

"Oh, I know she's smart as hell. She puts me to shame." I answer Charlotte and then turn to Dakota. "I'm just surprised you're into this kind of stuff."

"Charlotte's brilliant." Dakota and Charlotte exchange smiles. "She's made it all so fascinating. I can tell you more when we're on the plane, but I think I may have a new hobby."

"She has a new job if she wants one," Charlotte adds. "We could use more researchers like her."

"She said there's a good program for this kind of stuff at Highland if I wanted to take classes."

"But I'm also willing to just teach her some of the trade. It'd be nice to have someone out there who could have eyes on things for me."

"Part-time," Dakota adds when she sees my brows climb higher. "My first priority is still getting Seven Sins back up and running so that my staff has work again."

"I've already given them some shifts at the Avarice." I haven't had a chance to fill her in on everything yet.

"I heard." Her hand covers mine. "Thank you for that."

"Of course." I smile at her. "And don't worry. I've got plans I'll tell you more about on the way back."

"All right. What kind of research were you all able to do?" Charlotte looks between Hudson, Rowan, and me.

"Levi was able to find the governor's daughter. Well, find is an overstatement. He's got leads on his daughter, who went missing a few years back. It looks like she's in Europe. We think she might be the key to the third relic, or at least be able to lead us to it," I explain.

"We still don't know if it's only three or if there are more though," Rowan adds. "There's no indication he's working any other teams right now. I've reached out to contacts to see what information I could mine, but it seems quiet."

"Which doesn't make sense if he's closing in on what he needs. Getting this relic from the market, you'd think he'd be dying to get his hands on another. Or at least make fast work of going after all of us again, but everything from Jay indicates he's in a holding pattern. Like he's waiting on something." Hudson gives his thoughts.

"Waiting on what?" Charlotte asks. The question's rhetorical at this moment, but it's one we desperately need to answer.

"I fear that when things start moving again, it's going to happen quickly," Hudson adds.

"Agreed, and we still don't know what he plans to do with all of this." Rowan shakes his head in frustration.

"The daughter would potentially have answers though, right?" Dakota looks at me and then Charlotte.

"If she's involved, theoretically." I nod.

"So we need to find her then. Figure out if she's involved and see if she has information on it," Dakota suggests.

"Agreed." Hudson taps a pencil against the table.

"We need boots on the ground. Stalking her from a distance over tech is fine, but it's a poor substitute for being there. I can go if you want me to," Rowan offers.

Dakota shakes her head. "It should be Levi."

"Why Levi?" I frown, trying and failing to follow her logic.

"He's been following her and her friends closely on social media, right?"

I nod.

"Then he knows the most about her. What she likes. What she doesn't. If he has to make contact with her, he's the best bet. Not to mention he doesn't have any... attachments." Dakota explains her reasoning, and I hear Charlotte click her tongue, nodding along enthusiastically.

"I don't follow." I look between the two of them.

"He can seduce her." Charlotte gives me a sly smile. "Your brother's gorgeous. That face, those tattoos, the glasses, the broken cowboy-turned-hacker... I'd be tempted."

"I'll buy some glasses, and we can roleplay while you ride me." Rowan shoots her a look across the table. Her eyes rake over him in return.

"You'll read something to me tonight with them on?" Her voice has a teasing quality to it, but her eyes light in a way that makes me think she's half-serious.

"I'll let Finn read to you. You'll have my tongue busy with other things like you did last night."

I glance over at Dakota, and she's grinning wildly as her eyes dart back and forth between them.

"You're corrupting her, you know." I look at Charlotte.

"Happy to do it." Charlotte's sly grin spreads wider, and I shake my head, looking back at Dakota who winks at me.

"All right. Back on the subject at hand. We want Levi over there. Do you think he'll go?" Hudson looks at me for my thoughts.

"He'll go. He's already mentioned wanting to do it. I think he's eager to make some sort of progress however he can accomplish that. The explosion and the bombs at the Avarice rattled him in a way I haven't seen. He's usually calmer than I am, and he's been furious since he found out about Jay and the governor."

"Then let him loose on her." Rowan slices a glance in my direction. "Better to channel the energy than let it stay bottled up."

"You trust him not to do anything rash?" Hudson raises a brow.

"Absolutely. He's laser-focused and more controlled than anyone I know."

"And that's saying something," Dakota mutters under her breath, eliciting a round of amused chuckles from the table.

"Then when you get home, talk to him. See if he's willing to be on the ground for us there?" Hudson asks.

"Done." I nod.

"I'll keep working the research angle. Trying to narrow down possible leads on what the third is and if there's a fourth. I'll try to see if I can find anything on why he might want all of them. If there's a collector or some sort of occult purpose he could have in mind. Sometimes with these things, secret societies place value on them outside of whatever their religious purpose might have been. Other times, there's a collector who's obsessed, and depending on their assets, they'd pay a fortune for a complete set of something they've deemed worthy. The kind of sum that would fund a war chest." Charlotte offers up her theories, and we nod along.

"Well, here's hoping we find answers soon. Before the clock runs out." Rowan looks at me.

"Here's hoping," I echo.

We've bought ourselves some time, a truce, and I couldn't ask for a better team to be on this. I have more hope now than I've ever had, but we still need luck on our side.

FORTY-NINE

D AKOTA

"WHAT'S THIS?" I ask, puzzled. Grant's brought me to one of the conference rooms in the resort before he takes me for dinner and drinks downstairs. He has me standing at a table in front of the window that overlooks the side lot of the resort. There's a stack of portfolio pages laid out across it, and he nods to them.

"Open it."

I give him a skeptical look, but I open the folder. Inside is what looks like a detailed architectural drawing, a massive one judging by the different rooms. I tilt my head to see some of the writing and measurements as my eyes trace over the page down to the bottom where my heart stops.

SEVEN SINS SALOON

"Plans to rebuild?" I practically squeal the words. We discussed rebuilding briefly while we were on the flight home, but with the stakes that are still on the line for him, my problems seemed small in comparison. "You did this for me?"

"They're just some preliminary sketches from the architect I've worked with before. I thought it would give you a starting place to imagine what you could create."

"This looks massive though. Will it fit in the same footprint? Do I have enough to afford it?"

"It won't fit in the footprint downtown, no. But it'll fit out there." He nods to the massive lot below us.

"Here?" I raise a brow.

"Here."

"Grant... I appreciate it, but I worry about how we'll work together. I know we're in the honeymoon phase of this right now, but... Eventually, things will go back to a new normal. It was bad enough when you were my landlord; can you imagine if you were my boss? I really love our sex life, and I don't want to be sending you to sleep on the couch because you told me how to run my bar."

A laugh rumbles out of his chest as he turns the page over for me.

"No way on this fucking earth do I want to risk the couch or be your boss for that matter. Outside our bed anyway." He shoots me a charming little smirk. "This would be yours to run however you want. We don't even have to connect it to the resort if it would make you more comfortable. I just thought if it was here, I could keep you safe. No long walks to a car or long drives across town to get home at night."

"Right. Home. I still have to figure out where that's going to be."

"We'll get to that in a minute. But... what do you think of the plans? This one has a few floors to it. This other one has a bigger footprint, more sprawl with room for a stage and a mechanical bull pit."

"I have always wanted one of those." I nibble on my lip. I'm overwhelmed by choices. I never expected to have so many.

"I figured you would." He smiles at me. "This other one has a whisky bar built in."

"That doesn't sound like you had a hand in it at all," I tease him.

"I want somewhere I can drink and watch you work. It's one of my favorite things. You light up and your smile... fuck, it's amazing. Just like this." His fingers brush under my chin, and he presses a kiss to my lips. "Not to mention it's going to be better these days to watch all those guys make asses of themselves trying to get your attention, knowing it's my bed you're in at night. Turns me on to see the way you manage them."

"Okay. Maybe we keep the whisky bar then." I'm still getting used to the open praise that flows from his lips now. It's like he finally gave himself permission to say what's on his mind, and I love every moment of it.

"What else do you want? Whatever you want, we'll make it happen. And if you really don't want it here, we can discuss that too. I'd just want you to have extra security."

"I think I'll have to figure out my living situation first. Unless maybe we could build another apartment over whichever floor plan we build?"

"If that's what you want..." Something in his eyes dims at the suggestion. "We'd have to get it designated as a hybrid commercial-residential space. But the resort already has those if you wanted to build it here."

"I like the idea. Can we keep it as an option for now?"

"Yes. Can I show you another option though?"

"Of course." I look up to him, waiting for him to pull out his phone. I assume he has a property in mind. I can't imagine he's been looking for me, but then again, he has an army of under-lings he can order around to do his bidding, so one of them might have put something together for him.

"All right. Grab the folder so you can look through it some more and follow me."

"Follow you?" I give him a curious look.

"Yeah. I've got the idea up in my suite."

"Okay..." My brow furrows a little as I try to make out his plan, but I gather up the folder and follow him out of the room, down the hall, and up the elevator to the private residence floor where he lives. I've only been here one other time. We've been staying at the ranch since we got back from Ohio. It seemed like a more neutral space where we could negotiate where we were headed, and it also afforded me some room to roam while still having plenty of security. Getting to go for a ride any day I wanted was a bonus, and Kell has been letting me help out in the barns to keep busy.

When we get upstairs, he turns on the light and walks me through the kitchen to the island. Unlike the office we were in, there's not much on it. No folder full of properties for sale I might buy with the insurance money I'll be getting, and no clues as to what house he might have found for me.

"You think you could make this place work for you?" He whirls his finger around the room and looks at me expectantly.

"Work for me?" I repeat the question to make sure I under-stand him correctly.

"I want you to make this place ours." He studies my face, watching my reaction as my brow shoots up. "I know it'll prob-ably take a lot of work to feel like home for you. Give you a place you can bring Vendetta where she'll be happy and some-where that makes you feel comfortable too. But I can give you this." He pushes his black card across the counter. "And free rein to do what you want. Do it yourself. Have Hazel help you plan. Hire someone. I trust you. We're enough alike that I'm pretty sure I'll love anything you pick."

"We're enough alike? You're all business and luxury and rich leather and shiny things. I'm all vintage, worn edges, and messiness. How do you propose that's gonna work?" I give him a skeptical look, but the smile spreads in its wake because I can hardly believe he's suggesting letting me have control over this.

"I want it to feel like a home. However you decorate it doesn't matter. If you're here, and you love it, it'll feel like a home to me."

"Grant..." I press my hand to my heart, looking up at his brilliant blues and getting lost in them. "You're... I don't even know if there are words that are good enough to start."

"You could start with yes?"

I turn around, looking through the dining room, and then wandering into the living room and then the hallway and the master bedroom beyond that. There's a lot I wouldn't change. It's gorgeous the way it is, but it could use a little extra character here and there. I stop outside his closet where there's an old piece of furniture that looks like a torture device, a crossed tee at the top and a worn leather seat, with four horn-styled feet at the bottom.

"I think we can make it work if we get rid of the toys you used with other women." I nod to the obvious BDSM furniture. He bursts out laughing, and I cross my arms over my chest and raise a brow.

"That is a valet. You hang your suit jacket on this part, sling your tie over this, space for your cuff links here. And this drawer at the bottom is for your belts and any other accessories. It was my grandfather's. I brought it here from the ranch because Ramsey was never much on suits other than when they were mandated by the team for events."

"Oh." I feel a soft blush come over my cheeks. "Sorry. My imagination got the better of me."

"I like your imagination. So fucking much. I think we might have to try that out..." He presses a kiss to the side of my jaw. "But for what it's worth, I've only ever had family and the Kellys in here."

"And me."

"And you." His kisses drift down to my neck, and then he pulls back to meet my eyes. "Hopefully permanently, if we're agreed?"

"I don't think you say no to the head of The Quiet Horsemen, do you?"

"Rather you didn't." There's a wry smile on his lips as he presses them to my sensitive skin just beneath my earlobe. "If you need more convincing, though, I'm happy to help with that."

"I think I might," I whisper back because I'm so weak for this man that I can't even get through a day without him.

He walks me backward until the backs of my legs hit the leather of the valet. His hands ghost their way down my body, and then he kisses me, softly at first, until we both turn more desperate.

"Sit down," he demands as soon as we break.

I follow his orders. The worn leather is soft against the backs of my thighs, and he uses his foot to kick my boots wider so he can step between them. I watch as he pulls his suit jacket off, tossing it to the side and revealing the black dress shirt and the leather shoulder holster he wears underneath. His hands move to his belt, quickly undoing the buckle and pulling the leather free from his waist.

"Hands up." He motions for me to lift them above my head.

He presses my wrists together and uses his belt to secure them to the crossbar, wrapping and weaving the leather around until it's tight. I try to pull away to taunt him, but I'm surprised when it holds. A sly smile forms on his face, and then he hits his knees.

"Did you follow my rule?" he asks as his fingers slip under the hem of my dress and push upward. He grins when he finds me naked underneath and bends down to place a kiss between my thighs. "That's my girl. I like it when you listen."

He made me promise never to wear panties when the two of us go out together. It was part of the terms of our new agreement that gives him free rein to use me whenever he wants. One that he uses more often than not as an excuse to have his head between my thighs. A thing he says helps clear his head when he's working, and I'm certainly not complaining.

"I like you on your knees."

His brow raises in response, and a smirk spreads at the corner of his mouth.

"I have a gift for you. Something small to celebrate you moving in. If you can control that smart mouth of yours." He tries for a stern look, but his eyes dance with mirth.

"Yes, Daddy." I roll my lip between my teeth as I smile at him.

He reaches back for his jacket, pulling a small velvet bag from his coat. He opens it and turns out the contents into his palm, stretching his hand out to show me. It takes me a moment to realize what it is, and then my lips part as my eyes lift to meet his.

"Every bit of pleasure you get starts and ends with me. Always has. Figured this way we make it official." His eyes glint with my reaction—half shock and half amusement before it all melds into the same heady mix of devotion and desire that this man always manages to evoke in me. "I had it custom-made for you."

He's claiming me with this piece, one that makes my current jewelry pale in comparison because this one is horse-shoe-shaped with five diamonds embedded around the curve. Just thinking about how they'll make me feel has me desperate to have it on.

"Put it on me." I want him to be the one that does it, wearing it knowing he made it just for me.

"Me?" His face falters the slightest bit before his eyes fall between my legs. "Are you sure?"

"Positive. Just wash your hands with some warm water first. I don't know that we need to add temperature play to the mix today." I grin at him, and he hurries off to prep in the master bath before he returns to his kneeling position in front of me.

I talk him through removing the current jewelry and again through putting this one on. He's gentle and careful as he works, checking in with me at each stage to make sure he's not causing me any discomfort.

"The only discomfort is how badly I want you to fuck me right now," I reassure him as he finishes. By the time he leans back to admire his work and the way the horseshoe diamonds surround my clit, I'm ready for him to do his worst.

"Fuck... I thought it was nice in the box, but the way it looks on you? I'm going to need to get a picture of this pretty little pussy framed to sit on my office desk." There's a devilish smirk on his face, and a laugh tumbles out of me at the thought of it.

"Or I can just sit on your desk, and you can have your daily fix while you admire it."

He grins in response as his fingers trace over my tattoos on my right thigh. "See, this is why I need you at my side. Using this valet, sitting on my desk—you've got the best fucking ideas, Hellfire."

"Well, you made it easy to want to work hard. So many rewards today. A bar, a black card, and now jewelry. I guess I'll have to be good for you," I say softly, studying his face as his eyes search over mine.

"I'm glad you like them. Now spread wider for me so I can start working on earning mine."

I do as he asks, and he lifts one of my legs over his shoulder as he kneels down to start his perfect sort of torture, his tongue laving over my pussy and circling my clit as he toys with the new jewelry. I pull at my binds, desperate to touch him as he starts to fuck me in earnest with his mouth, using everything he has to make me beg—and it doesn't take long before I'm a whimpering mess under his touch.

"Grant... Please..." I plead with him as he pulls away, teasing me with the softest brush of the pad of his thumb over my clit. He loves this part—watching me squirm and telling him I need him almost as much as he loves the next part.

"Fuck, you're sexy all tied up like this. You know what I want, right?"

"Yes. I know."

"I'm so fucking close already from how good you taste. I can't take much more of the way you cry out for me," he mutters as he slips two fingers inside me, gently teasing me before he withdraws them again, licking the taste of me off before he moves to undo his pants. "The second you're done coming, I'm going to fuck that pretty mouth of yours. But first, I want to watch you soak this seat for me."

"Anything you want."

He bends down again, his lips locking around my clit, and he starts to suck as he fucks me with two fingers. I start coming within a few moments, his free hand digging into the flesh of

my thigh as I start to rock my hips up to fuck his face. I'm riding
out my release as I start to come so hard my legs shake.

"Oh fuck, Daddy," I curse as I bite down on my lower lip.
"Daddy, please. Fuck, yes. Right there. That's perfect." I cry
out for him loudly, and he holds me tight as I murmur his name
over and over. He lets me down slowly, my thighs hitting the
leather of the seat again while he continues to lick me clean.
"That's it. Be a good boy and lap it all up. Every drop. So good
for me," I murmur while I'm still coming down from the high.

I was quite possibly the luckiest woman on earth because
this right here is now a daily ritual for us. Him on his knees,
me coming on his face, and me telling him exactly how
perfect he is. And Grant Stockton eats up praise the same
way he eats pussy—like he's starved and I'm his only hope of
salvation. When he's eaten his fill, he rises again like a god
and runs his fingers under my jaw, staring down at me in
admiration.

"I love that filthy mouth of yours. Now open up so I can
fuck it," he commands, and I do exactly as I'm asked because
nothing makes me feel as good as I do when I'm with him.

His dick's already leaking, and I tease my tongue over the
tip, licking it up before I take him deeper. I can't run my fingers
up his hard thighs the way we both like because of the way my
hands are bound, but it's a new sort of pleasure to have it taken
away from me. To give him complete control of this and know I
can trust him.

He's loving it too. I can see it in his eyes as his fingers thread
through my hair and twist, grabbing a gentle fistful of it as he
starts to fuck my mouth, slow and steady at first until we both
get used to the pace.

"It's not gonna take long, and then we can get you to
dinner. But you get a taste first. Something to make you hungry
for how hard I'm going to fuck that tight little cunt of yours

later." He groans as I swirl my tongue under the base, teasing the sensitive spot there.

"That's my girl. That wicked little tongue of yours is so fucking talented," he mutters. "If you're good and eat all your dinner and dessert, I'll let you use one of your toys on me. See how hard you can make me come like that."

Well, fuck. The idea has me wet again already. I moan my enthusiasm over his cock, and he fucks my mouth faster, the tip teasing the back of my throat as he uses his free hand to stroke the base.

"But for now, we're gonna fill up this pretty mouth together." His fingers tighten against my scalp, and I can feel him start to come on my tongue. "That's my girl. Take it all. Swallow me down. I love watching that throat work to take everything I give you. So-fucking-perfect." He's cursing and murmuring soft broken praise as he fucks my mouth until he's spent, slowly pulling away and watching with wonder as he spills out over my lips.

"You're fucking gorgeous, you know..." He studies my face for a moment.

His thumb rubs over my lower lip, spreading his come like he's marking me before he leans down to kiss me. He takes his time, his tongue exploring mine as he reaches above me to untie the belt from my hands. He scoops me up after I'm loose, carrying me into the bathroom and setting me down on the counter. He grabs a washcloth, letting the water warm before he runs it underneath.

"Do you know what you want for dinner? We can eat downstairs, or I can take you into town or even the city," he offers as he wipes my lips, careful not to smear the rest of my makeup.

"Downstairs. As good as the city sounds, I'm too excited about getting to play after." I grin at him, and he slips the washcloth between my legs as his lips brush softly over mine. He cleans me up gently and then helps me down from the counter.

"I love the way your mind works." He presses his forehead to mine, and he plants another kiss on my lips and smiles.

"Good, because I happen to like yours a lot too." I'm madly in love with this man with no hope of recovery.

EPILOGUE

G RANT

A FEW WEEKS LATER

THE SKY IS STILL a brilliant blue as I walk across the meadow, the crop of aspens holding court around the small family cemetery. I kiss my fingertips and press them to the top of my mother's grave as I walk by and brush my palm over the top of my father's, clearing a couple of leaves that have gathered before I reach the man I'm here to visit.

It still hurts every time I see the stone facade with his name etched in it, the short span of years reminding me he didn't even make it to thirty. I settle down next to it, pulling out my flask and the two shot glasses I brought with me.

"Hey, old friend," I greet him as I set one on top of the stone. "I brought your favorite today because I have to tell you some things I don't think you're gonna want to hear. But I'd be a shit fucking friend if I didn't come talk to you first. Figure the good whisky might make it go down easier."

I pour his glass of Scotch and fill mine as well before I cap the flask and tuck it back into my pocket. I clink the edge against his and down the whole thing like it's the cheap stuff you shoot. I need the courage right now.

"I know it's been a minute since I've been out here. I hope you can forgive me. It's been a mess lately. So ugly there for a minute that I thought I might lose Dakota too. Things haven't been easy for her lately either. But she's a fighter, you know. Never lets anything get in her way, not for long anyway. You'd be so proud of her if you could see everything she accomplishes on her own." I chuckle. "She and Vendetta could take on the whole world all by themselves, I think."

There's no reply, but the whistle of a bird in one of the trees draws my attention skyward, and the way the leaves move, it feels like maybe he could be listening.

"She's what I need to talk to you about. The thing you're not gonna like much. Because I went and fucked up." I laugh at how I got here and bow my head, staring at a small outcropping of wildflowers starting to bloom on the edge of his grave. "I fell in love with her. I swear to you I did my best not to. I tried to stop it when I realized it was happening. But when she figured it out, well... you know how she is. She's still the same. If she wants it, she gets it... and for some stupid fucking reason I'll never understand, she wants me too."

I can almost see him sitting across from me. Laughing at me for getting myself into this situation. Telling me she'll have me by the balls for the rest of my life.

"That bit about the rest of my life? That's the part I'm here about. Figure you need to hear it from me first because I know you'll be the first person she runs to tell." I run my thumb over the edge of my empty glass. "I'm gonna ask her if she wants to try forever. Got a whole proposal planned out and everything. You'd be laughing your ass off at what a fool I'm gonna look like if you were still around.

"And before you say anything—I know damn well I don't deserve her. It would take my whole life to even come close to earning an ounce of her brand of love, but you know now, like you knew then, that I'll do anything for her. So I hope you can forgive me if you hate it. I'm hoping like hell you would have given us your blessing if you were here." I scrub my hand over my mouth, doing my best not to cry and failing. "I love her so damn much it hurts, and I just wish you could be here to see how hard I'm gonna work to make her happy."

I take a deep breath when I finally feel like I've let enough loose to recompose myself.

"Fuck. I'm sorry. I didn't mean to get so emotional on you. I just... wanted you to know." I grab his glass and pour it out in the grass in front of his headstone. "Cheers, old friend. I hope wherever you are, you know how much we miss you."

I tuck the glass into the other and start my long walk back to the house. Taking the chance to recite everything I want to say to her—all the things that'll probably go straight out of my head when I need them.

I'M anxious as we get to the top of the trail I've taken her to and tie off the horses. I throw the makeshift picnic bag Kit gave me over my shoulder, and I can't help but smile at the memory of how she squealed when I asked her to put it together for me. I didn't even tell her what it was for, but she knew anyway because she's known me well enough for years that picnics to romantic locations by trail ride aren't a thing I usually do.

Scratch that—it's not a thing I have ever or would ever do for anyone except Dakota.

"Thought we'd go up to the top of the tower. There's a nice view up there," I announce as I lead her in that direction.

"What's all this?" She looks at the bag, smiling.

"A picnic Kit put together for us."

"Oh my god. I love her food. How'd you talk her into that? Isn't she busy this week with all the guests?" Dakota's eyes drift over me.

"She is, but she makes time when it's someone she likes."

"And she likes you?" She gives me a teasing look.

"Well enough it seems. Mostly she was excited about me 'doing something relaxing for once,'" I explain, if only she knew how not relaxing this particular outing is going to be for me. I think I might be more tense than any meeting I've ever held before, and given some of the people I've done business with, that's saying something. But I want this—I need this, and after everything, it feels like there's no reason to wait any longer.

Jay has kept his end of the bargain, and Levi has an eye on everything he's doing through his phone. It's left us all feeling safe enough to resume business as usual for the time being. Life almost feels like it's back to normal while we work on our research and recon in the background. Minus the fact that Levi's in Europe hunting down leads, and I've been running the Avarice with Dakota at my side.

She's a natural at everything business, and I fully believe the second coming of Seven Sins will outstrip anything the town's seen yet in terms of drawing in new business. So I'm just grateful she's decided she wants to use the lot next to the Avarice to make it happen.

When we get to the top of the tower, I'm thankful there's a small overhang at the edge where I can lay out the food and drinks. Kit's even thrown in a bottle of rosé for good measure.

Something I hope we're about to open in celebration if I don't fuck this up royally.

"Dakota," I say quietly as she's distracted by pulling out the sandwiches and salads Kit packed. She looks up at me, her brow furrowed in question.

"Yes?" she asks, setting the last container down and turning her focus on me. I'm struck by how beautiful she is in this light, how perfect she is, and how I never in a million years thought we'd be standing here like this together. But it feels natural. Like everything about our lives and who we are was always going to lead to this place. "Everything okay?"

Her eyes search mine like she's worried by how long I'm taking to answer her, and I clear my throat.

"You see that spot over there? Where the sun is breaking through the clouds?" I ignore the question and point to a place in the distance where the forest fades and another large meadow opens up beneath a mountain. It's like nature's playing along and spotlighting it for me.

She shields her eyes and nods her yes.

"Do you think that's a good spot for the stables there and maybe putting a couple of paddocks on this side?"

Her brow furrows, and she blinks when she turns to me. "What do you mean? Is Hazel asking for your help with development now? I know she's working on that project with Beatrix and Madison, but isn't that beyond the ranch?"

"It's part of a new one."

"A new one? I heard someone talking in town about someone buying up Old Man Miller's property. Do you know what the new ranch is called?" She's still listening as she returns to absently unwrapping more of the food. I don't think she's understanding my meaning.

"What do you want to name it?"

Her attention snaps back to me then; her eyes go wide as she studies my face, and a smile spreads over my lips.

"*You* bought it?"

"I figured as much as you like to ride, you might want your own space. Plus, you've been doing such a great job with the penthouse. I want to see what you do with a ranch house."

Tears form in her eyes. "You didn't..." she murmurs. It's barely audible. She looks back and forth between me and the land.

"I did." I study her reaction as I worry about how quiet she's being. "Do you hate it?"

"What? No, I just... I don't know what to say. I always dreamed about that as a kid growing up, but I just thought it would never happen, you know? So much of the last few months feels like I'm living in a dream, and I don't know that I deserve any of it. I'm waiting to wake up." She swipes at the tear that's starting to form at the corner of her eye and gives me her own nervous smile.

"You deserve so much more than this. You deserve everything. Anything I can give you, I will. It just might take some time. But if you can give me that..."

"Of course. You're stuck with me. You should know that by now." Her fingers run over my forearm as I kiss her.

"I love you, you know," I say softly as I break the kiss.

"I love you too." She grins at me, but her brow furrows again when I pull out the box I've been hiding and drop to one knee.

"For better or worse?" I ask, and her hand goes to her mouth. The tears fall in earnest, and she practically shakes as she stares down at me. "I mean... knowing full well there's a lot of worse here, but I've been trying hard to make it better."

"Grant, are you serious right now?" she asks, and in answer, I open the box for her.

"It's my mom's. If you say yes, you can pick your own out. Whatever you want. I looked around, but it felt right to use this one to propose. I think she would have approved, given how much she adored you, but more importantly, I want you to know how serious I am. I know it hasn't been long officially, but—"

"Yes," she cuts me off. "I know what you mean. I feel the same way. I can't imagine anyone else I'd ever want to marry but you. So you're kind of on the spot here." A sweet laugh tumbles out of her and brings inexplicable tears to my eyes.

"Good, because I need it to be you. You're my everything, Hellfire."

"You're my everything too." She smiles through her own happy tears, and I take the ring out of the box to put it on her finger. "What if I want to keep this one though? Would that be okay?"

"Of course."

"I really loved your mom. She had such a good heart. Maybe a little bit will wear off on me." Her finger traces over the edges of the ring.

"Trust me. Your heart is every bit as big and pure and sweet. People just have to get through a few walls first—as they should. I'm going to spend the rest of my life making sure it stays that way."

WHEN WE GET BACK to the ranch house, my phone buzzes with a text, and I pull it out to see Levi's name flash across the screen. I swipe to open it, and it's a picture of a woman. She's sipping a cup of coffee and eating a pastry as she looks out across the city square, clearly somewhere in Germany or Austria, judging by the words scrawled on the chalkboard sign in front of the cafe door. She looks contemplative, worried even from the way her brow furrows.

My phone buzzes again, and another message comes through.

LEV:

Found her.

You'll never guess where.

Another photo comes through, one that appears to be of the same woman, only this time she's dressed in a way I can barely process. She's in all black from head to toe, her hair shrouded under a veil, as she walks with a group of women dressed the same. I blink and rub the heel of my palm over my eyes, but when I open them again, I'm still seeing the same thing on the screen in front of me.

He's right. I would've never guessed. Not in a million years. But we desperately need answers, and time is running out.

Do whatever it takes.

WHAT TO READ NEXT

THE QUIET HORSEMEN

Bull Rush - Hazel & Ramsey

QUEEN CITY CHAOS SERIES

Before the Chaos - Prequel Novella

Rival Hearts - Madison and Quentin

Mine to Gain - Beatrix & Cooper

SEATTLE PHANTOM FOOTBALL SERIES

Defensive End - Prequel Short Story

Pick Six - Alexander & Harper

Overtime - Colton & Joss

Wild Card - Tobias & Scarlett

ACKNOWLEDGMENTS

To you, the reader, thank you so much for taking a chance on this book and on me! Your support means everything.

To Kat and Vanessa, thanks isn't enough for all of your hard work. I'm so grateful to have such an amazing editing team.

To Autumn, for all of your tireless work supporting me and my books through all of the ups and downs. So grateful for you!

To Jaime, Ashley, and Mackenzie, thank you for everything you do to make it possible for me to have more time to write and for all your words of encouragement and support.

To Thorunn, thank you for your constant words of wisdom and support. Thank you for answering all of my research questions, cheering on the M.A.D. era., and holding my hand through this football season.

To my beta readers: Shannon, Tiffany, & Britt, for your thoughtful feedback and the unhinged reactions that keep me going when I have doubts.

To Eva and Kelly, thank you for holding me up during the doubts and celebrating with me every step of the way. This work is incredibly rewarding but it isn't always easy, and I wouldn't have made it this far without your support.

To my Content Team, thank you so much for all the support you give my characters, my books, and me. I wouldn't be able to do this without you, and I'm so incredibly grateful for every single edit and reel you create. When Hazel tells Dakota she wishes she had half her talent, know that it's all of you I'm thinking about!

ABOUT THE AUTHOR

Maggie Rawdon is a romance author living in the Midwest. She writes men with the kind of filthy mouths who will make you blush and swoon and the smart independent women who make them fall first. She has a weakness for writing frenemies whose fighting feels more like flirting and found families.

She loves real sports as much as the fictional kind and spends football season writing in front of the TV with her pups at her side. When she's not on editorial deadline you can find her bingeing epic historical dramas or fantasy series in between weekend hikes.

Join her readers' group on FB here:
https://www.facebook.com/groups/rawdonsromantics

f   facebook.com/maggierawdon

⊙   instagram.com/maggierawdonbooks

♪   tiktok.com/maggierawdon

Made in the USA
Monee, IL
21 March 2025

14197637R00236